THE

PAPER TRAIL

D.J. MacHale

This book is a work of fiction. Any references to historical events, real people, or real locales are used fictitiously. Other names, characters, places, and incidents are products of the author's imagination and any resemblance to actual events or locales or persons living or dead, is entirely coincidental.

Copyright © 2025 D.J. MacHale

An excerpt from this work was originally published in *Beyond Midnight* under the title *The Paper Trail (Vera)*

Copyright ©2023 D.J. MacHale

All rights reserved, including the right of reproduction in whole or in part in any form.

First paperback edition April 2025

ISBN 979-8-9876253-2-3

For Steve Kullback

FOREWORD

It's that time again. Settle in by the campfire and prepare for another tale of supernatural shenanigans. Or put your feet up on the couch. Either will do.

If you've read my collection of short stories titled: *BEYOND MIDNIGHT – Seven Peculiar Tales of Mystery and Suspense* you will be familiar with the story of Vera Holiday that was presented in the story: *THE PAPER TRAIL (Vera)*. Well, this is *THE PAPER TRAIL*, and Vera definitely plays a part, but hers is only one of several intertwining stories that occur in the sleepy town of Glenville, Wisconsin.

Note: there is no actual Glenville Wisconsin as far as I know. It exists only in my imagination and therefore on these pages. I've used the town name of Glenville in several stories, including the *Encyclopedia Brown* TV series, the *Pendragon* saga, and *The SYLO Chronicles* trilogy. I've probably used it several more times that I can't remember. I point this out in case some clever reader thinks to piece it all together and conclude that all of my universes are geographically connected. They aren't. Glenville is simply the name of the small town where I grew up, and I love using it. So, sorry. Nothing to see here. Move along.

For those who are familiar with my work, you'll know that the vast majority of my stories are aimed at young readers. Of course

I have many adult readers as well, but I try to keep the content suitable for everyone. Such is not the case with THE PAPER TRAIL. Putting it simply, in this story, shit happens, if only in my ability to use the word "shit". It's incredibly freeing. Muhahahaha! I mention this to avoid having a parent get their child a "D.J. MacHale book" only to discover it's not *The Monster Princess*. But you'll figure that out pretty quickly. The first chapter should do it.

One of the many reasons I love supernatural stories is that no matter what the particulars of the characters' journeys may be, and what uncanny and frightening experiences they go through, these stories all have something in common. They're mysteries. As a reader, I love trying to figure out what the author is up to. As a writer, I enjoy peppering in clues, large and small, that the characters use to try and solve their dilemmas. By doing that, I'm also challenging readers to do the same. I offer enough clues for them to be able to put it together, even if the lightbulb doesn't go on until the moment before I offer a big reveal. So stay on your toes, pay attention, and you'll probably be a better detective than the characters. And you can do it from the comfort of your couch.

I hope you have a fun ride.

And so we go.
D.J. MacHale

PROLOGUE

The middle-aged couple drove together in silence.

Too much and too little had already been said.

The wife was at the wheel of their burgundy Cadillac Coupe deVille, dressed in a conservative, sky-blue linen dress, complete with tasteful pearls, looking as though she was on her way to church services. Or to meet the press. Ordinarily her husband did the driving, but his thoughts were preoccupied with a myriad of more pressing concerns that fought for his attention. His wife took the responsibility of insuring that he was promptly delivered to what was expected to be the most impactful meeting of his life. Of both their lives. She chose not to share her concern that allowing him to drive when his mind was focused on everything except the road would have been negligent. And dangerous. He didn't like to be told that he was less-than-capable of anything, but he didn't argue when she took the driver's seat.

He was also dressed for an occasion, wearing a classic Glen Plaid three piece suit. He was a distinguished-looking gentleman in his late fifties with a full head of steel-gray hair and a neatly trimmed moustache. Ten years his wife's senior, they appeared to be the ideal midlife, prosperous, American couple. A closer look into their haunted eyes gave the only hint of the immense stress they'd been under.

It wasn't until they had nearly arrived at their destination that he finally spoke.

"Forgive me for saddling you with the responsibility," he said.

"I don't see it that way," his wife replied. "The choice is going to be yours. Whatever you decide, I'll support it. But you'll be making that choice."

"Thank you, but if circumstances prevent me from making that decision—"

"They won't," she said with loving confidence that she followed with a smile. "You'll get through this."

"Of course," he said, with a whiff of uncertainty. "I love you, Trish."

"And I love you. Please let me go in with you. This concerns both of us and—"

"No!" he snapped, startling her. He quickly softened and added, "I'm sorry. That was uncalled for. Yes, this will ultimately affect you. There's no getting around it. For that reason we need to limit your exposure. However this plays out, the less attention given to our family the better. At the risk of sounding melodramatic, it's my cross to bear."

She pulled into the circular driveway of the modern office building that was their destination on this sunny, weekday morning. Both were relieved to see only a few people milling around, none of whom were anticipating their arrival. She brought the car to a stop directly in front of the main entrance.

"See?" she said. "No reporters. Perhaps you don't need to be so concerned about the family being in the spotlight."

"Today, maybe."

"Then let me come in with you. Look, I'm all dressed for the occasion."

He took her hand and said, "And you're beautiful. But as much as I need and value your support, I don't want you there to witness this process. Call it ego, but I would hate for you to see me when I'm not at my best."

"Less than your best is far better than what these vultures have to offer."

He couldn't help but smile. He leaned forward and gave his wife a long, loving kiss.

"I don't deserve you," he said. "Go back to the hotel. I'm sure you'll be getting a call very soon."

"Maybe I should park and wait here," she said.

"No need, you'll be more comfortable in the room."

"All right, if you say so."

He gave her one last peck on the cheek, grabbed his briefcase, and opened the door. Before getting out, he looked back to his wife.

"Whatever happens, please know that I love you both."

"We know," she said. "Talk soon. Good luck."

With a quick nod he got out of the car and closed the door. He took a few steps backward toward the building with his eyes still on her as she waved and drove away from the curb. He waved back and stood watching until the car left the circular drive, melted into traffic, and was gone.

He was now on his own. With a sigh, he turned to face the building. To the left side of the entrance was signage that identified it as the Dane County Courthouse. On the opposite side was the identification that showed it was also the Madison City Hall. He had been there once before, and the meeting hadn't gone well. He had no reason to believe that this time would be any different. If anything, it would be worse as the list of accusations grew. At one time he thought he would welcome the process. He imagined it would be cleansing. The end of an ordeal. He soon came to realize that he had escaped one nightmare only to begin another. One that would involve his family. That was devastating, and he only had himself to blame.

He had a choice to make, and not the one he had entrusted to his wife. While he lamented the fact that he had put her in such an uncomfortable position, he had absolute faith that if the time came she would make the right decisions.

In that moment the choice he had to make was about creating the least painful path forward for those he loved. The way he saw it, he had two options. One would lead to months of investigation, public testimony and media coverage that would deepen and become more painful with each passing day. His family would have to endure endless scrutiny and live with the consequences for years to come. The other option would be devastating for all concerned, but would likely be forgotten once people grew tired of discussing it.

He had been weighing both options for weeks but hadn't come to a decision. One thing was certain: no matter what path he chose, there would be no happy ending. His ego played a role as well. If he made the latter choice he would be considered a coward for not fighting back the way he knew he was capable of. He was never one to give up on anything, but now he had his family to think about.

With the former choice he would forever live with the crushing weight of guilt.

In those few moments, the answer came clear. He knew what he had to do. He stood tall and walked toward the entrance of the courthouse. He stopped short of entering and turned his back to the glass doors. He reached into his briefcase, and pulled out a Smith & Wesson Model 19 revolver. Without hesitation he cocked the hammer, put the barrel in his mouth, pulled the trigger, and splattered his blood and brains against the glass doors.

His wife would not learn about what he had done for several hours.

It was 1990. She had yet to own a cell phone.

CHAPTER 1

Thirty Five Years Later

The first early morning rays of sunlight spread across the fall-colored, forested countryside of rural Wisconsin. The sole sign of civilization was the winding ribbon of pitted black asphalt that had followed this same route for over a century, revitalized only by infrequent repaving. It was a road traveled primarily by tractors and pick-up trucks, which made the sight of the long black limousine gliding along so elegantly, starkly incongruous. The sleek car navigated the turns with ease, respecting the overly conservative speed limit. It rolled past a weathered road sign which had been erected by the WPA decades before and was rarely updated.

TOWN OF GLENVILLE, WISCONSIN
POPULATION 10,000 (MORE OR LESS)
WELCOME

Glenville was a small, gray town that sat directly on the path to somewhere else. It was a place to stop for gas, a meal, or for directions to a more interesting place to find cheaper gas or a better meal. There were no Tesla charging stations or Trader Joe's markets. It wasn't a destination, unless one lived there, and the number of people who called Glenville home was in constant freefall. Its boom-years peaked in the 1950's when the town boasted several low-tech industrial businesses including a pulp mill, a foundry, and a tool-and-die manufacturer, all of which became obsolete when the world transitioned from low to high tech and grew considerably smaller. There remained enough work to keep the town alive, though barely. It held on because the idea of tearing up deep roots in search of a better way of life was not an option that most people living in this neck of the woods embraced. Glenville may have been firmly entrenched in another era, but it had been home to many families for generations. For those who remained, that was enough.

Most of the town hadn't yet woken up when the limousine turned on to Main Street, a five-block stretch of throwback shops with very few franchises. Half were shuttered, the victims of evolution and attrition. There were only two traffic lights, one of which functioned maybe half the time. The elegant, highly-polished limousine stopped at the first light as it turned red, though at this hour of the morning there wasn't much need to obey traffic rules. Once the car eased to a stop, the rear door opened, and its lone passenger emerged.

While the luxurious vehicle may have looked out of place, its passenger was a downright oddity. He was Black, stood well over six feet tall and looked to be somewhere in his fifties. The years had been kind to this slim, handsome gent who had a dusting of silver in his tightly-cut dark hair. One might have likened him to having aged like "a fine wine," though the bar for what was considered a fine wine in this neighborhood was not particularly high. He wore a midnight black, perfectly tailored three-piece suit, sported a dark bowler hat, and carried a black walking stick that was topped with a lion's head carved out of silver. His throwback, continental style screamed Savile Row, though no one in Glenville would have made that observation.

He stood next to the limo with perfect posture, taking in the town's tarnished charm with a bemused smile. If someone had been standing with him he might have said something mildly condescending like: "How endearingly quaint" before sliding back into the car to issue a "drive on" command that would quickly whisk him to a far more urbane destination.

Instead, he gave a slight nod to the driver. The car immediately pulled away, leaving him alone in the center of the intersection beneath the ancient, winking traffic light that swayed lazily in the breeze. He turned a graceful three-sixty to orient himself and let out a resigned sigh. He grasped his walking stick by the handle, lifted it to chest level and as if staking a claim, brought it down hard on the pavement. The surprisingly loud crack of sound reverberated off the surrounding buildings, rudely breaking the early morning quiet of the sleepy village.

Vera Holiday woke up with a start by a sound that wasn't particularly loud, but it was certainly unusual enough to rouse her.

She had lived her entire life in the modest house that sat a few blocks from Glenville's downtown. It had been built by her parents in the 1950's. When they both passed in the mid 1990's, ownership had fallen to her, their only child. She had no particular affection for the house, but since she lived alone it met her needs, and being the pragmatic sort, she had no desire to trade up or down. One of those needs was absolute quiet and while Glenville had an abundance of that, her property was particularly insulated by a thick ring of pine trees which is why an alien sound, no matter how subtle, wasn't missed.

What she heard was scratching.

The volume was muted by the thickness of the old-school plastered walls. There was no way for her to tell exactly where it was coming from, yet it was unmistakably emanating from somewhere inside the ancient walls.

"Damn," Vera muttered.

She had had similar issues in the past. A squirrel had once found its way into the house through a damaged vent near the attic. More than once birds had made a nest in the eaves of the roof. Each time she had a local handyman rid the house of the interlopers and make the requisite repairs, but the persistent critters would eventually find new ways in. It didn't happen often, but it was no less irritating when it did.

Vera irritated easily.

Without getting out of bed, she reached up to the wall and gave a few sharp bangs with her fist, hoping to scare off whatever creature had the temerity to trespass. The scratching stopped and Vera dared to believe she had solved the problem.

Until the scratching began anew. Distant yet incessant.

"Shit," she said and sat up. She would have to call her handyman to find and seal the entry point. The idea that a repair might trap an unsuspecting critter in her wall to die of starvation was the least of her worries. She was more concerned that a filthy varmint might start a family and encourage other visitors to follow along and chew through pipes and wiring.

"Can't catch a break," she grumbled and got up to start her day.

Karl Iverson awoke in the same instant as Vera, though it was a much more languid process. He would have preferred to remain unconscious until noon. Those few extra hours would have meant the difference between battling a hangover, or still being as drunk as when he'd fallen asleep. The choice wasn't his. He had to get to work.

Karl was as much at the mercy of the clock, as he was to his vices. Fortunately, his job didn't exactly require him to be sharp. It barely required him to be awake. Karl was known as "The Sweeper" because that's exactly what he did. The town council, which consisted of three people who met once a month whether they needed to or not, paid him to keep the sidewalks of downtown Glenville clean. Using a well-worn push broom, he'd start on one end of Main Street and sweep the sidewalk clear of dead leaves, trash, dog shit and cigarette butts. Yes, many folks in Glenville still smoked. Apparently they had not received the news that it would more than likely shorten their lives. Or perhaps that's why they smoked, hoping for a quicker exit. It would take Karl most of the morning to complete the sweep on one side of the street. In the afternoon he'd cross over and repeat the process on the other. Every day. Six days a week. Rain or shine.

Though no one said it in so many words, the job was charity. In his mid-sixties, Karl had no means of support other than a meager Social Security check. He had spent his entire life in Glenville, and though he wasn't exactly a beloved figure, no one wanted to see "The Sweeper" living on the very street he swept. Hiring someone to keep the sidewalks clean was one of the few signs of pride in their town that the people of Glenville showed. Many of the stores were shuttered due to lack of business, but at least the sidewalk in front of those shops, closed or not, was tidy, by God!

The small salary from his sweeping duties was the difference between being homeless, and affording a one-bedroom apartment near Main Street. That was the stipulation. To keep the job, he had to pay rent. Many scoffed at the set-up, saying that by giving him a job the town was essentially paying his rent which meant his Social Security money would surely be used to buy liquor. But no one tried to put an end to the arrangement because they liked their sidewalks clean. Despite the grousing, the set-up worked for everyone.

Except Karl.

On that morning he dragged his gray, bone-thin body out of bed and shuffled into the bathroom where he stood over the toilet to relieve himself, hands-free. Most of the urine made it into the bowl. Without flushing he stepped to the sink where he splashed cold water on his face to shock himself out of his stupor. It was a well-practiced routine, though this morning felt different.

Karl looked at his reflection in the hazy mirror to see a wizened face that would make Keith Richards cringe. Through bloodshot eyes he imagined the face of the younger man he once was. He once aspired to become a practical nurse but due to a string of bad luck, bad choices, and the genetic predisposition to addiction, he devolved into the wasted soul who stared back at him.

Karl was angry. About everything and everyone. It was his default position. Rarely did he channel that anger into something productive.

This morning was an exception. There's no telling why the idea popped into his head, but on that foggy, sour-breath morning he had the distinct sense that his time was running out. He felt that if he didn't make a change, his passing wouldn't be mourned as much as it would give relief to the community where he had spent his entire life. The small spark of pride that still burned somewhere deep in his miserable soul had fired to life.

"Enough," he said to himself. "Enough."

"Ow, Jee-zus!" shouted Ben Daniels, the cook and co-owner of the Rx Diner. He rubbed his aching hand after having touched the microwave that stood on the back-bar behind the diner's long service counter.

"What happened?" Holly Meade, the diner's sole waitress asked.

"Damn thing gave me a shock. What did you do to it?"

"Nothing, Ben," Holly said patiently. "I didn't do anything."

Holly was used to being blamed for anything and everything that went wrong at the Rx and always let it slide off her back. She was home from college after earning a degree from Northwestern in "What do I do now?" Her short-term answer was to move back to her hometown and work the morning shift at the Rx. She was a favorite of the regulars for she made a genuine effort to provide cheery service while taking the time to get to know them. It was far more enjoyable to be served by a cute, personable girl with a pony tail and a bright smile, than being snarled at by her irascible, perpetually sweaty bosses.

"So why did I get shocked?" Ben whined.

"You tell me," Holly shot back. "It's your microwave."

Ben gave Holly a suspicious sneer and went back to his griddle.

The Rx Diner was the hub of early morning activity in Glenville. Most every customer was a local who would stop by each morning for gossip, coffee, breakfast, and more gossip. The décor was straight out of the 1950's. Very little had been updated, upgraded, or replaced since Eisnenhower was in the Oval Office. The one nod to modern technology was the microwave that had just shocked Ben. Welcome to the 1980's.

"Morning Terri!" Holly said brightly to a newly-arrived customer.

Sheriff Terri Hirsch settled into a seat at the counter. In her mid-forties, Terri was as plain as the town she called home. Some would consider her "handsome," though she made a point to wear a touch of make-up to remind folks that she still had a glimmer of feminine sex appeal in spite of the fact that the pool of eligible bachelors in Glenville was drained and dry. She was born in Glenville, though her family moved to Chicago when she was in single digits. An only child, she grew up in the city, graduated from the police academy, married, had a daughter, and promptly got divorced from a man who was more interested in women who didn't carry a badge. Or a gun. And weren't named Terri. She moved back to Glenville with the idea of raising her child quietly, away from the intensity of the city.

Before returning to Wisconsin she applied to be a County Sheriff. Her resume and experience were impressive, which meant she was hired immediately. Her one request before taking the job was that she be based in Glenville. The county was more than happy to oblige since the waiting list for that posting was non-existent. Thus, her life had turned full-circle.

"Morning Holly," Terri said, then turned to Scott Wilson, a beefy guy in work clothes with ginger hair and a freckled baby-face that made him look ten years younger than his thirty-year-old body. His friends called him "Red," short for "Redneck Ed Sheeran." He sat at the counter finishing up a breakfast heavy on pancakes and syrup. And bacon. And hash browns. As with many diners it was called

"The Lumberjack Special" not that many lumberjacks ever ate there. But in this case it applied. Scott was indeed a lumberjack of sorts.

"Morning Scott. You in a hurry?"

"No. Why?"

"You left your truck running."

"I did?"

"You did."

"Dang!" he exclaimed. "I'm losing it. Thanks Sheriff."

He dropped a few bills on the counter and hurried out.

Terri looked to Holly and said, "And with that one considerate gesture I've earned my wages for the day."

Holly poured a mug of coffee for her and said, "That's why we love you, always looking out for us."

"That's me," Terri said. "Ever vigilant."

George Daniels, Ben's identical twin brother and co-owner of the Rx squeezed past Holly and groused, "Full house. Stop socializing."

"Morning George," Terri said brightly.

"Morning," George growled without stopping.

"Give the girl a break."

"Arrest me."

"Don't tempt me."

George was in a perpetual state of irk. He and his brother Ben were pushing seventy, at least fifty pounds overweight, balding, and always seemed to be out of breath. They were a cardiologist's dream, not that either of them had ever been examined by one.

Vera Holiday sat alone in her usual booth, the one furthest away from the front door. She had been coming to the Rx for her morning bowl of oatmeal for as long as anyone could remember, and as far as anyone could remember, she ate alone. Ironically, she knew most everyone who lived in Glenville because she owned the town's only pharmacy. As the pharmacist she knew who dealt with diabetes, hypo-thyroid, attention deficit disorder, high blood pressure and erectile dysfunction. She shared that information with exactly no one. Then again, she didn't have any friends to gossip with. Everyone in town gave her a wide berth since she showed no interest in conversing about anything other than what was necessary to complete a transaction. The most anyone spoke about her was to wonder why at her age and hermit-like tendencies she continued to self-dye her hair an unnatural shade of jet black. It was an incongruous show of vanity, and a poorly executed one at that.

As she sat staring at the newspaper (she refused to read the news on her smartphone) while savoring her gruel, she heard something that made the thick cereal catch in her throat.

It was a scratching sound coming from inside the wall next to the booth.

"Damn varmints," she growled to herself and leaned into the wall to get a better sense of where the critter might be.

The front door of the diner opened. Another customer had arrived who was not one of the regulars. All eyes went to the newcomer for it wasn't often that a non-local turned up at the Rx this early in the day, especially not one who looked as though he had come straight from Downton Abbey. First off, he was Black. That alone turned heads. There were few Black families in Glenville. People had deep roots in the town and most of those roots were decidedly White. Besides his skin color, his suit and mannerisms did not scream "country." And the bowler hat! No one in the diner had ever seen one, other than in an old-timey movie.

If the man felt uncomfortable being the center of attention, he didn't show it. He glided past tables to the last unoccupied booth a few spots away from Vera, who didn't notice him because she was focused on listening to the wall.

Holly spotted him the instant he stepped through the door and was right there with a stained menu in one hand and a steaming carafe of coffee in the other.

"Morning!" Holly said cheerfully. "Coffee?"

"Tea, if you please," the man said with a decidedly posh British accent. "Earl Grey?"

"Uh, no, it's Holly."

"Of course." The man gave her a warm smile and added. "I was referring to the tea. Earl Grey would be lovely."

"Oh, right," Holly said with embarrassment as she turned away to fetch his tea. "I knew that."

She didn't. No one ordered tea at the Rx. Earl Grey or otherwise.

"Miss Holly?" he called after her.

She turned back to him.

"Yeah?"

"A recommendation if you please. Whom might I speak with in order to learn about your lovely town?"

"Why?" Holly said with surprise, then realized how rude it must have sounded, so she re-set. "I mean, what do you want to know about Glenville?"

"I'm not sure myself. I am an author looking for local color and such."

"Well you came to the right place," she said as she gestured around the room with the ancient Bunn coffee carafe. "Local color is our specialty. But if you want to know where the bodies are buried, I'd talk to Sheriff Hirsch."

She gestured the carafe toward Terri.

"Brilliant. Thank you, Miss Holly. I will."

Holly smiled, a bit flustered. The man certainly was charming. And handsome. Nothing like the men who lived in Glenville who would sooner sport a grease-stained John Deere cap, backwards, than a natty bowler.

George Daniels rushed from the kitchen and hurried past the booth where Vera sat with her ear to the wall. George was always in a hurry, though no one knew why because he never seemed to arrive anywhere. Vera got his attention by raising her hand and snapping her fingers. George stopped short and took a deep breath to calm himself. Vera was always complaining about one thing or another.

The last thing he wanted was a debate over the correct temperature to serve oatmeal.

"Can I help you with something, Vera?" he asked, overly solicitous.

"You've got a rodent problem," Vera announced with authority.

George stood up straight. She might as well have said his food had given her Salmonella poisoning. He took a quick look around to see if anyone heard her.

"Why do you say that?" he asked in a strained whisper.

Vera tapped the wall and said, "Listen."

George leaned into the wall, listened, and declared, "Nothing."

"It's gone," Vera said. "Probably got spooked by us talking. But you've definitely got something in there. I don't know what. A squirrel. Or a rat."

"A rat!" George exclaimed, then realized he shouldn't be shouting "rat!" in his restaurant. He looked around quickly, hoping nobody heard.

"A rat?" he asked again, back to a whisper.

"Or something," Vera said. "If I were you I'd get an exterminator before somebody calls the health department."

"Let's not go there," he whispered, now breathing more heavily than usual. "I'd appreciate it if you didn't mention this to anybody."

"Who would I tell?" Vera asked, mildly insulted.

That was enough to satisfy George. Vera may have been annoying, but she was discreet. Her silence was confirmed when she made a zipping motion across her lips.

"I'll take care of it," George said and hurried off to somewhere.

Vera put her ear back to the wall.

The man in the dark suit approached Terri. Though he had removed his bowler he still looked decidedly out of place in this less than elegant blue-collar establishment.

"Pardon me, Sheriff Hirsch?" he said. "Forgive the intrusion."

Terri hadn't seen him enter the diner. She spun around, gave him a quick up-and-down and nearly spit out her coffee. She sat up a bit straighter and though she would never admit it, she felt a twinge of self-conscious embarrassment for wearing a particularly unflattering khaki uniform. She absently smoothed her hair, though her short bob didn't need smoothing.

"No problem," Terri said. "What can I do for you?"

The man gestured to the stool next to Terri.

"Might I?"

Terri nodded to the stool. "You might."

"Most kind of you," he said while sitting. "My name is Paper."

"Paper?"

"Yes. Fitting, I suppose, seeing as I am an author. Nonfiction, mostly."

"Is Paper your first or last name?"

"A family name. My forename is decidedly less interesting."

Though Terri was intrigued and a bit intimidated by the handsome man, she was still a professional and needed to act like one.

"What can I do for you, mister Author Paper?"

"The gracious Miss Holly tells me you are the one who knows, as she put it, where the bodies are buried in your charming town."

"Did she now?" Terri said and shot a quick look to Holly, who was behind the counter pretending not to be listening. "Well, if you want to know who lost their cat or the average amount we collect each month in parking fines, sure, I'm a font of knowledge."

Mr. Paper chuckled amiably and said, "Nothing quite so specific. I'm simply here to observe and soak up the atmosphere for

The Paper Trail

a book I'm writing about America through the eyes of an Englishman."

Holly placed a brown paper bag on the counter in front of Terri. "There you go, Sheriff. The usual: egg-white omelet, dry white toast, and a carton of 1% milk. I'll put it on your tab. Coffee's on the house."

Terri gazed at the bag, wishing Holly hadn't offered that decidedly bland gastronomic run-down.

"And there's your first observation," she said to Mr. Paper. "We're not exactly epicureans here."

"Who am I to judge?" Mr. Paper said, "As I said, I'm an Englishman."

He gave Terri a charming smile.

Terri and Holly exchanged looks. Both were taken by the gentleman. Holly broke first and focused on Mr. Paper.

"We don't have early grey tea," she said. "Is Lipton okay?"

"That would be lovely, thank you Miss Holly."

Holly went back to work as Terri stood and grabbed her bag of white-bread breakfast.

"Well, Mister Author Paper," she said. "Come by the Sheriff station and I'll tell you everything there is to know about our little town. It'll take about two minutes. It's on the north end of Main Street."

"Thank you, Sheriff. I most certainly will." He stood respectfully and gave her a slight nod, "Be seeing you."

Terri gave him an awkward smile. "Right," she said and headed for the exit.

Mr. Paper sat back down.

Holly was writing up Terri's tab with her back to the counter. She shook her pen. Out of ink. When she reached up to grab another, she saw reflected in a mirror above the back bar that someone else was now sitting next to Mr. Paper. It was a woman with long, flaming red hair who sat on the stool Terri had just vacated. Her back was to the counter.

"Be right with you, ma'am," Holly said over her shoulder.

"Pardon me?" Mr. Paper said.

Holly turned, and was surprised to see that no one was sitting next to him. She glanced around with confusion.

"Is there a problem?" Mr. Paper asked.

"I thought I saw—" She shook it off and added, "No. Weird. Should I bring your tea to the table?"

"No, actually. I quite like sitting here if that's all right."

"Quite," Holly said with a chipper smile, then turned and winced. She had never said "quite" before. Why had she suddenly turned into Mary Poppins? She had already forgotten about the woman she thought she'd seen.

In the back of the dining room, Vera gave up listening for varmints. With a shrug she dropped a few dollars onto the table and slid out of the booth.

A single, loud thump came from inside the wall. It was so sharp and violent that it made her jump while her spoon clattered about in the near-empty bowl of oatmeal. She let out a small, surprised yelp then looked around to see if anybody else had heard. She tentatively reached toward the wall, as if drawn to it. Her breathing was heavy with anticipation, and curiosity. She hesitated, then touched her fingertips to the wall's surface to feel...nothing. She pulled her hand away, grabbed her purse, and hurried out of the booth.

No one gave her a second look.

CHAPTER 2

Scott Wilson sat in his vintage (His word. It was just old) faded burgundy Ford 150 pick-up truck that was parked along the curb near the Rx Diner. He was trying to start the engine, with no luck.

"C'mon," he said, cajoling, as if that would make a difference.

He cranked the starter, it groaned but wouldn't turn over, compelling him to punch the steering wheel in frustration.

"Piece of shit!"

"What the problem?" Terri Hirsch asked as she approached.

"You sure it was running before?" Scott asked.

"Absolutely."

"Well it wasn't when I came out. Now it won't start."

"Out of gas?"

"Nah, I filled up last night. This sucks, I gotta get to work."

Terri pulled out her cell phone and said, "I'll call Charlie Dest to come give you a jump."

Scott took the key from the ignition, rolled out of the truck, slammed the door, and the engine instantly turned over. The two looked at the vehicle as if expecting to see some clue as to why the engine had changed its mind. Scott raised his hand to show that he was holding the truck's old-school ignition key.

"You need to get that serviced," Terri said.

"You think?" Scott replied.

He got back into the cab with caution for fear he'd break whatever spell had taken control of his vehicle and would decide to shut it down again.

Terri said, "Maybe drive straight to Charlie's shop and—" her eye caught something on the other side of the street. A boy and two girls in their teens hurried into an alleyway between shops.

"Can't do it now. I'm fallin' behind on the...Sheriff?"

Terri broke her focus and looked to Scott.

"Right. If you get stuck, call me."

"Will do, thanks."

Scott pulled away from the curb and accelerated slowly. He may have been in a hurry, but he didn't want to gun it in front of the sheriff.

It wouldn't have mattered. Terri's attention was back on the kids who had disappeared into the alley.

"Sheriff!" Karl yelled.

Karl Iverson, clutching his push broom, hurried to catch up to Terri.

"We gotta talk," he added.

Terri ignored him and stepped off the curb, headed across the street.

"Hey!" Karl bellowed.

Terri kept on walking without acknowledging Karl, leaving him standing there, frustrated.

"Your loss!" he shouted.

"Is there a problem, sir?" Mr. Paper asked. "I heard a commotion and came to investigate."

Karl turned quickly to see the British gentleman standing a few feet behind him, leaning casually on his walking stick.

"Who the hell're you?" Karl asked with equal parts curiosity and animosity.

"Simply a concerned stranger."

"You got that right. Can't say I ever saw anyone stranger'n you 'round here. No offense."

"None taken. Might there be something I can assist you with?"

Karl coughed out a laugh, stirring up the liquid emphysema that rattled through his lungs, the gift from years of Marlboro Red smoke.

"That's funny. It took a dandy stranger to ask me that question."

"Well then, is there?"

Karl shrugged, dropped the business end of his broom on to the sidewalk and pushed off.

"I wish," he said, and went on his merry sweeping way.

Mr. Paper offered him a warm smile that wasn't seen or appreciated, and strolled back to the Rx.

Terri stepped onto the opposite sidewalk and strode straight into the alley, where she'd seen the kids disappear. It only took a few steps before she smelled the distinct, skunky aroma of marijuana smoke. She stopped, counted to ten, braced herself, and continued on. It didn't take long before she came upon the scene she expected and dreaded to see.

"Morning, kids," Terri said lightly.

The three teens were relaxed on a ragged couch next to a dumpster behind the Glenville Furniture Emporium. They sprang to attention while the boy quickly swallowed the joint.

"Mom!" one girl shouted in surprise, as if to announce Terri's other identity to her friends.

"I wasn't aware that today was a school holiday," Terri said.

"It isn't," the boy, Jarod, said as he jumped to his feet. "None of us have—" he coughed, trying to dislodge the dry paper joint that was caught in his throat.

"None of us have first period," the girl, Wendy, said to bail out her choking friend.

"So you decided to put the free time to good use and get high," Terri said.

"No!" Wendy exclaimed. "Well, yes."

The other girl, Darcey, Terri's daughter, sat with her hand covering her eyes out of embarrassment, but more to hide the telltale evidence that she was thoroughly baked.

"You understand that recreational marijuana is illegal in Wisconsin. I'm assuming none of you have medical conditions that justify its use."

"I've been under a lot of stress lately," Jarod offered weakly.

"I'm sorry to hear that, but it doesn't qualify, unless you have a prescription card that says it does."

Jarod dropped his head.

"Are you going to arrest us?" Wendy asked.

"Who's holding?" Terri asked and made a silent wish that it wasn't her daughter.

Both girls looked to Jarod. His shoulders slumped as he reached into his back pocket and came out with a small plastic bag that held a few sorry buds.

Terri held out her hand.

Jarod hesitated.

"Are you serious?" Wendy exclaimed. "Give it to her!"

"This shit's expensive!" Jarod whined.

"Give it up, Jarod," Darcey said flatly.

Though it killed him to do it, he dropped the bag into Terri's hand.

"Go to school," Terri said.

Wendy and Jarod instantly brightened. Wendy jumped to her feet, took Jarod by the arm, and pulled him away.

"Thanks Sheriff," she said.

"Are you gonna tell our parents?" Jarod asked.

"I haven't decided," Terri replied. Not true. She had no intention of informing their parents but wanted the kids to squirm for a while.

"We'll never do it again," Jarod said, oozing sincerity.

"Don't push it, Jarod," Terri said. "Go."

The two ran off.

Darcey hadn't moved. She knew she wasn't going to get off that easily. Unlike Jarod and Wendy, her parent already knew what she'd done.

Terri didn't say a word. She wanted Darcey to squirm as well. A twenty-second lifetime passed before Darcey couldn't take it anymore.

"It's legal in Illinois," she said.

"That's your defense?" Terri asked. "Let's break this down. A, in Illinois it's legal for recreational use if you're twenty-one, not sixteen. B, this isn't Illinois. And C, whether it's legal or not, do you seriously think it's smart to get high before school?"

Darcey answered with a shrug. She had no defense.

Darcey did not look like a native of Glenville, because she wasn't. Her dyed pink-blonde hair and multiple ear-piercings weren't the only clues. Where the kids of Glenville lived in jeans and t's with logos of classic rock bands, Darcey wore long skirts and colorful tops she'd gotten while thrifting with friends when she visited her dad back in Chicago. There were no treasure-filled thrift stores in Glenville. The kids saw her as a unicorn. Some felt she acted like she was too good for them, others secretly envied her for the kind of style they'd only seen on TikTok. Either way, it was tough for her to make friends. Darcey had lived most of her life inside the Chicago Loop and went to public schools that were melting pots of race, religion, and creativity. She was an outgoing, flamboyant young woman who scored the lead in every school production, whether it be a drama, comedy, or musical. Her dream was to be a performer and had every reason to believe she'd succeed. Chicago was a city filled with opportunity.

Glenville was not.

"When did you start smoking weed?" Terri asked.

"When we moved here," was Darcey's curt answer.

That stung. Terri had moved them out of Chicago to raise Darcey in a less frenetic, wholesome environment. She figured that Darcey would eventually decide to move back to the city for college and beyond, but until then she wanted her daughter to spend her high school years without the pressures and temptations that came with living in a large city.

It wasn't going well.

"Whose idea was it?" Terri asked. "Was it that Jarod kid?"

Darcey stood up defiantly.

"No, Mom. It was actually my idea."

"So you sought out the one connected kid at school?"

Darcey laughed. "Yeah, that's it. I'm a total stoner who can't get through the day without being wasted."

"Don't be flip. I'm your mother, I can ask these questions. I'm also the sheriff."

"So it's really about you," Darcey shot back. "Tough call. Do you arrest your daughter? Or let her go and risk losing your job? Living here is turning out to be more complicated than you thought, isn't it? Big-city evils aren't exclusive to big cities."

"This doesn't have to be so difficult," Terri said.

"Well, yeah, it does. I gotta get to school."

Darcey walked past her Mom.

"Stop. Your eyes look like tail-lights. I'll take you to the station until it's out of your system."

"Fine, whatever. Park me in a jail cell," Darcey said and continued on. She turned back and added, "And Jarod isn't the only one who's connected. Most of the kids in this bullshit town smoke weed. That goes with the territory too."

She spun on the heel of her boot and headed out of the alley.

Terri had to take another deep breath. It wasn't yet seven thirty in the morning and the day had already turned to shit.

CHAPTER 3

Vera's pharmacy, *The Glenville Apothecary* was situated on Main Street a few blocks from the Rx Diner, which could be said about every other business in downtown Glenville. At least those that had not gone belly-up. Yet. For decades she ran the place on her own, which suited her just fine. The few times she hired help proved to be more trouble than it was worth since she spent more time and effort correcting their mistakes than she would have if she had performed the tasks herself. At least that's the way she saw it. Vera wanted things done her way, which in her mind was the only way. None of these hires lasted more than a few weeks, whether Vera fired them, or they became fed-up and quit in anger.

Now that Vera was rolling through her sixties, she was having trouble doing some of the more physically demanding tasks like stocking the higher shelves or keeping a high polish on the linoleum floors. Enter Mikey Harper. Mikey was a skinny kid with a buzz-cut who graduated high school the year before and had no desire to continue his formal education. He was a simple kid who lived with his parents. That was perfectly fine with him; less-fine with his parents. He took the job at Vera's pharmacy because he needed to work and figured she'd be retiring soon. His thinking was if he proved to be of value, Vera might one day leave the business to him. And why not? She had no family anyone knew of. Or a husband. Who better to leave the business to than someone who helped her keep it running through her golden years? At least that was Mikey's thinking, as delusional as it may be.

Proving himself to be of value was more challenging than he expected, due to Vera's rigid standards and her lack of respect for any opinion that wasn't hers. Still, Mikey had managed to last a year without annoying her enough to be canned or quitting in disgust, not that he hadn't considered it a few (dozen) times. He kept telling himself that if he was smart, one day the business could be his. Trouble was, he wasn't all that smart and there was little chance that Vera would leave her business to anyone. But other than an obsession with playing Fortnite, it was all Mikey had going on in his life, so he sucked it up and clung to the dream.

"Morning Ms. Holiday," Mikey chirped. He had dared to call her "Vera" exactly once. It didn't go well. He had to endure a lecture about how young people didn't have proper manners, respect, or an adequate work ethic. Mikey got the point after about thirty seconds, but politely listened to her rant, proving that "young people" could actually show respect. He'd even ditched his jeans and t-shirts to wear khakis and a polo shirt to look professional. Vera never once acknowledged his efforts.

Vera always arrived at the store at 7:30 sharp so Mikey made sure to get there at 7:20 to begin work on some project that made it look as though he'd been there for much longer. On that morning he was up on a ladder dusting the blades of the overhead fans.

"Don't you dare fall," Vera commanded as she walked by.

Her concern wasn't for his safety. It was about her liability.

"I won't," Mikey said brightly. "Morning!"

Vera walked on, nearly tripping over the store mascot, a chubby gray tabby tomcat of indeterminate age that had wandered into the pharmacy one day and never left. Vera named him...

"Bobcat!" she shouted. "Go away!"

Bobcat gave her an annoyed meow in response but didn't budge. Vera kept walking. The cat looked up to Mikey and meowed again. Unlike Mikey, Bobcat never showed respect.

The Paper Trail

"Don't look at me," Mikey said to the cat. "You tripped her."

Vera went straight for her tidy office in the back of the store. She kept her world in military-like orderliness, which was another issue she had with every one of her previous employees. Nobody could live up to her strict standards. At least Mikey came close, though she wouldn't acknowledge it. She carefully put her coat on a hangar and hung it in the office closet, with a few inches separating it from the other clothing. She pulled out one of her five arctic-white lab coats and removed the plastic wrapping that came from the cleaners. She always wore a lab coat at work. After all, she was a pharmacist and wanted to look the part. Each day after closing she'd drop that day's coat at the cleaners to be laundered and pressed. She never wore the same coat two days in a row.

Before donning the day's uniform, she'd fill Bobcat's food bowl and change his water, which was probably the main reason why Bobcat stuck around. He was a cat, not an idiot. She would then make a stop in the rest room to wash her hands, relieve herself, wash her hands again, and apply unscented moisturizer. She was then ready to don her armor and begin the day's duty of seeing to the pharmaceutical needs of the people of Glenville.

On that morning, once Bobcat was fed and watered, she entered the restroom, took one look, and screamed: "Mikey!"

Mikey was so startled he nearly fell off the ladder.

"Coming!" he shouted and scrambled down.

He ran to the back corridor to see Vera outside of the restroom, leaning against the wall, breathing hard.

"What's the matter?" he asked.

She looked at him with wild eyes. If looks could kill, well…

"You tell me," she said, seething, and motioned with her head toward the restroom.

Mikey walked cautiously toward the restroom, opened the door with trepidation, and immediately realized where this was headed. The toilet must have backed up because there was an unmistakable odor of sewage. Part of him didn't want to go in, but he convinced himself that Vera was so fussy, she was probably overreacting.

She wasn't. It might not have been a hazmat-worthy emergency, but it was definitely a disgusting mystery. Shit was everywhere, and not a small amount. There were unmistakable brown streaks smeared across the floor, the walls, and the mirror. There were even a few spots on the wall that looked as though wet turds had been flung about. A few still clung there.

"How the hell--?" was all Mikey managed to say.

"Don't pretend you didn't know," Vera said, accusingly.

"I didn't!" Mikey shot back defensively. "It was clean when I left last night."

"You're saying you didn't do it?"

"Seriously?" Mikey said indignantly. "Why would I? I'm the one who's gotta clean it up."

Good point. Vera downshifted and caught her breath.

"So who did? Are you sure it was clean when you left last night?"

Mikey thought back. "I don't know. Maybe not. I mean, last time I went in was like an hour or two before closing."

"We were busy," Vera said. "There were some out-of-towners poking around. It must have been them, or one of their annoying children. Little animals."

Mikey surveyed the carnage and said, "Whoever did this took some time to do it right."

"Right?" Vera asked sarcastically.

"I mean it's like they were angry or something. Were any customers angry?"

"Who knows?" Vera said. "I don't pay attention."

Mikey thought: *And maybe that's why they were angry.*

"I'll clean it," he said.

"Good. And hurry. We're not opening until it's completely clean. This is disgusting. I'm leaving until you're finished. Make sure it's immaculate."

"Sure," Mikey said with zero enthusiasm.

Bobcat was oblivious to the drama as he happily munched away at his breakfast.

Vera headed out, leaving Mikey to the dirty work. He took another look at the mess and had a thought he chose not to share with Vera. He didn't think this had been done the night before. It was too fresh, and wet. It had to have happened that morning, which meant it was done by somebody who had access to the pharmacy.

But who? And why would anyone do such a thing?

Vera had the same thought but convinced herself that it had to have been the out-of-towners and their demon children. To Vera, children were small, filthy animals. She used that opinion as an excuse for never marrying, not that she had the opportunity. The idea that some undisciplined child would smear feces on the walls of her spotless bathroom fit her image of children perfectly. Besides, she preferred to place the blame on random strangers rather than to think it was done by someone she knew. That would raise disturbing issues that couldn't be scrubbed away with a little 409 and bleach.

Breakfast at the Rx Diner was winding down. There were only a few stragglers left, which was more than usual because the appearance of Mr. Paper and the speculation over who he was and why he was in town kept a few regulars planted while the coffee and gossip continued to flow.

George Daniels was at the cash register totaling the morning's cash receipts. (Most locals still preferred to use cash for their transactions). Holly wiped down the empty tables and refilled the bottles of Hunt's ketchup and Log Cabin syrup while Ben Daniels cleaned up behind the counter in anticipation of the upcoming lunch shift. The Rx was all about breakfast. If they had to rely on their lunch business the place would fold, but the Daniels brothers kept the doors open for the few stragglers who wandered in for a burger or a sandwich. They certainly didn't need a waitress which meant Holly's day was done.

Ben was a fastidious man and meticulously wiped down every surface behind the counter. The board of health never had an issue with the Rx, not only because of Ben's freakish quest to maintain operating room like sterility, but also because it was rare for an inspector to visit the off-the-beaten-path town. The restaurant could have had an inch-thick layer of grease covering every work surface and never see a citation, but that wasn't Ben's style.

As he worked, inch by inch across every surface, he moved closer to the microwave that had given him a shock earlier that morning. Not only was the incident forgotten, the microwave was still plugged in. When he got to it, Ben didn't think twice about spraying its stainless still surface with Zep degreaser and wiping it down.

The instant he touched his cleaning rag to the microwave, a surge of electricity shot through him that knocked him backward as he let out an anguished scream of surprise and pain. George, Holly, and the few remaining customers looked in time to see him stumbling back and falling behind the counter. While George stood frozen at the cash register, Holly reacted quickly and ran behind the counter to see Ben flat on his back with his eyes open wide, staring at nothing.

"What happened?" she shouted as she dropped to her knees beside him.

"Fucking microwave," Ben managed to say. "Shocked the hell out of me again."

"Are you okay?"

"No!" he replied, annoyed. "That hurt like hell."

He was more surprised than hurt and the shock quickly wore off. Literally. George arrived and stood over his twin brother with his hands on his hips.

"Did you break something?" he asked.

"Thanks for your concern," Ben replied. "Help me up."

Ben wasn't a young man, nor was he light. Together with his twin they resembled an elderly, balding and grossly overweight

Tweedle-Dee and Tweedle-Dum. It was a struggle for them to get Ben back up on his feet in the narrow space.

"I don't understand how that could happen," Holly said.

"Because you're not an electrician," Ben shot back.

He grabbed the wood-handled mop he'd been using to swab the floor and approached the microwave.

"Neither are you," George said.

"I know wood isn't a conductor."

He reached the wooden handle toward the power cord.

"Maybe you shouldn't," Holly said nervously.

"Somebody has to," Ben countered. "The last thing we need is for somebody to get fried on our property."

Holly winced and backed away. George did too, making sure to keep Holly between him and his twin.

Ben slipped the handle behind the cord.

"You're sure that handle is wood, right?" Holly asked.

"Let's find out," Ben said.

He yanked the handle back, snagged the cord and pulled the plug out of the socket.

Everyone let out a relieved breath, even the few customers who were watching from a distance.

Ben dropped the mop, turned to his brother and said, "Lunch is cancelled. Call Malinowski Electric. I want this fixed before anybody else comes in."

"We can't afford to close," George cautioned.

"We can't afford a lawsuit," Ben shot back. "Call him."

Now that the danger was over and the adrenaline gone, Holly noticed a tremor in Ben's left hand.

"You sure you're okay?" she asked.

"No, I'm not. I already told you. I damn near got electrocuted. Finish cleaning up," he commanded, then followed his brother to the kitchen on shaky legs.

Holly was nearly as rattled as Ben. She looked to the microwave, which now seemed more like an infernal device than a benign kitchen appliance. There was scant little she understood about electricity, but she did know that it was unusual for an appliance to act like a live wire. Even if it did, the amount of power coming from a standard outlet shouldn't be enough to knock a two-hundred-and-fifty-pound man off his feet. Something was seriously wrong that needed to be fixed before someone got hurt.

She wasn't the only one interested in the odd occurrence. Observing the scene from outside through the diner's large front window, was Mr. Paper. He gave a slight shrug, turned, and continued on his way along Main Street.

Scott Wilson drove the few miles out of town to the site where he'd been working for the last few weeks. Scott was a surveyor, landscaper, and arborist. He was hired by a successful wealth management consultant from Milwaukee who, in Scott's mind, had more dollars than sense. The job was to clear a remote, wooded parcel of land the guy had purchased where he planned to build a weekend retreat. Scott had no issue with doing the job. Work was work. And once the construction of the house began, it would mean employment for the craftsmen in Glenville, himself included. What he couldn't understand was why someone from the city would want to spend his weekends in the middle of nowhere. Certainly, the lure of Glenville wasn't the fine cuisine served up at the Rx Diner. There was nothing around but dense forest and quiet, which was exactly what the man said he wanted. He saw it as an occasional antidote to the pressures of his job and the pace of the city. Scott didn't question his motives. At least not to his face. If he wanted a remote getaway surrounded by trees and mosquitos, he came to the right place. Scott was more than happy to take his money.

The first part of the job was to survey the property and mark the boundaries. Once that was completed, he felled the trees, of which there were dozens of all sizes. He then returned with his backhoe to dig out the stumps and grade the area for construction.

Up to that point it had been a simple gig that he'd have finished in a few days.

Driving to the site was nerve-racking. Given the finicky way his pick-up was behaving he feared that the engine might die as unexpectantly as it had started. The last thing he wanted was to be marooned at the remote site. He turned off the main (and only) road he'd taken out of Glenville onto a narrow dirt road he had marked with a bright orange ribbon tied to an upright stick.

The development of the area dated back to the late 1600's when French settlers cleared the area for farming. The side road was cut to give access to the fields but had since become overgrown with vegetation to the point of barely being visible. After several trips that Scott and his subcontractors had taken to clear the work site, the rutted dirt road that was originally intended for horse-drawn wagons was easily passable though barely wide enough for his pick-up to negotiate. Low stone walls that were overgrown with vegetation bordered the single-lane farm road. Scott marveled at the simple, effective craftmanship that was the result of pure brute labor. They weren't exactly the pyramids of Giza, but they had survived for generations and spoke to a long-forgotten history of the area.

When Scott made the turn at the orange marker, he felt relief that at the very least his suddenly quirky truck would get him to the work site. He slowed to under fifteen miles an hour so as not to bounce violently while travelling the rutted road. The last thing he needed was to damage the exhaust system. The truck was already giving him enough trouble.

It wasn't finished.

He was halfway to the site when he felt the gas pedal push to the floor, on its own. The truck instantly picked up speed as it dug into the soft earth, spewing dirt from behind like a cloud of brown exhaust. Scott had only a moment of confusion before he thought to pull his foot off the gas, but the pedal remained low as the bouncing truck picked up speed. Fighting panic, he jammed his foot onto the brake pedal, with no effect. He could not stop the truck. The narrow roadway followed a winding route, with the stone wall along one side and a line of trees along the other. Scott had a death grip on the wheel, frantically working to stay in the ruts for fear of rumbling off-course and a head-on collision with a tree. He desperately fought to control a vehicle that was uncontrollable, while wiping away the terror-tears that made it near impossible to focus.

He soon realized that the vehicle wasn't out of control. It was out of *his* control. The steering wheel spun abruptly to the right, leaving the newly-worn ruts headed directly for the stone wall.

"Fuck!"

He fought to steer back onto the dirt road, but he wasn't in charge. The truck barreled toward the wall and nothing he did could change that. He braced for impact, but there was a break in the wall that the truck hurtled through. Now he was careening through the forest. He thought to engage the parking brake. He didn't know what damage that would cause but he had to do something, so he pulled it.

Nothing happened. The truck continued its suicide dash through the forest.

Scott looked ahead to see the truck was bouncing along what appeared to be another road. It was overgrown and littered with branches, but it was definitely a road. Or had been at one time. The truck plowed over low obstacles while staying between the line of trees that stood as sentries along both sides of this second, forgotten roadway.

His final move of desperation was to bail out. Breaking a leg would be painful. Hitting a tree could be fatal. He pulled the door handle. It wouldn't open. He fumbled to release the door lock, but it was jammed. For better or worse, Scott was at the mercy of this runaway truck with no say as to how this terrifying journey would end.

His final thought was to relax. He'd heard that if one tensed up before an impact, the physical damage would be much worse. It was no more than an irrational choice that would undoubtedly not save him from severe injury, but might save his life. At least he had taken back a small bit of control over how this would end.

The truck charged through a thick grove of barren forsythia and emerged into a clearing. Scott was thrown forward against his seat belt as if the emergency brake had finally taken hold. The truck skidded and spun into a nauseatingly tight counterclockwise spiral. He had enough wherewithal to shoot a quick glance to his right to see that his luck had run out. The truck was careening sideways toward a stand of pine trees. He closed his eyes, wrapped his arms around his head, and said a quick prayer.

Terri sat at her office desk, filling out an incident report regarding Scott Wilson's finicky pick-up. It wasn't the kind of event that needed to be documented, but seeing as nothing much else happened in Glenville, relatively speaking it was big news. Making the report had the added benefit of giving her something to do other than lock horns with Darcey, who sat on a plastic chair in the lobby of the Sheriff's station with her arms folded.

Terri looked out of the window from her private office to see Darcey sitting there, pouting. So much for weed's mellowing effect. With a sigh, Terri got up and walked out of her office to stand behind the wall-to-wall counter that separated the private area from the public lobby.

"Talk to me," Terri said.

"I'm not a junkie," Darcey replied petulantly.

"I know that, but it bothers me that your coping mechanism is to get high."

"Why did we move here?" Darcey asked.

"Let's not go there again."

"Why not? You're worried about my coping mechanism; don't you think we should talk about why I need one?"

"You're right, I'm sorry."

"I lived on another planet for sixteen years. Chicago was my norm. It was part of me. This place isn't."

"You saw how bad things had gotten between your father and me," Terri said. "I didn't want either of us to be in that environment."

"Okay, fine. So you ran away. But why come here?"

"It was the only place I knew." Terri said.

"You moved away when you were a child! How well could you know it?"

"I wanted a complete break. A total change."

"You definitely got that!" Darcey said.

"Look," Terri said. "I wanted to get us out of the city. I always remembered Glenville as being a quiet, family friendly town."

"You got that right too," Darcey said, scoffing. "It's way-quiet."

"You don't have to live the rest of your life here, Darcey. I wanted you to meet some real people with simple values. When you graduate you can go to college wherever you want. After that you can choose to live anywhere in the world. But for now, this is where we're going to live."

"I feel like I'm frozen, Mom," Darcey said, less combatively. "You're asking me to be in neutral for the next two years. That isn't fair."

Terri's cell phone rang. She hesitated to answer, thinking it wasn't the best time to turn away from her daughter, but it was her job.

"Sorry," she said and took the call. "This is Sheriff Hirsch. Whoa, slow down. Are you hurt? Where exactly are you? Seriously? Why are you--? Never mind, I'm on my way."

She punched out of the call.

"Scott Wilson's been in an accident," she said. "That damn truck of his."

"Is he okay?"

"I think so, but he's all sorts of agitated. I have to go. How are you feeling?"

"You mean emotionally? Or am I still high?"

"Both. Can you go to school?"

"Not right this second."

"Then stay here until you can. Would you please do that?"

"Yeah, sure."

"I don't know how long I'll be. We'll continue this tonight."

"Fine."

"I hear you Darcey," Terri said sincerely. I just want what's best for the both of us."

She hurried for the door.

"I know what's best," Darcey called after her. "I'm moving back to Chicago to live with Dad."

Terri stopped short, hit with a bolt of emotional lightning. The announcement had too many implications to respond to quickly, or coherently.

"I'm sorry," Darcey added. "But..."

She chose not to finish the thought. She'd said enough.

"We'll talk about it tonight," Terri managed to say while desperately trying to force the news into a compartment she could close off long enough to focus on doing her job.

"Sure," Darcey said. "But I've made up my mind. Dad already knows."

Another shot to the heart.

"We'll talk," Terri said and hurried out of the door before saying something she'd regret.

CHAPTER 4

Once Vera left the pharmacy, she turned her attention to her other problem: the unwanted visitors who were scrambling through her walls at home. She considered bringing Bobcat to her house to be a mouser, but decided it wasn't worth the risk. Animals were creatures of habit. Changing their environment wasn't always the best for them and despite her constant complaints, she liked Bobcat and didn't want to stress him out.

No, this was a job for her trusty handyman, Denis O'Malley. Denis was a classic jack-of-all-trades. He could build, fix, re-build, paint, landscape and pretty much take care of any issues that a homeowner didn't have the skill or desire to tackle themselves. His business was one of the few in Glenville that boomed. His wife had died a decade before and Vera briefly considered firing up a relationship with him, but decided it wasn't wise to mix business with pleasure, which was a convenient excuse to not open herself up to change, or anyone else's annoying habits. Denis was the closest she came to having a friend in Glenville, though it was tempered by the fact that she paid him for his services.

Once Vera made the call, it took Denis no more than an hour to get to the house, assess the problem, put a fix in place, and report back to her as they stood on her neatly manicured front lawn.

"I've checked the whole place," Denis said. He wiped the sweat from his forehead with his shirtsleeve and re-positioned his well-worn Green Bay Packers baseball cap. "I didn't hear nothing, and I don't see where any critter could have gotten in."

"I'm not making this up," Vera said sharply.

"Didn't think you were. All I said is, I can't see where they got in. Varmints are smart. They know how to survive."

"So, what do I do?"

"I baited and put out a couple traps. Three outside and one in the kitchen near the sink in case they found a way in by the pipes. If they're hungry, they'll come sniffing around and we'll catch 'em."

"I don't want to run across some filthy animal in a trap with its neck broken," Vera said.

"Not that kind of trap," Denis said. "It's a cage. One way in, no way out. Totally humane. If we catch something, I'll take it out into the woods."

"And kill it," Vera said with a touch of revenge-anger.

"No, I'll set it loose."

"I'd just as soon you killed it," she said. "I don't want it coming back angry."

"It won't. Critters may be smart, but they don't go looking for revenge. That's a people-thing. I'll take it far enough away. All you've gotta do is relax and let me take care of it."

"I don't need this grief," Vera said.

"I know, this'll be over before you know it. I'll come back tomorrow morning to check the traps."

"Good," Vera said. She didn't add a "thank you" and Denis didn't expect one because that was Vera.

He got into his rust-bucket of a pick-up and drove off. Vera considered walking around the house to see where the traps were but decided she wanted nothing more to do with the problem. It wasn't yet ten in the morning, but she already felt end-of-the-day-weary. She decided to go inside, take a catnap to re-charge her battery, and give Mikey plenty of time to sanitize the pharmacy bathroom.

The house was quiet, as usual. She stood in the center of her living room and listened. After a minute she heard nothing and felt relieved enough to lie down on the couch, kick off her sensible shoes, remove her socks, close her eyes, and do her best to forget about annoying critters, both the two-legged and four-legged kind. Within minutes she was asleep. It wasn't a deep, nighttime sleep, but rather a light power-down nap where one hovers just below consciousness. It's a place where thoughts bleed into dreams with no way of knowing where one ends and the other begins. Vera thought (or dreamt) of a time when she was lying in a field not far from her house. It was a place she often went to as a little girl when she wanted to be alone. It was her happy place. She felt the warm sun on her face and a slight breeze that tickled her bare toes. It was a lovely feeling that took her back many years.

The dream-breeze picked up and in her semi-conscious state she worried that a storm might be headed in. It was enough of a concern that it pulled her out of the sweet memory and back to the reality of the moment.

But the breeze didn't stop. She could still feel it tickling her bare toes. The confusion got her conscious mind to start working. She was lying on her back, just as she always did in the field so she could feel the sun on her face.

She opened one sleepy eye and looked to her feet...

...to see a fat brown rat licking her toe.

A surge of adrenalin blasted the last bit of dopey sleep away as she screamed and pulled her knees to her chest. The rat was equally surprised. It let out a squeal and jumped off the couch, its worm-like tail slithering across the arm before disappearing. Vera sat up and pulled her feet under her. She instantly broke out in terror-sweat as her heart pounded. What should she do? She didn't want to put her feet on the floor for fear the rat was under the couch, waiting to pounce. This time it might decide to use its teeth rather than its tongue.

She sat there for a long minute, fighting panic. Once the shock had subsided and she could think clearly, she realized that she wasn't entirely sure of what she saw. It had all happened so fast. Was it an actual rat? Or part of her dream, brought on by the scratching in her walls?

She took a few deep breaths, and convinced herself that there wasn't a rat lurking under the couch, ready to tear flesh from her bare feet. She chuckled at how she had reacted like a frightened child. It was time to get up and get back to work. All was well…

…until she heard the snap of the metal-cage trap in the kitchen and the terrified shriek of the animal it had captured. It wasn't a dream. The rat was real. Her pulse spiked again. She quickly found her shoes and slipped them back on. At least she knew that the rat had been captured. This nightmare was over, thank-you Denis O'Malley. Now that she was fully awake and back in control, she wanted to see the beast that had dared enter her home.

She boldly strode for the kitchen but took a moment to collect herself before entering. The high-pitched squealing of the terrified animal continued as it thrashed against the metal cage. The sound made her stomach twist. If it had been up to her, it wouldn't be alive much longer and maybe that's what the rat sensed. She stepped into the kitchen and went straight to the sink where Denis had laid the trap.

The terrified squeals ended abruptly. Vera looked to the cage to see that the trap was empty. The little monster had escaped from the escape-proof trap. She looked around quickly, expecting to see the angry vermin cowering in a corner, but it was nowhere to be seen. She looked back to the trap and noticed that it wasn't empty after all. There was no rat inside, but something else was. Vera approached it cautiously and knelt down to get a closer look. Inside was something both familiar, and impossible.

It was a six-inch long black, plastic plaque with white lettering, the kind used on the door of an office. It read: **"Vera Holiday – Manager."**

Vera hoped that she was still dreaming.

Darcey sat in her mother's private office, not entirely sure of what her next move should be. She hadn't planned on springing the news about moving back to Chicago during an argument. She wanted it to be a calm and rational discussion where she could express how deeply and genuinely unhappy she was. Instead, it came out in the heat of battle. She knew how much it would hurt her mother and regretted having used it as a weapon. She didn't know enough about the circumstances of her parent's divorce to pass judgement on whose fault it was, preferring to believe it was equal. Whatever the reasons, her mother was bitter enough to move them several hundred miles away.

It hurt Darcey that her opinion wasn't even considered. It compounded the resentment she felt for having been brought to a town that held absolutely nothing for her. She felt that in spite of her rationale, Terri was only thinking of herself. The festering animosity turned their relationship toxic, something Darcey did not want. She loved her mother, she wanted her to be happy, but she couldn't get past the fact that the life she had known and loved had been taken away from her and replaced with a totally inadequate substitute while she had no say in the matter.

Darcey wiped her eyes and grabbed her pack. If she hurried she could get to school by third period. With a deep breath of resolve, she opened the office door to the small lobby to see that she wasn't alone.

Standing on the other side of the reception counter was a tall, well-dressed man wearing a bowler hat.

"Good morning," Mr. Paper said politely.

"Trick or treat?" Darcey said.

"I beg your pardon?"

Darcey dropped her pack and put both hands on the counter.

"What's your pleasure? Bottle of Bud? Shot of Jack? Or no, you look more like a wine guy."

Mr. Paper offered a confused look and said, "Forgive me, I understood this was the Sheriff's station."

"Sorry," Darcey said with a laugh. "It is. Dumb joke."

"I see," Mr. Paper said, though it didn't seem to Darcey as though he saw it at all. "I'm here to see Sheriff Hirsch."

"She's out on a call," Darcey said. "I guess there was a car accident."

"Oh, I'm sorry. I hope it isn't serious."

"Doesn't sound like it. You want to leave a message?"

"No need," Mr. Paper said. "I'll return a bit later."

"Can I tell her who you are?" Darcey asked. She was being efficient, but it was more about her own curiosity.

"Of course. I'm Mister Paper. I met the sheriff just this morning. She invited me to pay her a visit."

"Really?" Darcey asked, her interest level having jumped a few notches. "For business or pleasure?"

Mr. Paper cocked his head and smiled. "Is that the typical sort of question asked by a receptionist?"

"I have no idea. I'm not a receptionist. I'm her daughter."

Mr. Paper's smile broadened. He seemed genuinely pleased. "Brilliant," he exclaimed. "In that case I'll reply. It's business. I'm an author travelling through the states doing research on a book I'm writing about America through the eyes of an Englishman."

"And you're doing research in Glenville?" Darcey asked with an incredulous chuckle. "You realize Chicago isn't that far away, right? A lot more going on there. Trust me."

"I understand that, but my feeling is that there isn't much one could say about a city like Chicago that hasn't already been documented in a myriad of periodicals and books and film and television programs and—"

"I get it," Darcey said. "It's been done."

"What I'm looking for is unique color, and I've already seen enough of your town to give me the confidence that I've come to the right place."

"Seriously?" Darcey asked. "The only color I see here is gray."

"You seem like a creative young woman," Mr. Paper said. "Perhaps you aren't looking closely enough."

It was Darcey's turn to smile. It was the first time since having set foot in Glenville that someone recognized her creative bent. It didn't surprise her that it took someone from another planet to appreciate it.

"Okay Mister Paper," Darcey said. "Tell me one thing you've seen in this town that makes you think there's anything remotely interesting enough to write about."

Mr. Paper closed his eyes. It looked to Darcey as though he was blocking out the present in order to scan through his memory like it was a hard drive filled with recent memories. Or maybe he was just tired. After a few seconds he opened his eyes and looked squarely at Darcey.

"There's tension here," he said. "I've sensed it in more than one person I've encountered. It's an unsettling combination of complacency, and fear. There's a general sense that change is coming but with no certainty that it will be welcome."

Darcey held Mr. Paper's gaze with equal parts fascination and trepidation.

"I don't know what I was expecting you to say, but it sure wasn't that."

"At least that's my initial impression," Mr. Paper said with a slight shrug. "I've been here only a short while."

"Let me help you," Darcey blurted out without thinking.

"In what way?" Mr. Paper asked. "You've already explained that you find nothing remotely interesting about your town."

"It's not my town," Darcey corrected. "It never will be. Maybe if I see it through your eyes, I can make some sense out of why I'm here. Or why my mother is here. Or why anybody wants to live here. We could help each other out."

Mr. Paper cocked his head as if giving the idea serious thought.

"You're offering your services as a...what? A tour guide?"

"I guess so. Yeah. Or maybe a research assistant. That sounds better. You can't beat my price: free-ninety-free."

"Interesting. What's your name?" he asked.

"Darcey. I grew up in Chicago and now I'm living here in exile."

Mr. Paper nodded and backed toward the door.

"All right, Miss Darcey. Please inform your mother that you wish to assist with my research. If she agrees, we'll get to work."

"Brilliant!" Darcey exclaimed. "That's me trying to sound like a Brit."

Mr. Paper touched the brim of his hat and said, "Brilliant indeed. Be seeing you."

He spun gracefully, swept open the door, and strode out.

Darcey stood still for a moment, trying to gather her thoughts. She wasn't entirely sure of what just happened, or why she had volunteered to help a stranger she had known for roughly two minutes. The one thing she could say for certain was that those two minutes had been the most interesting she'd spent since landing in the wasteland of Glenville. She couldn't begin to predict what helping this odd man would involve, but for the first time in a very long while she had something to look forward to.

Whatever it might be.

Scott Wilson staggered away from his pick-up on wobbly legs. When the vehicle was spinning toward the trees, he felt certain that a devastating impact was inevitable. Instead, the truck side-slipped across the soft earth and abruptly came to a stop a few inches from a large pine tree. Scott had braced for an impact that never came. As soon as he realized he had stopped he threw open the door, which was no longer jammed, and fled from the truck in case it decided to come back to life.

The truck didn't move. The engine had stopped. The wild ride was over. He backed away from the possessed vehicle, grateful to be alive but without a clue as to what had caused the truck he had owned for the better part of an uneventful ten years to take off like that. It wasn't like it was a high-tech, self-driving Tesla with glitchy software. The pick-up didn't even have an electronic ignition. It was about as basic a vehicle as existed.

Once his heart rate dropped to under 150, he took out his cell phone and was relieved to see he had a few bars of cell service. He used it to call the first person who came to mind. Sheriff Hirsch. He wasn't even sure of what he blathered out to her, other than he had been in an accident. It was a relief to know she was on her way. He punched out of the call and looked back to his truck. He wasn't so sure he'd ever be able to drive it again.

"Well...fuck," he said with finality.

That pretty much said it all.

He looked around to see where he had landed. He was in a clearing that was surrounded by more tall pine trees. The only break in the densely packed forest was where the ancient road provided access to the otherwise empty area. There was scant vegetation for the ground was covered by a thick bed of pine needles that had been building up for centuries. His surveyor-mind took over and he wondered if this spot had once been developed. It could have been a homestead with a farmhouse that had long since fallen victim to the ravages of time. He looked for any hint of ancient habitation, like the ruins of a foundation or a ring of stones that could have marked a well. Though nothing popped out at him, he felt certain that the clearing had been man-made for the perimeter was a perfectly cut circle.

Scott was fascinated by history, especially that of his home town. He had read all about the native tribes of the Chippewa as well as the Oneida and the Forest County Potawatomi. Many of these native tribes farmed the land for centuries until white settlers began their steady encroachment. He wondered if he could be standing in an area that was once a small, native village. Or perhaps it was home to one of the earliest European settlers who brought with them the know-how to build the stone walls that delineated property lines. And Syphilis.

Speculating about the history that surrounded him was a far more pleasant way to spend the time waiting for the Sheriff than wondering why his truck had tried to kill him. Of course he knew that the truck wasn't sentient. It couldn't hold animosity toward him for not changing its oil often enough or driving on bald tires. Just the same, he kept a safe distance from the vehicle for fear it might spring back to life. The ticking of cooling metal was the only sound he heard, other than a slight wind that jostled pine branches.

After a few minutes he realized that there was no reason to wait for Terri in that spot. It's not like she was coming with a tow truck. He decided to follow the freshly gouged roadway back the way he had come to meet her at the intersection of the access road that led to his work site. With that resolved, he turned to head out…

…and saw that he wasn't alone.

A woman stood at the mouth of the roadway, ten yards from him. She was elderly with bare, filthy feet. She wore a plain cotton nightgown that had once been white but had since turned a tatty gray-yellow. What stood out most about her was that she was completely bald. She stood there, expressionless, with her hands at her side, looking directly at Scott.

Scott let out a short yelp of surprise before regaining his composure.

"Yo, lady, you scared me," he managed to say. "What are you doing out here?"

The woman didn't react.

"I said what are you doing out here?" Scott called, this time with urgency.

There was nothing right about this woman.

"You okay, lady?"

Still no response.

Scott fumbled for his cell phone.

"I...I'm gonna call the sheriff," he said. "Let her know you're here."

Scott turned away from the woman. Her unwavering stare was unnerving him.

"She'll drive us both out of here and—"

When Scott turned he saw another person who stood near the front of his truck. It was an African-American man wearing a red-plaid bathrobe. He was also elderly and like the woman he stood completely still, expressionless, looking directly at Scott.

"Wha...?" Scott blurted out. "Where did you come from?"

Scott turned in a third direction and saw yet another person standing inside the circle of trees. It was a teenage boy in jeans wearing a black t-shirt emblazoned with the red-and-white Hot Lips logo of the Rolling Stones. He had a mop of shoulder-length brown hair that covered his eyes, but through the tangle of hair Scott could see that he too was staring directly at him.

"Dude, what the hell?" Scott called out.

Scott's heartbeat shot back up as he felt the sharp edge of growing panic. He spun around to see that several more people had joined the party. There was a middle-aged woman with long, gray hair that reached nearly to her waist; a man who stood on one leg using a crutch for balance; and a young man wearing military fatigues.

Scott was at the center of the circle. Each time he spun around, he saw more people, all standing on the far reaches of the clearing, all silently staring at him. His mind couldn't comprehend who these people were and where they might have come from. There wasn't a house or any other building within five miles. He scanned the ever-growing circle of people, desperate for an escape route. He made one more turn to see that the bald woman was now standing inches from him with her nose right in his face. Scott froze in fear. The two held eye contact. Now that she was close, he saw that her eyes had a vacant, unfocused look.

"This is it," she whispered.

Scott screamed.

The sound of his terrified yelp was broken by the short, sharp chirp of the Sheriff's siren. Terri had arrived. He looked to the break in the trees that led to the overgrown roadway to see the Sheriff's Jeep moving slowly toward the clearing as it bounced over the ruts. Scott took off running for it as though it was the cavalry coming to the rescue.

"Sheriff!" he yelled, waving his hands as if she might not see him.

He dodged past the people who hadn't budged and ran directly to the driver's door as Terri stopped and lowered the window.

"Are you okay?" Terri asked. It was a logical question seeing as she'd gotten a frantic call about an accident, and he looked as agitated as she'd ever seen anyone.

"No I'm not!" Scott shouted. "Look!"

He turned around and pointed to the clearing.

It was as empty as when he arrived. Not a single soul was there.

"Your truck, I see," Terri said. "What kind of damage are we looking at?"

Scott took a few steps away from Terri's Jeep to scan the clearing.

"Are you hurt?" Terri asked.

"No," he said abruptly. "Get me out of here."

He hurried to the passenger door of the Jeep.

"What happened?" Terri asked.

"Just drive!" Scott shouted as he got in and slammed the door.

"Okay, no problem."

Terri drove further into the clearing, made a three-point turn and slowly drove out.

"Should I call Charlie Dest for a tow?" she asked.

Scott wasn't paying attention to her. He was leaning out of the open window, looking back into the clearing. There were no people there. What he saw instead was the lights of his truck flash as the engine growled to life.

CHAPTER 5

Ben Daniels, still wearing the grease-and-sweat-stained, yellowed-whites and grubby sneakers from his shift cooking at the Rx Diner, hurried along Main Street toward one of the two crosswalks that was controlled by a traffic light. He was on his way to the bank to deposit the morning's cash. Though Glenville had exactly zero-incidents of serious crime, he hated carrying around that much money. The job fell to him because his brother was stuck at the diner, waiting for an electrician to check out the rogue microwave. Reluctantly, Ben agreed to make the deposit, though in truth he was happy to get out of the diner for a while. The memory of the surprise jolt of electricity made it feel as though his hands were still tingling. He'd just as soon not go back until the problem was fixed.

He stopped at the curb and reached for the lamppost and the metal button that would trigger the crossing signal. He touched it and was instantly jolted by another strong shock that knocked him back a step.

"Goddamn!" he yelped.

For the first time since he was six, Ben wanted to cry. What was happening to him? He rubbed his throbbing hand and looked up at the lamppost as if he might see a telltale clue as to why he'd been shocked for the third time that day.

"What are you looking at?" Holly asked as she walked up to him. She'd finished her shift at the Rx and was headed home.

"I just got another…" Ben said, flustered. "There's a…"

"A what?"

"Touch the button," Ben commanded, pointing to the crosswalk control.

"Why?"

"Just touch it."

"You are a strange man," Holly said.

She stepped up to the lamppost, reached out, and touched the metal button.

Nothing happened.

"I'll be damned," Ben said, stunned.

"Anything else you need?" Holly said. "You want me to hold your hand and walk you across the street?"

"Don't be a wiseass," Ben said with a snarl.

"Just trying to help. See you tomorrow."

She gave him a short salute and continued on her way.

Ben stood staring at the button. He looked to the top of the pole, then back to the button. He reached out to try it again, but he wasn't one to tempt fate, so he backed off.

"Screw that," he said and stepped off the curb to cross the street…

…directly in front of an oncoming car. The driver saw Ben in time and jammed on the brakes, screeching to a stop a foot short of hitting him.

"Idiot!" the driver shouted.

"Screw you!" Ben shouted, threw him the finger, and hurried on.

Holly heard the screech and turned in time to see Ben flipping off the driver. She hadn't seen what happened, but was fairly certain whatever it was, it was Ben's fault. He'd never admit it though. Ben was adept at assigning blame to everyone but himself.

Holly's feet were sore from having been on them since early that morning. She couldn't wait to get to her apartment to lie on the couch, pick up a book and pretend she didn't hate her current situation. Why did she choose to move back to Glenville? Even her parents had left for a more colorful existence in the odd environs of Florida. Living in a world dominated by humidity and fast food sounded like the seventh level of hell to her, so she chose to idle in neutral for a while in the town where she grew up. At least some of her childhood friends still lived there. But after spending four years at Northwestern, she found she had little in common with friends who had chosen not to go away to school. Or anywhere. Reminiscing about old high-school times and crazy keg parties in the woods got old very quickly. Though she told herself it was only a temporary layover, she had no idea of what the next stop should be.

As was her habit, Holly lingered in front of Kaplan's Department Store to see if the window display held anything new and interesting. Kaplan's was the one store in Glenville that carried clothes she'd consider wearing. What caught her eye was a mannequin wearing a pretty, sleeveless, flowered sundress that she could imagine wearing on a date. That is, if she ever went on a date. In Glenville, the pickings were slim, not only in stylish clothing but in eligible young men. The guys she had crushes on growing up were either long gone, married with kids, or spent their nights doing shots and beers. Sometimes their days as well. Still, she could dream. She knew she wouldn't be stuck living there forever, it only felt that way.

As she stood in front of the store window admiring the dress, she saw in the window's reflection that a woman had stepped up behind her. Holly let out a gasp. She'd seen this woman before. Or thought she had. She had seen her reflection sitting at the counter of the Rx next to the handsome British fellow. It had to be her. She had a tangle of long, fiery-red hair that obscured half of her face. The other half of her face was now plainly visible. Even in the reflection Holly saw that it was marred by a hideous scar that cut diagonally across her cheek and over the bridge of her nose.

Holly spun around to face the woman, but once again, there was no one there. She quickly looked back to the storefront window, but saw only her own reflection. The display inside had three mannequins, one with longish, auburn hair. Was that what she'd seen? Was there an odd bend of reflected light that made it appear as though that mannequin was standing behind her?

And given her a facial scar?

That's what she told herself. Human nature will always reach for logical explanations, even when the logic is strained. She tore herself away from the window and hurried off without a second thought about the pretty dress.

She passed Karl Iverson who was nearing the halfway point of his morning sweep.

"You okay, missy?" Karl asked with genuine concern.

Holly didn't answer or even acknowledge him. She was on a mission to get home, lock the door and close herself off from this young day that she already wished was over.

Karl watched her speed away, thinking he should mind his own business. If she was going to ignore him, why should he care what her troubles were? But Karl wasn't one to keep his mouth shut.

"Did that lady spook you?" he called after her.

If Holly heard, she chose not to acknowledge him.

Nor did Mr. Paper, who had witnessed the entire scene while sitting on a bench across the street.

The drive back into town from the crash site was a silent one. Scott stared straight ahead the entire time and didn't offer any more than a quick "thanks" to Terri for picking him up.

Terri recognized the vacant look of shock on someone who was trying to process a harrowing incident. She hoped he'd volunteer an explanation as to what happened, but by the time she pulled into *Charlie Dest's Jalopy Service*, Scott hadn't said another word.

"Thanks," he said for the second time and opened the passenger door.

"Scott?"

Scott froze, as if he'd been thwarted mere seconds away from a clean escape.

"Yeah?"

"Can you tell me what happened?" she asked gently.

"I lost control of the truck," he said without looking at her. "It was lucky I didn't hit a tree."

"Lost control," Terri repeated thoughtfully. "You were in the woods a half mile away from the access road to your job site. Seems like there would have been plenty of time to get control back. What am I missing?"

"Wish I knew," Scott said. "There's something seriously wrong with that truck. It accelerated on its own and the brakes wouldn't grab."

Once he started talking, it came flooding out.

"I couldn't even steer," Scott added. "I guess I should be grateful I didn't end up wrapped around a tree, but I sure can't explain it. I didn't even know that old road was there."

"Seems like you had a guardian angel looking out for you."

Scott shot a look to Terri that was fraught with such genuine fear that it made her catch her breath.

"I don't know if I can drive that thing again," he said.

"I hear you, but don't give up so quick. Charlie will send out a wrecker to haul it in and give it a once-over."

Scott shook his head. "I doubt old Charlie has the chops to figure out what's wrong what that truck. Far as I'm concerned, it's scrap."

"Maybe so, but give him a chance."

Scott nodded and started out again.

"Is there anything else?" Terri asked.

"Like what?"

"Like I don't know. You're shaken up, anybody would be, but when I picked you up you were acting kind of, I don't know, panicked."

"Why's that weird?" Scott snapped. "I thought I was gonna die."

"It's not weird. I get it. But is there anything else you're not telling me?"

Scott took a long time before answering, which let Terri know that her instincts were correct. There was more to this incident than a truck with acceleration issues.

"Nothing that makes sense," he finally said. "But I'll tell you this much: that truck is haunted. Nothing Charlie Dest can do with a wrench will fix that."

Scott pulled himself out of the Jeep and slammed the door before Terri could ask any more questions that he didn't want to answer, or think about.

Terri watched the hulking man with the baby face amble toward the garage office with his hands shoved in his jacket pockets and his body hunched over in a closed, defensive position.

Something more had happened in that clearing. She was sure of it.

Her cell phone rang. A quick look showed her it was Vera Holiday. Terri's heart sank. Vera never called unless it was to complain about something that most people couldn't care less about. She took a deep breath, trying to shake away the thoughts of Scott and his strange accident so she could give Vera her undivided attention.

"Vera, hi," Terri said brightly. "What can I do for you?"

George Daniels put a call in to the electrician, Steve Malinowski, who promised him he'd be over to the diner as soon as he finished installing a dish antenna at a residence on the edge of town.

"A dish?" George said with exaggerated indignation. "I've got a serious situation here. Tell 'em they can wait for their Netflix."

Steve assured him he'd be over as soon as he could, and George hung up without saying good-bye.

"Asshole," he groused.

George's desk was wedged into a corner of the diner's kitchen. From there he took care of the business side of running the Rx. Where Ben kept the kitchen as clean and orderly as an operating room, George's small domain was a disheveled mess of invoices, old-school ledgers, purchase orders and a few plates with crusty, uneaten remnants of past meals. The twin brothers had an agreement not to encroach on each other's space or comment on their habits. The arrangement worked for decades. They stayed out of each other's way and the Rx hummed along smoothly. The incident of the mysterious shocking microwave was the first serious speed bump they'd hit since they opened their doors.

George was hungry. George was always hungry. You don't develop the kind of girth he and his brother sported without enjoying three (not so) healthy meals a day, supplemented by constant snacking and beer. With the diner closed for lunch, Ben wouldn't be cooking so George had to scrounge his next meal for himself. For George that was roughly akin to hunting and foraging in the wild. But he wasn't about to miss a meal, so he got up from his desk to begin the quest for nourishment.

He reached to close his laptop. When his fingers touched the top of the screen, he was hit with a vicious shot of electricity that was so strong he stumbled back a few steps. He would have gone down hard if he hadn't hit the wall behind him.

"Son of a *bitch*," he whined while massaging the ache that radiated from his hand up to his shoulder. He went from literal shock to anger in a nano-second. That's how he rolled. It was one of the few things he had in common with his brother. He wanted to lash out at someone, but who? He grabbed his cellphone and punched in the number for Malinowski Electric. He wanted the lazy electrician to drop whatever irrelevant job he was on and get to the diner, pronto. Something was seriously wrong with the power at the Rx and Malinowski should already be there to take care of it. If he had been,

George wouldn't have gotten shocked. Of that he was certain. If anybody needed to shoulder some blame, it was Malinowski.

"Hi, this is Steve," the voice said.

"Get your ass over here—"

"Leave me a message after the beep and I'll get back to—"

"Son of a bitch!" George snarled and hung up.

He was out of breath with a buzzing arm, and a mystery that he had no hope of solving on his own. It was at that moment that he saw movement on the floor. His eye went to the walk-in refrigerator to see water seeping out from under the closed, stainless-steel door.

"Jesus Christ, now what?"

The electric shock was all but forgotten. Replacing it was the worry that the refrigerator had crapped out and their stock of perishables was in danger of perishing. He walked to the door, sloshing through the slowly expanding puddle of water. He reached out for the steel door, fearing what he'd find inside. If the refrigerator had died, it would take weeks to replenish their stock, not to mention the repair. He didn't even want to think of the expense.

He grabbed the handle and yanked the door open. It was a relief to feel the familiar rush of refrigerated air. Maybe the compressor was still working. But where was the water coming from? He stepped inside to see that the single, overhead bulb was flickering. George thought for certain it was yet another clue as to what had gone haywire with their electricity. The winking bulb filled the refrigerator with an annoying, strobe-like effect, intermittently moving between dark and light. It was disorienting, but he wasn't about to leave without finding out what the problem was. He stepped in cautiously through the water, feeling the wetness that had quickly soaked through his scuffed no-longer-white New Balances. The quick flashes of light made it difficult to navigate, or find the source of the leak.

He looked to the back wall to see the electric panel that held the circuit breakers for the restaurant. The panel's door was partially ajar.

"Hel-lo," he said, cockily, as if he'd solved the mystery of the electric issues like some modern day Tesla. "Getting warmer."

He continued toward the panel that was on the wall between two stainless steel shelves that were packed with boxes of everything from bottles of ketchup to blocks of American cheese to dozens of eggs. He sloshed through a half-inch of water while keeping his eye on the panel for fear of veering off course due to the disorienting strobe. He had no doubt that whatever was causing the shocks, also had something to do with the intermittent power to the lights. He was feeling proud of himself for sleuthing this out and looked forward to pointing this out to Steve Malinowski once the idiot electrician finally decided to show up.

When he made it to the panel, he reached out to open it the rest of the way to see if any more clues would be revealed. He was about to grasp the metal door, when he remembered what Ben had said about wood not being a conductor. George chuckled, thinking himself quite clever for making the realization. Instead of opening the panel, he took one of the wooden spoons that was in a bin on a rack. He grabbed the handle, reached the spoon out for the panel, and gently used it to swing the door open wide.

He stood staring at a bank of breaker switches, having no idea of what he should be looking for. He took out his cell phone, turned on the flashlight, and directed the beam onto the panel. It didn't take an electrical engineer to see that something was definitely wrong. Every last one of the breaker switches was in the "off" position. According to these switches, there was no power at all being distributed through the diner.

"What the hell?"

He had no idea of how this might be causing a surge of power that lit up the appliances. It was counter-intuitive, but definitely wrong and needed fixing. He didn't need to pay an electrician to do that. He reached up to the panel to start flipping switches.

As he was about to touch the first, he stopped. He knew this could be trouble. There were random power surges electrifying appliances in the restaurant. Could this panel be charged up as well? He was standing in water. Wood may not be a conductor, but water certainly was. If he got hit with a jolt of electricity half as strong as when he touched the computer, he'd be fried.

He dropped his hand, preferring to let Malinowski take the risk. With that decision made, he turned to leave the refrigerator...

...and came face-to-face with a woman who stood a few feet from him. She wore a fuzzy pink bathrobe and stood in the water with bare feet, but what stood out was her long, wavy red hair that fell to her shoulders along and the vicious scar that ran diagonally across her cheek and nose.

George screamed, recoiled a step, and hit the breaker panel with his back. He may not have known much about electricity, but he was right to have been cautious about touching the panel. He screamed in surprise as a powerful surge of power coursed through his body. The once-flickering lights now burned bright and steady, lighting up the refrigerator like Main Street at high noon. George's body went into spasm as the power of the electricity held him tight, and liquified his brain. The smell of burned flesh filled the refrigerator, fouling the place in a way that would have been appalling to his fastidious brother. He opened his mouth to scream but the only sound that came out was a gasp that turned into a low death rattle.

Finally, the lights blew out. The refrigerator went dark, and George Daniels was released. He hovered there for a moment, but his dead legs didn't hold him upright for long. He slumped down and fell forward, splashing face-first into the water.

His eyes remained open. Wide. Dead. Unable to see that the scarred, red-haired woman was gone.

CHAPTER 6

Denis O'Malley faced off against Vera in the driveway outside of her house.

"Why would I do that?" he argued. "The only thing I put in that trap was dried fruit and Skippy peanut butter."

Denis was a laidback country guy who wasn't used to this kind of conflict. And accusation. Terri Hirsch was there, acting as a referee as she stood between the two of them. She wasn't worried that Vera would take a swing at Denis, but the woman was known to have a temper, so she wasn't taking any chances.

"It was a name plate?" Terri asked Vera. "With your name on it?"

Vera reached into her jacket pocket and held the name plate out for Terri to examine.

"It was from an office I had years ago," Vera said. "It was stuck in the back of a kitchen drawer. The only person who could have found it was him. Nobody else has been in the house."

"I never seen it before," Denis said defensively. "And I don't go rummaging through your drawers."

Terri chuckled at the double entendre.'

"Not funny," Vera said, chastising.

"Sorry," Terri said quickly.

"C'mon Vera," Denis said. "You know me better'n that!"

"Check it for fingerprints," Vera demanded.

"I don't believe it," Denis said with exasperation and took a step away to pace.

Terri looked at the plaque that she held in her bare hands.

"Lotta people had their fingers on this," she said. "Including me and you, Vera. I doubt I could pull a clean print."

Denis reached over and grabbed the plaque away from Terri.

"There!" he shouted. "Now it's got my prints on it. Arrest me."

Vera was ready to explode. She hadn't told them about her toe-licking run-in with the dream rat that had been caught in the trap, then not. She feared it would make her sound even crazier.

"Whoever did this has got it in for me," she said angrily. "Maybe it was the same person who smeared feces all over the bathroom at the pharmacy."

"Now you're accusing me of smearing shit on your walls!" Denis exclaimed. "What is wrong with you, woman? Have I ever done anything to make you think I'd pull something like that?"

Vera backed down. Denis was right. He had always been a good friend, and quite possibly the only person in town she hadn't offended in some way. Until then.

"Well, somebody's got it in for me," she said, deflated.

"It is strange," Terri said. "I'll head over to the pharmacy and check it out. I'm not exactly a CSI, but maybe something will jump out at me."

"Just so long as it isn't a rat," Vera said.

"Why would a rat--?" Terri asked.

"Nothing. Skip it."

"The best thing you can do is calm down and think about who might have an issue with you."

Vera snickered because that could be an extensive list. But she honestly didn't believe she'd done anything to anybody that was serious enough to justify the level of harassment she was getting.

"And lock your doors," Terri added.

"What's this town coming to?" Vera said. "I've never had to lock my doors."

"Start," Terri said. "And Denis, maybe it would be best if you steered clear of Vera for a while."

"No problem there," Denis said. "I'll be back for my traps when I'm not so steamed."

He turned and strode to his truck.

Vera had lost herself a handyman. And a friend. She actually felt a slight twinge of remorse. She truly liked Denis, at least more than she liked anyone else in town, and she hated to accuse him of doing such things, but there was no other plausible explanation.

"You okay?" Terri asked.

"No," Vera snapped. "Someone's got it in for me, and I don't like it. Would you?"

"I would not," Terri said. "Let me ask around. In the meantime, keep your doors and windows locked."

"Fine," Vera said. "And you be a sheriff."

That stung Terri, for Vera was questioning her professionalism. But Terri knew enough not to argue, especially since Vera had every right to be upset. She backed toward her County Sheriff Jeep and said, "I'll stop by later to check on you."

"No need, I'm fine," Vera said with petulance.

As Terri walked back to her vehicle, a cell phone call came in and she answered immediately. Glenville High School was calling.

"This is Sheriff Hirsch. Yes, I knew she'd be late. She should be there by now. She isn't? All right, thanks. I'll check on her."

Terri punched out of the call, stood by the driver's door of her Jeep, and took a moment to catch her breath.

"Gotta be a full moon," she said to herself.

Terri and Darcey lived in a salt-box of a rented house a few blocks from Main Street. It was so close to work that Terri often left the Jeep at the station and walked to and from home so as not to block her Subaru Outback that was parked in the garage in case Darcey needed it. A quick check of "Find My iPhone" told her that Darcey was at home. Or at least her phone was there and the two were never separated. She had no idea why Darcey would have gone home rather than to school, but given how they'd left things, she braced for more drama. She couldn't have been more surprised when she stepped through the front door and was greeted with a cheerful, "Hi Mom. Home for an early lunch?"

"Uh, no," Terri said with more than a bit of trepidation. "You're supposed to be at school."

"I know," Darcey said. "But this is just too good."

Terri was thrown. Not long before Darcey had delivered a gut punch by announcing she was going to move back to Chicago to live with her father. Now her daughter was as bright and happy as she'd ever seen her, at least since they'd moved to Glenville. Terri had gotten used to the teenage mood swings, but this one was extreme, even for her volatile daughter.

Darcey held two glasses of iced tea. It didn't tax Terri's detective skills to deduce that her daughter wasn't alone.

"Who else is here?" Terri asked, hoping to God it wasn't her bake sale of a friend Jarod.

"C'mon," Darcey said brightly. "We're in the middle of it."

Terri wasn't sure she wanted to know what her daughter was in the middle of. Darcey hurried into the living room with an excited bounce that made Terri wonder if she was using something more potent than weed.

"I think you two know each other," Darcey said.

Terri was surprised to see Mr. Paper stand up to greet her, like the gentleman he was.

"Hello Sheriff," Mr. Paper said cordially. "Forgive me for appearing at your lovely home but I thought this would be best in order to get your blessing."

Terri's head swam.

"Blessing for what?" she asked.

Darcey handed Mr. Paper a glass of iced tea and offered the other to Terri. Terri ignored her so Darcey shrugged and kept it for herself.

"I'm going to help Mister Paper with his book research," Darcey announced with excitement. "How awesome is that?"

"Uhh, I don't know how to answer that," Terri said.

"I realize this is all quite sudden," Mr. Paper said. "I came to see you at your station and met your daughter. When I explained to her what I was doing in your town, she was quite keen on assisting me by functioning as a guide of sorts."

"Of sorts," Darcey said and took a gulp of iced tea.

"A guide to Glenville?" Terri asked, incredulous. "You hate Glenville."

"Exactly!" Darcey exclaimed. "Who better to show him around than somebody who isn't blind to what this town is really about. It'll be a journey of discovery for both of us."

Terri already had more information thrown at her in one morning than in the entire time since they moved to Glenville. It was all getting dangerously close to overwhelming. She needed to sit, if only to take a few seconds to process this latest development. She dropped down on one end of the couch, gathered her thoughts, and chose her words carefully.

"Glenville is a small town where nothing much interesting goes on. Certainly not anything that would hold the attention of someone reading a book about it. Mister Paper, you've come to this town to do what? Soak up the atmosphere? Immerse yourself in the glorious waters of small-town America? I'm afraid you're going to discover those waters are pretty shallow here. I don't see how you can't get everything you need on your own in a few hours without the help of a research assistant, who is supposed to be in school by the way."

"Mom!" Darcey exclaimed with annoyance as she felt her opportunity slipping away.

"Ordinarily I would agree with you, Sheriff," Mr. Paper said. "But in the scant few hours I've been here I've sensed that those waters are far deeper than maybe even you realize."

"What is that supposed to mean?" Terri asked, chafed at the insinuation.

Mr. Paper sat on a well-worn easy chair across from Terri. It creaked when he sat, showing its age. Terri felt a slight twinge of embarrassment, but stayed focused on Mr. Paper who took a sip of iced tea, more out of courtesy than thirst, and placed the glass on the coffee table next to him.

"That is quite delicious, Miss Darcey," he said. "Thank you."

"You're welcome."

"It's from a mix," Terri said, impatiently. "Would you please answer my question?"

"Of course. Something is amiss in your town, Sheriff. I feel it. I'm sure you do too."

"I don't feel a thing," Terri shot back quickly. "There's nothing amiss in Glenville."

"Are you certain of that?" Mr. Paper countered.

"Dead certain."

"Perhaps you're too close to see. I've spoken to a number of people who have been experiencing unique phenomena. The gentleman whose vehicle seemingly has a mind of its own; the woman whose place of business has been violated; Miss Holly who is being haunted by disturbing visions; and the restaurant that has temporarily shut down due to an inexplicable electrical issue that is causing a dangerous health situation."

"Pretty freaky, right?" Darcey said with glee.

"How do you know about all this?" Terri asked, stunned.

"It's what I do," Mr. Paper replied as if it was a simple matter of fact.

Terri was rocked. This guy knew as much, if not more than she did about the issues she was dealing with. She had no idea that Holly was seeing disturbing visions. She'd have to add that to her plate because it would only be a matter of time before Holly would.

"What is it you're after?" Terri asked. "A sensationalized book about a haunted town? Glenville isn't haunted. These are all common issues that are coincidentally happening at the same time."

The Paper Trail

"And therein lies the dilemma," Mr. Paper exclaimed. "I don't believe in coincidence. In my experience, when a series of inexplicable phenomenon occur, there is often an underlying cause."

"That's crazy," Terri said with a snicker. "You're saying Scott's wonky truck and Vera's vandalized bathroom are connected?"

"I don't know that for certain, but it is possible. The connection could be something that happened in the past, or has yet to happen. Spiritual energy is very real, Sheriff. It can be exceptionally strong."

"Spiritual energy?" Terri exclaimed, incredulous. She'd heard enough and jumped to her feet. "We're done here."

She hurried for the front door, motioning for Mr. Paper to follow.

"Please Mom," Darcey plead. "You have to admit it's been a strange day. And it's only eleven o'clock!"

"Is getting high in an alley part of the voodoo mix?" Terri asked.

Darcey stiffened. "No. That's on me. What happened to those other people wasn't their choice."

Terri couldn't argue with that logic and felt a twinge of regret for having taken a shot at Darcey.

Mr. Paper stood and followed Terri toward the door.

"Please understand, Sheriff," he said. "I do not wish to add to your concerns. I simply wanted to point out that in my experience, the whole of what's happening in Glenville might be greater than the sum of its parts, to borrow a well-worn phrase."

"And what exactly is your experience?" Terri asked.

"My research has taken me to many unique corners of this Earth. I've studied multiple cultures, traditions, religions, cults, and unorthodox societies. I've learned enough to know that there aren't always logical answers to puzzling questions. Not everything can be explained using the standard of accepted rules."

"So you write fantasy," Terri said.

"It may appear that way to some," Mr. Paper replied. "But I assure you, it is not a fabrication."

"Look," Terri said. "I'm not going to argue with you. If you think there's something mystical going on here, that's your business. My job is to serve the people of this community. If you're going to continue snooping around, I have to ask you to keep your loony, forgive me, you're educated opinions to yourself. I don't need people running around thinking their town is haunted. It's tough enough living here without people having to worry about living in the Twilight Zone."

"You get no argument from me," Darcey said.

"I will certainly respect your wishes, Sheriff," Mr. Paper said. "But if you don't mind, I would like to remain here in your town until tomorrow."

"That's your call, you don't need my permission," Terri said. "So long as you don't cause a public nuisance."

"I understand completely. Might you recommend suitable accommodations?"

"I don't know what you'd consider suitable, but there's a bed and breakfast on Spruce Street. Tell Molly I sent you."

"I will, thank you."

"What about me?" Darcey asked.

Mr. Paper and Darcey looked to Terri, expectantly.

"Whatever," Terri said. "You want to go ghostbusting, be my guest. But school comes first."

"Deal!" Darcey exclaimed with joy.

"Thank you, Sheriff," Mr. Paper said. "I promise to stay out of your way, but if you feel the need to explore other possibilities for what is occurring, I'd be more than happy to assist you."

"Me too, Mom!" Darcey added.

"Thanks, I'm good."

"Miss Darcey, you can reach out to me after your school day is complete. I'll be about."

"I'll find you," Darcey said. "You're hard to miss."

"Then I'll be going. Be seeing you, both."

He gave a slight bow, and left.

Terri closed the door behind him and turned to Darcey.

"Is he for real?" she asked.

"I don't know. It's crazy. But it's kind of exciting. Right?"

"There's nothing exciting about what these people are going through," Terri said.

"C'mon Mom, you have to admit it's all so weird. This is the most my brain has worked in months. It's all probably just a goof, but at least it's something fun to think about."

"Fun?" Terri said. "That's not a word I'd use to describe anything that's been going on, but I won't stop you from doing...whatever."

Darcey threw her arms around her mother to give her a hug.

"Thank you. Who knows? Maybe I can help you help those people."

"Yeah, who knows?" Terri said skeptically.

She couldn't help but smile. It was the most affection Darcey had shown her in ages.

"I gotta get to school," Darcey said. "They'll probably call you wondering where I am."

"Yeah, probably."

"I have to stop at the station first. I left my pack there."

"Fine, whatever. Just get to school."

"Got it. I'll let you know as soon as we come up with something."

She hurried for the door.

"Darcey?"

Darcey stopped and turned back.

"I don't know that guy. He seems harmless. Odd, but harmless. If he tries anything you're not comfortable with—"

"Mom! You didn't raise me to be a victim."

Terri had to smile. "No, I didn't. But remember, I'm the sheriff. I have a gun. Feel free to remind him of that."

"Sure. It's a real conversation starter. Bye!"

With that, Darcey was gone.

Terri closed the door and stood trying to get her head around what had just happened. She didn't think for a second that there was some all-encompassing spiritual curse that had been cast on Glenville, but if it gave Darcey something to focus on other than moving back to Chicago, she was willing to humor her for a while.

What she couldn't do was open her own mind to the fact that there was any validity to what Mr. Paper was suggesting. That was a bridge too far.

Holly moved quickly toward home, past the stores on Main Street, keeping her eyes on the ground for fear of seeing another inexplicable image reflected in a shop window. As much as she had convinced herself that there had to be logical explanations for what she'd seen, she wasn't taking any chances. She kept moving, and was relieved when she made it to her front door without incident.

She lived in a fourth-floor walk-up on Main Street. The entrance was sandwiched between a beauty salon that specialized in dying elderly women's hair various pastel-colors, and a tattoo parlor that had a distinctly different clientele. Holly didn't frequent either. The front door to her building opened up directly to a steep stairway on top of which was a short hallway that led to four apartments. By the time she got inside she was already breathing hard. That didn't stop her from sprinting up the stairs to get to the safety and normalcy of her home.

Her apartment was inexpensively cozy and feminine without being precious. It was fairly large, nothing like the apartment she shared with two girls at Northwestern. Rents were reasonable in Glenville since there wasn't much competition. Or any. It was more than perfect for a single woman in her early twenties with a diner-waitress income. One large space served as a living room, dining room and kitchen. Double-doors led out to a large balcony where she would enjoy an afternoon Heineken while gazing down on Main

Street to ponder the mystery of why she had returned to this sad little town.

There was no such reverie that day. Or beer, for that matter. Holly entered quickly, even more breathless after the climb and quickly locked her door which was the only defense she had against scary things. The walk hadn't calmed her down. The more she thought about it, the more she was convinced that the woman in the reflection was not created by a strange refraction of light. She knew what she'd seen. Either she was hallucinating, or it was an apparition.

Neither explanation was comforting.

Holly dropped her backpack and went straight to her small dining table where she always kept a pad of paper for sketching. It was a calming habit she picked up in college where she took a few drawing classes and became quite good. One of the daydreams she had about her future was about using her artistic skills as a career. But how? She had no clue and in that moment, she didn't care. She was on a different mission. She flipped open the pad to a blank page, grabbed a charcoal pencil and sketched the image that remained in her mind's eye. She wanted to do it quickly, before details grew hazy.

When she saw the reflection in the diner, the woman's back was to her. In the window at Kaplan's she saw only half of her face, but that half left an impression. Holly quickly sketched a woman who might have been in her fifties, but the deep wrinkle-lines around her mouth could mean she was older. Or had lived a difficult life. It was an odd dichotomy. There were a few distinct features that she focused on and tried to capture accurately. Besides the long, wavy hair, there was the scar that traveled diagonally from the bridge of her nose to the base of her jaw. It looked angry. Whatever caused it was fairly recent. The sight of it made Holly wince, for even in sketch form it looked painful. Another bold feature was her eye. It wasn't the eye of an elderly woman, which was confusing. Perhaps the creases at the edges were the result of advanced age, or of pain. Maybe even grief.

Holly finished the sketch and was surprised to note that she was no longer afraid. She was saddened. This woman had a story to tell, and it wasn't a good one. Or maybe it was all a manifestation of her imagination.

With a sigh she dropped the sketch on the table and went to the kitchen for a glass of water. Her sprint home and up the stairs had left her parched. She filled a glass from the tap and downed it quickly. She rinsed the glass, put it in the drying rack, and headed back into the living room.

On the way she passed her stainless-steel refrigerator, and didn't notice that as she passed, a shadow swept by behind her, reflected on the silver surface of the refrigerator door.

Holly headed toward her bedroom, but stopped short when she caught sight of the full-length, antique mirror that stood between the bedroom door and the double-doors that led to the balcony. It was the first purchase she made when she scored the apartment. It was a true find in a small antique store and cost far more than she felt comfortable spending, but she fell in love with it if only for the ornately carved wooden yolk and pedestal that held it. Though it was prominently displayed as decoration, it had a practical use for each time Holly left her apartment, her last act was to stand in front of the mirror to check her appearance from head to toe. The mirror gave her the final go-ahead to start whatever adventure she was headed for, even if it was only a shift at the Rx.

In that moment, the mirror felt more like a nemesis. She didn't want to see her reflection, or more importantly, the reflection of anyone else. Unlike at the diner where several people were milling about, or Kaplan's department store where mannequins were posed eerily frozen behind panes of glass, there was nothing around that could be mistaken as a reflection of an old/young woman with a hideous scar and a sad eye. Holly dropped her gaze to the floor and strode past it quickly. Once by, she stopped abruptly. There was no way she could continue living in that apartment while constantly avoiding the mirror. It wasn't only silly, it was impractical. She was going to have to face up to whatever she might see.

She took a few steps backward until she was standing in front of the tall mirror. She only had to lift her gaze a few degrees to see herself, and whatever else might be lurking. She took a deep breath, lifted her chin, and looked into the mirror.

All she saw was a paranoid young woman with an Alice Through The Looking Glass phobia. Holly couldn't help but laugh over how childishly she was acting, but couldn't completely dismiss what she'd seen. On her small couch was a woolen blanket she'd often curl up with while reading or watching TV. She grabbed it and draped it over the mirror. It felt silly, but she wasn't taking any chances.

With a renewed sense of calm, she left the mirror and entered her bedroom.

Though it wasn't yet noon, Holly had been up since five and she was drained. She would normally eat some lunch then catch a quick catnap but since her appetite was non-existent, she decided to forego her usual routine and push on through the day. She might even go back to Kaplan's and spring for that flowered sundress. Holly didn't often treat herself. She barely made ends meet with the wages the Daniels brothers paid her. But every so often she splurged, as she did with the antique mirror. She made the snap decision that the dress would be hers.

She went to the bathroom to splash water on her face and wash away the last few hours of stress. She cupped her hands together, filled them with tap water and felt the exquisite joy of the bracing cold. Instantly reinvigorated, she filled her hands with water again and repeated the process, this time rubbing her eyes and cheeks. She dropped her hands, stood straight, looked into the mirror over the sink...

...and saw the woman directly behind her, peering over her shoulder.

There was a frozen moment of horror-movie shock where Holly was able to look right into the woman's eye that wasn't obscured by her hair. That one moment confirmed all of Holly's impressions. This was a middle-aged woman who had been through an ordeal. Holly looked straight into her eye.

The woman looked right back.

Holly screamed.

She spun around, but the woman wasn't there.

Holly stood still for a long moment, her pulse skyrocketing. She gathered her wits and ran for the living room. Before going for the front door she had the wherewithal to grab the sketch of the woman that was on the dining room table. She tore it from the pad, stuffed it into her back pocket and ran for the front door, grateful that the full-length mirror was covered.

CHAPTER 7

Vera Holiday's orderly life had suddenly become decidedly messy. She had no idea why or how someone would have gone through her kitchen drawers to find the nameplate from her old office and put it in an animal trap. Was it to frighten her by demonstrating how easily they could move in and out of her life, undetected? Why would anyone want to scare her like that? She wasn't exactly a beloved figure in town, but she had no real enemies. At least none that she was aware of.

The idea hit her that if somebody had gotten into her house, they might have stolen something. At least a robbery would make sense. The thief could be a psychopath who needed to leave a calling card to prove how easily he (or she or they) could enter her house. That might be why they used the nameplate. The thought didn't give her any comfort but at least it was a theory that made some sense. Or maybe she had seen too many serial-killer movies with contrived plotting.

When she entered the house, she took a quick inventory to see if anything was missing. She peered into the living room to see that the flat screen was still on the wall and the old-school Marantz stereo components were still in the bookcase. In the dining room she checked the cabinet for the "good" china that had been handed down from her mother that she never used. She also checked the drawer where she kept the tarnished silver flatware, also from her mother and equally unused. Nothing was missing. She went upstairs to her bedroom and to the dresser where she kept a few pieces of valuable jewelry that were as unused as the china and silverware. She had her mother and father's wedding rings and her mother's diamond engagement ring, along with a string of pearls from her grandmother that hadn't been worn since the 1970's. Everything was there. She thought about what else in her house might be worth stealing and came up empty. Her robbery theory wasn't holding water.

The scratching returned, making Vera jump as though the sound had physically touched a raw nerve. It was louder and more insistent than anything she had heard before. It was as though whatever creature was in the wall was intent on digging its way into the house. Her surprise turned to anger, and she banged on the wall behind her bed.

"Go! Get outta here!" she yelled.

The scratching stopped for a few seconds, then began again, only now it came from the wall opposite her bed. It was impossible for an animal to have traveled that quickly from one side of the room to the other, which meant the bold toe-licker had a friend.

Vera ran to the opposite wall and pounded on it with both fists.

"Forget the humane traps!" she shouted. "I'm getting traps that'll snap your scrawny little necks!"

The scratching stopped.

"Yeah, you better be scared," she said as she backed toward the doorway.

The scratching began again, this time coming from the wall next to the door. Vera leapt out of the way, banged her shoulder into the door frame and stumbled into the hallway. Whatever it was, it was on the move and now in the hallway wall.

"Bastards!" she screamed and hurried down the corridor, headed for the stairs.

The scratching grew louder. Vera heard scuffling and faint squealing. The creatures in the wall kept right up with her as she made it to the stairs and stumbled down, clutching the banister for fear she'd trip and fall. She had to keep from screaming as she imagined a dozen varmints tripping over one another, chasing her through the hidden areas of her own home. They were now in the wall next to the stairs, moving quickly, rattling the framed pictures of her when she was a little girl. Vera had to hold back terrified tears. Her focus was to get to the ground floor and out through the front door before the little monsters found a way out of the walls and into her world.

She made it to the bottom and hurried straight for the door. As she grabbed the doorknob, she was hit with a surge of indignation. How dare these creatures drive her out of her home? She let go of the doorknob and turned around to face the room.

"I'm coming back," she said with rage. "With poison gas."

She listened. All was quiet.

"Oh? Does that do it? Does that scare you?"

Her answer came from what sounded like dozens of animals in the wall surrounding the front door. They squealed and chattered and clawed in a response that was every bit as intimidating as Vera's threat.

Vera threw the door open and ran out, moving to get away from her infested house. Once she made it to the street, she stopped to catch her breath. What was her next move? She'd go to the pharmacy and make calls to find an exterminator. No more humane traps. She wanted her house fumigated. She wanted it to be a killing zone. She wouldn't set foot back inside until every last varmint who dared to enter was dead. And she wanted to see the bodies. Whatever exterminator she found would have to be willing to clean the place out afterward, even if it meant tearing into some walls. That was all right. Walls could be patched and repainted.

She needed to see carcasses. She didn't want an exterminator, she wanted an assassin.

Mr. Paper sat on a wrought-iron bench in front of Cassone's Bakery, one of the few businesses on Main Street that thrived. The bench was strategically placed to tantalize those who risked temptation by taking a seat directly in line of the delicious aromas that drifted from within. Mr. Paper wasn't seduced by the sweet smell of warm cinnamon buns. He was enjoying the vantage point from where he could see up and down Main Street.

"Lift your feet," Karl Iverson commanded.

Mr. Paper hadn't noticed Karl approaching with his broom and quickly stood.

"Forgive me," Mr. Paper said. "I was lost in thought."

"No need to move, I won't get dust on your shiny shoes."

Karl did a quick, expert sweep under the bench and pushed the debris off the curb onto the street.

"Street sweepers can take it from there," Karl said.

"You do quite the thorough job," Mr. Paper said as he sat back down.

"It ain't exactly tough work. I milk it, to be honest. I could sweep every inch of this street in a couple of hours, but I need the wages, so I stretch it out. Don't tell nobody."

"Wouldn't dream of it," Mr. Paper replied. "Do you enjoy the work?"

"I like getting paid, but I ain't gonna be doing it much longer."

"Oh?"

Karl sat down next to Mr. Paper who didn't flinch over the fact that a near homeless man with questionable hygiene was sharing his space.

"I'm gonna make the Sheriff an offer," he said with enthusiasm." You know her, right?"

"For all of a few hours now," Mr. Paper replied.

"She's a good egg, you know? I'm gonna offer my services as a deputy. Not like I'm trained for police work. It wouldn't be official or nothing. I don't need no gun. But I can be a help because nobody pays me any mind. I'm like wallpaper, you know? I'm always there, but I might as well be invisible. That lets me see things because nobody knows I'm watching."

"And you believe there are things that need to be seen?"

Karl scoffed and said, "Lot of secrets in this town. It might not seem like it to an outsider, but you don't need to peel back too many layers of this onion to find the rot."

"And you'd like to help Sheriff Hirsch peel back those layers?"

Karl looked down at the broom that had been his sidekick for years. He gave it a quick push to brush aside nothing.

"I've wasted a lot of time," he said. "As I'm gettin' toward the end, I wouldn't mind doing something a little more worthwhile."

"A noble sentiment."

"Not sure why I told you all that," Karl said. "Maybe cause you have no idea who I am and wouldn't judge me."

Karl looked up to see Darcey Hirsch halfway down the block, walking their way.

"Uh oh," he said. "Don't want my future boss' daughter seeing I'm a slacker before I even got the job."

He jumped to his feet and continued sweeping.

"Good luck to you, Mr. Iverson," Mr. Paper said.

"Thanks," Karl said and pushed off.

He thought of stopping to ask Mr. Paper how he knew his name, but didn't want to get busted by Darcey, so he let it go and continued on his way.

"I was right," Darcey said brightly as she approached Mr. Paper.

"About what?"

"You were easy to find. Here."

She held out a cardboard take-out box brimming with piping-hot, golden brown nuggets the size of large olives.

"Try one," she said. "A Wisconsin delicacy. One of the few things that make living here bearable."

"And they are...?"

"Fried cheese. With two dipping sauces. Ranch and honey mustard."

Mr. Paper did his best not to grimace with disgust and said, "That's quite thoughtful but, no."

"C'mon! You want to learn about this town? You gotta try fried cheese curd."

"Fair enough," Mr. Paper said with a resigned sigh.

He steeled himself and gingerly took a hot curd with two fingers as if it were diseased. He delicately dipped one end into the white sauce, only because it looked marginally less toxic than the bright yellow option.

"Careful, they're hot," Darcey warned.

After offering a weak smile, Mr. Paper took a small, exploratory bite. His eyes instantly widened with delight.

"That's quite delicious," he exclaimed and popped the rest of the deep-fried nugget into his mouth.

"I know, right?" Darcey said. "From your mouth to your heart and straight on to your arteries."

"Let me sample the other sauce," Mr. Paper said with genuine enthusiasm for the newly discovered delicacy. He swept up a healthy portion of honey mustard sauce and downed his second toasty curd with equal pleasure.

"I'm overwhelmed," he declared.

"Slow down or you'll be overwhelmed by the weight in your stomach. They sneak up on you."

"Noted. Shouldn't you be in school?" Mr. Paper asked.

"I just came from there. I checked in just before the lunch period and told the office I wasn't feeling so hot and had to go home. No big deal."

"Are you certain of that? I wouldn't want you to have an issue with your mother."

Darcey sat down next to Mr. Paper and said, "I've got way bigger issues with my mother than missing a couple of afternoon classes."

The two sat silently. Mr. Paper took another cheese curd, opting again for the Ranch sauce. Darcey joined him and dipped into the honey mustard.

"Were you serious about all that stuff?" Darcey asked. "About some spiritual thing making weird stuff happen? Or were you just messing with her?"

"I'm not one to mess with people, as you say. The situation might be far too dire to make light of."

"I don't know what all that means but I'm guessing the answer is you really do think something weird is going on here."

"As I said, I've traveled extensively and heard many stories. Some were exaggerated, others pure fantasy. But not all. The worrisome aspect is that when a genuine spiritual issue manifests a series of inexplicable events, those events rarely lead to happy conclusions."

"So in basic American English that means bad shit might be happening?"

"I suppose that's an apt characterization," Mr. Paper said. "Do you believe that's possible?"

"I don't know," Darcey said thoughtfully. She polished off the last bit of cheese curd to give her time to think of an honest answer. "There's definitely been odd things going on, but it's a stretch to say it's voodoo."

"Does that mean you won't consider the possibility?"

"No, I said I don't know. But I do believe everything can be explained, and not all explanations follow the rules of nature."

Her answer prompted Mr. Paper to offer a slight smile.

"I appreciate that you have an open mind," he said.

"Yeah, well, you gotta ride the wave, right?"

"Your mother is well respected," Mr. Paper said. "That's obvious even to someone who has been here for only a short time."

"I guess. It's different when she's your mother."

"I understand. But I do believe that the fair people of Glenville may soon be relying on her to help them through this unique time. Some have already turned to her, though she hasn't accepted the possibility that there might be a grander challenge in play. You are open to the possibility. That, in some small way, may have been what brought us together."

"What I'm open to or not doesn't count with her."

"Unless you want to help her. Is that something you're considering?"

Darcey gave the question serious thought, then said, "Yeah, I am. Might be fun."

"I'm glad you feel that way," Mr. Paper said. "Though I'm not certain that fun would be the most appropriate description of this endeavor."

"That's what Mom said."

"Did she? Let's hope we're both wrong."

Charlie Dest had worked as an auto mechanic in Glenville for most of his seventy-five years. His calloused hands were permanently stained from years of ground in oil and grease that no amount of scrubbing with citrus-scented pumice hand-cleaner would eliminate. Fortunately for him, most of the locals held on to their cars until one or the other died of old age, which meant his traditional skills still had value. He often lamented that folks who bought new cars would be better served by taking their vehicles to a Best Buy store for repairs. He was a slight men, with thinning gray hair and thick glasses who gave off an air of casual confidence that only comes from age and having been around the block more than once. Or twice.

There was no one Scott Wilson trusted more to retrieve his truck. To Scott, Charlie represented everything that was normal, and normal was what Scott desperately needed. He rode shotgun as Charlie maneuvered his flatbed wrecker along the well-worn access "road" toward the property where Scott was working.

"This where you lost control?" Charlie asked.

"Yeah," Scott answered perfunctorily. He hadn't explained much to Charlie about what had happened. As much as he was concerned about getting his truck out of there, he couldn't shake the images of the people he had seen, or thought he had seen, in that clearing.

"What'dya 's'pose happened?" Charlie asked.

"That's what I'm hoping you can figure out," Scott replied.

"I will," Charlie said with authority. "The Ford one-fifty ain't exactly a complex piece of machinery."

Scott appreciated his confidence, but didn't share it. Whatever caused his truck to take off on him couldn't possibly be attributed to a simple mechanical issue. The fact that the pickup wasn't a complex piece of machinery, as Charlie put it, was all the more maddening. How could multiple, low-tech, independent systems simultaneously go haywire?

"Over there," Scott said, pointing. "Follow the tracks through the break in the stone wall."

Charlie turned the wrecker out of one set of ruts into another.

He let out an impressed whistle and said, "Definitely was a road here. Long time ago. Makes me feel like that Indiana Jones fella out here uncovering something ancient."

Scott didn't share Charlie's enthusiasm. He wanted nothing more than to get his truck out of there and never set foot in these woods again.

"Not much further," he said.

Scott looked ahead and caught glimpses of something bright yellow through the trees. It wasn't a color found in nature and definitely wasn't there earlier.

"You see that?" Scott asked. He was questioning his own sanity and hoped someone else was riding with him on the crazy train.

"You talking about the yellow?" Charlie asked.

Scott let out a relieved breath. He wasn't hallucinating.

"Yeah."

"Might be a digger," Charlie said as they drew closer.

"Weird," Scott said. "It wasn't there before."

As far as Scott knew, there were no other clearing jobs happening in the area. As they bounced closer, reality hit. It was indeed a digger. A CAT 450 backhoe. It was the kind of powerful tool that Scott was using to dig out the tree stumps at his job site. As they drove into the clearing, Scott realized there was still more to this mystery.

It was his backhoe.

"What the hell?" he muttered under his breath.

"That your rig?" Charlie asked as he drifted to a stop.

"Yeah," Scott said, barely above a whisper.

"Why'd you drive it over here?"

Scott wanted to scream out: "I didn't!" but didn't want Charlie to think he was losing his mind, though he feared it was a distinct possibility.

"I'm using it at the site I'm clearing," was all Scott said.

It didn't answer the question, but it was enough to satisfy the mechanic because Charlie's focus had already gone to the challenge of how to get the pick-up truck onto the flatbed. He got out of the wrecker and ambled toward the truck. The slight man was perpetually stooped forward, his odd posture the result of being hunched over fenders working on engines for most of his life. He looked inside the truck to see the keys were still in the ignition. For a brief second he thought that Scott was being careless by leaving the keys, but realized that nobody would be coming out there with the intent of stealing a truck, so he chose not to point that out. The kid seemed upset enough.

Charlie got into Scott's truck, turned the key, and the engine growled to life. No problem. He glanced toward Scott to get a reaction.

Scott hadn't gotten out of the wrecker. He was staring at the backhoe that sat on the opposite side of the clearing. There was no question in Charlie's mind that Scott was shaken up, but decided it wasn't his duty to try and make him feel better. The best he could do was go about his business and load the pickup. He went back to his wrecker and as he got in, Scott got out and wandered toward his backhoe.

Charlie fired up the wrecker and maneuvered it into position in front of Scott's pick-up, which was no easy task given the size of his flatbed and the relatively small clearing. Once in position he dropped the back end of the bed and went to the truck to start the engine again.

"What're you doing?" Scott asked.

"Gonna drive it up," Charlie replied.

"Don't," Scott cautioned.

"Why not?"

"What if it goes crazy again?"

Charlie wanted to argue that it would be far easier to drive the pickup the few feet up and onto the flatbed than dealing with the cable and winch, but the fearful look in Scott's eyes told him not to bother.

"Good point," Charlie said and began the laborious process of cabling up the pickup in order to winch it onto the flatbed. Ten minutes later the truck was loaded and secured.

"Let's go," Charlie called to Scott.

"You go on," Scott said. "I gotta drive the backhoe back to the work site. I'll call for somebody to come pick me up."

"Suit yourself," Charlie said. "I'll let you know what I find after I give it the onceover."

He was more than happy to get out of there and drive back to town alone. Scott was starting to spook him. Charlie put the wrecker in gear and slowly rumbled out of the clearing.

Scott took a quick glance around, fearing that he'd see one of the odd people, but no one was there. He took a breath and headed for his backhoe. He had no idea how it had gotten there, and quickly convinced himself that it was probably some kids screwing around.

He was about to step up into the seat when the vehicle rumbled to life.

Scott froze. His throat closed up. His thoughts flashed through the possibilities of what could have made that happen, but he drew a blank.

"Charlie!" Scott yelled.

The wrecker was nearly out of the clearing.

Scott took off after it on a dead-sprint. He'd hire somebody else to retrieve the backhoe. He wanted nothing more to do with the haunted place.

CHAPTER 8

Vera had gone directly from her home to the Sheriff's station where she stood across the 1950s era Formica reception counter from Terri.

"There are rats in my walls," she wailed. "Hundreds of 'em."

Mr. Paper and Darcey sat on plastic chairs behind Terri, quietly observing.

"That's horrible," Terri said calmly, though her mind was already running to the possible challenges she'd face in dealing with a rat infestation in Glenville. Was there really such a thing as a Pied Piper she could reach out to?

"Sounds like a job for an exterminator," she said.

"You don't get it," Vera said, distraught. "This isn't normal. It's a massive infestation."

"I understand, but there isn't much I can do. No crime has been committed."

"What about the name plate that showed up in that trap? O'Malley was the only person who could have done that. And the desecration of my bathroom at the pharmacy?"

"Are you saying I should arrest Denis? There's no proof he had anything to do with the nameplate and I'm not seeing a connection between a vermin infestation in your house and the vandalism at the pharmacy."

Vera was becoming so frustrated that she physically shook. Getting no satisfaction out of Terri only made it worse.

"Fine," Vera finally said. "I'll call an exterminator. But I want you to investigate what happened at the pharmacy."

"It's on the very top of my list," Terri said. "I'll be there later this afternoon."

"Good."

Vera stood staring at Terri, not knowing what else to say.

"Very good," she added. "I'll be expecting you."

She turned quickly and strode out of the station.

"Well that sucks," Darcey said. "How're you gonna figure out who smeared shit around her bathroom?"

"Please don't be crude," Terri said.

"But that's what happened, isn't it?" Darcey shot back.

"Yes but if there wasn't...wait, why are you still here?"

"Oh yeah, I'm still a little buzzed from this morning," Darcey answered. "I'm almost good to go. But get back to the shit."

Mr. Paper wisely chose not to comment.

Terri had to take a breath to keep from teeing off on her daughter. Once calm, she replied, "Without security video or a witness I don't see how we can identify a suspect. It's not like I'm going to be doing DNA analysis of the...the--"

"The shit," Darcey said.

"Thank you, yes," Terri said.

"It's quite the mystery," Mr. Paper offered. "As I said, I've found that multiple conflicts occurring simultaneously could be indicative of a larger issue."

"What exactly is that supposed to mean?" Terri asked impatiently.

"Are there any open crimes on your books?" he asked. "Mysteries that haven't been solved? Questions that haven't been answered? In my experience, unsettled business might lead to other conflicts that seem unrelated, yet prove to be anything but."

Darcey was eating up every word that Mr. Paper offered, as if he were the wisest of sages. She jumped to her feet enthusiastically and stood between him and her mother.

"Are there Mom? I mean, other unsolved crimes?"

Terri looked between the two as they waited for an answer.

"You're taking a long time to answer," Darcey said. "A simple yes or no would—"

"No!" Terri spat out. "Nothing ever happens here. Especially not something that would lead to the kinds of things that—"

The front door burst open, and Holly came charging in.

"I think I'm going crazy," she announced, breathless.

Terri stood with her mouth open for a long moment.

Darcey couldn't help but smile.

"And here we go," she said under her breath to Mr. Paper as she sat back down next to him.

"Why is that?" Terri asked, trying to sound level-headed while keeping from screaming in frustration.

"It started this morning in the diner. I thought I saw, no, I know I saw a woman sitting next to Mr. Paper at the counter. In a reflection. But when I turned around, she wasn't there."

"I remember the moment," Mr. Paper offered. "You did seem quite confused."

Terri shot him a stern *please be quiet* look.

"Is that all?" Terri asked.

"I wish!" Holly exclaimed anxiously. "Walking home after my shift I saw the woman again, in the reflection of Kaplan's window. Then when I got home, I saw her standing behind me in the reflection of the bathroom mirror."

"Ooh, like in a horror movie," Darcey exclaimed.

"Darcey, please," Terri said, chastising. Then to Holly she said, "You're sure it was the same woman?"

"Yes! Either I'm going out of my mind, or I'm being haunted."

"You're not being haunted," Terri said.

Darcey looked to Mr. Paper and shrugged as if to say, *I wouldn't be so sure.*

"And you're far too level-headed to be hallucinating," Terri added. "There must be a more realistic explanation. You're seeing reflections. Light can play tricks, especially with reflections of—"

Holly slapped her sketch of the woman down on the counter.

"This is no trick of light," she said. "I sketched that after I saw her in Kaplan's window."

Darcey and Mr. Paper stood and approached the counter to look at the sketch along with Terri.

"Wow, you're good," Darcey said with genuine admiration.

"That's pretty much exactly what she looked like," Holly replied.

"That's remarkably detailed," Terri said because she didn't know what else to say.

"Might I offer an opinion?" Mr. Paper said.

"I don't think it's appropriate that you—"

"Yes! Please!" Holly said quickly.

Terri bit her tongue. Mr. Paper gave another quick glance at the sketch and nodded as if it was exactly what he expected to see.

"A vision that specific must be coming from a real place."

"You mean like the Twilight Zone?" Terri asked sarcastically.

"That's the second time you referred to such a place," Mr. Paper said with confusion. "Is it a locale I should be familiar with?"

"I think you're a little too familiar with it," Terri said. "Forget I mentioned it."

Mr. Paper tapped his own forehead and added, "I mean it could be coming from somewhere in here. Perhaps, Miss Holly, this is someone you met long ago and have since consciously forgotten. Or an acquaintance of someone you've seen in pictures. You might not have met her at all, at least not in the traditional sense. It could be someone you saw in passing when you were away at university. Why you're seeing visions of her, I cannot begin to speculate but she most likely is very real. If you determine who she is, it might explain why she's haunting you."

"Please don't use that term," Terri cautioned.

"So you don't think I'm crazy, Mr. Paper?" Holly asked.

"Oh, you may very well be crazy, but I don't doubt that you've actually seen this woman at some point."

Holly frowned and said, "Oh. Well, thanks. I think."

"What would you like me to do, Holly?" Terri asked.

"I don't know. Nothing, I guess. I just needed to tell somebody. At least that makes it real and not something that only exists in my head."

"Maybe you should consider seeing a doctor," Terri said.

"Sure. Why not?" Holly said with a snicker. "There must be a load of competent psychiatrists in Glenville."

"Zing!" Darcey said over her shoulder.

"I'm going to do what Mr. Paper suggested," Holly said. "I'm going to try and figure out who she is."

"I'll keep my eyes open," Terri said, though she didn't believe for a second that she would miraculously cross paths with this mystery woman.

"Thanks, Sheriff. I feel better sharing this with somebody."

"I wish I could give you more help, Holly," Terri said. "If you see her again, try to talk to her. And please tell me what happens."

"I will."

Holly stood there awkwardly, not sure of how to make an exit.

"Okay, then, bye," she finally said then gave a quick wave and headed out.

Terri, Darcey, and Mr. Paper watched her leave, then shared looks.

"So this book you're writing," Terri said. "Is it a ghost story?"

"Why do you ask?" Mr. Paper replied.

"Oh I don't know. You seem to know a whole lot about odd things."

Mr. Paper picked up his walking stick, rounded the counter and headed for the door.

"I have learned a thing or two on my travels," he said. "And I must say, I am truly enjoying my visit to your lovely town. Thank you for humoring me, Sheriff. Will you be joining me, Miss Darcey?"

"I'll catch up," Darcey said.

"No you won't," Terri said. "You can make the last two periods at school."

"Oh, right," Darcey said with no enthusiasm. She glanced at Mr. Paper, fearing he might let it out that she'd already signed herself out.

He tipped his bowler hat and said, "Good luck, Sheriff. Be seeing you."

With the fluidity of a dancer, he opened the door and breezed out.

"He's starting to creep me out," Terri said.

"He's just interested," Darcey said. "And interesting."

"Am I the crazy one for letting you hang out with him?" Terri asked.

"I'm a big girl."

"No you're not."

"Well, I am. But I promise, if anything feels sketch, I'll come straight to you."

"Fine."

"You have to admit, there's some weird shit happening."

"Again. Crude."

"I want to help you figure out what's going on."

In that moment, Terri saw her daughter as a competent woman and not a little girl who needed taking care of.

"Thank you," she said.

Darcey rounded the counter and hurried for the door.

"I'll pick up dinner," Darcey said. "What sounds good?"

"We're not in Chicago. There's no take-out here."

"Oh, right. I forgot. This place sucks."

"I'll cook. Be home by six. Now get to school!"

"Love you, Mom. Bye!"

Darcey pulled open the door and headed out with no intention of going to the school.

"We need to talk about Chicago!" Terri called after her.

Too late. Terri was left alone to try and understand why her dull town had suddenly developed a decidedly strange edge.

The Glenville Hardware Store was a throwback to a simpler time with well-worn wooden floors, barrels filled with every nail and screw imaginable and a limited yet adequate selection of hand tools. The entire place was permeated with the sweet smell of lubricating oil.

Ben Daniels stalked the aisles, scowling and shuffling his way along until he found what he was looking for: a heavy-duty pair of rubber gloves. He brought them to the checkout counter and dropped them in front of a young sales clerk with residual acne scars and a 1980's style mullet that reached down to his shoulders. Danny Reynolds normally worked at the checkout after school and on weekends but decided he needed cash more than geometry, which was why he was working in the middle of the week during school hours.

Ben was breathing hard and sweating as if the search for the gloves had been physically taxing. Danny took one look at him and envisioned having to jump over the counter to pump out CPR. If only he knew how to do CPR.

"You okay buddy?" Danny asked.

"Just ring it up," Ben shot back.

"No problemo. Cash or credit?"

"Credit."

Danny rang up the order and said, "Swipe your card. Or stick it in if you have a chip. Or tap it if—"

"I'll swipe it," Ben said curtly as he pulled out his wallet.

"Funny how they call it swiping," Danny said. "Sounds like you're ripping something off."

Ben didn't think it was all that funny, so Danny gave up trying to be amiable. When Ben touched the POS device on the counter, he was hit with a shock that was so brutal it nearly knocked him off his feet. He yelped and took a step back.

"Whoa, dude, you okay?" Danny said, wide-eyed.

Ben's heart rate leapt back up to dangerous. He massaged his hand and stared at the POS device as if it was a sentient trap. Tears welled in his eyes from pain, surprise, confusion, and rising anger.

"Charge it to that card," he barked.

He tossed the card onto the counter, swept up the gloves and hurried out of the store.

"You gotta sign!" Danny called. "And your card!"

Ben ignored him and kept moving, leaving Danny alone and confused. He looked at the POS machine with curiosity. With a mischievous gleam in his eye, he reached out with both hands and grabbed the device as if hoping to get the same kind of jolt that hit Ben.

Nothing happened.

Disappointed, Danny swept Ben's card through the machine to complete the sale.

Holly went straight from the Sheriff's station to the Rx Diner. The last people she expected to get any help or sympathy from were George and Ben Daniels, but she had formed a plan to investigate her mysterious, red-haired woman and needed to get to George's office. It was all about the Wi-Fi. The cell service in town was even less stable than the wonky traffic light on Main Street and Holly had no intention of going back to her apartment just yet. The Rx was the one place she knew of that had decent WiFi.

When she entered through the front door she was momentarily surprised that the dining room was dark and quiet. With all that had happened since that morning she'd forgotten about the strange electrical problem that forced them to close for lunch.

Once she remembered, her fear was that the power had been cut off, which would mean no WiFi.

There was a simple way to find out. The light switches were located near the door to the back of the diner, but to get to them she had to walk past the service counter, behind which was the mirror where she had first seen the scarred woman. She braced herself, kept her eyes on the floor, and hurried through the dining room without so much as a glance to the mirror. She went straight to the row of wall switches, reached out, and hesitated. Had the electric problem been fixed? Could touching the light switch give her a shock? After a quick look around she grabbed one of the plastic-laminated menus. Plastic isn't a conductor. Or is it? She reached the large menu out to the line of switches and flipped them up. The overhead lights kicked on.

The diner had power. She went through the door which led to the far end of the kitchen where George had his desk. After flipping on the kitchen lights with the same menu, she shoved aside some of George's mess and laid her sketch of the woman down on the surface. With her phone, she took a picture of it. Once satisfied that the photo was decent, she attached the photo file to a text message, wrote an accompanying text, and sent it on its way.

"What the hell are you doing?" Ben barked, making Holly jump with surprise.

"My God, you scared me!" she exclaimed.

"You don't work lunches," Ben said as he showed dominance by going right for the desk, forcing Holly to take a step back.

"I know," she said. "You're not even open. I needed WiFi."

"Why?" Ben asked with a sneer. "To watch your Tik Tok?"

"I'm sending a picture to my mother. Why doesn't this town have decent cell service?"

"Why can't you do that at home?"

"Because..." Holly fell silent. She didn't want to explain why she was afraid to go home. "Because I need to send a picture and WiFi is better here. Is the electricity fixed?"

"I don't know, I've been running errands."

"Oh, right," Holly said. "Did you figure out how to use the cross walk?"

"You're hysterical."

"What's with the rubber gloves?" Holly asked.

Ben cautiously reached out with a rubber-gloved hand and touched the printer on his desk. Nothing happened and he sighed with relief.

"I'm not going to risk getting shocked again," he said.

"Or you could just fix the problem."

"Are you done here?" Ben asked, irritated.

Holly reached past him to grab her sketch that was still on the desk. Before she could pick it up, Ben slammed his open hand down on it, making Holly push back in surprise.

Ben stared down at the picture, with both hands now on the desk as if he needed support.

"What the hell is this?" he asked, sounding as though it was an accusation.

Holly was again surprised by his sudden shift of tone.

"Nothing," she said. "Just a sketch I did."

She reached around Ben to grab it, but Ben didn't lift his hand from it.

"Who is it?" he asked cautiously, as if he didn't really want the answer.

"Just somebody I saw."

"You saw this person?" Ben asked, incredulous. "Where?"

Holly was not about to answer that question. At least not fully.

"Around town," she said. "I don't know who it is, so I took a picture of it to send to my mom. She used to live here so I thought she might know somebody who—"

"Go home," Ben barked.

"What?"

"I said go home!"

Ben had always been a gruff character who Holly never warmed to, but this odd behavior was particularly aggressive, even for him.

"Fine," she said. "Can I have my sketch please?"

Ben grabbed the paper and crumpled it up.

"What is wrong with you?" Holly cried. "You had no right to do that."

Ben didn't try to defend himself. It was as though the fight had gone out of him. He simply sat down in the desk chair with his back to Holly.

Holly didn't know how to react. Something was wrong but she had no idea what it might be.

"All right," she said. "Fine. I don't know why you did that, and I don't really care."

She waited for a reaction, but got none so she backed away.

"Maybe you should go home too," she said. "This electric thing has got us all on edge and—"

She stepped back into a puddle of water.

"Oh man, now what?" she said.

She placed her phone down on the desk, and followed the source to see that it was coming from underneath the walk-in refrigerator door.

This broke Ben from his stupor. He looked to her, then to the floor and saw the water.

"What did you do?" he demanded.

"I didn't do anything! Why do you blame everything on me?"

"Is the compressor out?" he asked.

"How should I know?"

She strode through the water, headed for the refrigerator. "If it is it probably had something to do with the electric weirdness." She reached for the metal door handle. "George is going to absolutely go out of his mind."

She grabbed the handle pulled open the door...

...and screamed.

CHAPTER 9

Mr. Paper and Darcey strolled casually together along Main Street. With his chin up and the rhythmic ticking of his walking stick on the pavement, Mr. Paper's discerning gaze traveled across each storefront as if perusing the works in a museum of fine art.

Darcey kept stealing quick glances up to him, fascinated by the man, and by the man's fascination with the dying town.

Mr. Paper said, "I take it by your furtive looks that there is something you'd like to say but have yet to find the right words."

"Sorry," Darcey said, more than a little embarrassed. "Rude."

"What's on your mind?"

"All that stuff you said, about how some crime or unsettled business might be why people are being spooked. Do you believe that?"

"I believe it's possible. Societies function much like the human body or a complex machine. It's a perfectly calibrated ballet where every action impacts the other. Throwing a hammer into the works would most likely cause havoc."

"But that's science. This is a whole 'nother thing."

"Is it? The human spirit is every bit as powerful as the relatively pedestrian physical mechanisms it creates."

Darcey gave him a double-take and said, "Now you're talking in riddles."

"Life is about balance. For every action there is an equal and opposite reaction."

"Again. Science. Einstein, right?"

"Sir Isaac Newton," Mr. Paper said. "His third law of motion. Who is to say there isn't a fourth? One that applies to the spirit as well as to physical reality. For example, your desire to leave your mother, to live with your father in Chicago. That is certain to have a dramatic and lasting impact on many lives."

Darcey stiffened.

"I don't get the connection," she said curtly.

"It's an example of how every action has a ripple effect that goes beyond the action itself. That must be considered with every decision one makes."

"Yeah well I can't see the future, all I know is it's not working for me here."

"Yes but the question is, why? Understanding that will tell you if you're running toward something, or away."

"What if it's both?" Darcey asked.

"Very possible. In that case you need to weigh the alternatives to try and mitigate the upheaval caused by the ever expanding ripples."

Darcey stared at the ground for a few more steps then said, "You seem pretty wise in an old-guy British kind of way. I'm thinking it's mostly because your accent makes you sound smart and you've got some major balls to wear a hat like that around here. But I'll pretend that you're not full of BS and ask what you'd do if you were me."

Mr. Paper chuckled and said, "I can't pretend to see the world through the eyes of a young girl, even one as intelligent and precocious as you. But I will say that no matter who you are or what challenges you face, you must always look forward. Sometimes that means taking a step back to try and understand what it is you want as opposed to what you don't want."

Darcey considered this and said, "How did this get to be about me?"

"We were talking about the concept of balance, and the implications of it being upended."

"Let's stick with Glenville."

"Agreed."

"So what do we do?" Darcey asked.

"There are two possible explanations for what has been happening. One is that the unsettling events are random. That would mean there are multiple, unrelated occurrences. Coincidences. That would make our investigation far more difficult and quite possibly unnecessary."

"So we're looking for something that connects them?"

"That would be the second explanation. If that can be established, it would be the first step in understanding the conflicts and ultimately lead to their resolution."

"There's a third," Darcey said. "The people in this town are a little bit looney. I know. Living here is definitely driving me nuts. There's a chance that none of this is real."

"I suppose mass delusion is a possibility," Mr. Paper said. "Ideally we will make that determination. My suggestion is that we start by speaking to the individuals who have been affected. Listen to their stories. The goal is to determine if there is a common denominator. Perhaps you should begin with Mr. Wilson, the fellow who has been having automotive issues. Do you know him well?"

"Well enough to talk to him. What about you?"

Mr. Paper scanned the street to see Karl Iverson on the opposite sidewalk, sweeping around the cement planters in front of an abandoned florist shop.

"I'll have a chat with Mister Iverson."

"The Sweeper?" Darcey asked. "What's his problem?"

"I don't believe he even knows himself," Mr. Paper replied.

"Uh, okay. Whatever that means."

"Keep one thing in mind," Mr. Paper said. "If these events do prove to be connected, it will most likely lead us to a single individual who is the key to it all."

"So we're looking for a culprit?" Darcey asked.

"That implies villainy, which may or may not be the case. Let's say we're searching for a nexus. Something or someone who ties this all together."

"Got it. I think. We'll compare notes later," Darcey said with growing enthusiasm.

She started to run off, then put on the brakes and turned back to Mr. Paper.

"I get what you said about balance. I'll definitely think about it."

"I have no doubt that you will," Mr. Paper said. "Whatever decision you make going forward, I'm delighted that you've chosen to join me on this journey."

"Are you kidding?" Darcey said with a laugh. "It's the best thing that's happened to me in forever!"

She turned and ran off. Mr. Paper watched her go, took a wistful breath, then strode across the street headed for Karl Iverson.

"It appears as though your task is nearly complete for the day," he called out to the man known as The Sweeper.

Karl kept his head down, focused on getting his broom behind a cement planter to dig out a few stubborn cigarette butts. He attacked the work with vengeance, frustrated by the trash that was resisting his best efforts. Mr. Paper stood behind him, leaning on his walking stick with both hands.

"Have you given more thought to the proposal you plan to offer Sheriff Hirsch?"

"It's all I've been thinking about," Karl groused. "Sweeping don't require a whole lot of concentration."

"And?" Mr. Paper asked.

"I'm kiddin' myself. Nobody wants me working for them. They barely tolerate me sweeping up their trash."

He angrily dug at the last cigarette butt and finally wrangled it into his dust pan.

"I suppose it's the bed I made," Karl said. "I never had much time for people and now they ain't got time for me."

"I'm sorry to hear that, Mr. Iverson," Mr. Paper said. "But I do believe you're right about something."

"Yeah? What's that?"

"It may be time for a change."

"You're right. Anything's better than this."

"That's a positive way of seeing things," Mr. Paper said. "But change can be difficult. I hope you can accept that whatever comes next, it will be for the best."

Karl stopped sweeping and looked straight at Mr. Paper.

"You some kind of philosopher?" he asked.

"No, just an observer. Good luck, Mr. Iverson. Be seeing you."

He tipped his hat and walked off. Karl watched him go for a moment, then dropped his broom onto the sidewalk. It fell with a clatter and settled with the brush hanging off of the curb. With a sigh, Karl strode off in the opposite direction, leaving his trusty broom behind.

Darcey had no intention of going to her last few classes of the day. School could wait. Maybe forever, since she expected to be back at her old school in Chicago very soon. Her adventure with Mr. Paper was all that mattered. It was thrilling to think they were dealing with next level spiritual issues that might change everything she knew about how life worked, and since she was grappling with an existence that was mundane at best, the idea that there could be more to life than mind-numbing routine in a town on life-support gave her hope that a better future was possible.

Flush with excitement that the curtain was about to go up on a decidedly more interesting life, she couldn't wait to get to Scott Wilson's house to grill him on what he'd seen that morning. As she stood on the curb, waiting for the light to change, she glanced across the street to see a little girl on the opposite curb who looked to be no more than seven. She was waiting to cross the street in the same direction Darcey was heading. It was an odd sight, and not only for the fact that it was midday when kids were supposed to be in school. The girl was wearing a faded, yellow nightgown that went below her knees. And she was barefoot. Darcey couldn't take her eyes off the girl, who stared directly ahead with her arms straight at her side and her eyes closed. Darcey wondered if she might actually be asleep standing up.

A pick-up truck rolled by, momentarily blocking her view of the girl. When the truck drove past, Darcey caught her breath because the girl's eyes were open, and she was staring back at her. The two held eye contact for a long moment, then the girl raised her hand and gave Darcey a small wave. Without thinking, Darcey waved back as a town bus drove past, once again blocking her view. When the bus cleared, Darcey gasped again. The little girl was no longer there.

Darcey opened her mouth to call out, but had no words. She scanned the street, but there was no sign of her. Unnerved, Darcey went on her way, while glancing back for any sign of the odd little girl. Part of her felt as though there was a simple explanation for what had happened. She also feared that she might now be one of the victims of whatever supernatural force had descended on Glenville.

Vera Holiday left the Sheriff's station, adrift. Hers was a life that had always been about consistency and regimentation. Since she lived alone and ran her own business, she made the rules without discussion or pushback. She had no one to answer to, no one to compromise with, no one to tell her what to do, and no obligations to anyone but herself. Every choice she made was calculated for maximum efficiency. Now, forces beyond her control had upended that orderly existence. It was not only unsettling, it enraged her.

She lived in a perpetual state of frustration because in her opinion, most everyone she dealt with turned out to be incompetent, oblivious, or just plain stupid. It wasn't an attitude that was conducive to making friends, not that she wanted any.

Now that she found herself in a situation that was out of her control, she had no one to turn to for support. Her one friend, Denis O'Malley, was the most likely suspect to be guilty of harassing her. The kid who worked for her, Mikey Harper, was just a kid in a lengthy line of kids who came and went. Though he was more reliable than most, she had no intention of reaching out to him for advice or comfort. Sheriff Terri Hirsch was proving to be as incompetent as she feared when her hiring was first announced. She didn't believe that a city girl, and a divorcee to boot, could possibly know about the needs of simple, small-town people. She hadn't had any direct dealing with Terri, until that day, but had no faith that this woman had the ability to determine who was harassing her. That ineptitude, while not surprising, made her blood boil. She decided that once the dust settled she'd petition the county to have her useless, big-city ass run out of town, along with her snotty daughter.

All that righteous indignation did nothing to help her in that moment. Though she would never admit it, even to herself, she was afraid to go back to her house. She was too frazzled to go to the pharmacy because she didn't want to show vulnerability to her clientele. She needed time to think and form a plan of action, so she walked to the far end of Main Street and the throwback Motor Lodge called The Cozy Rest that had been there since she was a little girl. She never had a reason to set foot in the place, but felt that this was as good a time as any to change that, if only to grab a few precious hours to rest and reset.

"Vera Holiday!" exclaimed Sherry Terri as Vera entered the office. Sherry was a heavyset, middle-aged woman who was known for her perpetual smile and heavy-handed use of eye make-up. Sherry had owned and managed The Cozy Rest for the better part of two decades. She logged more hours behind the counter to service her guests than she did in her own home. That was okay by Sherry. She loved meeting new people and enjoyed hearing about where they came from and where they were headed.

She was nothing like Vera.

"I need a room," Vera said curtly. "Might be staying the night or a few days. I don't know yet."

Sherry gave her a sly smile and said, "Why Ms. Holiday. Is there an assignation in your future?"

"Don't be crude," Vera snapped. "My house is being fumigated."

Sherry dropped her smile and said, "Oh. Too bad." She slid an old-school key on a plastic fob across the desk to Vera and added, "One can always hope!"

Vera shot her a vicious look that chilled Sherry.

"Room Six. Ground floor. Stay as long as you'd like. I'll give you the locals rate."

Vera snatched the key off of the counter and headed for the door.

"Enjoy your stay!" Sherry called out with genuine sincerity.

Vera didn't acknowledge her and stormed out, leaving Sherry to shake off the frigid Vera-wind that had blown through.

Room Six was small but clean. If Vera had been inclined to look beyond the practical, she might have said that it was actually cozy, as the name of the motel promised. In that moment, such adjectives meant nothing to Vera. She needed a refuge where she would feel safe for the time it took to rid her house of vermin. Brilliant sunlight streamed in through the large window next to the door, so the first thing Vera did was close the Venetian blinds. That effectively closed off the outside world. The simple room offered only two places to sit: a small table with two chairs that was a place to drink coffee or eat a pizza, and the bed. Neither were ideal. Vera chose the bed. She sat down with her back to the wall and immediately took out her cell phone to search for an exterminator. The only one listed in Glenville was Denis O'Malley. That was a non-starter. Fon Du Lac offered several choices, but that town was a three-hour drive away. Vera's heart sank. She wanted someone to get on it right away, but had to resign herself to the reality. She found some Cozy Rest stationary, and began making a list of names.

As she wrote *A-1 Exterminators*, a name which didn't speak to the quality of their work but to their intent of always being first on the alphabetized exterminator list, there was a knock on her door that was so soft she wasn't entirely sure it had happened. She stopped writing and listened. A few seconds later, there was another knock.

"Who's there?" she called out brusquely to insure that the interloper would know she didn't appreciate the interruption.

No response.

"Hello?" she called.

The reply was another soft knocking.

She tossed down the pen with annoyance and went for the door.

"I just checked in," she yelled. "I don't need housekeeping."

She looked through the peephole to see nothing.

"Go away, Sherry!" she called out, putting an exclamation point on her demand in case she hadn't made her feelings clear enough.

She headed back for the bed but before she could sit, there was another gentle knock. She stopped short, spun on her heel, and stormed back to the door.

"I said I don't need housekeeping!"

She threw the door open. Nobody was there. She leaned out, looked right, and left, but saw no one.

"Sherry?" she called out.

No reply. She slammed the door, this time making sure to put on the safety chain though she felt certain whoever it was had gotten the hint and had given up trying to do whatever it was they were there for. Vera went back to the bed to continue compiling her list.

Another knock. This time more insistent.

"What the hell!" she exclaimed.

This time when she looked up, she saw a silhouette through the closed Venetian blinds causing her to let out an involuntary yelp of surprise. Someone was standing outside of the window. Whoever it was, wasn't tall. It could have been a child. They stood frozen, directly centered in the window.

As surprised as she was, Vera didn't hesitate. She jumped up, ran for the door, pulled off the chain, opened the door and leaned outside.

"What do you want?" she demanded.

Nobody was there.

She tried to call out, but the words caught in her throat because she was too stunned to form a coherent response. Her anger quickly morphed into confusion. She pulled the door shut, threw the dead bolt, and attached the chain. She then backed away from the door, keeping her eyes on the window. The silhouette was gone, which offered some relief. Instead of returning to the bed, she went to the window and pulled the cord to close the drapes, effectively cutting off all light from outside. Her next move was to use the room's old-school telephone to call Sherry at the front desk to complain about being harassed. She got as far as grabbing the receiver from its cradle when another soft knock was heard. Vera slammed the phone receiver down, steeled herself and went back to the door. Rather than open it, she changed direction and headed for the window where she violently pulled on the cord to sweep the drapes open.

There was no silhouette.

She moved to the center of the large window and stood directly in front of it, her nose only a few inches from the closed blinds. She reached up, hooked her finger around one of the slats at eye level, and pulled it down to reveal a pair of brown eyes staring back at her. There was a frozen moment where she thought the eyes weren't human because they were surrounded by short, gray fur.

She didn't scream. The shock was too great for her to do anything but stumble backward. Her hip caught the edge of a dining chair. She was knocked off balance and fell to the floor, landing hard on her hip. When she gathered her wits enough to look back to the window. There was still no silhouette. She pulled herself up, using the chair to help her climb to her feet. She went right back to the window and pulled the drapes shut. From there she backed away, more cautiously this time, and sat on the bed. All thoughts of writing out a list of exterminators was gone. She yanked down the bedcovers, crawled underneath, and pulled them up over her head. It was a juvenile act that she performed unconsciously. She had no plan or purpose other than to sooth herself.

She closed her eyes and fought back tears because in those few moments she realized that whatever was happening to her had nothing to do with her house, or the pharmacy, or the Rx Diner for that matter. It was all about her, and there was no place in Glenville where she could hide.

Until that morning, Scott Wilson's life had been one that could best be described as unremarkable. He was born in Glenville, played sports from elementary school through high school, had one long-time girlfriend who moved on from him when she left town to attend Villanova University and never returned. He went into his father's landscaping business, and eventually took it over when his father aged out. He had a few relationships that hadn't grown into anything long-term but never quite went away. He always found someone to spend a Saturday evening with that sometimes, if the stars aligned, stretched into Sunday morning. He made enough money to get by, mostly because getting by in Glenville didn't take much. He had all that he needed: A small house with a manageable mortgage, a handful of drinking buddies, and enough clients to keep him busy but not so much that it prevented him from fishing a few days a week. He even had the foresight to stash a few dollars into a 401k.

Scott's life was sweet and simple. The best way to describe his frame of mind was contented.

Until that morning.

Now the best words to describe Scott's frame of mind were confused, angry, desperate, frustrated, and most of all frightened. There was nothing that had happened in his life up until that day that could have prepared him for what he had gone through over the past few hours. There was no logical explanation for any of it, which meant he began to question his sanity. Scott prided himself on being a problem solver, a fixer, but he had no idea of how to fix this particular problem because he didn't understand what it was. The best he could do was compartmentalize the events, ignore them, and focus on going about his normal day, in spite of the fact that his day was anything but.

With his haunted pick-up truck in the care of Charlie Dest, Scott needed wheels, so he turned to his ancient Honda Civic that hadn't been driven since Netflix's primary business was mailing out DVDs. The reliable car was in fine shape, other than a dead battery that needed to be replaced, which is exactly what he was working on in his driveway when a visitor approached.

"Excuse me, Mr. Wilson?" Darcey said politely.

Polite or not, it made Scott jump. He spun around quickly, which prompted Darcey to take a step back.

"Whoa, sorry," she said.

Scott took a moment to register who it was, and relaxed.

"Darcey. Sorry," he said. "I'm kind of on edge. Obviously."

"My fault. I didn't mean to surprise you."

"You didn't," Scott said. "I mean, you did but, it's okay."

Scott was still shaking as he went back to work installing the new battery which was actually quite old which meant there was no guarantee it could do the job any better than the one he was replacing. Darcey didn't know much about him other than that his friends kidded him about the whole "Redneck Ed Sheeran" thing, which was something she had to agree with, though she stopped short of using his nickname "Red" in case he might take offense. To her he was simply another townie that was barely on her radar.

Until then.

The Paper Trail

"Something I can do for you?" Scott asked.

"Maybe," Darcey said. "I want to ask you about what happened this morning."

Scott stopped working. So much for ignoring his problem.

"Why? What did you hear?" he asked.

"That your truck got a mind of its own and you crashed out in the woods."

"Yeah, that's one thing."

"There's more?" Darcey asked.

"Why do you want to know?"

"Mr. Paper has an idea that there might be—"

"Who?"

"The British guy who's writing a book."

"Oh, right. What's his deal?" Scott asked.

"He travels a lot and sees weird things like this happen in other places. So I'm helping him try and connect the dots."

"There are dots?"

"You aren't the only one who's had strange things happen to them today."

Scott felt a surge of relief in a misery-loves-company kind of way.

"Really? What else happened?" he asked.

"Maybe we should share stories," Darcey said, slyly, ready to trade information.

Scott gave it a half-second thought, and slammed the car hood closed.

"I gotta charge the battery," he said. "Let's go for a ride."

"Deal," Darcey exclaimed, and they both hopped into the car.

The engine groaned and complained but ultimately turned over. There was still enough juice left in the old battery to crank the starter. Scott backed out of his driveway and drove with no particular destination or plan other than to keep moving so the battery would charge.

"You first," Darcey said. "What else happened to you?"

Though he'd told Terri and Charlie Dest about his *Mr. Toad's Wild Ride* took through the forest, Scott hadn't told anyone about the strange people he saw in the clearing.

"I guess a mechanical issue can be explained," Scott finally said. "I don't know how, but there has to be a reason that makes sense. What I saw beyond that? Nothing about that makes sense."

Darcey's heart raced. This was exactly the kind of thing she was hoping to hear. But she didn't press. It was obvious that Scott was reluctant to share his story. She didn't want to push him so far that he'd have second thoughts about opening up.

"Do you believe in ghosts?" he asked.

Darcey had to catch her breath. "Uhh, maybe. Did you see a ghost?"

"I don't know. I don't know anything anymore. There are a whole lot of things going on I never thought could happen. Once you go there, anything's possible."

"What did you see?"

She held her breath with eager anticipation for she felt that whatever Scott said next could change everything.

"People," Scott began. "Right after I crashed. There was a bald old lady. A kid wearing a Stones t-shirt. A soldier. An old guy in a bathrobe. There were a bunch more but they're blending together in my head."

"Out in the woods?" Darcey asked with confusion.

"They shouldn't have been there. But they were. And then they weren't. Either I was hallucinating, or—"

The words caught in his throat as he glanced into his rearview mirror.

"—shit."

"What?"

Darcey turned around to see that a vehicle was driving behind them. Closely. And not just any vehicle. It was Scott's pickup.

"Is that your truck?" Darcey asked.

"Yeah."

"That's good. It's fixed."

"Only one problem," Scott said.

"What's that?"

"Nobody's driving."

Darcey focused on the driver's side of the truck. No one was behind the wheel.

"Oh my God," Darcey said with a gasp. "How--?"

"I don't know," Scott shouted. "Ask your Mr. Paper."

The truck suddenly accelerated and slammed into the Honda, jolting them. Darcey let out a surprised yelp as Scott struggled to control the little car.

"This can't be happening," Darcey cried out.

"Welcome to my day," Scott said through clenched teeth.

He turned the wheel hard, slid into a turn and accelerated. The pickup kept going straight for a moment, then it too made the tight turn and followed.

"That's impossible," Darcey exclaimed.

Apparently it wasn't.

Scott jammed the gas pedal to the floor and sped through an industrial area lined with warehouses that had long ago been abandoned when business in Glenville dried up. The newer pickup had far more power. It sped forward, caught up quickly, and slammed into the rear of the Honda again, making the little car fishtail. At that speed it was hard for Scott to keep it from spinning out of control, but he managed to stay on the road and keep going.

The driverless truck sped up. Darcey and Scott braced, expecting another impact. But the truck maneuvered around the Honda and shot forward until it was driving alongside, keeping pace. It was an unnerving sight, since no one was behind the wheel.

"Maybe we should stop," Darcey said.

Before Scott could respond, the pickup turned into the Honda on Scott's side. Scott had no choice but to steer away. The move avoided a collision, but sent the Honda careening off the road.

The car sped across a narrow parking lot headed straight for the cement wall of a shuttered warehouse. Scott spun the wheel, slammed on the brakes, and skidded sideways, coming to rest short of slamming into the wall. They rocked to a stop, safe, but the pickup kept coming, Darcey screamed because the truck was headed straight for her. She cowered and covered her head.

Scott quickly pulled her down and covered her with his body to shield her, but the truck skid to a stop short of a T-bone collision.

All had gone strangely silent, the only sound coming from the ticking of hot metal and the heaves of terrified breathing. Scott and Darcey cautiously sat up and looked to the pickup, through its windshield, to the empty driver's side.

"What do we do?" Darcey whispered.

Scott didn't reply. The fixer didn't know how to fix this situation. The two sat there for a 30-second lifetime.

Suddenly the pickup lurched. Its tires spun on the fine gravel, caught, and sped backward. It traveled twenty feet, skid to a stop, then jumped forward.

"Oh God no," Darcey said with a gasp, fearing that the haunted truck had moved back in order to get up speed to ram them. But the driverless truck made a sharp turn and sped off, bouncing over the curb and landing back onto the road where it drove off. Darcey and Scott kept their eyes on it until it was out of sight.

"Holy shit," Darcey exclaimed.

"Yeah, holy shit," Scott said.

He angrily threw the Honda into gear and peeled out.

"Where are we going?" Darcey asked.

"I'm dropping you back in town."

Darcey was rattled, but Scott was pissed. Beyond pissed. He drove aggressively, past any safe speed limit. Compared to what they'd just been through, it was like a leisurely Sunday drive. Darcey didn't say a word. She wanted Scott focused on his driving. Her immediate concern was getting out of that car in one piece. It only took a few minutes for them to get back to Main Street where Scott pulled over and stopped. Darcey looked to him to see his eyes were set dead ahead, fired up and focused.

"Out," he commanded.

"What are you going to do?" she asked.

"I'm going to end this," he said through heavy breaths.

"How?"

"I'm going on offense."

"What does that mean?"

"Get out, Darcey. Tell your mother that whatever happens, it's because I stopped being a victim."

"Okay. Sure."

Darcey opened the door and slowly got out to stand on shaky legs.

"Maybe you should talk to her before you do anything."

"I already did. There's nothing she can do. It's on me."

"Be careful, okay?" Darcey said.

"I think that ship has sailed," Scott replied. "Close the door."

Darcey hesitated, but closed the door. The moment it shut, Scott hit the gas and shot forward. He made a sharp U-Turn, accelerated, and sped out of town, headed after his pickup truck.

Headed for the woods.

CHAPTER 10

George Daniel's body lay where he had fallen. His eyes still open; his heart still dormant. Only now he wasn't alone.

Terri Hirsch stood over him, along with George's brother Ben, who looked about as pale as poor, dead George.

Terri took photos of the body, which was something she had never done before, even when she worked in Chicago.

"We can't move him until the medical examiner gets here," Terri said softly.

"It's okay," Ben said. "Not like he cares."

Though she was no forensic expert, Terri had a pretty good idea of what had happened. Between the dark scorch marks across George's face and hands, his burned shirt, and the blackened breaker panel, there was little doubt as to what had caused his death.

"Why is the breaker box in the refrigerator?" Terri asked.

"That's how it was set up when we bought the place," Ben replied with a hint of defensiveness. "Never had a problem with it. Until now."

"The investigation should give us some answers as to what happened," Terri said. "Between the water, metal racks and—"

"There's something going on with the power," Ben said curtly. "Seems like everything in this place is charged up. Don't touch anything."

"Okay. They'll figure that one out too. I'm so sorry, Ben."

Ben's response was a tired shrug of acceptance.

Terri added, "He was a good man."

It was the right thing to say, so Ben didn't call her out on a comment they both knew wasn't true. She gently took his arm to guide him out of the freezer.

In the kitchen, Holly was sitting at George's desk with her head in her hands. She'd been crying since she found his body.

"You okay?" Terri asked.

"He knew something was wrong with the electricity," she said through hitching breaths. "He was trying to get it fixed. He shouldn't have gone in there."

"The county medical examiner will be here soon," Terri said. "Let me give you a ride home, Ben."

"I'd rather stay with George," Ben replied.

"You go," Holly said. "I'll stay."

"No!" Ben snapped.

Terri and Holly shot surprised looks at him.

"I mean," Ben went on. "I want to spend some quiet time with my brother."

"I understand," Terri said.

"Alone," Ben said with finality.

"Sure thing," Terri said, then to Holly she added, "Let's head out."

Holly was too numb to do anything but go along. Discovering a fried body had that effect.

"I realize I don't need to say this Ben," Terri said, "But the coroner needs to see things as they are."

"Don't worry, I won't touch anything," Ben said with a sarcastic snarl, as if insulted by the request.

"I know, but I had to say it."

Holly touched his shoulder as a gesture of warmth and said, "I'm so sorry."

Ben recoiled as though her touch had delivered another electric shock. Holly pulled back quickly, surprised by his violent reaction. She looked to Terri, who gestured that they should leave.

"I'll be back when the coroner gets here," Terri said to Ben.

Ben kept his eyes on the floor. Once Holly and Terri left, he dropped his head into his hands, pressing his palms into his eyes to stem the flow of tears. He took a deep breath, then reached into his jacket pocket and pulled out the crumpled sketch that Holly had made of the scarred woman. He pulled it open, placed it on the desk, and ran his hand over its surface to flatten it. As he stared down at the wrinkled image, his heart raced. The drawing was remarkably detailed, right down to the woman's eye, which seemed to be staring back at him. He began to tremble, as if an eruption of emotion were building. His bottom lip quivered; his right eye twitched; his hands shook, but he didn't break eye contact with the image of the woman in the sketch. His focus was finally interrupted by a sweet, short chime that took him by surprise if only that it wasn't familiar. He glanced around with curiosity until the chime sounded again, calling his attention to the cell phone on his desk.

Holly's phone.

Ben automatically leaned over to see what the chime was about and saw that Holly had received a text message. The picture-icon of the sender was a woman who looked like an older version of Holly. The I.D. name was a simple: *"MOM"*.

Ben focused on the previous text that Holly had sent to her mother. It was a photo of the sketch. Ben's gut twisted. The text from Holly that accompanied it was: *"Does this woman look familiar?"*

The return text that had just come in was in all caps. It read: "MY GOD! WHERE DID YOU GET THAT? CALL ME!"

Ben trembled. He reached forward, ready to delete the text.

"Ben?"

Holly walked tentatively back into the kitchen, headed his way.

Ben swept the paper sketch off the desk.

"Sorry," she said. "I think I left my cell phone on the—" She spotted the phone on George's desk. "There it is."

As she reached for it, Ben shot his hand out and grabbed her wrist.

"Ben?" Holly asked with confusion and a little fear.

After a tense moment, he let her go and sat back.

Holly, unnerved, snatched her phone and backed away.

"Let's talk when things aren't so crazy," she said and hurried out.

Ben sat at the desk, staring at nothing. He tossed the crumpled sketch on to the desk, looked at it for a moment, then reached down and opened his desk drawer. Inside was a tool with an orange grip that was attached to a foot long metal bar with a metal two-pronged fork on the end. Ben hesitated as if unsure he wanted to be looking at it, let alone touching it. He took a deep breath, reached for it, and held it up as if admiring it.

He turned to the refrigerator and called out. "I'll handle it."

Darcey needed to catch her breath and be normal.

She had finally calmed down after the harrowing ride that challenged her belief in reality. Prior to that adventure she had been excited about helping Mr. Paper with his research, never truly thinking she'd discover anything out of the ordinary in the painfully normal town. It was meant to be nothing more than an interesting lark. Now she feared what else might be lurking, waiting to put her in its strange crosshairs. Part of her wanted to go to her room and hide under the bed. Another part of her was charged up and curious about what else she might find.

Curiosity won.

As much as she wanted to know more, she needed to go about it in a way that felt normal, and safe. Mr. Paper had said one of their goals was to find a common denominator that tied the strange events together. He called it a nexus. He was clearly an old-school guy who went about his investigation by actually speaking with those involved. She had other ideas. Safer ideas. Ideas that she felt had a far better chance of yielding results. Quickly.

She turned to Google.

Darcey returned to the safety of her house and the normalcy of browsing the internet. Sitting comfortably at the dining room table she fired up her laptop and did a search using the names of the people who had had incidents that morning: Scott Wilson, Vera Holiday, George and Ben Daniels, Karl Iverson, and Holly Meade. She felt that if a search turned up something they all had in common, it might point her in a direction that would make sense.

At first it was frustrating, as most internet searches tend to be. Most of what came up were articles about people with the same names but had nothing to do with the subjects who lived in Glenville. She followed dozens of meaningless links, came up empty time and again and feared that she was giving too much credit to the almighty, all-knowing internet.

She changed her search from "all" to "images," thinking it would be easier to eliminate dead ends if she could see faces. She scrolled through countless pictures. Some were candid shots of people who felt the need to post pictures of every banal moment of their lives on social media. Others were about selling things, still others were taken from published articles. The first picture she recognized was a head shot of Holly Meade. It was her official university graduation portrait. Following the picture link didn't offer much information, other than that she was from Glenville and majored in Communications at Northwestern.

She was getting close to giving up when she saw a photo of two men wearing business suits and standing on cement stairs that led up to large, carved, double doors set in an elaborate, arched frame. To Darcey it looked like the entrance to an old, gothic church. The men looked to be in their late thirties and stood stiffly, as if the last thing they wanted to do was pose for a photo. The picture caught Darcey's eye because they looked vaguely familiar. It wasn't until she read the caption that she realized she knew exactly who they were. It was George and Ben Daniels from the Rx Diner, though thirty years younger and a hundred pounds lighter.

"The years have not been kind," Darcey muttered.

The caption read: "Doctors Benjamin and George Daniels of the High Point Institute."

"Doctors?" Darcey said aloud.

The idea that those surly Tweedle Dee and Dum characters might actually be doctors was nearly as farfetched as having been chased by a driverless truck. The best part about the discovery was that she had found another name. She opened a second window, went to Google, and added "High Point Institute" to the list of names in her search, while refining the Daniels' brothers names to include "Doctor" and "M.D."

"Seriously?" Terri called out.

Darcey looked up to see her mother standing in the doorway, looking as drained as if she'd been up for days though it was barely past one in the afternoon.

"Mom!" she called out. "I think I found something."

"Why aren't you in school?" Terri asked with strained patience.

Darcey was momentarily thrown. The fact that she hadn't gone back to school for a few hours seemed insignificant compared to the dramatic events that were unfolding.

"This is way more important," Darcey argued.

"Don't tell me what's important," Terri barked. "I'm done debating with you today."

The events of the morning had pushed Terri into foul-mood territory.

"I'm sorry," Darcey said, "But Mr. Paper and I were—"

"Mr. Paper," Terri said with disdain. "Not a good day for that guy to be poking around."

"Or maybe it's the perfect day," Darcey shot back. "I was in Scott Wilson's car. We were chased by his truck, but nobody was driving it. And then—"

"Hold on, why were you in Scott Wilson's car?" Terri asked, incredulously.

"I was asking him about what happened this morning. With his truck. He's scared Mom. He told me to tell you that whatever happens it's because he's going to stop being a victim. I don't know what he's going to do but it can't be good."

Terri's head swam. She had to sit down.

"I don't understand," she said.

"Tell me about it! It was like the truck could think and it was coming after us and tried to run us off the road. I know that's crazy, but I swear that's what happened. That's not all. I did a Google search of all the people who had strange things happen today. I think I found a common denominator. Have you ever heard of the High Point Institute?"

Terri stiffened.

"Where did you hear about that?" Terri asked.

"It came up on the Google search."

Terri looked to the laptop screen to see a bold headline that read: "The High Point Institute." She stared at it for several seconds, then reached over and closed the laptop.

"You're done," she said with finality.

"What?" Darcey said, stunned. "Why?"

"There's too much shit going on today," Terri said.

That surprised Darcey, if only because her mother rarely used crude language.

"I know! That's why I'm trying to help Mr. Paper," Darcey argued. "And you too. Scott said he saw people--"

"George Daniels is dead," Terri said. "He was electrocuted in the diner less than an hour ago. I can't get the smell of burned flesh out of my nose. Or my clothes. I came home to change my uniform. I've got to get back to the Rx before the county M.E. arrives."

"Holy shit," Darcey said, stunned.

"Yeah, holy shit," Terri echoed. "I don't know why this storm hit Glenville, but it has nothing to do with supernatural karma, and I don't need that Paper character putting those ideas into people's heads. Especially not yours."

"Okay, fine," Darcey said curtly. "If you have a better idea about what's going on I'd love to hear it."

Terri shot her a look that was akin to a bull having caught sight of a red cape. Darcey immediately realized she'd gone too far.

"Do not talk to that man again," Terri said through gritted teeth. "Go to your room."

Whatever leverage Terri's anger gave her over Darcey evaporated with that command. Darcey was her mother's daughter and did not appreciate being given mandates.

"Seriously?" Darcey said, flippantly. "My room? I'm not ten."

Terri didn't back down.

"My house, my town, my rules," she said while staring her daughter down.

"Or what?" Darcey shot back. "No TV tonight? Or maybe you'll take away my phone. Yeah, that'll teach me. Or maybe you'll tell my father when he gets home. Oh wait, he doesn't live here, does he? I guess I'll just have to tell him myself. I'll do that when he comes to pick me up this weekend."

Darcey stood up and grabbed her laptop.

"Leave it," Terri commanded.

Darcey hesitated, then put it back down, and laughed.

"Wow, you really are taking away my privileges," she said. "All because I'm trying to help you."

"I'm trying to protect you," Terri said.

"From what?"

Terri gave the question some serious thought and said, "I'm not sure."

"That's okay," Darcey added. "You won't have to worry about me much longer. I'm done with your house, your town, and your rules."

Darcey stormed off, headed for her room.

Terri sat staring at the floor, her heart racing. After a long minute, she looked to the laptop and opened it, revealing the web page that said: "The High Point Institute."

"What the hell?" she muttered to herself.

Karl Iverson's apartment was in an ancient building a block off the north end of Main Street's commercial district. There were eight identical one-bedroom apartments in the sad brick structure, seven of which were vacant. It wasn't exactly a luxury rental, but as Karl often put it: "Beggars can't be beggars." Nobody knew what that meant, but figured he understood how lucky he was to have a roof over his head, no matter how low-grade it may be.

Karl had never entertained a visitor. The only time someone else set foot in the apartment was when a social worker from the state showed up for a surprise visit to make sure he wasn't living in squalor. He welcomed the solitude. Quiet was good. It suited him to be the only resident in the building.

Karl was a creature of habit. His day of Main Street-sweeping always began at nine a.m. He'd start on the northeast end of the commercial district and work his way south, reaching the far end of the commercial district by eleven-thirty. There'd he'd break for lunch, which consisted of a thermos of Lipton Chicken Noodle Soup and a half-sleeve of Saltines (A favorite meal of seven-year-olds with the sniffles). By noon he'd move to the west side of Main Street and sweep his way back north. By two thirty the circuit would be complete. From there he'd sometimes pay a visit to Smerlo's Market to replenish supplies (usually more soup and Saltines) and then head for home.

His afternoons were often spent reading books he had checked out from the local library. Yes, Karl had a library card and usually spent his Sundays there, roaming the stacks. His authors of choice were Jack London and Louis L'Amour. He also watched whatever sports on TV that his rabbit ear antennas could capture. Dinner consisted of anything he could nuke that came from a can (usually Hormel chili or Dinty Moore beef stew) and his one splurge item: a can of diet Dr. Pepper. His drink of choice was Budweiser, but he was never able to stop at one. And beer was expensive. One of the conditions of his employment was that he stop drinking. He was mostly able to stay dry, but lately it had become more difficult in large part due to the recent self-appraisal of his life. The night before was not a good night, as proven by the hangover he suffered through that morning.

Like Scott Wilson, Karl's life was simple, though perhaps not quite as sweet. Now that he was getting closer to the end than the beginning, he had come to the realization that over the course of his life he had never challenged himself. Never strived. Never took risks. He had always convinced himself that getting-by was good enough. He had worked for years as a janitor at a large hospital where the biggest challenge was avoiding contact with the staff or patients. That may have suited his desire for solitude, but it did nothing to build self-esteem, or social awareness, or (God forbid) friendships. Karl was a hermit who lived and worked in plain sight. He might as well have been a ghost.

If asked, he would not have been able to say why, so late in the game, he felt the urge to make something more of himself. Perhaps it was an inspirational passage from one of the books he'd been reading. Or maybe it was something he saw in a TV drama. It could have been from watching the joy of a post-touchdown celebration in Lambeau Field, or when he would step aside to let a group of laughing kids run past on their way home from school. It may even have been during one of the many moments when he sat on the curb, sipping his soup, watching cars drive by carrying people who all had a destination. Or maybe it was while he witnessed the slow but incessant erosion of the town where he had spent his entire life. He saw the physical and spiritual degradation of Glenville, and felt the same downward spiral happening to himself.

He had no idea if his plan to provide pseudo-deputy services to Sheriff Hirsch would be wanted or needed. She might laugh him out of her office. But knowing that he was going to give it a shot gave Karl a sense of purpose he hadn't felt in a very long time. Or ever. He took to heart the words of advice from the British stranger who said that change could be difficult, and hoped that he'd accept that it was for the best.

That was fine with Karl. Change was what he needed.

Once back in his apartment, he went straight to the threadbare easy chair where he spent most of his home-time and put his feet up on the mis-matched ottoman. It was a simple moment of pleasure he always looked forward to because it provided welcome relief to his aching feet and knees after the hours of sweeping.

That afternoon he didn't get the usual feeling of sweet relief. What he felt was nothing. His immediate thought was that he might actually be getting into better shape and no longer had the same need for rest and recovery. It heartened him, thinking that he might not be as physically decrepit as he feared, which would bode well for his chances of scoring a deputy job. He sat with his eyes closed, daring to let his thoughts drift to what the next phase of his life might hold. He wondered if he might actually get a uniform. And a badge. The image made him smile.

It was then that he became aware of an unfamiliar sound. A buzzing. It didn't seem to be electrical, or mechanical. It was so faint he needed to swivel his head to try and determine the source. It wasn't coming from the kitchen, or the ancient Zenith television or from his inner ear. The sound was faint but distinct. It appeared to be coming from his bedroom. As much as he didn't want to pull himself out of the chair he'd just relaxed into, his curiosity got the better of him, so he hoisted himself up and went to investigate.

He was about to step through the bedroom doorway when a fly flew past his head. The sound was unmistakable as it passed by his ear. Karl swatted at it, but the insect had already flown beyond his reach. He was ready to look for a rolled-up newspaper to go on a fly-hunt, when he heard more buzzing coming from the bedroom. The fly had friends. The thought hit him that he may have left dirty dishes out. Nothing attracts flies like congealed chili. A quick scan of the room showed no dishes, but they could have been on the floor on the far side of his bed. That had happened once or twice. Or a dozen times. He walked toward the bed to get a look on the far side when he registered something that made him stop short.

His bed was unmade. Nothing unusual there. The only time he did anything with the bed sheets besides sleep in them was on laundry day, which happened once a month. Maybe. What froze him was that the blanket and sheets were piled haphazardly, but in such a way that it looked as though someone was in the bed. Of course, that was impossible. Still, he had to be sure and approached cautiously.

As he drew nearer, the sound of buzzing flies grew more intense. He could now make out that there were several flies hovering over the pile of bedsheets. Had he left a bowl of stew there? He didn't remember eating anything the night before, but the flies had to be there for a reason. He stepped closer to the bed to see that what he thought was impossible…wasn't. There was indeed someone lying there, asleep. Whoever it was must have been thrashing about for they had twisted themselves up in the sheets before settling.

Karl was torn between running out and calling the Sheriff, and confronting the interloper. Karl's hotheadedness took over. The idea that somebody dared to come into his home, defile his privacy and pass out on his bed of all places, was too much to let slide. His anger built, quickly overcoming the fear that this person might actually be dangerous.

"Get yer ass up, Goldilocks!" he commanded while yanking the sheet back from the intruder's face. "What the hell do you think you're—"

What he saw was impossible, yet there it was. Lying in the bed, with flies buzzing around his head, was Karl himself.

He backed off quickly as if pushed by an invisible force. He slammed into his dresser, knocking over a table lamp that crashed to the floor. He didn't notice. His attention was focused on the face of the man who was lying in his bed.

A hungry fly landed on his cheek.

Karl's cheek.

Holly hurried away from the Rx, not sure if she'd ever be going back. It wasn't solely due to George's grisly death. George and Ben had consistently blamed her for everything that went wrong with their restaurant, large and small. Holly would easily blow off their accusations because she understood that the brothers had old-school sensibilities and massive egos that never allowed them to admit fault. They were harmless. Annoying but harmless. And she needed the job.

This was different. Ben's reaction went beyond the expected shock and grief over the sudden death of his brother. His decidedly frosty attitude toward Holly made it clear that he somehow felt that it was her fault. But this wasn't a problem like a defective microwave or a customer who complained about cold oatmeal. George was dead, and Ben had a temper. She feared that if for whatever misguided reason he blamed her, she could be the target of his anger and who knew how that might come out? As she hurried home, all thoughts of the scarred woman were pushed to the bottom of the list of her concerns.

They wouldn't stay there for long.

Her cell phone vibrated. Her mother was trying to FaceTime. Holly hesitated to answer because she knew why her mother was calling and she only wanted to deal with one problem at a time. She also didn't want to share what had happened to George. Not yet. It was all too raw. She didn't want her mother to worry, but couldn't ignore her. Whenever she ducked a call, her mother assumed something bad had happened. This time she'd be right.

Holly made the snap decision to answer, and not mention George's death. She hurried into a small park that was sandwiched between buildings, stood to the far end for privacy, pasted on a smile, and answered the call.

"Hi Mom!" she said with false cheer.

"You didn't answer my text," her mother said, clearly irked.

Nancy Meade was an older version of Holly. They both had the same positive personality, quick smile, and auburn hair, but in that moment there was nothing remotely bubbly about her. Holly sensed it instantly, even with the stuttering FaceTime connection.

"Sorry," Holly said cautiously. "I got caught up with some stuff."

There's an understatement, Holly thought.

"Where did you get that sketch?" Nancy demanded, deadly serious.

It took a moment for Holly to remember what her mother was asking about since George's death had taken center stage in her thoughts. Her parents were Glenville natives. If, as Mr. Paper suggested, the mysterious woman was someone Holly had seen in the past, she thought it might be someone her parents knew from town. Holly figured it was a longshot, until she saw her mother's reaction.

"I drew it," Holly replied.

"That's impossible."

"Why? Do you know who it is?"

Nancy wiped away a tear and said with a hitched breath, "Yeah. Yeah I do. It's my mother, Hols."

Holly's knees went weak. She had to sit on the park bench she was leaning against. It was all she could do to keep her hand steady while holding the phone.

"Grandma Claire?" she managed to say.

"Yes, but I don't see how you could have made that sketch. There are no pictures of her looking like that, and I certainly didn't describe her that way to you."

Holly struggled to grasp what her mother was saying while balancing it with what she'd seen.

"I don't understand," Holly said. "If she never looked like that, how can you be sure it's her?"

"I said there were no pictures of her like that," Nancy said, her voice breaking. "But that's exactly how she looked toward the end."

Holly's gut clenched. Though she had never met Grandma Claire, she felt as though she knew her through the wonderful stories her mom shared. To think that her grandmother had ever been in such a horrible state was difficult to imagine.

"What happened to her?" Holly asked. "You told me she had cancer and died young. This woman looked tortured. I mean, that scar."

Nancy wiped away tears while trying to regain her composure.

"She was sick, but it wasn't cancer," Nancy said. "To this day I don't know the actual diagnosis. Schizophrenia? Bi-Polar disorder? Dementia? All the above? Your grandfather kept the details from me, and I kept them from you. It wasn't until years after her death that I learned the truth."

"And that was...?" Holly asked.

"She was troubled, Hols. I guess that's putting it mildly. She was in such terrible shape that Grandpa had her committed to a psyche ward. To keep her safe. But he was convinced the treatment made her worse. They had her on powerful drugs that caused hallucinations. They eventually resorted to shock treatments."

"My God," Holly said, reeling. "Is that what caused the scar?"

"That's what they claimed but as extreme as those treatments are, they don't cause physical scars. She was disfigured. Horribly, and not just her face. She had burns all over her body that weren't discovered until--" Nancy had to take a moment to compose herself, then said, "Until the autopsy."

"How did she die?"

"Your grandfather kept it from me until he was near his own death. I didn't want to share it with you because--"

"Just tell me."

"She killed herself, Hols. They said it was the result of a psychotic break. I don't fully understand what that is or if it's even true, but she jumped from a balcony inside the hospital."

"Oh my God," Holly said with a pained gasp.

"Your grandfather filed a malpractice suit against the hospital and the horrible doctors, but nothing came of it. Small town. People take care of their own. Dad didn't have the money for lawyers and eventually gave up."

"So nobody was held accountable?" Holly asked.

"No. I've tried not to think about it, but your sketch brought it all back. I'm sorry for unloading like this but seeing it was overwhelming."

Holly wanted to apologize for having put her mom through this agony, but she had issues of her own, so she pressed on.

"Grandpa kept all this from you?" Holly asked.

"He said he didn't see what good could come from putting that all on a little girl. I didn't share it with you for the same reason. Shortly before she died I begged Grandpa to take me to the hospital to see her. I'm ashamed to say I wish he hadn't because I saw her at her worst. I'd rather remember her this way, back before things turned for her."

She held up a snapshot of a woman with long red hair, hugging her young daughter. Holly's mother. The woman looked joyful and proud, nothing like the woman Holly had seen in the reflections. But it was unmistakably the woman Holly saw reflected.

"I'm sorry I kept this from you, sweetheart," Nancy said.

"It's okay, Mom. I understand."

"Now help me to understand," Nancy said. "How could you possibly have drawn this?"

Holly was still trying to process what she'd just learned. She wasn't about to add to her mother's pain and confusion by telling her that she'd been having visions of her dead, mutilated mother.

"I can't explain it," Holly said.

She was able to fabricate an answer that had a shred of truth to it. "It kind of came to me in a dream. Maybe I heard stories about her when I was little. You must have talked about her problems at some point. Maybe with Dad. You might not have realized I was listening."

"Maybe," Nancy said, unsure. "But I can't imagine what I might have said."

"Who knows? It could have been something simple that you didn't even realize you were saying. You know how kids are. They're sponges."

"I suppose," Nancy said.

"I'm sorry, Mom. I had no idea it would cause you so much pain."

"It's all right, you couldn't have known. I should have been more open with you."

It hurt Holly to lie, but until she understood exactly why she'd been seeing the visions, she wasn't about to compound her mother's anguish.

"We'll talk about it some more," Holly said. "How about if I take some time off and come for a visit?"

"Can you do that?" Nancy asked. "Those two jokers rely on you."

"I don't think it'll be a problem," Holly said.

"Then I'd love to have you come."

"Great. I'm going to jump now and let this settle. Then we'll talk, okay?"

"Okay, good, I love you Hols."

"I love you too, Mom. Bye. Whoa, wait."

"What?"

"The hospital where she died. Do you remember what it was called?"

"How could I forget? It was The High Point Institute. Why?"

"Just trying to get the whole picture. Talk soon."

She punched out of the call to stare at her phone, and the sketch of her poor, tortured grandmother. Grandma Claire. Mr. Paper was right. This was someone from her past, though she had died long before Holly was born. Now she knew, but the question remained as to why she was seeing the vision. Her first thought was a disturbing one. If her grandmother suffered from mental illness, could it be a condition that she had inherited? It was a possibility she did not want to accept, though it seemed more likely than the scenario where she was being haunted by an actual spirit. There were no easy or comforting answers.

Holly needed to move. She stood up, jammed her phone into her pocket and strode out of the park, headed for home.

She wasn't alone.

Standing close to the building that bordered the park was Ben Daniels. He watched as she hurried away and glanced around to see if anyone had noticed him. Satisfied that he hadn't been seen, he cautiously stepped out to follow her.

CHAPTER 11

When Scott Wilson drove in pursuit of his haunted truck, he was consumed by fear, anger, and the indignation of being toyed with by...what? A ghost? Magic? Demonic forces? He believed in exactly none of that, but couldn't blame it on his own sanity, or lack thereof, because Darcey Hirsch had seen it too. What had happened was real, and he was determined to put an end to it.

He sped out of town, desperate to catch up with the renegade truck, but after running through a stop sign and nearly t-boning a crossing Camaro, he forced himself to take a breath and regain some semblance of control. His gut told him there was no need to catch up with the truck anyway. He was certain of where it was going. There were more important questions he needed answered. What was it about that clearing? Why was it drawing him there? Why was it targeting him? And most importantly: what the hell was "it"?

Scott didn't believe in ghosts. Years before he was one of the few kids who wasn't terrified while watching the kid-horror show *Are You Afraid of the Dark?* He was far too pragmatic to appreciate such silliness, even as fiction. Some would say he didn't have much of an imagination, and he couldn't argue with that. That's what made the morning's events all the more maddening. His practical mind desperately searched for logical explanations, but came up empty. Ultimately, that's what pushed him on. He wanted answers that would assure him all was right and normal with the world. What truly frightened him was the possibility that the world might not be as right and normal as he thought.

His biggest challenge was to keep his nerves in check. He needed to be in control, not only of himself but of the situation. What made it difficult was not knowing exactly what he was headed into. The most potent fear is that of the unknown. He wished he had thought to bring his shotgun. Even a baseball bat would have been better than nothing. Not that either of those weapons would be effective against a rampaging truck driven by no one, but at least they would have given him a sense of power, false as it may be.

All these thoughts were raging when he reached the turnoff that led to his worksite, and then to the newly cut roadway that would take him to the clearing. Though his Honda wasn't built for rough terrain, he had no trouble navigating the ancient roadway since so many larger and much heavier vehicles had already cut the way. The route was bumpy, but his car only bottomed out once. He was more concerned that the Honda might suddenly take over. But he maintained control, which made him wonder if that was because he was doing exactly what "it" wanted him to do. Was he kidding himself to think he could take charge and end the nightmare? Or was he being manipulated as easily as when he went helplessly along for the ride when his truck was calling the shots?

As he neared the clearing he looked ahead to see his prediction was correct. His yellow backhoe was still there, along with his truck. It gave him no satisfaction, only confirmed his theory. When he and Darcey were being harassed by the pickup, it wasn't to run them down. It was to get his attention.

It was luring him back.

And here he was.

The first thing he did after driving into the clearing was to do a 180 so that the nose of the Honda was pointed toward the roadway. If he had to make a quick exit, he didn't want to be jockeying around to make a three-point turn under pressure. Once the car was in position, he shifted into park, took a deep breath, and got out. He left the engine running, again, to facilitate a hasty exit.

He stood behind the Honda and scanned the area. There was nothing out of the ordinary, other than his backhoe and pickup truck.

"You got me here," he shouted. "Now what?"

His answer? The Honda's engine shut down.

Scott's heart sank. He wasn't in control. Not even a little. The only reason he was able to drive himself there was because he was doing exactly what was expected of him.

"Why am I here?" Scott called out.

He didn't want to appear desperate and afraid, but he was desperate and afraid.

"It's okay dude, relax."

Scott spun around to see the kid in the Stones t-shirt leaning against the trunk of his car.

"Who the hell are you?" Scott managed to ask. "Why are you out here?"

The kid responded with a dismissive snicker, as if it was an idiotic question.

"What do you want from me?" Scott added.

"It's no big deal. We just want you to do what you do."

"We?"

The kid walked toward Scott. Scott tensed up. There was nothing remotely threatening about the kid, except that he was there. The kid continued past Scott, giving him a thumbs up and a smile.

"Relax," the kid said. "Everything's cool."

Scott saw that he had a heavy, silver, skull-ring on his thumb.

The kid continued until he was halfway to the backhoe where he stopped and turned back to Scott.

"That's your digger, right?" he asked.

"Yeah."

The kid nodded thoughtfully, then continued walking. He sauntered to the far edge of the clearing, looking at the ground. He scuffed through the fallen leaves and pine needles as if searching for something. In spite of his fear, Scott was now intrigued and had to fight the urge to pepper the kid with questions. It was clear he had an agenda and Scott wanted to hear what it was before pushing back.

The kid looked up and around at the trees as if getting his bearing, then focused on Scott.

"Here's good," he said.

"For what?" Scott asked.

"To dig. That's what you do, right?"

"Why don't you do it?" Scott said. "You drove it here, right?"

"Digging's only half of it," the kid said.

"What's the other half?" Scott asked. He had the sick feeling the kid was asking him to dig his own grave.

"We need a witness."

"Witness to what? What am I digging for? Buried treasure?"

He forced a chuckle, hoping to get the kid to lighten up. It didn't work. The kid didn't think it was funny.

"Buried treasure," he repeated. "Good one."

"So why do you want me to dig?"

The kid looked down and kicked at the dirt. He gouged out a small trough with his heel, then reached down and picked up something he'd uncovered. He brushed it off, and held it out for Scott to see.

The kid said, "To find me."

He held a heavy, tarnished, silver skull-head ring.

Karl stood frozen, staring at…Karl.

Was he dreaming? Hallucinating? Was it a sick joke and this wasn't a human body at all, but a lookalike dummy that somebody put in his bed to antagonize him? It didn't seem to be a dummy; it was too realistic. The flies certainly thought so. Karl stood there for the longest time, unsure of what to do. He found the courage to shuffle back to the bed for a closer look and hovered over the still form, staring down at what seemed to be his own dead body while fighting multiple conflicting emotions. The only thing keeping him from screaming out in anguish was that he didn't understand how it could be possible.

Karl hadn't been in the best of health. In addition to the emphysema he had a congenital heart problem. It was a race to see which disease would get him first. He'd known about his health issues for years but did nothing to take care of himself. He didn't like doctors, or trust that they could actually help him. Beyond his hesitation, he simply couldn't afford health care. The sidewalk sweeping job certainly didn't provide health insurance and medication was expensive. He knew that his time was limited, which was another reason why he'd been taking stock of his life. Though he never imagined the end to be like this.

Was it the end? In spite of his revulsion, he tentatively reached for the body's hand to feel if it was actually flesh and blood. He tried to swallow, but had no saliva. He pulled back. He didn't want to touch the body, but he knew he had to. He steeled himself and clasped the wrist.

It was warm. This was no dummy. The sensation of grasping what appeared to be his own hand was too much for Karl to bear and he recoiled. Tears rolling down his cheeks. What was happening? What was he supposed to do? He was at a total loss until a realization crept through the chaos.

The hand was warm.

He went back to the bed and this time he grasped the wrist with no hesitation. It took a few seconds, but he felt it. A pulse. It was faint, but there. The flies had jumped the gun. The body wasn't a body. Yet.

Karl instantly clicked into go-mode. Answers could wait until after he got help. His singular focus was to save the life of the person lying in his bed, whoever it was. He didn't have a phone, cell or otherwise, so he hurried out of the apartment, and headed for Main Street to find someone who could make the 9-1-1 call and summon an ambulance.

He saw a woman walking her dog, or more specifically, picking up her dog's poop.

"Hey! Lady!" Karl shouted.

The woman was a block away and didn't hear him, or deliberately ignored him. She scooped the poop and hurried off, disappearing down a side street. Karl chose not to run after her when he saw a man across the street who was unlocking a door between shuttered stores.

"Hey! Buddy! I need help!"

The man didn't give The Sweeper the courtesy of a glance. He opened the door, stepped inside and quickly closed it. It felt to Karl like the man was deliberately shutting him out.

"Bastard!" Karl yelled.

Karl had been a tolerated fixture on Main Street for several years, and had gotten used to being ignored. He didn't mind it at all. In fact, he welcomed it. He had no desire to make small talk with anyone. Over time he came to realize that most of the good citizens of Glenville were repulsed by him. They needed their sidewalks cleaned, but wanted nothing to do with the lowly wretch who had the responsibility. He took satisfaction in knowing that they needed The Sweeper more than he needed them.

Until that moment.

He ran to a shop that sold Christmas ornaments, year-round, only to be faced with a "Closed" sign. The shop next to it had a faded "Radio Shack" sign over the door that proved it hadn't been open for quite some time. Next to it was a music shop that had gone out of business by only selling LPs. The retro vinyl craze had not found its way to Glenville. Karl's desperation grew as he was confronted with the limitations of a town that was ebbing life.

His eye finally caught movement one block ahead, near the Rx Diner. Charlie Dest, the mechanic, was in the process of loading a car onto his flatbed. Karl ran for him.

"Dest!" Karl called. "Charlie Dest!"

Charlie was focused on the job and didn't react as Karl ran up behind him.

"Call nine one one," Karl said, breathless. "There's a guy in my apartment gonna die. He needs an ambulance."

Charlie moved to the front of the car to make sure the winching cable was secure, then headed to the cab to pull the car up. Karl followed right behind him.

"This ain't about me, Dest. It's about saving somebody's life."

Charlie ignored him. He opened the cab door, ready to climb in.

"Don't be an asshole! He's gonna die!" Karl shouted.

He grabbed Charlie's shoulder to stop him from entering the cab, but his hand passed through the man as if he wasn't there. Stunned, Karl took a step backward.

"The hell?"

He reached out again to try and grasp Charlie's arm and grabbed nothing but air. It was as though Charlie Dest was an illusion. Or a ghost.

Karl stood looking at the man, speechless.

The kid with the mullet who worked at the hardware store, Danny Reynolds, approached the wrecker from the sidewalk.

"Excuse me," Danny called out. "Is the Rx closed?"

"Beats me," Charlie replied. "It's usually open this time of day."

"Door's locked," Danny said. "I got Ben Daniels' credit card. He left it at the hardware store. I don't want him thinking I'm using it."

Charlie snickered, "Yeah, he'd probably think that. Go round back. They should be there."

Karl stood between the two, listening to the exchange, trying to understand what was happening.

Danny was about to go around to the back when he saw the Sheriff's Jeep turn onto the street that ran behind the Rx. It was followed close behind by a van marked: "County Coroner." Danny wanted no part of whatever that was.

"I'll stick it in the mail slot," he said. "If anybody asks, that's what I did, okay?"

"Whatever you say," Charlie replied.

Danny headed toward the front door of the diner.

"Hey kid!" Karl called out as he ran after him. "Stop for a second, would ya?"

Danny leaned over and dropped the credit card in the mail slot that was built into the door.

Karl reached out to grab his shoulder, but his hand passed through Danny's body without causing so much as a ripple.

Danny walked away, unknowing.

Karl stood there for a long moment, trying to make sense of what was happening. He looked at his two hands as if they might offer some clue. He clasped them together. They felt solid enough. Karl couldn't fathom what had suddenly happened to the people of Glenville. His thoughts went back to that morning when he was ignored by a few people, including Terri Hirsch. Being treated as though he wasn't there was nothing new to Karl, but that wasn't like Sheriff Hirsch. He hadn't given it a second thought, until then. Was he now living in a ghost town? Literally?

There was another possibility. One that was far more disturbing, but would answer some questions. The more he thought it through, the more it made sense. With that realization, Karl relaxed. He understood. The pressure was off.

He walked slowly back to his apartment, taking in the sights of Main Street. He knew every inch of that street, every crack in its sidewalks. He took some small bit of pride in knowing that the job he did may have been menial, but he did it well. In the end, it was all he had. Once he was back in the apartment he headed straight for the bedroom.

The body was there, as he had left it. It now made sense. He was not going to be a deputy, or one of those people who drove through town, headed for somewhere. Anywhere. If Karl had one regret, it was that he hadn't made a single human connection that might have helped him travel a different path. A less lonely one. The issue didn't solely define the last few years of his life. It went back decades. He had intentionally made himself invisible. People had often reached out to make a friendly connection or to ask for support. He ignored them. He couldn't help but wonder how things would have been different had he bothered to listen. To hear. When the time came that he was the one who desperately needed someone to hear him, nobody cared to listen.

Karl clenched his hands. They felt solid, though he knew they weren't. He looked down to the body and once again grasped its wrist and felt a slight pulse. It didn't last. After a few final beats, the pulsing ceased. It didn't come as a surprise. He sat down on the edge of the bed and took one last look around at his sad bedroom. He sighed, laid down, and allowed his spirit to rejoin his body.

And the flies returned.

On Main Street, Mr. Paper strolled along with his chin up. He came upon the broom that Karl had dropped not long before. He picked it up and held it out in front of him, admiring it as though it was a noble sword. He placed it upright against the building with reverence, then took a step back, tipped his hat out of respect, and continued on his way.

CHAPTER 12

Holly hurried into her apartment and went straight for the dining room table. It was the one spot where she could summon more than one bar of cell service. Barely. Armed with the information her mother had given her, she Googled "*High Point Institute, Glenville Wisconsin,* and *Claire Meade.*" With only two bars of cell service, it was maddingly slow for the Google Gods to search the internet. As she waited, her gaze drifted to the full-length mirror that was covered by the blanket.

Had she actually been visited by the spirit of her grandmother? Or was the explanation more in line with the half-truth she told her mother? When she was young had she overheard stories of the tragic last days of Claire Meade? Was that information lurking somewhere deep in her subconscious, waiting to leap out at her? Holly wasn't sure what scenario was more disturbing: the possibility that her mind was conjuring deeply embedded memories, or the revelation that ghosts were real?

The only solid truth was that her grandmother was a tortured soul who died a horrible death. Was it suicide brought on by the demons of mental disease? Or was she driven to the edge by doctors who had mistreated her to the point of physical abuse?

The Google page finally loaded, and she immediately saw a link to a story about a *Wisconsin Woman* who committed suicide at a *Renowned Medical Facility.* Holly clicked the link. Mercifully, the story loaded quickly, complete with two black and white photos. The first was one she was familiar with. It was a portrait, probably taken at a Wal-Mart, of her grandmother. It was the same photo that her mother had framed and was sitting on an end table in her living room. There was no hint of distress in her bright eyes and warm smile. This was the image Darcey had of Grandma Claire. Her long hair was styled in classic 1970's fashion: big and dramatic with curling-iron ringlets that cascaded to her shoulders. She was looking straight into the camera with confidence. It tore Holly's heart out, knowing what the future held for her.

The second photo meant nothing to her, at first. A closer look made her catch her breath. It was a posed shot of two men in business suits standing on cement stairs below ornate double doors built into a brick edifice. The picture may have been taken thirty years before, but she recognized the men. The caption confirmed it. They were identified as *Doctors Benjamin and George Daniels.*

Doctors. The doctors who had been (mis)treating her grandmother.

Holly's heart raced. Her ears rang and her breathing sped up to the point where she was in danger of hyperventilating. Was this possible? She knew nothing of the Daniel's history prior to them owning the Rx Diner. The idea that in an earlier life they had been practicing physicians seemed impossible, but her day had already been nothing short of impossible. She dropped her phone, stood, and paced while trying to add this new revelation into the strange equation that had been developing. The myriad of incredible information made it difficult for her to think straight. She needed help.

She picked up her cell phone and forced her thumbs to punch out a text. It read: *I know who the woman is. I think I'm in trouble. Please, PLEASE come to my apartment ASAP.* She hit "send" and the text went out to Terri Hirsch.

The text was delivered to Terri's cell phone, though she didn't see it. The phone sat on the front passenger seat of her Jeep that was parked behind the Rx Diner. Terri stood next to the County

Coroner's van, observing the two techs who struggled to carry the stretcher that held George Daniels' burned, lifeless body.

The Coroner, a short, solid woman named Jackie approached Terri while pulling off her rubber gloves.

"He was a miserable cuss, but nobody deserves to go out like that," she said.

Jackie wasn't known for being delicate.

"How soon can I get a cause of death?" Terri asked.

"Some time tomorrow. Things are slow. That's good news in my world."

"Any early guesses?" Terri asked.

"Seems like he got a severe jolt of electricity from that breaker box, which should not have been in that refrigerator by the way. What genius designed that? It could have led to ventricular fibrillation, especially if he had a history of heart disease. The autopsy should give some answers."

A man wearing dark coveralls with the logo *Malinowski Electric* approached the two.

"What's the deal, Steve?" Terri asked.

"I don't know what to tell you," he replied. "The wiring is old, but sound. I can't find any problems, other than the breaker box being in the refrigerator. What genius designed that?"

"That's what *she* said," Jackie said. "And by she I meant me."

Terri said, "So then how was it possible that George was, uhh…?"

"Roasted?" Jackie offered. "Let's just say it."

"Beats me," Malinowski said. "Wherever the juice came from, it wasn't from any lines in this building."

"Well it came from somewhere," Terri said. "Could you please stay on it?"

"Will do," Malinowski replied and headed back to the diner.

"Be careful!" Terri called out to him.

Malinowski replied with a casual wave over his shoulder.

"You okay?" Jackie asked Terri. "You're looking a little, I don't know, fried. And I don't mean like fat old George here."

Terri offered a polite chuckle, in spite of the poor-taste comment.

"I'm fine," she replied. "A lot going on today. Is there a full moon?"

"Let's hope not. I like it when things are slow. I'll be in touch. Where's the brother?"

Terri looked to the diner with concern.

"I don't know. I thought he was going to stay with George until you got here."

"Ben Daniels is a nasty old coot too. Don't quote me on that, I don't want him spitting in my food when I eat here."

She walked to the van, slapped the side panel a few times and shouted, "Saddle up boys! George's last round-up."

The Coroner's team boarded the van and drove off. Terri gave them a quick wave, then headed for her Jeep. She got in quickly and drove off, without checking her phone for messages.

Holly sat at the dining table, reading the article for the twelfth time. The sentence that jumped out at her was: *The deceased, who left behind a husband and young daughter, had a history of severe depression, according to her physicians.*

Her physicians.

Ben and George Daniels.

Her bosses.

Her asshole bosses. (May George rest in peace).

How did they go from being physicians to ornery old men who owned a sad little restaurant? Did they know she was Grandma Claire's granddaughter? There were no statements from the family. Her family. Nor was there any mention of a lawsuit, which followed what her mother told her. Her grandfather didn't have the resources to go after the hospital. The only comment came from the director of the institute who expressed his condolences and said what a sad occurrence it was and blah blah blah. There were no details about how her grandmother got to the point where, under professional supervision, she was able to commit suicide by leaping from the tallest point inside of the very medical building where she was supposedly receiving care. Or why she was scarred with burns that covered her body. That news, or lack thereof, also followed what her mother had said: a small town takes care of its own. Apparently her grandmother wasn't extended the same courtesy. Holly didn't know any of these answers, but as she stood there, fighting back tears, she vowed to find them.

She might have read the article yet another time, had she not heard the faint sound of a door lock engaging. It was such an innocuous sound that if she hadn't been on edge she might not have heard it. In that moment it registered like a gunshot. She instantly dropped her phone and spun around to see that someone had quietly entered her apartment. In her haste she had forgotten to lock the door.

It was locked now. Ben Daniels had made sure of that. He stood with his feet planted apart, his eyes focused on Holly.

"Ben! Jeez! Don't you knock?"

"Sweet little college girl," Ben said through clenched teeth. "Just waiting for your chance. How did you do it? Was it a generator? Did you rig something from the main line? Did you intend to make him suffer?"

"What? No! I didn't kill George."

"I suppose I should take some blame," Ben said. "I didn't make the connection until I saw that sketch. You planned this all along."

"I did not kill George. But if I'd known who you were and how you tortured her, I might have considered it."

"Why? Who was she to you?"

"She was my grandmother."

"Is that so? That makes even more sense now."

Ben took a step toward her. Holly stood and backed toward the kitchen.

"How could you torture her like that? You were supposed to help her."

"We had no choice. She was like a rabid dog; a threat to herself and everyone else. We had to control her."

"So you drugged her and burned her?" Holly cried.

"And we took the fall while the Director walked scott-free. If you want to blame somebody? Blame him. Your grandmother wasn't the only casualty. We were all just part of the machine and did what we were told. And what was our reward? They pulled our license and tossed us to the curb. Such hypocrites. Now all we have to show for it is a pathetic restaurant in this pitiful town. If anyone deserves revenge, it's me."

"You're lucky you didn't land in jail," Holly said, her confidence growing along with her anger. "You should leave now or that's where you'll end up. Terri Hirsch is on her way."

If Ben feared the imminent arrival of the sheriff, he didn't show it.

"You had it all figured out," he said. "But you made one very big mistake."

Ben lifted his hand to reveal the device with the orange handle: An electric cattle prod.

"You didn't kill both of us."

Terri Hirsch drove up and parked in front of the Glenville Apothecary. One perk of living in such a small town was that she always found a parking spot directly in front of her destination. Just like in the movies.

She had promised Vera Holiday that she'd investigate her vandalized bathroom, though she had no expectation of learning anything that would lead to a suspect. The best she could hope for was to keep Vera from launching into another angry tirade. She opened the car door and was about to step out when she remembered her phone. She snatched it from the passenger seat, gave it a quick look, and saw Holly's text.

"Crap," she said, exasperated.

She did a quick check of the time. *When did that text come in?*

With a sigh, she reply-texted: *I'll be there shortly, tell me what's up.* She was about to hit "send" but thought better of it.

"I hate texting," she said to no one.

Rather than send the text, she dialed Holly's cell number.

Holly's cell phone rang. It was sitting on the dining room table where she had dropped it. She glanced at it to see that Sheriff Hirsch was calling. After a look to Ben, and a quick calculation, she reached for it.

"Leave it!" Ben demanded and sprang toward her, leading with the electric prod.

Holly was forced to back away, leaving the phone on the table, still ringing. Ben had her cornered. If she made a break for the front door he would certainly hit her with a four-thousand-watt jolt of electricity.

"Is that what you burned her with?" Holly asked. "Did you treat all your patients that way?"

"It's crude, but effective," Ben said. He was in no hurry because he was in control. "Less expensive than pharmaceuticals. That made the Director happy. All we did was follow his directives and with him it always came down to money. "

"You're blaming what you did on your boss?" Holly asked with disdain. "You were just following orders?"

"Welcome to real life, college girl."

Holly backed away into the kitchen area, looking for something, anything she could use to defend herself. Her eye caught a wooden block that sat on the counter that held carving knives.

"Don't make this worse, Ben," Holly said in a desperate attempt to calm him down, as she moved closer to the knives. "You're upset about George. If you just leave I'll forget this happened."

"And let you get away with murder? If you think I'd do that then you're as demented as your grandmother."

Holly realized there was no reasoning with him. If she had any hope of getting out of this situation alive, she had to act. She quickly reached for the block of carving knives, grabbed one and spun back, holding it out toward Ben.

"I didn't kill him," she said vehemently. "I couldn't."

"You say that as you hold a knife on me," Ben said.

"I'm defending myself!"

She may have been brandishing a large, lethal carving knife, but her voice cracked, and her hand wavered.

"You don't have it in you to use that," Ben said, smug.

He lunged at her, leading with the electric prod. Holly swiped at him with the knife. Ben easily side-stepped the attack and grazed her other arm with the electric prod. There was a short, sharp crackling sound as Holly yelped in agony. But rather than debilitating her, the pain kicked her into adrenalin-fueled survival mode. She took another swipe at Ben. This time she connected. The knife sliced across the top of his arm. He grunted more out of surprise than pain. He hadn't expected her to fight back. He dropped the cattle prod, and Holly ran for the door.

Ben clasped his sliced shoulder and picked up the prod. When he stood back up, his face was directly in front of the microwave oven. The shadowed image of a face appeared in the reflective glass window of the oven's door.

George's face.

"Kill her," the apparition commanded with venom.

Ben glanced at his brother's image and with renewed rage, charged for Holly.

Terri sat in her Jeep, impatiently waiting for Holly to answer her phone. When the call was finally connected she heard a brief, bright recording: "This is Holly. Who are you?"

Terri punched out of the call and clicked into triage mode. Which problem was more pressing? Calming an angry woman by trying to determine who smeared shit around her bathroom? Or calming a frightened woman who thought she was in trouble and called for help? And wasn't answering her phone.

Terri pulled the door shut and fired up the engine.

"Gotta be a full moon," she said, and peeled out.

Holly made it to the door and desperately fumbled to unlock the dead bolt, but Ben was on her too quickly. She spun around and grabbed his hand that held the cattle prod, struggling to keep it from touching any part of her body. Ben was larger and more powerful, but Holly had the strength of a cornered animal. She kicked out, hoping to hit his knee. She scored with a sickening crunch. Ben screamed and crumpled to the floor. Holly stumbled backward, off-balance and fell onto her back in the living room.

Ben was up on his feet before she landed.

"It ends now," he said, seething. His injured shoulder didn't stop him. He clutched the cattle prod and stalked toward Holly.

Holly, still on the floor, backed away, defenseless. She passed the mirror that was covered by the blanket and in an act of desperation, yanked the blanket off and flung it toward Ben, hoping to trip him and slow him down. The blanket fell at his feet and Ben kicked it away, laughing. He re-focused on Holly, his rage building.

"This is for my brother," he declared.

A sudden calm came over Holly. In that moment, the moment before her death, she was at peace. She actually smiled. It made Ben hesitate. He wanted to see fear in her eyes, knowing she had only seconds to live. He'd seen that look before. Many times. It excited him. But Holly wasn't looking at him. Her eyes were focused on something else.

For Ben's benefit, she pointed to what she was looking at.

The mirror.

Ben looked. What he saw made his knees buckle.

In the full-length mirror was the reflection of Holly's Grandmother, Claire. Her long red hair was a wild mess that cascaded over a savagely scarred face. Now that Holly had a full view of her, she saw that her grandmother was barefoot, wearing a fluffy pink bathrobe over a yellowed nightgown. This time, the image didn't frighten Holly. She welcomed it.

Ben, on the other hand, stood frozen. He looked back into the room, expecting to see the woman standing in front of the mirror, but there was only her reflection.

"How?" was all he could mutter.

Holly scooted back further and got to her feet.

Ben approached the mirror and stood defiantly in front of the image of Claire Meade. Ben knew exactly who he was looking at. The years hadn't erased the memory of the woman, his patient, who had leapt to her death.

"This is a trick," he said. "How did you do this?"

"I didn't," Holly said with confidence. "This is on you."

While Ben couldn't grasp how he could be seeing this woman, this dead woman, what happened next pushed him to the edge of madness.

Claire moved forward, stepped out of the mirror, and into the living room, fully fleshed. The image in the mirror turned into her actual reflection as she walked away from it, moving toward Ben.

"You aren't real," he said with rising panic as he backed away. "I watched you die."

Claire didn't react. She kept walking, slowly, her eyes locked on Ben, backing him out of the double doors that led to the balcony.

"You're an apparition," Ben cried. "A memory."

Holly stood aside, watching with stunned wonder as Claire drew closer to Ben.

"You can't hurt me!" Ben shouted as if trying to convince himself. To make his point, he thrust the cattle prod toward her threateningly.

When Claire saw the weapon she stopped, and smiled. The wild look in her eyes could have stemmed from madness or ecstasy, the two being remarkably similar. She raised her arms as if ready to take flight, then quickly dropped them. In the next instant, as if they'd been summoned, a flock of crows erupted from the mirror in a dark mass of feathers and fury. The flock split in two to fly past Claire on either side, headed directly for Ben.

Ben screamed in terror and took a few steps back, swinging his arms, fighting off the birds that swarmed him, pecking at his head and hands, screeching with anger. He stabbed at the flying attackers with the cattle prod to no effect.

Holly crouched down, covering her head for fear the crows might turn on her.

More crows flew from the mirror, an insidious, growing storm directed at Ben.

Claire stood her ground, watching with wide eyes.

Ben backed up, furiously swinging the cattle prod, trying to keep the onslaught away.

"Ben!" Holly shouted. "Stop!"

Too late. Ben, still flailing, backed into the railing and lost his balance. With one last wave of crows that seemed intent on finishing the job, Ben fell over backward, off of the balcony.

Holly screamed.

On the street below, Danny Reynolds was walking by, headed back to the hardware store. He heard Holly's scream and looked up in time to see something falling his way. He jumped toward the building out of instinct, but he needn't have bothered.

Ben Daniels landed on the windshield of a car parked at the curb with the violent, booming sound of wrenched metal and crushed bone. His head shattered the windshield as a blossom of blood trickled through the channels of the newly created spider web of cracked glass. His neck was bent at an impossible angle as if snapped by a hangman's noose. His right arm was twisted around his misshapen neck. His hand still clutched the cattle prod with the business end jammed into his cheek. The sound of the surging electricity that was burning dead flesh was drowned out by the whooping of the car alarm that was triggered on impact.

Ben's eyes were open. When Danny spoke about it afterward, he said he felt as though the man was focused on him. In that moment he reacted exactly as one would expect. He screamed. It was an involuntary, primal response at having witnessed a sudden, violent death.

Terri's Jeep screeched to a stop directly behind the death car. (Once again, she got the perfect parking spot). She jumped out and rushed to the front of the wrecked car to see Ben's body. She didn't need the expertise of Jackie the Medical Examiner to tell her that he was dead. She had to fight the urge to break down and cry because the Grim Reaper had paid another visit to Glenville.

Danny continued screaming as he pressed himself against the wall as if trying to get further away. Terri rounded the car and went to him.

"Danny," she said while gently holding his shoulders. "Take a breath. It's okay."

"It's not okay," Danny cried, inconsolable.

"Look at me, Danny," Terri said calmly. "I need you to focus and talk to me."

Danny tore his eyes away from Ben and looked to Terri. Seeing her helped him begin the return to Earth. Terri gently maneuvered him around, so that his back was to the death scene.

"That's good," Terri said. "Deep breaths. I need you to tell me what happened."

In the apartment, Holly remained crouched on the floor, hugging her knees. The shock of seeing Ben fall to what had to be certain death left her paralyzed. The moment he went over the railing, the crows flew away, without leaving so much as a stray feather to show they'd been there.

Claire remained standing in the open doorway, never having gotten any closer to Ben than that. She took a step back into the apartment and slowly turned around to face Holly.

Holly was surprised to see that it was now a different woman who stood across from her. It was still her grandmother, but the scar on her face was gone, as was the fiery glint of madness in her eyes. Claire now resembled the woman that Holly had known through the photograph on her mother's end table.

Holly wiped away her tears and did her best to collect herself.

Claire approached her and knelt down. She reached out to touch Holly's cheek but stopped short of actually making contact.

"I wish I could have known you," Claire said. Her voice was soothing. It immediately put Holly at ease.

"I do too," Holly said.

Claire's eyes glistened with tears, but they were happy tears. She offered Holly a warm smile, then stood and walked toward the mirror.

"Grandma Claire?" Holly called out.

Claire turned back to her.

"I don't understand any of this," Holly said.

"I know," Claire said. "I'm not sure I do either, but I do know that it's right."

With that, Claire faced the mirror, and stepped into the frame.

"Wait!" Holly yelled and ran for it. When she got there, all she saw was her own reflection looking back at her. She knelt down, having been hit with a surge of mixed emotions. Above all she knew that whatever else had happened that day, she took heart that her Grandmother was now at peace.

Terri led a shaken Danny Reynolds to her Jeep where she helped him into the back seat. The car alarm had mercifully stopped chirping.

"Wait here," Terri said. "I'll need to get a statement. Okay?"

Danny nodded. He was a mess and would do whatever she asked. His top priority was to keep from looking at the car that sat a few feet away with a bloody and broken body splayed across its hood.

Terri closed the Jeep's door and punched a number into her cell phone. As she waited for an answer she walked to the death scene. Ben had a gruesome ending. She considered pulling the cattle prod away from his burnt cheek but didn't want to disrupt what might be a crime scene. It wasn't as if the electric charges were hurting the guy anymore. She took a few steps back and up to the balcony that Ben appeared to have fallen from. She backed into the street to get a better perspective when the call was answered.

"Jackie. No, I know you don't have a report yet. I've got something else for you. It's the brother. Yes. Just as dead."

As Terri listened she glanced around at street level until she saw someone sitting on a bench directly across the street from Holly's apartment building.

Mr. Paper.

"Understood. I gotta go. Send the wagon to Main Street. Near the hardware store. You won't miss the scene. I'll be here."

She punched out of the call and walked across the street. When Mr. Paper saw her approach, he stood politely.

"Good afternoon, Sheriff," he said with his usual charm. "This is proving to be quite the day."

"You're pretty calm for someone who just witnessed that," Terri said. "I assume you did witness it."

"I did and believe me I'm doing my best to maintain an even keel."

"I'm starting to wonder why you're always conveniently turning up," Terri said.

"It does seem coincidental," Mr. Paper said. "Then again, I've been covering quite a bit of territory. With so much drama unfolding, it would be more surprising if I managed to avoid it all."

Terri looked to Holly's building, calculating the sight lines.

"Tell me what you saw," Terri said.

"The poor man backed across the balcony, flailing his arms as if desperately fighting something off."

"Like what?" Terri asked.

"From what I could see, he was flailing at nothing. There was no one else on the balcony. He was wielding that orange device like a weapon against what seemed to be an imaginary foe."

"No one else was near him?"

"No. No one. The poor man backed into the railing and flipped over the edge."

"You're certain nobody was with him?" Terri asked.

"Absolutely."

"So he didn't jump intentionally?"

"I don't believe so," Mr. Paper replied. "If I were to venture a guess, I'd say it was an unfortunate accident."

Terri nodded thoughtfully as her analytical wheels spun, calculating the possibilities.

"Two brothers in the same day," she said wistfully.

"Perhaps he was distraught over his brother's death," Mr. Paper offered.

"Maybe," Terri said as she rolled the idea around. "You're a witness now. I'll need an official statement. Would you come by the station?"

"I'm at your disposal," Mr. Paper said, tipping his hat.

"There's one thing we agree on," Terri said. "I don't believe in coincidences either. I can't help but think that you being here is somehow tied into what's been happening."

"I'm not surprised you feel that way," Mr. Paper replied. "But I assure you, I have no personal connection to any of the people who have been affected."

"Right," she said, oozing skepticism. "I've changed my mind about letting Darcey work with you."

"She is a bright young woman," Mr. Paper said.

"She is, and she has other things to worry about. So please, don't contact her anymore."

"I understand completely," Mr. Paper said. "I will respect your wishes."

Terri nodded and made a move to leave.

"There is something I hope you consider," Mr. Paper said.

"What's that?"

"I understand your skepticism regarding my theories regarding underlying issues that may be triggering these events. It's not a common occurrence by any means. But I hope you are at least open to the possibility."

"At this point I'm open to everything," Terri said.

"I'm glad to hear that. And a caution: if you do come upon a common denominator, you must also be open to the fact that it might not be a finding you'll be comfortable with."

"I'm not comfortable with any of this," Terri shot back.

"I'm only suggesting that you may have to deal with a difficult truth. But it's one you'll have to accept, no matter how disturbing."

Terri walked back to Mr. Paper, stood a few feet from him, and stared straight into his eyes.

"Is there something you're not telling me?" she asked.

"I'm only giving you the benefit of my experience."

Terri continued to stare at him, as if trying to read his mind. Failing that, she said, "As much as I'd love for you to leave town, I'm asking you to stay for a while. Who knows where this investigation might lead?"

"I wouldn't consider leaving," Mr. Paper said.

He tipped his bowler hat once again and strolled off.

Terri headed back to the scene, spent the next few minutes taking pictures, after which she covered Ben's body with a silver space blanket. As she waited for the coroner, she spent most of her time securing the area with yellow crime-scene tape and keeping gawkers from getting too close. She also let Danny go. He had finally calmed down, so she asked him to head home and give his statement the next day when the shock had worn off. She wanted to hear from him once he was thinking straight. Danny was more than happy to get out of there.

When Jackie arrived with her team, Terri quickly gave her what little information she had, then moved on to the next task. She needed to speak with Holly. When she arrived at Holly's apartment, the door was slightly ajar. She knocked, and cautiously poked her head in.

"Hello?" Terri called.

"Come on in," Holly called out brightly.

Terri pushed the door open to see Holly sitting at her dining table, calmly drinking a Heineken.

"Hi Sheriff," Holly said. "Want a beer?"

Terri entered tentatively and went right to the table.

"I could use one, but no. Are you okay?"

"I am now."

Terri sat across from Holly, uneasily, for she didn't know what to make of the situation and Holly's oddly placid demeanor.

"You texted you were in trouble," Terri said. "What happened?"

Holly took a long swig of the Heineken, which Terri took as an indication that she might not be as calm as she first appeared. She put the bottle down and took a deep breath, as if preparing herself to re-live something she'd just as soon not have to.

"I was afraid Ben was going to blame me for what happened to George and do something stupid. I sure got that right."

"He came here to confront you about George's death?"

"Confront? That's an understatement. He tried to kill me. Look at this mess."

She gestured for Terri to look around at the apartment, and the aftermath of the struggle. Furniture was knocked over, shattered glass was everywhere, and a bloody knife was on the floor.

"He attacked you with that knife?"

"No, with a cattle prod. Nice, huh?"

Terri flashed on the image of the cattle prod still clutched in Ben's dead hand.

"The knife was me," Holly added. "Probably saved my life. Is he dead?'

"Yes."

Holly nodded in understanding.

"Did he go over the rail while you were defending yourself?" Terri asked.

"No, I was nowhere near him."

"Then what made him go over?"

Holly gave the answer some thought and chose her words carefully.

"I'd say it was guilt," she finally answered. "It sure wasn't regret, but there had to be some guilt."

"About attacking you?"

Holly pushed her phone across the table for Terri to see.

"Guilt over what he did to her," she replied. "What they both did to her."

On her phone was the photo of Holly's Grandma Claire.

"This is the woman you've been seeing?" Terri asked.

Holly nodded. "My grandmother. I learned that from my mother. Grandma Claire died before I was born."

Terri did her best not to show a reaction and remain analytical, but her gut was twisting.

"You're telling me the woman you've been seeing all morning, is your dead grandmother?"

"Freaky, right?"

"I...I'm having trouble understanding, Holly."

"You and me both. Did you know that George and Ben used to be doctors?"

Terri stiffened as if this was news she didn't want to hear.

"I didn't," she said.

"Apparently Grandma Claire had psychological problems. Like, serious ones and she was committed to an institution. Those two clowns were her doctors. According to my mother they mistreated her to the point that she was driven to suicide. Read the article. It's all there. Except for the malpractice stuff. Apparently it was all covered up. Ben admitted to most of it before he attacked me. Though he didn't take any blame, big surprise. It was all a blur because, well, he was trying to kill me. Like always he pointed the finger at somebody else."

"Who?"

"He said they treated difficult patients roughly because the hospital's Director told them to. Apparently it was the cheapest way to keep them under control. Imagine that. Torture for the budget. I'd sure like to know who that guy was."

Terri swallowed hard and asked, "Does the article mention the hospital? Or the Director?"

Holly took the phone back and scrolled through the article.

"The High Point Institute. The Director was a guy named Everett Kane. Ever hear about him?"

Terri took a long time before answering.

"I'll look into it," she said.

Holly took a swig of beer and said, "Good. I'd really love to find that guy."

CHAPTER 13

Vera Holiday spent the better part of the few hours after checking into the Cozy Rest hiding under the bed covers. She knew it was childish, and impractical, but she needed the comfort that came with shutting out the world like a frightened six-year-old, even if the only protection was a threadbare bed sheet and a pilled-up woolen blanket.

Vera was an educated person. A woman of science. Her entire worldview was fact-based. There was no room for anything spiritual or, God forbid, supernatural to exist in that orderly world. As she cowered beneath the covers, she challenged herself using the Socratic method to run through multiple scenarios that would explain what she'd been experiencing. None held water. She felt certain she was missing something. An "X" factor. Whatever it was, she had confidence that once she found it the pieces would fit together logically and provide her with the tools to end it. Perhaps she'd even get some measure of revenge against whoever was behind the harassment. But because she couldn't produce that missing piece, her anger grew. Perhaps worse was her rising frustration over not knowing where, or to whom, to direct her ire.

Her indignation grew stronger than her fear. How dare someone harass her like this? She was never a victim and wasn't about to become one now. It was time to get back to work. God only knows what Mikey was getting up to at the pharmacy. With renewed resolve, she threw off the blankets and jumped out of the bed, determined to get back in the game. Her only moment of concern came when she was about to open the door. What was it that had been outside? She hesitated, steeled herself, pulled the door open, and cautiously peeked out.

"Vera!" Sherry Terri exclaimed.

Vera literally jumped when she saw the overly-enthusiastic woman outside of the door.

"What are you doing out here?" Vera exclaimed.

"Sorry, girlfriend, didn't mean to surprise you," Sherry said. "I wanted to check in to see if you needed anything. Extra towels? Ice? We don't have Wi-Fi I'm afraid so I can't—"

"I'm fine," Vera said sharply. "I might be checking out. I don't know yet."

"Oh," Sherry said, disappointed. "You've only been here a few hours I don't have to charge you for—"

"I said might," Vera snapped. "I'll let you know."

"No problem," Sherry said brightly. "You do you."

Vera started to walk off but had a thought.

"Were you looking in my window?" Vera asked. "A few hours ago?"

"No, of course not!" Sherry immediately replied, mortified. "Was someone looking in at you? I didn't see anyone--"

"Never mind," Vera said and stormed off.

Sherry was left shaken. The idea that there might be a lurker around her cozy Motor Lodge was a disturbing one. She glanced around nervously, then hurried back to the lobby and locked the door.

The Glenville Apothecary was a short walk from the Cozy Rest, made shorter by the quick pace Vera kept. Her first order of business was to find an exterminator. The sooner she did that, the sooner the nightmare would be over. She reached the front door to discover it was unlocked. Had she forgotten to lock it?

She went inside to see a woman at the cash register buying Advil and a toothbrush. Ringing her up was Mikey. It gave Vera a moment of calm. Mikey had actually opened the store for business. He must have finished the clean-up and then took the initiative to allow customers in. For a moment she genuinely appreciated the kid and thought he might be worth keeping around.

"Thanks ma'am," Mikey said as the customer left the cash register.

"Hello Vera," the woman said as they passed each other.

"Maggie," Vera replied. "How's the arthritis?"

"Not going anywhere," Maggie said with a shrug and headed out.

Vera approached Mikey at the counter.

"It's all cleaned up," Mikey said tentatively. "Like it never happened. I thought you'd want me to open."

He braced himself, ready to be chastised for having somehow blundered.

"You thought right," Vera said, though stopped short of thanking him.

Mikey beamed, as if he'd just been anointed employee of the year.

"Would you mind staying up front?" Vera asked. "I've got some business that needs doing."

"Sure!" Mikey said. He enjoyed helping customers. It was more interesting than mopping floors, stocking shelves, and wiping down shit-covered walls.

"I'll be in my office," Vera said.

As she walked to the rear of the store, her confidence grew. She had a plan. She was being pro-active. She'd find a qualified rat-killer because that's what she wanted. A killer. She might have to spend a few nights sleeping at the Cozy Rest while the poison did its job, but that would be okay. She wanted nothing left alive.

With renewed confidence, she opened her office door, stepped inside...

...and screamed.

Mikey came running. He found Vera on her knees inside the office door.

"What the matter?" Mikey cried for the second time that day.

"Why?" Vera said through tears.

"Why what?" Mikey asked.

He looked into the office and saw it. Vera's desk chair had been moved to the center of the room. On the seat, resting upright against the backrest was a wooden board.

Nailed to the board was Bobcat. Dead.

He hung there, belly-out with all four paws hammered into the board. The animal was sliced open from neck to abdomen, revealing its guts. The poor cat wasn't torn apart, it had been surgically splayed open up as though being dissected.

Mikey took one look, turned away, and vomited.

"Why did you do that?" Vera cried.

"I didn't!" Mikey sobbed while wiping his chin. "I swear Vera. I didn't."

Vera struggled to get to her feet and dragged herself closer to the grisly scene. Though she would never admit it, she liked Bobcat. The stray cat reminded her of the cat she had when she was a child. She hadn't had another pet until Bobcat showed up. Now he was gone, having suffered a gruesome death. Vera couldn't help but think that all the horrors of this day were tied together. She had no idea what she had done to deserve any of it.

She stood in front of the grisly scene, mesmerized by the tidy array of entrails that had been left perfectly in place within the shell of Bobcat's carcass. She had performed necropsies on many animals, including cats, but never on one she cared about. Or had a name. Other than the fact that it was there, there was nothing unusual about the display, except for something that caught her eye. Tucked between Bobcat's duodenum and transverse colon was a foreign object. It stood out because of its color (white) and its sharp-angled edge. Only the tip showed. The rest was buried in Bobcat's guts.

Vera's scientific curiosity took over and she reached for it. She grasped the corner between her thumb and forefinger and gently pulled. With a wet, sucking sound, the foreign object was released from the viscera. It was plastic, a few inches long and a half inch wide. Vera took a close look and let out a gasp.

"What is it?" Mikey asked, still sitting on the floor near his puddle of vomit.

Vera took a few involuntary steps backward, her mind racing to nowhere. She backed into an easy chair she used for reading and fell into it while staring at the plastic strip.

"Ms. Holiday?" Mikey whined with confusion.

Vera let her hand drop onto the arm rest and stared into space.

Mikey managed to stand and go to her. He knelt down to get a look at what she'd pulled out of Bobcat, with no intention of touching it.

"Vera Holiday," Mikey read.

It was an I.D. badge.

"I swear to God, Vera, I didn't do this. Maybe when I was cleaning the bathroom somebody got---"

'It's okay," Vera said. "I believe you."

Vera was remarkably calm. Mikey couldn't tell if she had regained control or had plunged off the deep end.

"What is that thing?" Mikey asked.

"It was my I.D. badge from a job I had a very long time ago," Vera said, sounding eerily detached as if her thoughts had traveled back to that time.

"This is really fucked up," Mikey said. "Sorry."

"Yes, it is," Vera said.

Mikey reached for his cell phone.

"I'll call Sheriff Hirsch," he said. "She'll figure out who did this and—"

"No," Vera said abruptly.

"C'mon Vera!" Mikey said, momentarily forgetting decorum. "This is serious. Somebody's got it out for you."

"I want you to call her, but not yet. I need to deal with this myself."

"How? And do what?"

Vera stood up. She was back in control.

"Wait one hour," Vera said with certainty. "Then call the sheriff and tell her to meet me at the High Point Institute."

"What's that?"

"She'll know."

"This is crazy," Mikey said, his voice shaking. "If some nut case is out there who kills and guts cats, who knows what he's capable of?"

"Or she," Vera said.

"Whatever. We should call the Sheriff right now."

He started to input Terri's number, then stopped.

"I don't know her number."

Vera gently put her hand over his to stop him.

"Please," Vera said. "It's on me to deal with this."

"Then I'll go with you to this High Point place," Mikey said, trying to sound more confident than he felt.

"No, I told you, this is on me. Wait an hour, then call the sheriff. Would you please do that for me?"

Mikey wasn't happy with the plan, but he knew that once Vera got something into her head, there was no getting it out.

"One hour," he said with authority. "I'll leave Bobcat like that so the sheriff can see him, but I'll clean up my puke. Sorry for that."

"No need to apologize. Thank you, Mikey. You're a good kid."

If nothing else, that rare compliment left Mikey speechless.

Vera left the pharmacy and headed back to her house. Fortunately, she had her car keys in her coat pocket. There was no need for her to venture inside. She wanted no part of whatever was going on in there. She opened the garage and got into her ancient Saab. She couldn't remember the last time she'd driven it and feared that the battery might be dead. But the trusty car sputtered, chugged and the engine turned over.

"This has to end, now," she said to no one.

CHAPTER 14

Scott Wilson sat on his backhoe and deftly gouged another shovel-full of dirt from the short trench he had created. Though it was a heavy, powerful piece of machinery, Scott managed the work with surgical precision.

When he'd made the first gouge, the kid had called out an admonishment. "Whoa, easy! You're not digging up tree stumps."

"Then what am I digging up?" Scott called out. "And how deep is it?"

The kid didn't reply. He backed away until he was at the pick-up truck and stayed there, watching Scott work.

Scott controlled the powerful shovel as deftly as if it was a hand-held trowel. He scraped away no more than a few inches at a time. With each pass he looked down into the deepening trench to see if he'd uncovered anything. He often wondered if he'd missed his calling and should have gone into archeology. He figured he'd moved enough dirt over the years to qualify.

When the pit was nearing three feet deep, he felt a slight hitch as the shovel made its pass. It was subtle, but enough for Scott to feel it. He backed the vehicle away, jumped off, and walked to the edge of the trench to see what it might be. He looked down, then quickly recoiled.

"Jee-suz!" he exclaimed.

The kid didn't react.

Scott now saw the hole for what it was. A grave. He wiped nervous-sweat from his forehead and took another look down. What the shovel had bumped over was a foot wearing a black, rotting, high-top sneaker. Scott glanced at the kid who hung close to the pick-up truck as if needing it for protection. The kid wore black high-top Converse sneakers.

Nothing Scott had experienced that day made sense, but it wasn't until that moment that he accepted the world didn't work the way he thought it did. It was a seemingly impossible conclusion, but it made things clearer.

He looked to the kid and asked, "Is that you down there?"

The kid shrugged and nodded.

"You said you want me to be a witness?" Scott said. "You want me to tell people you're here? Is that all?"

The kid shook his head "no." His confident air was shaken, as if finding the body was as disturbing to him as it was to Scott.

"Then what?" Scott asked.

The kid pointed to the other side of the clearing. Scott looked to see the elderly Black man in the plaid bathrobe standing alone, pointing to the ground at his feet.

"Shit," Scott said.

Darcey waited until her mother left the house before returning to the dining room, and her computer, determined to find answers. The fact that Terri told her to back off only compelled her to dig in harder. What harm would it do? She was moving out in a few days. As a bonus, by going against her mother's wishes she felt as though she was exacting a small bit of revenge for having had her life turned inside out. She knew it was petty but didn't care.

Unfortunately, after twenty minutes of searching, she came up empty. She Googled every possible combination of names of the affected people, along with *High Point Institute* and *Glenville Wisconsin*. The only thing she found was an article about some poor woman who committed suicide. She also came across the name of the Director of the High Point Institute: Everett Kane. Diving deeper proved fruitless. She chalked it up to the fact that not everything existed on the internet, especially not the accounts of events that happened back in the 1990's. That was a lifetime ago. It might as well have happened in the 1890's. Her plan of short cutting the investigation by relying on Google led to a dead end. She was faced with a choice: Stay home, as her mother asked, no, ordered her to do, or seek out Mr. Paper to continue the investigation.

It was an easy choice. She left the house.

She found Mr. Paper sitting at a table outside of Cassone's Bakery, sipping tea from a chipped ceramic mug while nibbling a scone.

"You're becoming a regular here," Darcey said as she sat next to him.

"I finally succumbed to the heavenly aromas that waft from this establishment," Mr. Paper said. "However, I'm afraid we should not be conversing."

"Seriously? Did my mother get to you?"

"She's concerned about your well-being and would prefer that you concentrate on your studies."

"That's one way of putting it," Darcey said, scoffing.

"How else might you put it?"

"For one, she wants to control me. Two, I'm moving back to Chicago, so it doesn't matter what she wants. And three..."

She didn't complete the sentence.

"Three?" Mr. Paper asked.

Darcey backed off from her tirade and gave a genuinely thoughtful answer.

"Something's off with her," she said. "It's been a messed-up day so maybe it's just stress. That guy getting electrocuted sure didn't help. But she's normally pretty open about stuff. I usually don't agree with her, but at least I understand where she's coming from. This is different."

"Do you sense that she is not being completely forthcoming with you?" Mr. Paper asked.

"Maybe. But that's too simple. She's dealing with a lot of stuff, so I think it's more than that."

"She may be upset about your decision to live with your father."

"Doubt it. She'd say so. She's not shy about letting me know how she feels about pretty much everything to do with me. And my father."

Mr. Paper took a sip of tea and dabbed the corners of his mouth with a thin paper napkin. "In my last brief conversation with her I pointed out that if it does indeed turn out to be an underlying issue at play here, it would likely prove to be disturbing. Those types of inciting incidents are never joyful."

"If that's what's bothering her then it means she buys that something bigger is happening."

"It seems she may be open to the idea," Mr. Paper said.

"The sooner we figure out what it is, the sooner we can help her end it."

"That would be a welcome outcome," Mr. Paper said. "However, I must respect her wishes. We can no longer chat."

"Okay, fine, that sucks, but we're already chatting now so let's take advantage. Scott Wilson and I were chased by a truck that nobody was driving."

Mr. Paper raised an eyebrow. "Interesting."

"What about you?" Darcey asked.

"I'm afraid there's been another death. The other Daniels brother is no longer with us."

"Are you shitting me?"

"I'm afraid I cannot attest to that, one way or the other. I'm unfamiliar with the term."

"How'd he die?" Darcey asked.

"It appears to have been an accident. He fell from a balcony."

"Damn. Was it suicide?"

"Perhaps."

"This is crazy!" Darcey exclaimed. "No wonder Mom's flipping out."

"That might follow, but she's a strong woman."

"Yeah but this is going beyond," Darcey said. "I don't know what to do."

"Your instinct to search the internet for connections was a good one, but it's limited."

"I found that out."

"I've learned that using traditional methods is often the most effective. The web gives you access to the world, but your concern is here, with Glenville. If you're delving into the past of a particular area, you might want to focus on more pointed resources."

Darcey gave this some thought and brightened up with an idea.

"That makes total sense," she said, and stood up. "We're going to figure this out, even if we're on our own."

"I hope you're right, for your mother's sake."

Those slightly ominous words didn't sit well with Darcey, but she shook it off and left Mr. Paper to finish his tea and scone.

She knew exactly where to head next.

Scott now understood.

He didn't question or hesitate. Once it became clear what he was in the middle of, he set his mind to the task and didn't falter. The rhythm was the same. He would position the backhoe near the spot he was directed to and carefully dig until he came upon more grisly remains. He would then back the vehicle away and approach the hole, often making sure that the evidence was sufficiently revealed by cautiously reaching down into the grave with a hand shovel to gently scrape away more dirt. He ultimately became numb to the horrid task.

There were no coffins. The holes had been dug and the bodies tossed in with no more respect than would have been given to a dog. The remains were in various states of decay. The cloth of their clothing had rotted away to reveal gray, molding flesh that clung to brittle bones. A few skulls had been unearthed. Those were the worst. Though the eyes had long since disintegrated he still felt as though they were looking up at him from their lonely resting places. While it was difficult to tell much from the bodies since they were in such an advanced state of decay, the clothing told a more definitive story. Some wore nightgowns, others blue jeans and t-shirts. There were a few corpses that wore simple dresses that at one time must have been brightly colored but had faded to a dull bone white.

He found more than one child.

While there might not have been enough left of the physical remains to officially identity any of them, he knew exactly who each one was. When he finished with a grave, he'd stand over it, make the sign of the cross, say a silent prayer, then scan the clearing to learn of his next task. Each time he would see someone new standing over another spot, indicating where he should dig next. He saw the elderly bald women. He saw more young men who wore jeans and flannel shirts. He saw the young women in their pastel-colored dresses. And he saw the children. He saw who each one was and how they looked in life. He knew exactly who he would find each time he dug down to uncover their corrupted remains.

With each new dig, the occupant would stand vigil as if to make sure the job was done properly. He grieved for each of them for he felt as if he knew them. Once Scott found the body, he would look to see the spirit was no longer there, while another had taken its place in another part of the clearing.

As he worked he tried not to focus on the gruesome task itself, but rather on what this unholy graveyard might represent. Were these victims of a mass murder? The casualties of some deadly virus? A cult that had lived off the grid? Clearly this was not an ancient burial ground. The clothing they wore made that abundantly clear. It made it all the more disturbing to know that it hadn't been eons since these people had lived. The extent of the decay told him they might have died only a few decades before. That was in his lifetime. How was it possible for this to have gone undiscovered? In the very town where he grew up?

He was no longer afraid. He was grief-stricken.

When he said his prayer over the grave of a man with one leg who was buried with a crutch, he looked up to determine his next task and saw that he was alone. He took that to mean he had found them all. He staggered back a few steps to stand on the edge of the clearing where he could view the entire area. He had been so focused on the individual tasks that he hadn't dared to appreciate the scope of the site.

There were twenty-five open graves scattered haphazardly. All held the remains of people who had lived unique lives. Who had families. Who were dumped into unmarked graves that were hidden deep in the woods where no one would come to mourn and lay flowers. Scott was overcome. He fell to his knees, crushed by the weight of this terrible discovery, and wept.

Once he pulled himself together, his grief turned to anger. Who was responsible for this? What kind of monster, or monsters, would do this? Most importantly, why? If nothing else, the realization of what had been happening to him that day became clear. He wasn't the target of a malevolent force. His truck had not turned against him. He was chosen because he had the ability to do exactly what he had been doing for the last few hours. The words of the kid in the Stones T-shirt said it all. They needed Scott to be a witness. He wasn't about to try and understand how forlorn spirits could interact with the living. That would be left for another time and for those smarter than him. His task was to tell the story of these poor souls. To let the world know that they were here.

Scott now understood.

His Honda was parked with its nose facing the road he had cut earlier that morning. The road that the spirits had cut for him. He swore he'd use it to bring the world to this unholy site and give these spirits the closure they deserved.

The town library was an ancient structure that was constructed in the 1920's, when Glenville was a growing town and people read books made of paper. It hadn't changed much since. It was one of the more interesting structures in town, looking more like a European castle than a government building. It had a weathered, red-brick façade, with a circular tower that housed a special reading room for those who wished for a private nook to kick back and get lost in a good book.

That nook hadn't been used in ages, other than by horny kids looking for a secluded spot to hook up.

Darcey had never set foot in the building. Her first thought when she entered was that she had stepped back in time. The bookshelves were wooden, the tables polished oak. They even had a rack of wooden pull-out drawers that contained Dewey Decimal System cards. The pervasive smell was a blend of wood polish, dried paper, and aging leather. The only nod to contemporary times were the two outdated IBM PCs that were set up near the circulation desk, as well as the colorful dust jackets on the shelved books.

"No fucking way!"

The voice echoed through the cavernous room.

Wendy Tipton, Darcey's weed-smoking partner from that morning approached her carrying a stack of books.

"Never thought I'd see you here," Wendy said.

"Yeah, surprise," Darcey said.

"Wait. Are we in trouble? Is your mother going to arrest us? My parents would kill me if—"

"No, it's cool," Darcey said.

"Thank God," Wendy said, relieved. "If that happened I could kiss Notre Dame good-bye. Or anywhere else for that matter. I'd be stuck here rearranging books that nobody reads for the rest of my life."

"You work here?" Darcey asked with a touch of incredulity.

Wendy placed the stack of books down onto the circulation desk.

The Paper Trail

"It's better than babysitting. Or working retail. That's like death. Then again, everything in this town is like death."

Darcey didn't want to tell her that she was only a few days away from escaping, so she gave a safe reply: "I hear you."

"What are you doing here?" Wendy asked. "You must know that everything here you can get with your phone."

"Not everything," Darcey said. "I'm looking for books on local history. Anything that shows what businesses used to be here."

Wendy gave Darcey a long, inquiring look and said, "Oh. I thought you might be looking for something boring."

Darcey laughed. "It's for a history report. I tried the internet but there isn't a whole lot that's been uploaded about Glenville. Almost nothing, actually. Big surprise. Do you have anything like that?"

"Maybe," she said. "Probably. But do you seriously think I know all the books in this place? All anybody wants to check out are bestsellers. Not that we get that many."

"Is there a librarian who'd know?" Darcey asked.

"Yeah, but she only works a couple hours a day, and she's gone already. It's not a tough job."

"There must be a local history section," Darcey said.

"If there is it would probably be downstairs, in the stacks. Look down there unless you're allergic to dust."

"I'll risk it," Darcey said and headed for the stairs in the back of the building that led down to the basement, and the seldom-visited archives. She descended the creaky, wooden stairs and found herself in a dark basement. She took a few tentative steps, looking for a light switch, and was surprised when the overhead lights came on automatically, triggered by her movement. It was a cost-saving device that would insure the lights only went on when someone was there.

The old-school, harsh neon light revealed a large room that encompassed the entire footprint of the building. The stacks were aptly named. There was one long aisle that separated multiple rows of bookcases that nearly reached the ceiling. To get a book from a high shelf would require a step ladder. The far end of each row of bookcases ended before reaching the side walls, creating walkways on either side of the large space. The far walls were taken up by more shelves of books. It was an ancient-book wonderland and Darcey had no idea where to begin. If Wendy had been an actual librarian, she would have referred her to the computer or the ancient card files to track down the location of whatever book she wanted. But she wasn't so Darcey had to search.

She walked slowly down the center aisle, scanning from side to side, looking for book titles that would hint at what each section contained. Each time she took a few steps a new light would buzz to life while the light behind her shut down. The result was that Darcey traveled in a moving cocoon of light, glimpsing at titles of books on various subjects. There was a travel section with tourist guides that had been obsolete for thirty years. She saw cookbooks, biographies, how-to guides, self-help books, and military histories.

Darcey grew increasingly frustrated because she was only scratching the surface of what these stacks contained.

She thought, *this is going to take forever.*

As she neared the end of the center aisle and hadn't seen anything that remotely hinted at local history, she feared it was all a waste of time. Her patience had run dry, and she was about to give up when she sensed that a light had turned on far behind her. Had someone else come down to the stacks?

"Wendy?"

She turned around to see that the light at the bottom of the stairs was burning, but nobody was there. She figured the ancient motion detectors weren't all that efficient. They probably hadn't kicked on in ages. A moment later, the light went out and the aisle was plunged into darkness. Darcey didn't give it another thought and continued on, figuring she'd at least continue to search both sides of the center aisle before giving up. When she reached the far end, she heard the distant crackle of electricity flowing through neon tubes that indicated the light behind her had activated again. She turned to start making her way back...

...and saw she wasn't alone. A man stood directly under the light at the far end of the aisle, twenty yards away. He wore dark clothing with his hands in his pockets. His feet were apart as he stood perfectly still. Chillingly, he seemed to be looking straight at her.

"Something I can do for you?" she called out, trying to exude confidence she didn't have.

The light went out. The far end went dark. The man became invisible.

Darcey's danger-radar pinged. She did a quick look around to see if there was another exit she could use to get back upstairs. There wasn't one. Fire laws weren't as restrictive when this building was constructed. But a fire was the last thing on her mind. To get out, she was going to have to walk back the way she'd come in, past where the man had been.

She heard the crackle of electricity as another set of lights surged to life. It was the next section closer to her. When they came on, Darcey let out a short yelp of surprise. The man was there, still standing with his hands in his pockets. Still staring at her. Only now he stood an aisle closer.

"You gonna say something?" Darcey called, challenging him.

The man didn't respond. As she stared back at him, trying not to show fear, she realized that he looked familiar. Who was he? It took a solid ten seconds before it came to her.

"Mr. Iverson?" she called out. "Karl Iverson?"

The light went out again and the aisle went dark.

Darcey wasn't sure if she should be relieved that it was someone she knew, or worried that he was acting strangely. She didn't know him all that well, only that he was The Sweeper. He wasn't sociable, or friendly, though he seemed harmless. There were no rumors about him being a maniac killer or a loner bomb-builder.

"Karl Iverson?" she called out to the darkness. "I'm Darcey Hirsch. Sheriff Hirsch's daughter."

She hoped that if he knew that, he'd think twice before doing something stupid.

"You're making me nervous, dude," she called out.

It was a vulnerable position. She was alone under the light while he was hidden in darkness. She feared that another light would go on, this time even closer, and he'd be in her face.

Another light did come on, though it was further back, at the stairs. Karl was under it.

"What are you doing, Karl?" Darcey called.

Karl motioned for Darcey to follow him, turned, and walked into a side aisle and out of sight.

"That's not creepy," she said to herself.

Her fear notched down a tick. She reasoned that if the guy wanted to hurt her, he would have done it where she stood, trapped in a dead end. Trusting her instincts, she slowly made her way back the way she had come. Each time she passed a side aisle she held her breath and prayed that he wouldn't spring from the shadows. It was like walking through a real-life amusement park spook house.

She made it back to the head of the aisle at the bottom of the stairs. The moment she stepped into the light that Karl had walked away from, the light went out. Darcey froze. This was her chance. The way was clear. She was a breath away from running for the stairs, when another light went on at the end of the side aisle Karl had walked down. She took a few cautious steps forward until she could peer into that aisle.

Karl wasn't there.

"Karl?" she called. "Why are you messing with me?"

Darcey wanted nothing more than to get the hell out of there. But why did Karl want her to follow him? Again, if he wanted to hurt her he would have done it when she was trapped. Right? RIGHT? She felt certain that Karl had some other purpose in mind, and she wanted to know what it was. After a deep, bracing breath, she walked cautiously into the aisle toward the area that was lit up.

"Okay I'm here," Darcey said. "What do you want?"

She peered over the tops of the books on both sides, looking past them into the adjacent aisles, expecting to see Karl staring back at her, while praying she wouldn't. Her gaze caught something else. It was the cover of a book that was face out. It's title: *"Wisconsin, Then and Now."*

"Holy shit," Darcey exclaimed.

She'd found it: the section with books on local history. In her excitement she forgot about how she'd gotten there. Her entire attention went to the books. She quickly scanned through the volumes, looking for anything that was specifically about Glenville. She glossed over title after title, row after row. There were volumes about Madison, Milwaukee, Lake Geneva, the NFL Packers, bike trails, hiking trails, camping sites, Governors, Notable People from Wisconsin including some guy named Vince Lombardi, and more than one book about cheese. There seemed to be books on everything except what she was looking for. It was as if Glenville didn't exist.

She was about to give up when she saw it. Not a book about Glenville. Better. The title was: *Welcome to the High Point Institute.*

"Oh my God," Darcey said.

She grabbed the book to discover it wasn't so much a book as it was a thick, full-color brochure that was bound in a leather cover. When she opened it the spine crackled as if it had never been cracked. It was a slickly made, expensive looking, sales tool that spoke glowingly about the wonderful facilities, staff, research, and health care that the institute provided. Darcey quickly scanned through pages of photographs that showed a campus that had an architectural style much like the Glenville Public Library. Apparently the buildings had been around since the early 1900's and the text spoke of how the medical care they provided was state of the art.

One of the first pictures she came upon was a large, formal portrait of an older man in a suit. He had a full head of perfectly combed gray hair and keen eyes that spoke of his intellect. The caption said he was the Director of the Institute, Dr. Everett Kane.

The text was a quote from him, welcoming all those who sought care and comfort at the institute.

    Darcey was too excited to focus on the text. She was drawn to the pictures. Besides the beauty shots of the campus, there was a slick two-page spread featuring the opulent main lobby with a gorgeous neo-classical fountain and a breathtaking, three story high stained-glass window that overlooked it. Several pictures showed patient rooms that rivaled what could be found in a high-end hotel. There were multiple photos of the staff, both posed and candid. It struck Darcey that those photos made it seem more like a high school yearbook than a promotional brochure for a hospital.

    She turned the page and saw the photo that launched her on this mission. It was George and Ben Daniels standing on the cement stairs of what she now realized was the main entrance of the High Point Institute.

    There was an entire section that clearly meant to characterize the staff as friendly, caring family folks. Several charming amateur snapshots showed them at holiday celebrations, birthday parties and vacations. Some felt vaguely familiar, though she couldn't identify them. After all, these pictures had been taken decades before.

    As she flipped through the pages, not sure what she was hoping to find, she lamented that she couldn't share this with Mr. Paper. At least not if she was going to obey her mother. She had already crossed a couple of red lines by continuing the Google search, talking to Mr. Paper, and now standing in the basement of the library holding what she felt sure was a significant piece to the puzzle. Could things get any worse with her mother if she showed this to Mr. Paper? She decided to make that call after she got home with the brochure in hand.

    She turned one last page and saw a picture that made her catch her breath. It was a candid shot of the Director, Dr. Kane, with his family in front of a Christmas tree. It was him, his wife, and his four-year-old daughter.

Darcey stared at the image, trying to grasp what she was seeing. She wanted to come up with an explanation that was anything but the obvious one. The impossible one. Her heart pounded. Sweat broke out on her forehead. She wasn't sure if she should cry or laugh or put the brochure back on the shelf and forget that she'd seen it.

She was having trouble breathing. She had to get out of that basement, so she took off running for the stairs, still grasping the bound brochure. She ran up the stairs and headed straight for the front door.

"Hey!' Wendy called to her. "You gotta check that out!"

Darcey kept going.

Wendy thought for a second that she should go after her, but instead shrugged and said, "Who cares? She probably doesn't have a library card anyway."

She went back to her homework.

As Darcey went out of her mind.

CHAPTER 15

The High Point Institute was situated in a wooded area five miles north of downtown Glenville. Vera knew the way there. She'd driven it for the better part of ten years. It sat on a huge parcel of woodland that had been deeded to the institute by a trust that had existed for well over a hundred years. The turnoff from the main road once had a tasteful wooden sign to mark it, but that was long gone. The turnoff itself was almost gone as well. The untended bushes on either side of the entrance had grown wild, obscuring the turn while weeds poked up through the cracked asphalt. The turnoff went unnoticed by most everyone who drove past, except for those who knew.

Vera knew. She made the turn and winced as branches scratched at her car's finish. Fortunately, once she drove past the bushes that ran parallel to the main road, the lane was clear. Since it was a private road, there was no reason for anyone to be driving it unless they were visiting the institute. It was a barely two-lane road that wound through a thick pine forest on the way up to a knoll, upon which sat the structure. It was always a breathtaking moment for Vera when her car emerged from the dense forest to reveal a view of the impressive building.

It was built in the 1920's during what was considered the Gilded Age of architecture, an era when barons of industry built fabulous European-style mansions to display their wealth. High Point was a sprawling, five-story structure built mostly of red brick, with five round turrets that gave it the feel of a medieval castle. It was designed and built to be a hospital and operated as such for the entirety of its functional existence.

That existence ended decades before when High Point closed its doors. When the last of the staff left, the doors were locked, and the grand old building abandoned. Years of research hadn't settled the question of who controlled the trust that had originally leased the property to the hospital so there it sat. Empty. Waiting for a savior that had yet to come. Or a wrecking ball.

An imposing wrought-iron fence circled the property, with tall brick pillars spaced twenty yards apart to anchor it. The entryway was through massive iron gates that were set between two of the tallest pillars. Vera feared that the gates would be closed and locked but found them swung wide open, with a heavy padlock dangling from a central latch. It was as if someone was expecting a visitor. She drove through the pillars, along the road that cut through weeded grounds that once sported a manicured lawn, and onto the circular driveway to park directly in front of the main entrance. She got out and looked up at the dozen cement stairs that led to a pair of imposing wooden doors in an arched frame. It was an entrance she had rarely used. Normally she would park around back and enter through a nondescript entryway.

"Such a beautiful old hellhole," she said to no one.

She climbed the stairs, expecting, and hoping that she would be locked out. Not only were the doors unlocked; one was ajar.

Vera gently pushed the door open and entered the building's lobby. Though long-neglected, this five-story atrium was still breathtaking. It was designed to be an impressive first look at the opulent interior and it didn't disappoint. The floor was a mosaic of intricately detailed Venetian tile. A grand marble staircase led to a second-floor balcony over which was a massive stained-glass window that, while darkened with ages of accumulated grime, still rivaled anything found in a medieval cathedral. Each of the five floors held a balcony that ringed the open space, capped by a glass dome that had grown cloudy from lack of care. The centerpiece on the ground floor was an immense marble fountain that once had a constant flow of water that cascaded from multiple tiers of Roman-style cisterns. It was now filled with dust and debris.

It made Vera wistful to see how this showplace from another era had fallen into such a sorry state of decay. It was a fleeting sentiment, for there was no love lost between her and anything that had to do with the High Point Institute. When she left for the final time, she vowed never to set foot in the place again.

Until ghosts from her past beckoned.

Vera left the atrium and walked slowly through the tomb-like building. The only sound came from the broken bits of plaster that were crushed beneath her shoes as she walked. With each step, more vivid memories returned. Memories she had suppressed for years.

She had been hired as a research assistant out of grad school and went to work in the institute's department that specialized in live animal research. She was fascinated by the biology of it all and thrilled to be on the forefront of research that was used to produce pharmaceuticals that would improve the quality of health care.

Her boss, a Doctor Abernathy, was an amiable old gent she enjoyed working for, but he retired a year into Vera's employment and died soon after. She was immediately promoted to the position of lab manager by High Point's director, Dr. Everett Kane.

The department became her domain to run as she saw fit.

At any given time, they had hundreds of animals involved in multiple projects. There were bins and cages filled with rats and mice, dozens of rabbits, dogs, cats, pigs, and monkeys. More arrived every day to replace the animals that had died by design, euthanasia, or as a result of testing. Death and suffering were constants that Vera became inured to. While her interns might have blanched at the task of exposing a monkey's brain in order to attach electrodes that would monitor the animal's reaction to pain, Vera only saw the science.

The lab was a lucrative source of income for High Point, thanks to the contracts they were awarded by pharmaceutical companies that thirsted for the data they produced. Yet there always seemed to be budget issues, which rankled Vera. She ran a tight operation and suspected the real issue had to do with the institute's director, Doctor Kane, and his never-ending quest to maximize profits. Whatever the reason, she was constantly forced to tighten her budget which made it increasingly difficult to function efficiently. Her recourse was to bypass many government regulations that mandated the humane treatment of the test subjects. It was an easy decision because she saw these regulations as intrusive, expensive, counter-productive, and unnecessary.

Not everyone agreed. Several interns resigned over disputes regarding Vera's callous treatment of their subjects. Vera fired even more. Her questionable practices were never challenged by Doctor Kane, as long as the lucrative contracts kept coming. Since Doctor Kane didn't interfere with Vera's management of the lab, it made it all the more devastating for her when he didn't hesitate to throw her under the bus the moment the state of Wisconsin came knocking to investigate multiple complaints filed against the lab, the institute, and her directly. During the inquest, Vera argued that the state only focused on one side of the story and didn't appreciate the value of the research. Who cared if the animals had been somewhat neglected?

The state did. Vera was fired and the department was shut down. Soon after the entire institute was shuttered. It was one of the last major employers in a town that was struggling to remain relevant. Fingers were pointed at Vera, but she was unfazed. She truly believed she had done nothing wrong and was used as a scapegoat to hide the transgressions of many others on the staff, including Doctor Kane himself.

Once her tenure at High Point ended, Vera re-invented herself. Using money she had been saving since high school and a pitiful severance from High Point, she went back to school and obtained a degree in pharmacology. Years later she returned to the town and opened the Glenville Apothecary. The history of her lab, and the High Point Institute, was mostly forgotten.

Though apparently not by everyone. The mysterious appearance of Vera's office name plate and the I.D. tag pointed directly to her time at High Point. The evisceration of her cat elevated the taunts to a threat. She felt certain that someone had arrived through the mist of time who held a grudge. There were plenty of suspects who had it out for her back then. The self-important tree-hugging animal activists, the disgruntled employees she fired, even the state investigators. They treated her as a villain, though she never admitted to any fault or apologized for anything she did while performing her duties.

Now she was back.

The lab was in the basement of the East wing, isolated from the rest of the building. It was so remote that no one in other areas of the hospital had ever heard a peep, screech, or howl coming from Vera's domain. She descended into the basement with trepidation. What would she find? Was someone lying in wait? She cursed herself for not thinking to bring a flashlight. Without the overhead lights she had to rely on the slight bit of daylight that found its way into the depths. It was a dark, gray world that met her when she hit the bottom of the stairs.

She wished she had brought her gun.

The lab was on the far end of a long corridor, a short distance from the crematorium where the carcasses of thousands of dead animals, large and small, were disposed of. Oddly, there was enough light to navigate. That didn't seem possible, given the depth of the corridor yet she had no trouble seeing. When she neared the lab she saw even more light seeping out from under the door. How could that be? Before she could take another step, she heard a sound that instantly shot her back in time. It was an intermittent, mechanical clatter that came from inside the lab. Though she hadn't heard it in decades, she knew exactly what it was.

And it meant she wasn't alone.

Terri Hirsch wanted nothing more than for this day to be over, yet the challenges continued to pile up. If she was being honest, she didn't particularly want to go home and face Darcey either, for they would surely have it out over her decision to move back to Chicago. Terri hadn't had a chance to breathe, let alone call her ex-husband to get his opinion. Did he really want Darcey to live with him? Or was it his way of getting back at her for the divorce and moving his daughter away? And would he be wrong? Did she have the right to pull Darcey out of a life where she was thriving to bring her to this sad, rural town? Terri feared that her personal reasons for the move may have clouded her judgement when it came to what was best for her daughter.

Terri imagined that the three of them would get on a Facetime call to discuss the situation like rational people, knowing that inevitably one of them would say something that didn't sit well with someone else, a snarky insult would follow, and the rational discussion would devolve into a free-for-all melee' that would end with Darcey headed out the door. What made the situation so incredibly difficult to deal with was that Darcey's rationale for wanting to leave Glenville might be justified.

The conflict made her sick to her stomach, and incredibly sad. But she couldn't dwell on it because her nightmare of a day was far from over. She still had to deal with the aftermath of two gruesome deaths, two people who were convinced they were being haunted, an irrational woman who was being harassed by an unknown antagonist, and a stranger from England who was trying to convince her that their town was haunted.

Not a typical Tuesday.

She intended to let Vera's issue wait until the next day, until she got a frantic call from Mikey Harper. That shot Vera straight back to the top of her to-do list. She left the remains of Ben Daniels in the capable hands of Jackie's team and headed to the Glenville Pharmacy.

When she pulled up to the drugstore, Mikey was outside on the sidewalk waiting for her.

"She told me to wait an hour before calling you," he said, breathless. "But I couldn't. She'll be pissed, but I couldn't."

"Take a breath," Terri said. "What's going on?"

"I wish I knew. You gotta see this."

He led Terri inside and headed straight for Vera's office.

"It must have happened while I was cleaning the bathroom," Mikey said, frantic. "I was in there a while, but the front door was locked. I don't know how somebody could have gotten in, done that, and left without me knowing, but they did."

"I get it," Terri said. "Show me."

"Get ready," Mikey said. "It isn't pretty."

He opened the door to Vera's office and Terri's eyes immediately went to the crucified and eviscerated Bobcat.

"My God," she said with a gasp.

She allowed herself a brief moment to feel sorry for herself for having to deal with yet another level of horror, then clicked right back into professional mode. She quickly deduced that Mikey was either innocent of this ghastly crime, or an incredible actor. She'd known Mikey for a while. He was a good kid. There was nothing about him that made her think he could have done anything so depraved. She had to assume he was telling the truth. At least until proven otherwise.

"That smell is my puke," Mikey said. "Sorry. I was going to clean it up, but I couldn't stand being in here with Bobcat like that."

"Where's Vera?" Terri asked.

"Gone. That's why I called you. When she saw Bobcat she was really upset but then she got all calm. It was weird, like she went numb or something. She told me to call you in an hour and tell you to meet her at the High Point Institute."

Terri's knees went weak. There it was again. The High Point Institute. She had to force herself to stay in the moment and not let her thoughts spin off into speculation land.

"She went there?" Terri asked.

"Yeah. I never heard of it, but she said you'd know what it was. She's gonna be pissed at me but I couldn't wait the whole hour."

"It's okay, you did the right thing."

Terri grabbed her cell phone and called Vera's number. She heard the phone ring, then heard it ringing live only a few feet away.

Vera's cell phone was on her desk.

"She forgets to carry it around," Mikey said with a shrug.

Terri punched out of the call.

"Did she say why she was going there?" Terri asked.

"No! She wouldn't even tell me what it was. Do you know?"

"Yeah, I know."

"This is freaking weird, Sheriff."

"I know. We'll sort it out. Don't touch anything, alright? It's a crime scene."

"Don't worry. No chance of that."

"I'll bring her back and we'll figure out what's going on. You okay with that?"

Mikey nodded quickly, though he wasn't truly okay with anything that had happened.

"I'll be back as soon as I can," Terri said. "Close the pharmacy. Go home if you want."

"No, I'll stay. It's kind of my job."

"You're a good kid, Mikey. We'll figure this out."

Mikey gave her a weak smile that said, *I hope so.*

Terri strode back through the pharmacy and went straight for her Jeep to make a trip she had been dreading for a very long time.

Stepping into the lab was both strange and familiar for Vera. Familiar for obvious reasons. This had been her second home for three years. Strange because the overhead fluorescents were burning, which meant electricity was coming into the abandoned building. The plastic bins that once held hundreds of small rodents lay empty, as did the large and small cages. A thick layer of dust covered the counters and operating tables.

None of that mattered. Vera was focused on the clattering sound that was coming from the room that had once been her office. She moved with trepidation past the empty cages toward the closed door. If nothing else the sound proved her instinct to come to the institute was the right one, though it gave her no satisfaction. She stepped up to the door, gently pushed it open and looked in to see an elderly man in a white lab coat sitting at the desk behind an old-school Royal typewriter. He was hammering away at the keys, hunting-and-pecking out the letters with his index fingers, just as she remembered him doing so many times in the past. It was impossible, yet apparently not.

"Doctor Abernathy?" Vera said, barely above a whisper.

Abernathy looked up over his half-glasses to Vera, who stood at the door clutching the doorknob in a death-grip.

"Vera my dear! Good of you to come! Close the door please."

Vera's head swum. As she closed the office door she had to hold on to the doorknob for fear she might pass out.

"You can't be here," she said, barely above a whisper, as she closed the door.

"Why not? I used to run the place, remember?"

"But you're dead."

"Indeed I am, but do the dead ever truly leave?"

Abernathy was a jovial old man with a twinkle in his eyes and a quick smile. He looked like a kindly country doctor that's often depicted in TV shows. Wise, yet firm. And strangely, alive.

"I'm dreaming," Vera said as she made an unsteady walk to the desk and sat in a wooden chair that faced Abernathy.

"If only that were true," he said as he typed a few last letters then looked at her over the top of his glasses. "It isn't."

"What's happening to me?" Vera asked, numb.

"That's the wrong question, my dear. What you should ask is what *happened* to you."

"I don't understand."

"I hired you because you were an idealist with a marvelous, inquisitive mind. The idea that our work here would better people's lives was what brought you to me. But that didn't last, did it?"

"I...I suppose not," Vera stammered. "It was far more challenging than I anticipated."

"Challenging," Abernathy repeated as if trying the word on for size. "Yes, that's one way of putting it. We were not only dealing with rigorous scientific protocols; we were charged with the care of living creatures. Most lived in, shall we say, less than ideal circumstances."

"There were so many," she said softly, revisiting a dark memory.

"There were indeed. But they weren't just numbers, were they?"

"Yes they were!" Vera argued. She was less disturbed about having a conversation with her dead boss than about being challenged over how she had run the lab. "If we cared about them, treated them like, I don't know, pets, it would have driven us insane."

Abernathy chuckled, "Your word, not mine."

"I treated them well enough," Vera said with confidence.

"You say that as if you actually believe you had compassion for our subjects."

"I did!" Vera exclaimed.

"Well you certainly had an odd way of showing it," Abernathy shot back. He was becoming less jovial by the second. "By all accounts you lost sight of the fact that we were dealing with living beings that experienced pain and suffering."

"They were animals."

"Animals that were undernourished and lived in their own filth." He flipped through some papers on the desk and pulled one to read from. "What was it you said at the inquest? Quote: *"I had a budget that was reduced most every quarter. I couldn't meet it* without cutting some corners. Knowing these creatures would soon be dead, I didn't feel the need to feed them as if they would have normal lifespans. I only did what was expected of me and a big part of that was hitting my budget numbers, which I always did."

Abernathy dropped the page and looked straight at Vera.

"You must have been so proud," he said with sarcasm.

"I did what needed to be done!" Vera shouted.

"Did that include torture?"

"I didn't torture the animals!" Vera argued. "Not beyond the discomfort that was expected and accepted within the parameters of the experiments."

"Is that so?" Abernathy said. He flipped through more pages until he found the one he wanted. He read: *"At times when she became particularly stressed, she would take one of the larger rats and squeeze it until it either suffocated or until she broke its neck. That always seemed to calm her down."*

"That was testimony from a disgruntled employee I had to fire," Vera said. "How did you get those transcripts?"

Abernathy found another page and read: *"We had a large Rhesus monkey, Old Harry, who had electrodes planted into his brain to conduct a neural reflex study. Vera would often send electric impulses through George's brain that had nothing to do with the study. She wanted to see him twitch and squirm. She actually enjoyed it and giggled with each involuntary spasm as if George were a puppet she could play with for her amusement."*

"I didn't design the experiment," Vera said.

"Nor did you follow the protocols. Do you deny that?"

"I'll tell you same thing I told them at the inquest, I did what the experiment called for."

"Perhaps, but that wasn't all you did, was it?"

"I have no regrets."

"None at all?"

Vera started to answer but held back.

"There are pages of testimony here," Abernathy said. "All recount a disturbing pattern of abusive behavior toward these subjects that resulted in suffering and premature death. You went out of your way to abuse them."

"They were animals!" Vera repeated.

"Not that it will change anything, other than to satisfy my own curiosity, but what was going through your mind when you intentionally hurt these creatures?"

Vera held back as if she didn't want to answer, but finally couldn't help herself.

"It was their fault!" she blurted out.

"Please explain," Abernathy said coldly.

"They weren't here to be treated, or cured," she said defiantly. "They were here to die. I was constantly dealing with pain and death. It was overwhelming. I resented them for that."

"Are you saying you felt as though it was their fault for simply being here?"

"I'm saying they were the cause of my own agony. I had to relieve the stress somehow." She took a deep breath and added, "All right. Fine. I'm not proud of everything I did, but given the circumstances, if I had to do it over again, I'd do the same thing. They were animals. My peace of mind was more important. And Doctor Kane knew exactly what was happening."

Abernathy stared at Vera with a mixture of pity and disdain.

"I'm not deaf to what you're saying," he said with compassion. "When I ran the department I had similar feelings. I won't deny that. It never bothered me while in veterinary school, and beyond, but there was something about this laboratory, this hospital, which brought out an anger in me that I could easily have channeled toward the animals."

"Then you know!" Very exclaimed with relief, as if she'd been tossed a lifeline.

"I do. And do you know how I dealt with it?"

"Tell me, please."

"I retired. I had the wherewithal to recognize the danger. Dare I say the evil. It wasn't like me at all, but it was real. I left before doing something ghastly. It may have been a coward's way out, but it cleared my head. I had no regrets other than having to live with the guilt of what happened once you took charge."

"But you understand," Vera said.

"Yes, I understand. I understand that you chose a path far different than mine."

He pulled the paper from his typewriter with one quick snatch.

"It will all be documented in my report."

"What report?" Vera asked. "What are you doing here? Did you smear the shit around in my bathroom? And kill my cat?"

"Me? No. Perish the thought."

"Then who did?"

"I'm afraid you'll soon find out."

Vera heard the sound of a cage rattling in the lab. She spun around to shoot a look at the closed door.

"Who else is here?" Vera asked with alarm. "Is there some other ghost haunting me and—"

She turned back to Abernathy, but he was no longer there. Neither were the pages of his report. Or his typewriter. Vera's office looked the same as it did on her last day of work. It was filled with nothing but dust and memories.

A cage outside of the office rattled again.

Vera snapped a look back at the closed door. Who or what was out there?

Terri didn't speed out of town with her lights flashing. She drove well within the speed limit because she was in no hurry to get to the High Point Institute. She had only been to the property once as Sheriff and didn't set foot inside the building. The place was so remote that most people didn't know it existed. Or had forgotten. She didn't want to risk having any curious explorers stumbling upon it, finding their way inside and getting hurt, so she put a heavy padlock on the front gate and hoped that no one was foolish enough to try and scale the high fence.

When she emerged from the woods to see the institute building, a cold shiver ran up her spine. This place had a history, and it wasn't a pleasant one. If it had been up to her, the entire structure would be bulldozed, and the property returned to nature.

She drove to the front gate and was relieved to see that it was closed and locked. The padlock was doing its job. She got out of her vehicle and walked to the gate to see something that made no sense. Vera's Saab was parked at the bottom of the stairs that led to the front door. How did it get there if the gate was padlocked, and she held the only key?

"This day just keeps on getting better," Terri said to herself and headed back to her Jeep to fetch her over-burdened key ring. It held several dozen keys that belonged to various padlocks, door locks, bicycle locks and equipment locks that had been entrusted to her by the good people of Glenville. They gave their duplicate keys to her in case theirs were lost, which meant she had to go through the painstaking process of trying them one at a time until she found the right one.

"And here we go," she said as she tried the first key.

Vera kept her eyes on the closed office door. The cage-rattling sound continued and was soon joined by another. And another. Within seconds it sounded as though an earthquake was rattling every last cage. After having a chat with her dead boss, she had no desire to find out who was beyond the door causing the ruckus.

"This isn't happening," she said to herself.

While she didn't think she was actually dreaming, she knew that none of what was going on could be real. Her mind had to be playing tricks on her. It had happened before. When she worked in the lab, she often felt as though the animals were watching her.

Sometimes she heard whispered voices, as if the creatures were talking to one another. She could never make out exactly what was being said, and didn't question how animals could be whispering, let alone in English.

She made some of them pay the price for conspiring against her. All it took was a not-so-gentle neck-squeeze.

Vera knew she needed help. In that brief moment she decided to seek out a therapist. Someone who had no connections to Glenville or recollection of the High Point Institute. She'd tell the truth, about everything. Even if it meant losing her pharmacy license. She needed to get right and calm her brain. Having made that decision, her confidence grew. Certainly, with some work she could exorcise the ghosts that had been haunting her that morning, and for the last few decades.

The sound of rattling cages grew more frantic. It didn't faze her for she now had a plan. She stood up and strode boldly for the office door, ready to walk past her hallucinations and out of the institute, forever this time. She'd get in her car, drive home, and start the process of healing. Yes. It was a good plan. In that one sweet moment, Vera felt ready to start on the road to a new and healthier life.

She grabbed the doorknob, yanked the door open and stepped into the lab.

The sound of clattering cages died instantly. There wasn't so much as a fading echo from the cacophony. All was deathly quiet.

But Vera wasn't alone.

The cages were occupied. All of them. There were rabbits, small dogs, and a few kittens. And rats. Lots of rats, both white and black. Larger cages held monkeys of all sizes. Even Old Harry was there with the top of his skull exposed to reveal his brain and the electrode terminals that had been fused to his bone. Larger cages on the floor held a few goats, some larger dogs, and several small pigs. Vera looked to the white-plastic bins to see silhouettes of mice, gerbils, and hamsters. There had to be several hundred animals. None moved. None made a sound. They were all eerily still.

And they were all staring at her.

The only thing that kept Vera from screaming is that she knew it had to be a paranoid delusion. Animals didn't have the capacity to focus like that, and certainly not collectively.

"I have no guilt," she said to the assemblage, though in reality she was saying it to herself, still trying to convince herself that everything she had done in the past was justified.

She forced herself to walk for the door, moving slowly, not wanting to provoke any reactions. She didn't believe for a second that the room was actually filled with animals, but she moved as if it was. She tried to keep her eyes on the floor but stole a few quick glances to see that the animals all kept their gazes locked on her. Following her. While she was convinced that the scene was being conjured from the depths of her subconscious, she was grateful that the cages were latched. There was nothing these animals could do to harm her.

That's when she heard the unmistakable, metallic squeak of a cage door opening.

She turned slowly to see that one of the cages was indeed open. Inside was a Rhesus monkey. Vera stared at the little primate, who opened its mouth and hissed at her.

Vera gasped. Was this monkey going to jump out at her? She took a step backward toward the exit. Her eye caught movement on the other side of the room. One of the rats had nudged open its cage door. It was followed by another, and another. Tops of plastic bins were pushed up as sniffing rat-noses poked their way up and out.

Old Harry pushed open his cage door. His eyes were locked on Vera's. She recognized those eyes, but not from the distant past. She'd seen them earlier that day, staring at her through Venetian Blinds at the Cozy Rest Motel.

What was going on? Why was her brain creating this impossible scene?

The Rhesus Monkey let out a scream. It was a signal. A rallying cry that stirred the animals. More rats pushed up and out from their bins and jumped to the floor. No sooner did they hit the ground than each one got to its feet and scurried toward Vera. Other cage doors flew open as animals jumped out of confinement, headed her way.

Hallucination or no, Vera wasn't about to stand there and let these animals attack her. She ran for the lab door, threw it open and escaped into the corridor, slamming the door behind her. She backed away as the door was pummeled and scratched at from inside by dozens of animals. Vera gathered her wits and ran, stumbling along the dark corridor with one goal in mind: get out of the building to her car.

Behind her, the lab door crashed open.

Vera didn't stop or look back to see what was coming. She ran, tripped and fell to a knee but got back up and kept going. Behind her she heard the sounds of hundreds of clawed paws scurrying across the linoleum. If she fell again, they'd be on her.

Vera turned the corner at the end of the hallway and was momentarily out of the sight of her pursuers. She kept moving but was still a long way from the stairs that led up to the first floor and the atrium. She feared the animals would catch her long before she reached them. She spotted an open door and made a snap decision. She jumped through it and quickly closed and locked it behind her. She stood still and held her breath. If any of those beasts had seen where she went they'd surely batter down the door as they did at the lab. If they hadn't seen her, perhaps they'd pass by and hunt for her through the rest of the building, giving her time to sneak out behind them, head in the opposite direction, and escape to her car.

She put her ear to the door. The sound of the approaching animals grew louder. The taunting screech of monkeys joined the scuttling of claws and hoofs on the linoleum floor. Vera held her breath. They'd be at the door in seconds. She had the brief, sickening thought that they might smell her. After all, they were animals. She cursed herself for not realizing that sooner. Glancing over her shoulder she saw that she was in a closet. It was large, with empty metal racks along one wall. It had once been the domain of the janitorial staff. There was no way out other than through the door she was leaning against. She prayed that she hadn't trapped herself in a dead end.

She heard the wave of animals approaching and had to force herself not to whimper. They were nearly there. If they smelled her, she'd certainly feel the thump of their bodies being hurled against the door. She closed her eyes and prayed to a God who had never heard from her in the past. She braced herself.

The barrage didn't come. The sound of the animals receded. Her desperate gamble had paid off. Vera instantly thought ahead to her next move. She'd wait a few seconds to make sure there were no stragglers, then leave the closet and hurry back the way she'd come. There was a loading dock past the office where the animal deliveries were made. It was the last sight the creatures had of the outside world. Now it would be Vera's escape route. She took a shallow breath and listened for any other animals in the hallway.

She heard nothing from the outside.

What she heard was on the inside.

Scratching.

It came from the walls, as it did in her house, and the Rx Diner. Something was behind the walls, scratching furiously. It wasn't until that moment that she made the connection between the scratching she heard elsewhere and the impossible events that were happening at High Point. Had she imagined those earlier scratching noises as well? Had this hallucinatory odyssey begun the moment she woke up that morning? It made sense, but it raised the question: why now? Why was this the day her mind decided to snap? Why not yesterday? Or the week, month, or year before? What was different about today?

There would be plenty of time to dive into those questions in therapy. It was more important to be diving into her car and getting away. Vera gave one last listen at the door. Convinced that the pursuers had passed by, she moved to unlock the door, but froze when something dropped onto her hand. It was a dusting of plaster that had fallen from above. She slowly looked up.

The ceiling crumbled directly over her head. Whatever had been digging from inside had broken through. Vera was hit with chunks of plaster. Dust got into her eyes, blinding her. She quickly rubbed away the debris and looked up again to see that crumbling plaster was the least of her worries. Directly over her head was a large, dark hole that had been eaten, clawed, and torn open. She stared up at it in horror, only to have a waterfall of mice drop down. They landed on her head and got tangled in her hair. They fell onto her shoulders and clawed at her blouse. Several found their way to her collar and slipped down along her neck. They slithered inside her blouse, and they bit. Their teeth were tiny but sharp. Vera was hit by what felt like hundreds of tiny bee stings.

She swatted them away, tore them off of her clothes and pulled them from her hair. In spite of the vicious attack, she had the wherewithal not to scream, which would certainly summon the other attackers. She continued to tear the mice off with one hand, while fumbling to open the door with the other.

The mice kept coming. Hundreds cascaded from the wound in the ceiling. Most hit the floor and moved to climb up her pants. Vera kicked at them and stomped them under foot, crushing their tiny skeletons and squirting blood from under her shoes. She was oblivious to their squeals of pain, and the gore.

Finally, she managed to open the door and half jumped, half fell out of the closet. She stayed focused and turned to head back toward the loading dock, but she was stopped by a waterfall of mice that came tumbling out of another, larger hole that had been clawed open in the ceiling. She was cut off from that escape route and had no choice but to run in the opposite direction. She continued tearing mice off of her and had the brief thought that for a hallucination, it seemed all so very real.

She had only one way out. Through the atrium. That was okay. Her car was waiting at the foot of the stairs outside the front doors. As long as she could avoid the wave of vermin that had been chasing her, she had a chance. She threw the last mouse off and sprinted for the stairs at the far end of the subterranean corridor. She reached them in no time and ran up, taking two at a time. It was the most exercise her 60-year-old body had been through in decades, but she didn't falter. Adrenalin will do that. And terror. She bounded up the stairs and quickly covered the short distance through the corridor that led to the atrium. She didn't see a single animal along the way and dared to think that they were searching for her in other parts of the vast complex, or maybe her brain had simply given up on conjuring the nightmare.

The light ahead meant freedom. She was nearly at the atrium. She was going to get out. She even allowed herself a moment of anger. These animals had been the cause of her anguish decades before and continued the onslaught today. In her mind this only justified what she had done to them years before. They were beasts then and they remained beasts today. Her only regret was that she couldn't make more of them suffer for what they had done to her. Thoughts of revenge weren't far off. But she first had to get away. She hurried into the warm light of the atrium and immediately realized she had made a grave mistake.

The animals hadn't given up. They were not hunting for her throughout the rest of the sprawling institute.

They were waiting for her.

Vera ran into the atrium and stopped near the dry fountain. She looked around for an escape route and realized there wasn't one. She was surrounded. The animals were everywhere. Mongrel dogs stood menacingly in front of the exits. Rats swarmed the floor, taking up most every inch of space, crawling over one another, all looking to Vera. Monkeys had climbed up onto the fountain and looked down on her, screeching. To Vera it sounded like taunting laughter. There were far more animals than had ever been in the laboratory at any given time.

On the marble stairs that led up to the second-floor landing was Old Harry. He sat on the tenth stair overlooking the lobby like a stoic judge, surrounded by several other monkeys. He had the air of a wise old monarch, with the top of his skull removed to reveal his brain and the imbedded electric terminals. While the other animals were agitated and ready for action, Old Harry sat calmly, overlooking the scene.

Vera focused on him. The two held eye-contact.

It had come to this.

Terri grew more frustrated with each failed attempt at finding the key. There were at least fifty keys on the ring, most of which weren't labeled, or had some useless marking like: "Front #1" or "Padlock" which meant exactly nothing to her. She made a mental note that she wouldn't put another key on the ring unless it was clearly labeled. Better yet, let everyone be in charge of their own damned keys.

"I know it's going to be the last key I try," she said to herself, then chuckled, realizing that of course it would be the last key she tried.

As frustrating as it was, there was another emotion at work. Dread.

She took a moment to look through the fence at the imposing structure that was the High Point Institute. It gave her the same uneasy feeling she'd experienced the most recent time she'd been there. She wanted it, and its history to be forgotten and buried, but feared the incredible events that had been haunting Glenville that day meant it wouldn't happen. While she wanted nothing more than to jump back in her Jeep and leave it behind, her job description didn't allow for that, no matter what her personal feelings were.

She went back to searching for the key.

Vera stood frozen, surrounded by hundreds of angry animals. Trapped. Strangely, she was no longer afraid. She was angry. Being cornered by these varmints was a validation of how she felt about the creatures when she ran the lab. The animals had her trapped back then as well. Her resentment may have gone dormant since she left High Point, but it never left her completely. It not only came flooding back, it was compounded by the fact that these animals had dared to band together to physically threaten her. It didn't matter that it was a conjured hallucination, it was evidence of her deep seated hatred of these beasts.

Back then, her only way to alleviate the anger was to lash out. To torture. To strangle the life out of the monsters. A single squeeze would snap a fragile neck, though death wasn't always instantaneous. Those were the most gratifying times. She didn't want it to be quick. She wanted them to suffer. She wanted to feel the life drain from their bodies. Those precious moments would quell her anxiety for a while, but it would inevitably build again until she would need another death-fix.

She had the brief thought that perhaps Doctor Abernathy was right. There was something about this hospital that fostered evil.

The only true relief came when she was fired from High Point, though she resented the fact that Doctor Kane had turned on her. After all, his policies encouraged atrocities that were far worse than anything that had gone down in her lab. She enjoyed a slight measure of revenge when the institute closed shortly after. In the years since she managed to push the anger deep into her subconscious, knowing full well that one day it could resurface.

Today was that day.

Vera locked eyes with Old Harry. He sat there calmly, for he had the upper hand. It only intensified her rage.

"What is it you want?" she said through gritted teeth. "Revenge? I won't give you the satisfaction."

She walked slowly toward the stairs while rats skittered around her feet. A few nipped at her ankles, Vera ignored the sharp jabs of pain.

"I suppose some therapist will tell me how this illusion was a manifestation of my guilt, but they'd be wrong. I have no remorse. If anyone should feel guilty it's the companies that ordered the testing, and Doctor Kane for accepting their projects. And their money. I had no choice. I was as much a victim as you were."

The mongrels that guarded the exits let out deep, guttural growls. Vera had no doubt that if she made a break for any door, the dogs would attack. The fleeting image of being brought down by a pack of angry dogs, followed by what would surely be a swarm of rats tearing at her flesh killed any thoughts of escape. Her mind may be conjuring the situation, but the pain she felt from the nipping of the rats felt all too real.

She made it to the foot of the stairs, directly below Old Harry and his minions who watched her dispassionately.

"How is this going to end?" Vera called out to him. "With an apology? Is that it? Do you want me to admit I treated you badly? No, that's too simple and it wouldn't be sincere. I have no regrets. The next move is yours. What is it you want from me?"

As if in answer, the circle of animals drew tighter around Vera. The dogs closed in. The rats swarmed over her feet and clawed at her pants leg. Though she had convinced herself that this was all happening in her mind, Vera was afraid. The idea of being set-upon by vengeful beasts with sharp claws and teeth was too horrifying to imagine. Though she knew it was all being created in her mind, she couldn't bear to give these creatures the satisfaction of taking revenge on her.

There was only one way out. A way with which she was all too familiar.

"I control my own fate," she said to Old Harry with determination.

She slowly reached up to her neck as the dogs drew closer and the rats climbed up her pants legs.

"I'm going to kill every last one of you, once and for all."

"Finally!" Terri said triumphantly.

She hadn't had to go through the entire ring of keys. There were a good ten or so left. The lock was slightly rusted but fell open easily. Terri pulled it off of the latch and pushed the two doors of the heavy gate open. After a short drive she was at the entrance. When she got to Vera's car, she saw that the keys were in the ignition. That wasn't unusual. People in Glenville left keys in cars. And didn't lock front doors. Yet they put padlocks on their equipment and gave their duplicate keys to Terri. Go figure. As she stood peering into the car, she heard the unmistakable sound of a lock being thrown. She stood up quickly and looked over the top of Vera's car to the front door of High Point.

"Vera?" Terri called out.

She had to suppress her overwhelming feelings of dread, and do her job. She circled Vera's car and climbed the stairs. She thought about pulling her service Glock, but a quick assessment told her to keep it holstered. Eerie feelings didn't justify drawing one's weapon. She got to the top of the stairs and stood in front of the door. This is as far as she'd gotten when she returned to Glenville as an adult. She had checked to insure that the door was locked, and it was. Now, she was able to push it open with her foot. Had it been locked a moment before?

"Vera? It's Terri," she called.

Still no response. Terri took a cautious step inside and waited for her eyes to adjust in the dim light. Compounding her sense of dread was an inexplicable yet overwhelming feeling of sadness. This was once an elegant building. The giant stained-glass window alone was breathtaking. Great care had gone into the institute's design and construction. Now it lay empty and lifeless, like a shriveled corpse. A corpse that she wanted buried.

"Vera? It's Terri Hirsch!"

Terri had no idea where to find her. The message was to meet her here, not where she'd be once she got here. The last thing Terri wanted to do was to search the sprawling building. She walked further into the atrium, gazing up at the stained-glass window that had a colorful, idealized depiction of a green pasture populated by grazing sheep and cattle. There were horses trotting across a manicured, grassy plain and trees in full, colorful springtime blossom. Though the glass was crusted with the accumulated grime of decades, the beauty of the craftmanship shone through. Terri imagined how it might look with a little help from a power washer. It was a brief moment where she could appreciate what the building had once been.

The feeling ended quickly when she took a step and nearly tripped over something. She looked down and let out a scream.

She'd found Vera Holiday.

The woman lay on her back with her eyes open and bulging. Her two hands were clutching her throat.

Terri didn't need to examine her to know the truth.

Death had once again paid a visit to Glenville.

An hour after having discovered Vera's body, Terri sat on the front steps of the institute, shellshocked. The Coroner's van was parked in front of Vera's Saab.

Gotta call Charlie Dest to come tow that away, Terri thought. It was one of the more mundane chores she knew she'd have to deal with in the coming days. At that point she welcomed the mundane.

Jackie exited the building and sat down next to her.

"Bet you're missing Chicago about now," she said.

She looked to Terri for a reaction but got none.

"What the hell, Terri?" the Coroner went on. "I always thought Vera was too mean to die."

"Any thoughts about what happened?" Terri asked.

"I can't believe I'm saying this again, but we'll know more after the autopsy. The preliminary inspection tells me it was ligature strangulation."

"What exactly is that?"

"Looks like she strangled herself.'

"My God."

"Nice, huh? Not something you see every day. Or ever. At least we know how the Daniels boys bought it. Zap. Splat. They say things happen in threes, right?"

Once again, Terri chose to ignore Jackie's less-than-delicate comments, though she hoped she was right about things happening in threes.

"There's no rush," Terri said. "She has no family that I know of."

"Good, because she's got to take a number. So much for business being slow."

"I'm calling the County for help. Probably Madison too," Terri said. "This goes way beyond my job description."

"I hear you. What are the odds of three violent deaths in the same day?" Jackie asked.

"Too great for me to wrap my head around. I need another set of eyes. Or two. I'll try to get some investigators down here tomorrow."

"Why do you suppose she came out to this old place to off herself?" Jackie asked. "I'm surprised she even knew about it. Vera rarely ventured from downtown."

"I believe she used to work here," Terri replied.

"No shit!" Jackie exclaimed. "That fits. Nothing good ever happened at this place. At least that what I heard."

Terri replied with a shrug.

"One thing's a little strange," Jackie added.

"Only one?" Terri asked and they both actually chuckled.

"The cuffs of her pants were shredded, like she'd been walking through a pricker bush."

"What does that mean?" Terri asked.

"Damned if I know," the Coroner said as she stood up. "That's your job to figure out. It'll be in the report. I'll be in touch. Right now I've got to figure out how to make room in the wagon. I've still got Ben cooling back there."

Jackie headed back up the stairs into the institute to join her team, leaving Terri with more questions than answers. She drove back to town and went straight to Vera's pharmacy. She needed to tell Mikey that his boss was no longer his boss. She also had to document the scene with photos and pick up poor Bobcat. She thought of refrigerating him at her office, but the idea of putting the remains in the same fridge where she stored her yogurt actually made her gag. She decided to press upon Doc Scofield's veterinary clinic to take care of poor Bobcat for a few days.

Terri had no idea what would happen with Vera's business. As she told Jackie, Vera had no known family. It would fall to Terri to hunt down any possible relations to inform them of her death. Ideally, she'd find someone who would want to know, and take care of her burial. They might even lay claim to the pharmacy. Whether she found someone or not, she would shortly turn the issues over to the county to sort out.

What she could not do was rid herself of the horror that was happening to her town, and the growing sense of inevitability that Mr. Paper's theories may hold some water.

CHAPTER 16

The sun was nearly down by the time Terri dragged herself home on what felt like the longest day of her life. The last thing she wanted to do was cook dinner. The most effort she wanted to put into preparing a meal was pulling the cork on a bottle of Cabernet. But she had to consider Darcey and knew it would be better to have their discussion over pasta and salad.

The house was dark, which was unusual. Darcey had the habit of turning on lights in every room she entered and leaving them on when she exited.

"Darcey?"

Terri was hit with the sinking feeling that her daughter had already left for Chicago. The last words they had together were spoken in anger. Had she actually taken off? The Subaru was still in the driveway, so she hadn't driven anywhere. Her ex couldn't have gotten there so quickly unless the plan to pick Darcey up had already been in place. She didn't want to consider that possibility. She may not see eye-to-eye with Darcey's father on most issues, but he wasn't conniving. Nor was Darcey.

"Darcey?" she called again.

"In here," came a quiet reply.

Terri could breathe again. She entered the living room to find her daughter sitting on the couch. In the dark.

"Were you sleeping?" Terri asked as she turned on a table lamp.

"I wish."

Terri sank into an easy chair across from the couch with her focus on Darcey, who had the puffy-eyed, post-crying look.

"What's the matter?" she asked with trepidation.

"You knew I didn't want to move here," Darcey said softly. "You knew I would hate it."

"Darcey I—"

"Let me finish," Darcey said sharply.

Terri sensed a change. Something was up that went beyond their usual argument over living in Glenville. Darcey couldn't even make eye contact. That wasn't at all like her confidant daughter.

"You said you wanted us to live somewhere less hectic," Darcey said. "I didn't agree with you, but I understood. You wanted to get distance from Dad. I didn't agree with you, but I understood. I understood when you told me the most important thing two people could share was honesty. Even if it was painful. I agree with you on that one."

"What's this about, honey?" Terri asked gently.

Darcey tossed the leatherbound High Point Institute brochure down onto the coffee table in front of her mother. Terri picked it up and opened it to the cover page. It took a moment for her to register what it was, and when she did her heart sank.

"My God," Terri said with a sigh.

Darcey finally made eye-contact and said, "Everett Kane?"

She snatched the brochure from her mother and flipped to the page that showed Doctor Everett Kane with his wife and young daughter posing happily in front of a Christmas tree. She held it up for Terri to see.

"That's Granny Trish," she said. "Which means that little girl is you. I even recognize the ornaments on the Christmas tree. We still use them! I don't know what else to say but, what the fuck?"

Terri took the brochure back and gazed at the photo, then did a quick flip through the rest of the brochure.

"I had no idea this existed," she said, lamely.

"Yeah, well, surprise."

Terri placed the book on the table slowly, buying a few more seconds to collect her thoughts.

"I wanted to protect you," she said.

"No!" Darcey shouted. "Don't spin this. Just tell me the fucking truth."

Terri took a long minute to choose her words. She always knew this conversation had to happen. She had run it over in her mind hundreds of times, but hadn't found the right opportunity to bring it up. Or the courage. Now, she had no choice.

"Everett Kane was my father," she began. "Your grandfather. He died when I was five. That's when Granny Trish went back to using her family name."

"Why?" Darcey asked. "To disassociate herself, and me, from him. From that moment on it was like he never existed."

"All you told me about him was that he and Granny Trish had a short relationship, and they broke up when you were a baby. That was a lie?"

"It was."

"Do you remember him?"

"I do. I'm so sorry you had to find out this way."

"Yeah, whatever. Move on."

"What I'm going to tell you I didn't learn about until I was an adult. Granny Trish kept it from me, just as I have from you. It wasn't until she was near the end that she opened up. I can't say that I'm glad she did. Ignorance is bliss, right? She told me things I always suspected, but didn't want to believe. I still don't. Hearing it had a profound effect on me that wasn't good. I wanted to spare you that."

"Just tell me," Darcey said, impatiently.

"My father was the Director of the High Point Institute. I was young and have only a few memories of the place. I do remember him walking me around the hospital, proudly showing me off to his staff. Everyone was sweet to me, but I had the sense, even at that age, that the people who worked there were afraid of him. They seemed nervous, as if fearing they might say the wrong thing It didn't make sense, because as far as I knew, he was a loving father who told me silly stories and sang songs at bedtime. That didn't wash with the image of someone to be feared."

Darcey picked up the brochure and gazed at the picture, trying to imagine the dichotomy of a man that Terri was describing.

"My memories of the institute are vague," Terri said. "They're all blended, except for one visit that stuck with me. I don't know how old I was. Maybe three or four. We were in his office. It was large, with heavy wood-frame furniture and an ornate rug, like a living room. A floor to ceiling bookcase lined the wall behind an imposing desk that was so high I had to push up on my tip-toes to see over it."

Terri closed her eyes, recalling memories that transported her back to that moment.

"He wanted to play hide and seek. He loved that game. Or pretended to. While he sat at his desk with his eyes covered, I hid behind a potted plant. He probably saw me right away, but pretended to search and then acted surprised to find me as though it was the best hiding place in the world."

"That's the only memory that stuck with you?" Darcey asked skeptically.

"No. Then it was his turn to hide," Terri said, her voice dropping low. "I covered my eyes, counted to ten then ran all over the office, looking behind chairs and couches but I couldn't find him. It wasn't like there were many places to hide, and I got frustrated. I peeked out of the office door to see if he was in the corridor. He wasn't. My frustration changed to confusion and then fear because it made no sense. I had searched everywhere possible. I still remember the sense of panic because I couldn't comprehend what was happening. I called out for him, but got nothing back. That was the worst moment. I called to him again, and by this point I was crying. I still remember the feeling of being alone in that room, with nobody to reassure me that everything was okay. It was silly, I know, but I was a toddler. As I ran for the door to get out and find help, he called my name. He was standing in front of the bookcase. One section was swung out, like a door. There was a room behind it. A hidden room. That's where he'd been. I ran to him and hugged him, but I couldn't stop crying. I still remember the feeling of the course wool of his suit jacket as I pressed my face against his chest. He laughed and said it was just a game, and I shouldn't take it so seriously. It bothered me that he didn't understand why I was so upset. I tried to explain, but he scoffed and said I was being silly. He was totally dismissive. Cold, even. It was my first glimpse at the other side of his personality."

Terri took the brochure and looked at the picture through tears. Darcey couldn't tell if her reaction was wistful, or she was torn over the fact that her father might not have been as wonderful a person as she wanted him to be.

"When I was five they told me we were moving. No reason. No explanation other than he wasn't going to work at the institute anymore. I don't even remember packing, that's how quickly we left town. Mom tried to make a game out of it, like we were going on an adventure, but it felt more like we were escaping. It was a whirlwind. Being in a new home was difficult, but I loved having my father around. At first, anyway. My memory of him back then was that he was always in his home office on the phone angrily yelling at someone. And he drank. Often. Mom told me not to disturb him because he was working on an important project. She didn't tell me what it was, and I was too young to care. All that mattered was how much I missed our old life."

"Really?" Darcey asked with more than a little sarcasm.

"Touche'," Terri replied. "But I'd lost more than that. My father had changed. He stopped singing to me and the silly stories ended. Less than a year later, he died."

"How?" Darcey asked. "He wasn't that old."

"There's no good way to say this," Terri said stoically. "He shot himself. In front of the Dane County Courthouse where he was going to stand trial."

"Jeez," Darcey muttered.

"I was devastated. Mom and I barely talked about what had happened. It was just so sad. Whenever I tried to ask questions about how he'd gotten to that point, she shut me down. It was clearly painful for her, so I didn't push. We became consumed by the business of building a new life. As I got older I recognized how she was struggling so I didn't put pressure on her to talk about him and why we left Glenville. It wasn't until she was close to death that she finally opened up."

"What was he going to be on trial for?" Darcey asked.

"It was a laundry list of charges, criminal and civil, all having to do with the High Point Institute. There were a slew of lawsuits being prepared. Nothing was ever put into the public record because he died before trial. Nothing was proven or disproven. All that's known came from rumors and anecdotes."

"About him?" Darcey asked.

"About how he ran High Point. It was a psychiatric rehab facility. There were disturbing stories about how the patients were treated. It was said that they were used in research, like guinea pigs. The use of unregulated psychotropic drugs was rampant. The staff was underqualified to manage patients who were dealing with such extreme issues and used cruel methods to keep them under control. Apparently the patients were either heavily sedated, or flying off on hallucinatory rampages. There were rumors of multiple deaths, but negligence or malpractice were never proven."

"No one in town knew what was going on?" Darcey asked.

"They may have, but by the late eighties, Glenville was a dying town. High Point was the number one employer. Their research projects kept it solvent so apparently that was my father's main concern. He supposedly turned a blind eye to the atrocities in order to keep the money train rolling with contracts from the government and big pharma. No one dared talk about what was actually going on for fear of retribution, or of the hospital being shut down. Whatever records existed that might have held clues to the atrocities went missing. If even half of the stories were true, those records would provide information that would be an embarrassment to a lot of people, especially those who had research contracts with High Point. But investigators never found them, and my father died."

"Your mother told you all that?" Darcey asked.

"She told me some, the rest I found out on my own. A few years ago I got access to the preliminary interviews that were done by the DA who was building the case. It was all so horrifying, but at the end of the day, all they had were statements and allegations from former patients and their family members. No one who worked there agreed to testify. Who knows what the truth was and what was embellished? But there were enough accusations and lawsuits being readied that my father was forced to resign. Once he was gone, the place fell apart and shut down."

"And he killed himself over it," Darcey said solemnly.

"His death ended the criminal investigation and the lawsuits. We'll never know what actually happened. There was no justice. For anyone. My father didn't prove his innocence, nor did his accusers get the satisfaction of having someone held responsible."

"What about the victims?" Darcey said. "What justice did they get?"

"They didn't. It all just went away. Now you see why I didn't want to share this with you. It's a dark family legacy. That's the entire truth."

Darcey couldn't sit still any longer and jumped to her feet.

"No it isn't" she exclaimed.

"What more can I say?" Terri said, plaintively. "That's what happened."

"You can tell me the truth about why we're here. You've been selling this place like it's some kind of old-fashioned, golly-gee-willikers Main Street Disneyland. All I've seen is a gray, depressed town filled with people who would rather live somewhere else but don't have the money or the balls to leave. It's like this place is cursed. From what I've seen today, maybe it is. It's just like Mr. Paper said."

"Please don't bring him up—"

"Why not? Seems like everything he's been saying is true."

"I don't know what's true," Terri shot back. "There are only rumors and people's opinions and who knows how unbiased those are?"

"So you think your father was innocent?" Darcey asked.

"I want to believe that," Terri replied. "I need to believe that."

"Okay," Darcey said. "Let's pretend it's all exaggeration and rumors. I still want to know the real reason why we're here."

Darcey sat back down on the couch, leaning forward toward her mother, expecting an honest answer.

Terri had to wipe away tears before she could go on.

"I truly don't know how much responsibility falls to my father for what happened back then," Terri said. "But there were enough accusations that the institute had to shut down, and he has to take responsibility for at least some of that. It hurt this town. This isn't the Glenville I remember. I might be painting a rosy, imaginary picture, but I do remember it as a warm, wonderful place. I haven't been lying. I wanted to move here so you could grow up in a quiet, safe environment. But I also wanted to come back for myself, and I wasn't forthcoming about that. I took the job as sheriff to try and give back. I don't think for a second that I can change things, or undo what happened or bring this town back from the dead, but I felt like I had to do something to make up for whatever role my father may have played in the nightmare. And that's the God's honest truth. I took you away from a life you loved so that I could sooth my own conscience, and for that I'm sorry."

Terri took a deep, troubled breath and added, "You have every right to be angry with me. I can understand why you want to move back with your father. If that's really what you want, I won't try to stop you."

As painful as telling the truth had been, Terri felt a sense of relief for having shared it with the one person who deserved to hear it. Less comforting was the uncertainty of what would happen next. She had lobbed the ball squarely into Darcey's court. The two sat silently, staring at the floor.

"I don't know if I should be angry or relieved," Darcey said. "I wish you'd told me the truth a long time ago."

"I do too," Terri said. "I'm so sorry sweetheart."

Darcey got up and sat on the arm of the chair next to Terri. She leaned over and hugged her mother, releasing a flood of emotions from Terri that came out in tears.

"I'm sorry you had to go through all that," Darcey said.

"Bringing you here was selfish," Terri said. "I don't want to lose you."

"You won't lose me, Mom. But we have to figure out where to go from here. Now we can do it with no secrets."

"Right, no secrets. When did you get so wise?"

"I've always been wise," Darcey said. "At least now you know it."

Terri laughed, prompting Darcey to laugh with her.

They sat together, holding each other for several moments. Terri didn't want it to end for fear of what would come next.

"Can we make dinner?" Darcey said.

"Seriously?"

"Yeah, I'm starving."

"Me too," Terri said with a relieved laugh.

Preparing the fusilli (not easy to find in Glenville) with a salad of field greens and radicchio (equally difficult to find) was a welcome respite from the day's drama. For a brief time they were able to enjoy the simple pleasure of being a mother and daughter who remembered how much they loved one another, and enjoyed each other's company. While cooking they talked about movies, kids at school, the impossibility of finding clothes in a town that placed no value on style, the joy of not having to deal with traffic, and the challenge of generating interest in staging a drama-club version of *Les Misérables*. When they ate, Terri poured Darcey a glass of inexpensive Chianti (which was surprisingly easy to find in Glenville). Though the wine was too bitter for Darcey's taste, she appreciated the gesture and took a few sips.

Clean-up was quick, but as it neared completion, both allowed difficult thoughts to creep back. With no discussion they returned to the living room and sat across from one another, ready to face the inevitable.

"There's a lot going on," Darcey said. "Can I go first?"

"Please."

"I talked to Dad about moving back. At least in theory. He's cool with it, but he said he wants to talk to you first. We should all Facetime."

"Agreed," Terri said. "I just don't want it to be contentious."

"It won't be because it's not about you two."

"Fair enough."

"I don't know what I'm going to do," Darcey said. "But I'm not going to leave right away."

"I'm glad," Terri said, barely hiding her relief.

"Don't be," Darcey said. "You won't like the reason."

"Honey, other than the meal we just shared there isn't anything about this day I've liked. Fire away."

"Okay, I'm glad you told me everything. It doesn't change the way I feel about living here but let's not deal with that right now."

"Because...?"

"Because I want us to figure out what's going on. Way too many strange things have happened for it to be coincidence. Three people have died. I was chased by a truck that nobody was driving. Holly thinks she's been seeing ghosts, and you still haven't figured out who was harassing Vera Holiday. Did I miss something?"

"Unfortunately, yes," Terri said. "Holly thinks the woman she's been seeing is the ghost of her Grandmother who was a patient at High Point and committed suicide there."

"Fuck me!"

"Easy now," Terri scolded.

"Here's one for you, why did The Sweeper follow me down to the stacks in the library and lead me to that High Point brochure?"

"Karl Iverson? That's how you found it? What did he say?"

"He didn't say anything. It was totally creepy. Did he have something to do with High Point?"

Terri ran her hand through her hair and sighed. "I think he might have worked there."

"Of course he did," Darcey said sarcastically.

"That's not all," Terri said, and took a deep breath. "Vera Holiday is dead. It looks like another suicide. I believe she also worked at High Point."

Darcey stared at her mother, stunned, for several seconds, then said, "Another suicide. All tied to that hospital. What are the odds of that?"

"Long," Terri said.

"I know you don't want to hear this Mom, but it's exactly the kind of thing Mr. Paper warned us about."

"I don't believe in ghosts."

"Neither do I," Darcey said. "But I'm starting to."

"Go back to what you said. Karl Iverson directed you to that brochure?"

"He did. I have no idea why, but everything seems to be pointing to High Point as the common denominator. He *literally* pointed to that High Point brochure in the library. Maybe he wants us to know something."

Terri mulled that over, then grabbed her phone and checked the time.

"Okay Sherlock," she said. "It's only seven o'clock. Let's pay a visit to Mr. Iverson."

"Seriously? You want me to go with you?"

"Why not? He led you to that brochure. Let's find out why."

CHAPTER 17

Downtown Glenville was quiet. There were no bars or restaurants that stayed open past seven. It took only a few minutes for Terri and Darcey to drive to Karl's apartment building and park directly in front, of course.

Darcey looked out of the Jeep's window at the seedy building.

"It's kind of a...a—"

"A dump," Terri said. "Better than living on the street."

"Whatever works," Darcey said.

They got out of the Jeep and headed straight inside. The hallway leading to Karl's apartment was lit by bare bulbs in ancient ceiling fixtures that created more deep shadows than light.

"So quiet," Darcey said. "So creepy."

"Karl's the only tenant. That's something Glenville has going for it. We take care of the homeless, though I guess that isn't saying much since he's the only one."

Terri had helped Karl move in to the apartment a few months before. Getting him off the street was one small victory in her campaign to give something back to the town.

They stopped at his door and Terri knocked quietly.

"I don't hear a TV," Darcey said. "He could be asleep."

Terri knocked again, a bit harder, and the door opened a crack since it hadn't been shut tight. She shot a look to Darcey, who shrugged. Terri eased the door open and leaned in.

"Karl? It's Terri Hirsch. You decent?"

No reply.

"He must be out somewhere," Darcey offered.

"Really? Where?"

"Good point," Darcey said. "He's probably asleep."

"Karl?" Terri called louder. "Can we come in?"

Still no reply. Terri leaned in further, and quickly recoiled.

"Oh God," she said, with surprise.

"What?" Darcey asked.

"Go wait in the Jeep," Terri ordered, and stepped further into the small apartment.

Darcey ignored the command and stuck with her mother. Terri turned on an overhead light and scanned the room that functioned as a living room, kitchen, dining room, and closet.

"It's neater than I thought it would be," Darcey said.

"I said go outside," Terri said, insistent.

"I thought we were doing this together?" Darcey shot back, then added, "I smell it too, Mom. Something died."

Terri chose not to argue and made her way to the bedroom where she glanced in to see the unmade bed and its occupant.

"Oh Karl," she said with sadness.

She flipped on the overhead light. The single bare ceiling bulb cast harsh light, making the grizzly scene appear even more macabre. Terri's first impression was that there was no sign of a struggle other than a lamp on the floor.

Darcey peered into the room over her mother's shoulder.

"I've never seen a dead body before," she said.

Terri walked in slowly, surveying the scene. She leaned over the body to get a closer look to insure it was indeed Karl Iverson, and though there was little doubt that he was dead, she placed two fingers to his neck to check for a pulse. His cold, gray skin was all the proof she needed.

Darcey leaned over Terri's shoulder to get a better look.

"I wonder if it was suicide," she said. "A lot of that going around."

Terri gave Darcey a disparaging look.

"Sorry," Darcey said.

"The M.E. will determine how he died," Terri said.

"Can you tell how long he's been dead?"

"I can guess. Looks like rigor's already set in. His skin is gray, and there's the smell. I'm no expert but I'd say several hours."

"Then why did I see him in the library this afternoon?"

Terri caught her breath. The situation had gone from a routine, natural death scene, to another macabre piece in the day's impossible puzzle.

"We should go," Terri said, and gently pulled the top sheet over Karl.

As they walked out of the front door to the street, Terri was already on the phone to the Coroner.

"No Jackie, I'm not shitting you. Address is two twenty-four Glenville Road. Apartment one-D. The door is unlocked. Yes, I know. I know. I know! Think of all the overtime you're getting. Thank you."

Terri ended the call and said to Darcey, "Are you sure it was him in the library?"

Darcey ignored the question and said, "Hi Scott."

Scott Wilson stood in front of Terri's Jeep.

"Scott," Terri said, surprised. "Everything okay?"

"No," he said, obviously shaken.

He stood on weak legs, swaying, looking ready to pass out.

"I've been driving around, trying to make sense out of what I saw before coming to you, Sheriff. Couldn't do it."

"What's going on?" Terri asked. She hoped he was going to tell her about he and Darcey being chased by his truck and not add something new to her plate.

"I already told her about your truck," Darcey offered.

"It's not about that," Scott said softly.

Terri deflated. Her plate was about to get another serving.

"At least not all of it," he added. "Better that I show you."

"Can it wait till morning?" Terri asked.

"It shouldn't," Scott replied.

"What is it?"

"You gotta see for yourself. If I tell you, you'll think I've gone crazy."

"Okay, where is it?"

"At that site in the woods where you picked me up. Your Jeep's got a spotlight, right? We'll need it."

"I'm coming with you," Darcey said.

"No!" Scott shot back quickly. "This is Sheriff-business."

"I'm part of this," Darcey argued. "I was chased by the ghost-truck too, remember?"

"I...I don't know, Sheriff," Scott said, hesitatingly.

"How bad is it?" Terri asked.

"Can't imagine anything worse."

"Is it dangerous?"

Scott shook his head.

Terri looked to her daughter, torn.

"I'm not a child, don't treat me like one," Darcey said with confidence.

"That's not the point. It's about protocol," she said.

"Seriously? Is there anything about today that's followed protocol?" Darcey asked.

Terri gave a sigh of resignation and looked to Scott.

Scott shrugged and said, "Suit yourself. Don't say I didn't warn you."

"Alright, let's go," Terri said with authority.

There wasn't much conversation as they drove out of town. The silence gave Terri the chance to think. She couldn't help but conclude that whatever they were about to see, it would have something to do with the nightmare that had descended on Glenville. She didn't feel as though they had to fear Scott, but was glad to have her Glock on her hip.

Bouncing along on the newly-cut ancient roadway through the woods was treacherous. The Jeep's headlights could only do so much to light the way. It was like driving through a dark, claustrophobic tunnel.

"Don't drive all the way in," Scott instructed.

Terri stopped short of entering the clearing.

"Now what?" she asked.

Scott's hands were shaking. His forehead glistened with sweat. Terri feared he was on the edge of losing it.

"Talk to me Scott, why are we here?"

Scott turned to face Darcey and said, "You don't have to see this."

"Yes I do," she said with conviction.

Scott looked to Terri and said, "Shine your spotlight into the clearing."

As Terri lit up the spotlight that was affixed to the side of the Jeep, Scott got out and walked to the front of the vehicle.

"Is he okay?" Darcey asked.

"I don't know yet," Terri replied.

The two got out and joined Scott, who gestured ahead.

Terri grasped the spotlight and shone it forward.

"What am I looking for?" she asked.

Scott didn't reply. He knew she'd understand soon enough.

Soon enough came quickly.

"Oh my God," Darcey said with a gasp.

Terri quickly reached into the Jeep and grabbed a high-powered Sunitact flashlight. She fired it up and took a few steps into the clearing, sweeping its beam across the grisly scene.

"It's a graveyard," Scott said. "Twenty-five graves. Unmarked. Nobody knows they're here. Except for me. And now you two. And whatever dirtbag buried them here."

Terri walked in a daze, unable to comprehend how such a gruesome situation was possible. She walked to the edge of one trench and shone her flashlight down on the skeletal remains of someone wearing a rotted Rolling Stones t-shirt and black Converse high-tops.

She recoiled in surprise and revulsion. Darcey peered into the grave, turned away, and vomited.

"Did you do this?" Terri asked, stunned.

"If you mean did I uncover them, yes."

Terri gave a quick, motherly touch to her daughter's shoulder and said, "Stay here."

Darcey wiped her chin and nodded. She had no desire to see any more.

Terri walked past a few more open graves, shining the flashlight down to view the remains of the occupants. Her stomach twisted and her head went light, but she kept her professional composure.

"Everything that happened today was about getting me here to find this," Scott said. "My truck brought me here. Twice. It was being controlled."

"How? By who?" Terri asked, incredulously.

"By them," Scott said, gesturing to the graves. "Their spirits brought me here and told me where to dig."

Terri gave him a quick look, which Scott rightly took as skeptical.

"I get it," he said. "If somebody told me that I'd think they were nuts too. Or hallucinating. Or bullshitting. But those graves are real. The bodies are real. You see 'em, right?"

"I believe you," Darcey said weakly.

"Look at their clothes," Scott added. "This isn't some ancient burial ground. I saw 'em all. The way they were in life. The old men and women, the kid with the Stones shirt and the veteran with one leg. Couple of little kids, too. See for yourself. They each showed me exactly where to dig. And I know why."

"Why?" Terri asked.

"They want people to know they're here. They must have families. People who care. They deserve to know. I'm going to shout it out on social media and call the newspapers and TV stations and keep on shouting until somebody can figure out who did this to them so these poor souls can get some peace. Or justice. I wanted to bring you here first in case there's something official that's gotta be done. Like autopsies or investigations or whatever."

Terri was clearly shaken and kept her composure by spewing practiced official protocol.

"I'll call this in to the DCI," she said. "They'll send an investigating team from the crime scene response unit."

"How are they at investigating ghosts?" Darcey asked.

"Let's not go there," Terri said quickly.

"Too late," Darcey said.

"I'm not telling you what to do, Scott. I'm asking you. Don't broadcast this until the investigators can do their job. We don't want this turning into a circus."

"Okay, I'll hold off on telling anybody until you say it's time. But once you do, the whole world is gonna know about these poor people."

They left the scene and headed back to town. Terri drove Scott directly to his house. He was drained, mentally and physically. Before he got out of the Jeep he said, "I know I'll probably be a suspect, but I'm no killer. They've been in the ground since I was a kid."

"I doubt anybody's going to think you did it," Terri said. "But you'll have to talk to investigators about how you found them."

"They'll think I'm nuts. Do you think I'm nuts?"

"I don't know what to think," Terri said. "I won't lie, it's overwhelming."

"That's one word for it," Scott said.

"Try to get some rest," Terri said. "I'll take your statement tomorrow."

Scott snickered and said, "Yeah. My statement. I gotta go on record to say I'm being haunted. Nobody's gonna believe that."

"I do," Darcey said.

"One step at a time," Terri said, which was the most non-committal response she could produce.

Scott nodded, got out of the Jeep and lumbered toward his front door.

"You did the right thing, Scott," Terri called to him.

Scott nodded thoughtfully and said, "I know that. It's the one thing I'm sure of."

Terri drove straight to her office, knowing it was going to be a long night. She didn't ask Darcey if she wanted to be dropped off at home because she knew what the answer would be. While Darcey sat in the outer office on her cell phone, Terri made calls to the County Division of Criminal Investigation in Madison to mobilize a forensic team. Once those wheels were set in motion, there was nothing more to do but wait. She left her office and sat down next to Darcey on one of the ancient plastic chairs.

"They're going to assemble an action team that'll be here in the morning," she said.

"Shouldn't you do something to the grave site? Like, rope it off?"

"That can wait," Terri said. "Only three people know about it. Scott, me and you."

"And the person who did it," Darcey said.

"Yes. And the person who did it. Assuming it was only one."

"How are you doing, Mom?" Darcey asked with genuine concern.

"Well, considering we just discovered a mass grave in my jurisdiction, on top of the four other deaths that happened within hours of each other, I'd say I'm holding up pretty well."

"Don't forget about the ghosts."

Terri closed her eyes as if trying to shut out that last comment.

"Right," Terri said. "I think I'll stay focused on problems I can somewhat understand."

"Me too," Darcey said. "Only I'm looking at this like there might be some kind of spiritual stuff going on."

Terri gave a resigned chuckle and said, "And how's that working out for you?"

That was the open-door Darcey needed. She sat up straight and spoke with enthusiasm.

"You said there were rumors about lots of deaths at the High Point Institute, right?"

"You think those are graves of patients who were secretly buried in the woods?" Terri asked, incredulous. "That's too horrible to even comprehend."

"It is, but hear me out. You told me there were lawsuits and criminal charges in the works, and your father spent all his time in his office working on something. He could have been getting ready to defend himself."

"I suppose, sure, makes sense."

"But then he killed himself. That tells me he didn't think he stood a chance."

Terri let that sink in, then said, "That would mean the accusations against him were true."

"Maybe, but nobody would testify. The prosecutors needed the hospital records for proof. What if your father had them? He must have had access. He was the boss. What if he took them away when he left and hid them from the prosecutors?"

"The only reason to do that would be if they proved he was guilty."

"Exactly," Darcey exclaimed. "If they proved his innocence, he would have turned them over."

"So you think he was guilty," Terri said flatly.

"I don't know," Darcey said quickly. "I'm trying to see this from the point of view of the spirits. It's like Scott said. They want the truth to come out. The records would show the truth. If your father took them, maybe Granny Trish kept them. She might have put them in a safe place and--"

Terri jumped to her feet as if propelled by raw emotion and said, "I am not basing an investigation on the motivations of spirits from beyond the grave."

She strode quickly back to her office. Darcey followed right on her heels.

"Maybe you should. I've seen things, Mom. Other people have too. I don't know what Scott saw out there, but he's convinced those people are not exactly resting in peace. They want closure. And justice. Whatever happened at that hospital could have put twenty-five people in the ground. Who knows how many more victims there were?"

"There is nothing tying those victims to the hospital."

"What about the Daniels brothers? They both worked at High Point and now they're dead. Same with Vera Holiday, and now Karl Iverson. All dead. All connected to that hospital. This is exactly the kind of thing Mr. Paper was talking about—"

"Mr. Paper!" Terri shouted. "There's more going on with that guy than he's admitting. I can't believe some effete author from England just so happened to stop off in our sorry little town."

"I agree," Darcey said. "He sure seems to have figured out why all these odd things are—"

Darcey suddenly stopped talking.

"What?" Terri asked.

Darcey's mind was sparked with the beginnings of an idea.

"Mister Paper said a series of unexplainable events can sometimes be triggered by a single, unresolved situation. A common denominator. He called it a nexus. Something that ties the events together."

"And you think that's High Point?" Terri said, skeptically.

"Maybe. Probably. But he said it could also be a person."

"Your grandfather is long gone. So is Granny Trish."

"I know. I'm not talking about them."

"Then who?"

"It might be you, Mom."

Terri opened her mouth to respond, but no words came out.

"It was your father who ran the hospital," Darcey said with growing enthusiasm. "Every time something happened today, people came to you. You're at the center of this whole thing."

"Because I'm the sheriff."

"You're more than that," Darcey said. "You said it yourself. You moved us here to try and give something back to the community. You may be doing more than you imagined. Your being here might have triggered everything."

"That's ridiculous."

"Is it? What's happened is real. I don't know if it's actual spirits or some kind of group psychic phenomenon, but shit is happening. I think if we want it to end, we've got to figure out exactly what happened at that hospital. We need to find the truth. You might be the best person to do it."

Terri sat at her desk and put her head in her hands.

Darcey watched her, not sure of how to react. She chose to stay quiet and let her mother wrap her head around what she'd just said.

Terri looked up, wiped her eyes, and focused on Darcey.

"I don't believe in ghosts," she said with finality. "Whatever it is that made this town go crazy, I do not accept that it has anything to do with the supernatural or that I am in any way responsible. I've been nothing but a friend to these people."

"I know. You're not the problem. But you might be the solution."

"Stop!" Terri said. "You're asking me to prove that my father was a monster who was responsible for those victims buried out in the woods."

"I'm asking you to find the truth. Do you have any idea what happened to those hospital records? That would tell us—"

"I said stop!" Terri barked.

Darcey backed off, surprised by such an angry outburst.

"I'm not going down that rabbit hole," Terri said.

"Why not? You're a living connection to the hospital! The Director's daughter! If anybody could figure out what happened back then, it's you."

"I was a little girl!" Terri cried.

"Try to remember some things he did after he resigned. Letting the world know what happened might help those people to truly rest in peace."

"And find justice?" Terri asked.

"That too."

Terri nodded, giving thought to what she would say next.

"Look at me, Darcey," she said, and locked eyes with her daughter. "He was my father. I loved him. I will not stand in the way of the investigation, but I will do nothing to help them."

"But—"

"Listen to me," Terri scolded, shutting Darcey down. "What happened to those people took place years ago. Decades. Nothing will bring them back. It could only destroy what little is left of my father's legacy, and open old wounds. I won't do that."

"I thought you came back here to try and heal those wounds," Darcey said coldly.

Terri stiffened.

"Go home," she said. "I'll wait here for the action team."

"Why, if you're not going to help them?" Darcey said with disdain.

"Go," Terri commanded.

Darcey turned to leave, holding back tears.

"Darcey?" Terri called.

Darcey looked back.

"Maybe you're right," Terri said. "It might be best if you moved back to Chicago."

This struck Darcey like a gut-punch, but she didn't argue.

"I'll call Dad tomorrow," Darcey said, sadly. "Good luck, Mom."

Darcey headed for the door. Terri briefly made a move as if to head her off, but stopped. It was an excruciatingly difficult choice to make, but she made it.

She let her daughter go.

CHAPTER 18

Darcey didn't head home. She didn't call her father. There was only one person she wanted to speak with, so she headed straight for the bed and breakfast on Spruce street where he was staying.

"This is exactly how I expected to find you," Darcey said as she stepped into the inviting living room.

Mr. Paper sat in a well-worn leather easy chair, reading a book, enjoying a cup of tea held in a delicate porcelain cup.

"Miss Darcey," Mr. Paper exclaimed warmly. "What a pleasant surprise."

Entering the room was like travelling back to the turn of the previous century. It was tastefully appointed with heavy furniture, flocked wallpaper, and oil portraits that made it feel more like a museum than a contemporary inn. A small fire crackled in the hearth, adding the only sound beyond the rhythmic ticking of a grandfather clock.

Mr. Paper seemed right at home, with his suit jacket draped neatly over the arm of a nearby chair and his bowler hat resting on the table next to the tea pot. He looked every bit as fresh as he did the moment he stepped out of the limousine that morning.

"I don't think you're surprised at all," Darcey replied flatly.

"Please sit, would you like a cup of tea?" Mr. Paper asked.

"No," Darcey said as she sat in a wooden rocker across from him.

"To what do I owe the pleasure of this visit?" Mr. Paper asked.

"There's a reason you came here, and I don't think it's about writing a book," Darcey said, all business. "I want to know what it is."

Mr. Paper offered her a bemused smile and said, "Are you certain of that?"

"Four people are dead who weren't this morning, and that's not counting the twenty-five graves out in the woods. I have a feeling you already know about those. So yeah, I'm certain."

Mr. Paper took a sip of tea then settled back into his chair.

"There seem to have been quite a few developments since we last spoke. Please, tell me what you've discovered."

Darcey unloaded, relating everything that had happened in Glenville since that morning. The harassment of Vera Holiday, and her apparent suicide; the seemingly natural death of Karl Iverson, and the appearance of his ghost; the deaths of Ben and George Daniels along with the visions that Holly Meade had seen. She ended with Scott Wilson's haunting that led to his discovering multiple graves in the woods. She also told him about the High Point Institute and the allegations of malpractice that forced it to shut down. She finished by revealing that the director of the hospital was her grandfather, who committed suicide when Terri was five years old.

Mr. Paper listened attentively, while taking an occasional sip of tea.

"And then there's you," Darcey said. "You didn't give any specifics, but you pretty much told us why this is happening. How did you know?"

"As I said, I've come across similar situations in my travels. The details vary but the overall scenario is invariably the same."

"Okay, if you're such an expert, tell me what I should do now."

Mr. Paper gently placed the porcelain cup and saucer onto the table and folded his hands in his lap.

"I'm afraid I don't know," he said. "And if I did, it wouldn't be my place to tell you."

Darcey stared at him, slack jawed.

"Who are you?" she asked.

"You are an astute young woman. You've correctly surmised that my visit here is not solely to do research for a treatise about America. Though I suppose a book might result from this incident. I've yet to decide."

"So then why are you here?"

"I believe you've seen enough today to understand that the nature of mankind is far more complicated than biology dictates. The lifeforce that lives within each of us is every bit as vital to one's existence as flesh and bone. Perhaps more so. While a physical being may die, the spirit that makes us who we are, our very essence, does not. It simply moves on to the next level of existence. It's the natural course of events for every being. That is, unless closure has eluded them in life."

"Isn't dying pretty much closure?"

"For one's physical self, yes. But if death occurs before one's journey is complete, the spirit will continue to seek that closure. It happens far more often than you can imagine."

"So that's what's happening?" Darcey asked. "A bunch of spirits are floating around here trying to get closure?"

"It appears so."

Mr. Paper poured himself another cup of tea.

"Are you certain you won't join me?" he asked.

"Are you asking me about tea, or something else?"

Mr. Paper chuckled and said, "Tea. Your journey is your own."

"I can't believe I'm saying this, but are you a ghost?" Darcey asked with trepidation.

"Goodness no," Mr. Paper responded quickly. "Though you aren't the first to have asked that question. I suppose I can best be described as a medium. I've made the study of spiritual phenomenon my life's work, and as such I've developed a remarkable aptitude for connecting with lost souls. Honestly, I can't say whether it's a gift or a curse. I can sense when there is a particularly powerful anomaly, which is what brought me to Glenville."

"So, you saw this coming," Darcey said.

"Specifically, no. But I sensed conflict, so here I am."

"Why? What's the point if you're not going to help fix things?"

"I've already done quite a bit to that end. My very presence opened a door that has allowed the spirits to interact with the living. What happens beyond that is entirely up to those involved. It's not my place to interfere."

Darcey couldn't sit still any longer. She jumped to her feet and paced nervously while Mr. Paper calmly sipped his tea.

"Bad stuff happened at that hospital," Darcey said. "People were tortured. Some died. Who knows how many? If what you're saying is true, these spirits are looking for…what? Revenge? Justice?"

"Perhaps both. Or they may simply want the world to know the truth about the tragedy of their lives, and deaths."

"My mother is the nexus, isn't she?"

"That's quite possible."

"But she doesn't believe any of it. No, worse, she doesn't want to know the truth."

"Understandable. Which leads to another possible scenario."

"What's that?"

"You, Miss Darcey. You may be the nexus."

Darcey froze. Until that moment she believed she was operating on the periphery of the trouble. She wanted answers but other than going on one particularly terrifying car-ride and spotting what may have been a few ghosts, she didn't feel as though she was a part of it.

Until then.

"If your grandfather was indeed the author of these poor people's misery and your mother is unwilling to seek the truth, perhaps it is your destiny to ease their pain."

"How?" Darcey asked.

"That would be up to you," Mr. Paper said. "But if their desire is to bring the truth to light, you might very well be the one to help them."

"But there's no proof of what really happened, or who those people are out in the woods," Darcey argued. "Every witness is either dead or long gone. Unless--"

Her mind raced ahead with an idea.

"Unless?" Mr. Paper repeated.

"I'm not sure," Darcey said. "I'll be back."

Darcey headed for the door.

"Miss Darcey?" Mr. Paper called out.

She turned back to him.

"A warning. When a conduit to the spirit world has been opened, the innocents who seek closure aren't the only spirits who are able to pass through."

"What does that mean?" Darcey asked.

"It means you should be very careful."

Though it was approaching midnight, Terri Hirsch was wide awake, assaulted by a myriad of thoughts that battled for control of her emotions, and quite possibly her sanity.

Ever since the disturbing details of her father's involvement with the High Point Institute began to creep into the consciousness of her younger self, she steadfastly clung to the belief that whatever had happened at the hospital, whatever atrocities had occurred, her father could not have known. If he had, he certainly would have put a stop to it. And maybe he did. Her hope was that Everett Kane had been the voice of reason who chose to shut down the lucrative business, rather than allow it to continue along its horrid path. In her mind, Everett Kane may have actually done something heroic.

That's what she told herself for years. Over time she came to believe it. Though as she grew older there were many nights when she lay awake, wondering if her loving father had been a cold-hearted monster. Rather than fading with time, the reality that she could be deluding herself grew stronger. That concern was her principal impetus to enter the Illinois State Police Academy. Being a sheriff gave her some measure of satisfaction that she was performing a valuable public service. However, it was a stressful career. The drain on her time and energy made it difficult to raise a daughter, while nurturing a relationship with her husband. In the end, though she was loath to admit it, her job may have been a significant contributor to their divorce.

Doubts about what had happened at the High Point Institute continued to haunt her, and compelled her to return to Glenville. The County Sheriff's Station was thrilled to have someone with her experience request to be based in the sleepy town, a post no other sheriff wanted to touch. Once she took the job no one made the connection between her and Everett Kane, and she wasn't about to reveal it.

For months, the stress-free job helped to quell her uneasy feelings about whatever role her father played in the decades-old drama, if only because she felt as though she was having a positive impact on the people of Glenville. The residents embraced Terri, grateful for her steady hand. They quickly came to trust her ability to manage conflicts, from directing emergency services to tracking down lost dogs, to giving a second chance to a homeless man who owned his own push broom. She became a mother hen to the residents, and as much as Terri joked that she was significantly over-qualified, she loved the job. Every day she found joy in performing acts as simple as being the caretaker of people's spare keys or filling in as a crossing guard at the elementary school. She was even asked to speak at the graduation ceremony of Glenville High.

The one downside was a big one. Darcey loathed being there. While Terri understood her daughter's feelings, she weighed it against the good she was doing, and the fact that for Darcey it would be a temporary sojourn. She hadn't shared with her daughter how the experience of being Glenville's sheriff was having a profound and positive effect on her own mental health. Darcey had no idea of the turmoil she had been struggling with since childhood because she wanted to be seen by her daughter as a strong, capable role model.

Despite Darcey's protests, Terri was confident that she had made the right move. She held on to the hope that Darcey would eventually embrace life in the small town and see these few years as a unique experience that would benefit her for the rest of her life.

On balance, Terri felt as though everything was working.

Until that morning when the shit hit the fan.

In the span of eighteen hours, the sleepy town of Glenville had been rattled by events far more devastating than the steady encroachment of technology and the accompanying death spiral into irrelevance. Four people were dead. Twenty-five unmarked graves had been discovered. There were multiple reports of inexplicable phenomenon, all coming from credible individuals who were not prone to hysteria, including her daughter. Perhaps most troubling was the common denominator to all these incidents: The High Point Institute and by extension, her father.

Terri felt the town deserved a second chance and dared to believe she was playing an important role in its resurrection. However, whatever progress had been made was now crumbling under the weight of what? Vengeful ghosts? Karma? Or was it simply a series of horrible coincidences, fueled by the onset of mass hysteria brought on by a stranger who had inexplicably arrived at the moment the trouble began?

Who exactly was Mr. Paper?

Terri prided herself on being a pragmatic problem solver. She knew she had to push aside her anxieties in order to do her job effectively. There would be an exhaustive investigation. That much was certain. By the time the sun came up, Glenville would be overrun by state and county investigators. News crews wouldn't be far behind. She wasn't entirely sure what role she would play, other than as a witness. While she was confident in her ability to lead the investigation into the deaths of the Daniels brothers and Vera

Holiday, the presence of multiple unmarked graves escalated the situation beyond anything a small-town sheriff was capable of.

Karl Iverson's death would be relegated to a sad footnote.

How she dealt with the storm would go a long way toward deciding whether or not she would remain sheriff. Of that she was certain. It wasn't that she feared being accused of anything other than being in charge when the storm hit. She didn't think for a second there would be charges filed against her. But being the one who was driving the bus when the wheels came off was not a good look. She may be asked, or forced, to transfer to a different district. Once the dust settled, decisions would be made. Some by her, some by her superiors. Until then, the best she could do was cooperate.

To a point.

Terri clung to the belief that her father wasn't the architect of the abuses that the High Point Institute was accused of. She wanted to believe that he was an innocent victim of circumstance. For years she had done her best to convince herself of that. It was the bedrock her own story was built upon. But with the revelation of the graves in the woods, she could no longer ignore the accusations and had no doubt about what narrative would emerge. Rumors that had been lost to time would resurface. Families of the victims would be found. Explanations required. Restitution demanded. Since her father couldn't defend himself, he would likely be considered the villain and take the blame. It would be the easiest, most tidy outcome.

Inevitably, it would be revealed that she, Sheriff Terri Hirsch, was the daughter of the devil. It would come as a shock to the people who had embraced her. They would feel betrayed. It could very well be the end of her stay in Glenville, and her career.

She wanted to prove that her father was innocent, or at least the innocent pawn of a corrupt institution. But that didn't seem likely. Therefore, the best she could do was squash any evidence that might point to his guilt. There was no doubt that the investigation would lead directly to the High Point Institute itself. Did that old building still hold secrets that could point to her father's complicity in the atrocities?

Her fear was that the world was about to find out.

Darcey gambled that her mother wouldn't be returning home that night, and probably not for a while after that. There was no way to know how long it would take for the county to assemble a large investigative team and deploy it to Glenville. It could be as little as a few hours but more likely not until the next day. Darcey knew that Terri would want to be at the station to greet them and therefore wouldn't risk going home to sleep. At best she'd catch a quick nap at her desk. She would need the rest because when the team landed the real work would begin. Twenty-five bodies would be exhumed, a job that could take weeks. Terri would be tied up for a very long time and that gave Darcey free reign to follow her plan.

She went home, grabbed a flashlight, and jumped in the Subaru. She slowly rolled out of the driveway with the headlights off for fear that a nosy neighbor might spot her and call Terri to ask why her daughter was out for a joyride in the middle of the night. It was somewhat paranoid, but her emotions were spiked by the fuel of surging adrenaline. Heading into the unknown will do that.

Darcey wasn't sure of where she was going. The address she found on-line wasn't familiar. She had to trust that Google Maps knew more than she did, and a location that hadn't been searched for in decades wasn't deleted. She punched the information into the app, held her breath, and was rewarded with a map that clearly showed the route.

With a relieved sigh she memorized the directions and shut her phone down. She didn't want to risk having her mother track her. She put the phone in the glove box, fired up the headlights, stepped on the gas, and headed for The High Point Institute.

It wasn't a long drive. The route led her to a spot five miles from the center of town. With her phone off, she inadvertently sped past the semi-obscured turnoff but quickly realized she'd gone too far, doubled back, and was soon driving cautiously along the narrow road that wound through the pine forest and up to the plateau that held the old hospital.

Now that she was growing close, the importance of her task began to weigh on her. While the impetus was to seek closure for the victims, she couldn't ignore the fact that this was also her story. Her family's story. The person at the center of this nightmare, the possible architect of the horror, was her grandfather. While she never knew the man, Darcey wanted to uncover the truth, not only for the victims, but for herself. Hopefully, it would be proven that he was unjustly accused of the atrocities. But what if he was guilty? Was that something her mother could live with?

Darcey had her doubts, but she also had the image of all those moldering victims lying in unmarked graves forever burned into her memory. This was the reason why Mr. Paper came to town. Those spirits were denied the ability to rest in peace. They deserved better.

Steeled by that thought, she drove on.

When the institute first came into view, she had to catch her breath. Her mother's speculation that there had to be a full moon that day was correct. Light from the bright, rising satellite backlit the tall towers of the imposing building, making them appear like dark sentinels that had stood guard for a hundred years.

"Fuuuuck..." she said with a low, lengthy gasp.

As impossible as it seemed only a few hours before, this was a ghost story. If any place had ever fit the description of a gothic haunted house, it was the High Point Institute. She was immediately hit with an overwhelming sense of foreboding. While her mission was simple and specific, she knew she had to stay focused and not dwell on the mind-bending reality that there were spirits at work, and according to Mr. Paper's warning, not all of them would be friendly. She feared that if she let those thoughts run rampant, she'd spin the car around, hit the gas, and never look back.

The massive, wrought-iron gates were wide open. As she drove through she saw an open padlock hanging from the heavy-duty gate latch. She wondered why her mother hadn't locked the entrance, seeing as a woman had committed suicide there that very day. She drove to the main building and stopped at the bottom of the cement staircase that led up to the main entrance. She recognized the stairs and the church-like wooden doors from the picture of the Daniels brothers that had been taken decades before. When they were young. And thin. And not dead.

One of the two front doors was wide open. Strange. It wasn't like her mother to miss that detail. Darcey couldn't help but wonder if the gate and the doors had been left open for a reason. But by whom? She got a firm grasp on her flashlight and climbed the stairs. Up until that moment her plan had gone smoothly. From here on things would become more complicated.

She wanted to find her grandfather's office. The idea first came to her when her mother told the story about playing hide and seek in that office and being frightened because she thought her father had magically disappeared. Of course, it wasn't magic. He was hiding inside a secret room that he accessed through a hidden door built into his bookcase. The idea of a secret room fascinated Darcey. Why did he have one? What was its purpose? Most intriguing, what secrets did he have to hide?

One of the unresolved issues concerning the High Point Institute was the mystery of what had happened to the hospital's records. Was it possible that Everett Kane had them hidden away in that secret room? There was no indication that they had been destroyed. Or even moved. Apparently none of the employees or patients spoke to that. Did that mean they still existed somewhere inside? If so, a logical place for them to be kept, and hidden, may have been the secret room that only Everett Kane had access to.

It was a longshot. Darcey realized that. But if she were right, those records could hold the information about what had happened to those twenty-five people, as well as any others who had been treated, or mistreated at the hospital. At the very least the records would indicate who their next of kin were. It might also be the definitive answer as to whether or not Everett Kane was culpable for the atrocities.

Those records could be evidence, or exoneration.

For Darcey, it was worth trying to find out which. The only issue was that she had no idea where the office might be. The High Point building was massive. It could take hours to find it. All she could do was start looking.

When she stepped through the front door, a nervous twitch tickled her stomach. A woman had committed suicide there only a few hours before. Though she was the daughter of a sheriff, Darcey had not become inured to the more disturbing aspects of her mother's job.

As unsettling as the thoughts of Vera Holiday's tragic demise may have been, they were forgotten once Darcey viewed the sad and spectacular atrium. What immediately drew her attention was the enormous stained-glass window that began on the second floor landing and soared above the center stairway. It glowed with light from the full moon, bringing out its colorful, grimy glory. She did a slow turn to take in every detail of the abandoned space: The majestic yet crumbling fountain, the marble stairway, the balconies that ringed the five-story atrium that was capped off with a dome of cut glass that caught light from the moon, making it sparkle through the layer of time and grime. It brought a feeling of life to a building that otherwise had none.

Darcey was awestruck. She hadn't expected to find such grand details inside a building that from the outside appeared grim at best. Everything about this five-story atrium spoke of a rich past that must have been inviting to those who first entered, whether as patients seeking help, or to entrust the care of their loved ones to the renowned staff. At least that's how the brochure characterized them. Renowned. A better word to describe them might be infamous. This atrium was an enticing come-on, ripe with promise and professionalism that must have filled the victims with a needed sense of hope, false as it may have been.

Behind the curtain held a much different story. That's where Darcey had to venture. But where to start? She fired up the flashlight and chose a random path. There were open double-doors to her right. It was as good a place as any to begin her search. She walked slowly across the atrium, keeping her eyes and the flashlight's beam on the floor to avoid tripping over anything. The only sign of life were the dozens of fresh footprints that were left in the thick dust that covered the tiled floor. Darcey figured they must have been made by her mother and the coroner's team that had removed Vera's body. She wondered which of the footprints were Vera's. What path had she taken to get here, and why had she chosen this spot to kill herself?

Oddly, Darcey also noticed what looked to be animal tracks that were large enough to have been made by good-sized dogs. It added to her already spiking anxiety that there might be wild animals lurking throughout the abandoned building. Maybe coyotes. Or bobcats. She saw other prints that looked as though they might have been made by hooves. She had the sickening thought that wild animals could have gotten to Vera before her mother did. That was an image too grim to dwell on.

Darcey caught a flash of movement beyond the open double doors, and quickly shone her flashlight that way. Had she actually seen something? Or was it a trick of (moon) light? She moved forward, more cautiously. As she drew nearer to the doorway she could see that the opening led to a short corridor with another set of double doors on the far end that were closed. There were several open doors on either side of the corridor that could have led to patients' rooms, or offices, or exam rooms or she didn't know what else. She hoped they were offices, and that her search for Kane's would be a quick one.

There was a sharp sound of a squeaky door hinge, followed by the faint but unmistakable sound of a door shutting. Darcey froze. This was no trick of light, or her imagination. She was not alone. She resisted the urge to yell out: "Hello? Who's there?" That's what characters did in horrors movies, and it made no sense to her. If some maniac killer was hiding in the shadows he wouldn't reply: "Oh, hi. Yes, I'm right here."

Instead, Darcey killed the flashlight and continued on. She'd come too far to be frightened off that easily. There was enough moonlight to help her see, so she cautiously took a step through the open doors, stopped, and listened. The hospital was dead silent, which is how she was able to make out the faint sound of heavy breathing. The first door to her left was the only one that was closed. She had to fight the urge to turn and run, which was something the characters in horror movies never did. They always kept looking, which usually led to a grisly death. But this wasn't a scenario devised by a screenwriter to frighten an audience. There wouldn't be a maniac with a chain saw behind the door. Would there?

Darcey approached the closed door and listened. Again, she heard the faint sound of someone who seemed to be panting, as if out of breath. Was it an animal? A cornered animal would be trouble. She quickly figured out a way to minimize her risk. She grasped the door handle with her left hand, her flashlight with her right. She took a breath, flipped on the flashlight, and yanked the door open while shining the light inside. She gave a wide berth for whatever was inside to run out past her.

Nothing sprang out. Cautiously, she stepped forward and peered into the room while sweeping the flashlight beam about. She soon saw the culprit.

Crouched against the far wall hugging her knees was a little girl wearing a tattered yellow nightgown. She had long, wavy blonde hair that obscured her face. She was indeed breathing heavily, whether it was from running around, or out of fear. Multiple explanations came to mind as to why this forlorn little girl was hiding in this abandoned hospital. It was the final thought that landed.

She had seen this girl before.

"It's you," Darcey said with surprise. "Today. In town. That was you, wasn't it?"

The little girl looked at her through strands of matted hair, and nodded.

"What's your name?" Darcey asked gently.

"Millie," the girl said through hitched breaths.

"Hi Millie. I'm Darcey. Why are you here?"

Millie sniffed and said, "I don't know."

"How did you get here?"

Millie shrugged and scooped strands of hair behind her ear, revealing a precious face. Her piercing blue eyes blazed with what Darcey took to be fear.

"It's okay," Darcey said with compassion. "I'm not going to hurt you. Are you alone?"

Mille shook her head.

"That's good. Who else is here?"

"Everyone," Millie said softly.

Darcey's questions only led to more questions.

"Who are they?"

Millie slowly got to her feet.

"You shouldn't be here," Millie said, and started for the door.

Darcey quickly moved to block her way. Millie stopped but faced Darcey with defiance. She might not have been as frightened as Darcey thought.

"I need to ask you a silly question, Millie," Darcey said. "Are you a ghost?"

Millie cocked her head slightly, like a dog that had heard an unfamiliar sound.

"A ghost?" Millie asked. She gave the question some thought, and said, "I don't know."

Darcey shrugged off the odd answer and said, "Let's go find the others."

Millie backed away as if the idea frightened her.

"You should leave," Millie said, with force.

"I will. As soon as I find something I'm looking for. Maybe the others can help me."

Darcey wondered if maybe the "others" were homeless squatters who had taken up residence in the abandoned hospital. Karl Iverson might not have been the only homeless citizen in Glenville after all. They might even know where the offices are. The more she thought about it, the more it made sense. She felt silly thinking this little girl was a ghost.

"Would you please take me to them?" Darcey asked.

Millie wiped away tears.

"If that's what you want, but you don't belong here."

Darcey stepped out of the way and Millie hurried out of the room. She scampered down the corridor, headed for the closed double doors on the far end opposite the atrium. Darcey was right after her. When Millie reached the doors, she turned back to Darcey.

"They're here, but I don't want to talk to them. I don't like most of them."

"That's okay," Darcey said. "Thank you, Millie."

"Please tell them you don't belong."

Darcey thought that was an odd comment to keep making. Whoever was beyond those doors would surely know she didn't belong.

"I will," Darcey said. "Thank you."

Millie stepped out of the way and gestured to the door, beckoning for Darcey to enter. Darcey took a deep breath, braced herself, then pushed the door open and boldly walked through.

CHAPTER 19

When Darcey stepped through the double doors she was instantly hit with bright light that was in such contrast to the dark corridor that she was momentarily blinded. Before her eyes could adjust, she sensed another odd change. The quiet hospital was no longer quiet. She heard the unmistakable sounds of people interacting and the soft scuffle of movement. And music. It was non-descript wallpaper-music designed to create a subconscious, calming vibe.

As Darcey lowered her hand and gazed about, her first thought was that she was dreaming. It was the only knee-jerk, logical explanation that made sense. The fact that daylight was streaming in through high windows when it was after midnight was the least impossible sight. She found herself in a large common room filled with patients, most wearing pajamas and bathrobes, along with staff people wearing green scrubs. An elderly woman sat at a table staring at a puzzle though she made no move to add pieces. A young boy who looked to be Millie's age lay on the floor moving a toy truck back and forth. Back and forth. Back and forth. A teenage girl sat cross-legged on the floor in the middle of the room, rocking while humming a non-descript tune.

There were several table-and-chair sets along with threadbare couches scattered randomly. The people wearing medical scrubs looked to be staff. They were peppered throughout the room but paid no attention to the patients. One read a magazine. Another played solitaire. One woman painted her fingernails.

A teenage guy who seemed to be more in the moment than most, sat on a couch watching TV. Darcey saw it was an old sitcom her mother used to watch called *"Cheers."* Watching along with him were two people in wheelchairs who seemed to have been there in body only for they stared at the screen vacantly, with no sign that they were registering the playful banter between Sam and Diane.

There were several other patients of various ages scattered around the room who appeared to be just as out of it, as if they had been drugged into a state of catatonia. Some had restraints on their wrists, keeping them strapped into the chairs.

Darcey's belief that she was dreaming didn't last once she realized what she was seeing. These weren't squatters. She had found herself among spirits who were reliving a past moment at the High Point Institute. Was this another manifestation of Mr. Paper's influence? Millie's words now made more sense. Darcey didn't belong, and she didn't know what it meant for a living person to be walking among spirits. Did they know she was there? Or was this like watching a movie and she was solely an observer, herself a ghost of sorts?

"Who are you?"

Darcey spun quickly to see an older African-American man in a red plaid bathrobe leaning on a cane for support.

"You talking to me?" Darcey asked hesitantly.

"Who else?" the old man asked. "You must be a newcomer. They don't let visitors back here."

So much for it being a movie.

"I...I'm looking for something," Darcey said. "Do you know where Everett Kane's office is?"

The gruff old man stiffened.

"Why would you want to know that?" he asked.

"I, uh, I have an appointment," Darcey said, thinking fast.

She sensed that someone else had stepped up behind her and spun around quickly to come face-to-face with the kid who had been watching *Cheers* but now stood uncomfortably close. He looked to be around her age, had long hair and wore a black Rolling Stones t-shirt.

"You carrying?" he asked in a whisper. "Sometimes they don't check close enough when people first get here."

"No, I'm not."

"Shit," the kid said. "This place sucks."

He headed back to the TV and his gorked-out friends.

"I'd be careful about that Doctor Kane," the old man said.

"Why?" Darcey asked.

"Forget it," the man said and hobbled away. "I didn't say nothing. Just be careful."

It was the second time in an hour she had been given that warning.

Darcey was startled by a screeching sound that was somewhat human and completely out of place. No one else seemed to notice or react. Another short screech echoed across the room. It came from a woman sitting in a chair near a window wearing a bright pink, fuzzy bathrobe. In spite of her shrill outburst, she didn't seem agitated at all as she lifted her chin to let the sun warm her face. Darcey was drawn to her because she was one of the few people in the room who showed any sign of life, even if it were to screech out an annoying sound.

"Hi," Darcey said as she approached the woman cautiously. "I'm Darcey."

When the woman turned to her, Darcey had all she could do to keep from gasping. The otherwise pretty woman had a vicious scar that was slashed across her face from one eye, over her nose and across the opposite cheek. It was red, angry, and fresh. The woman could have been anywhere from forty to sixty. She had beautiful, auburn hair without a trace of gray that fell in soft curls past her shoulders. Now that she was close, Darcey saw deep wrinkles around her eyes that hinted at the kind of past pain that would leave emotional scars far more hurtful than the one slashed across her face.

Darcey knew her. She'd seen the sketch. It was the spirit who was haunting Holly Meade. It was her grandmother.

"Hello, I'm Claire," the woman said. "Have you seen my friends?"

"I don't think so," Darcey replied, unsure.

"Look," Claire said as she gestured out of the window.

Flying in a circle around a large, leafy tree that sat in the middle of a grassy courtyard were several black crows. A dozen more were perched on branches near the window. Claire had been screeching out a call to them.

"I watched so many of them hatch and grow to take their first flight," Claire said with pride. "Their nest is right there in the tree, almost close enough to touch."

"They're beautiful," Darcey said, though she wasn't particularly fond of crows or found them to be all that beautiful.

"Aren't they?" Claire said enthusiastically. "I know it's silly, but I'd like to think they know I'm here and a part of their lives."

"Not so silly," Darcey said.

"I wonder if they'd come to me," Claire said with childlike enthusiasm. "I'd love to have one perch on my arm."

"They might. You should go out and try."

"I wish I could," Claire said with a resigned shrug. "They don't let me outside anymore."

Darcey was about to ask why when the woman's attention was caught by something that changed her demeanor from wistful to alert.

"What is that wretched woman up to now?" Claire said with concern, her voice dropping two octaves.

Darcey looked outside to see that a woman had entered the outdoor courtyard from a door on the far side and was walking with purpose toward the crow-tree. She wore a white lab coat that identified her as a medical professional, but that wasn't the first thing

Darcey registered. She knew the woman. She was much younger than Darcey's image of her, but it was unmistakably her.

Vera Holiday.

Though Darcey understood that she was among spirits from the past, seeing someone she'd known in life, who had died that very day, was next-level disturbing.

"No," Claire muttered with concern. She stood and pressed her hands against the window pane and shouted, "Leave them alone!"

The woman was too far away to hear Claire through the window.

A custodial worker wearing dark blue coveralls entered the community room. He was a slight man with stringy, graying hair who went about the business of emptying trash cans into a large bin on wheels.

Claire saw him enter and called out, "Mister Iverson! Help me!"

Darcey snapped a look to the man, and let out a short gasp. Though he was decades younger and considerably less worse for wear, she recognized him.

Karl Iverson was back.

"Please Karl," Claire pleaded. "She's doing it again."

Karl didn't react. He didn't even give her the courtesy of telling her to leave him alone.

"Don't waste your breath," the kid in the Stones t-shirt called out. "He ignores everybody."

Claire tried to open the window, but it was locked tight.

"What's going on? Why are you so upset?" Darcey asked.

"That wicked woman puts out poisoned birdseed," Claire cried. "I keep getting rid of it, but they won't let me go outside anymore. Who's going to save them now? Will you save them?"

Darcey was reeling. Millie was right. She didn't belong there. Before she could think of a reply, Claire let out an anguished cry.

"My God, no!"

Coming out of the building to follow Vera across the courtyard was a man who also wore blue coveralls. He was another custodial worker, but instead of a broom, he carried a shotgun.

Vera stopped several yards from the tree that held the crow's nest and pointed up to it.

Claire let out a scream of agony that finally got the attention of the staff in the room who had been oblivious to the patients up until then. They looked at one another, as if expecting someone else to make the first move.

Karl went about his business of emptying trash cans, ignoring the fuss.

Claire banged on the glass with the palms of her hands. "Stop! My God stop!"

The crows grew agitated, as if they sensed the danger. They continued to circle the tree, but their path was tighter as if they wanted to protect their nest while letting out agitated cries.

The maintenance worker shouldered the weapon, took aim, and fired. One crow was instantly blown out of the sky and plummeted to the ground, a bloody pulp.

Claire let out a pained cry, as if she herself had been shot.

As gut-wrenching as the scene was, Darcey knew it wasn't actually happening in that moment. She was witnessing the shadows of a past event. There was nothing she could do to stop it.

The worker took aim again and fired. Buckshot tore apart the crow's nest, blasting it to dust. The circling crows seemed to understand that the battle was lost. The entire flock scattered and flew away, abandoning the tree that had been their home.

That was more than Claire could manage. Serenity had transformed into uncontrollable rage. She tore herself from the window and started for the exit. The orderlies, a man and a woman, finally sprang into action and ran to head her off. They grabbed her arms to restrain her, but Claire's anger gave her strength that made her difficult to control. She pulled against their grasp in a struggle to free herself.

"They're killers!" Claire screamed. "Murderers!"

Darcey watched helplessly.

The patients hardly noticed. The kid watching TV turned to see what was happening but didn't budge from the couch. A door on the far side of the room flew open and a man wearing a doctor's white lab coat rushed in and headed straight for the melee. Without a second's hesitation, he grabbed Claire around the neck in an aggressive chokehold.

"Stop it!" he commanded. "Calm down!"

"Murderers!" Claire shouted.

Her words were cut off by the chokehold. That was all that Darcey could stand. Ghosts or no, seeing this elderly woman being strangled was too much and she ran for the group.

"You're hurting her!" she admonished.

She grabbed the doctor from behind, trying to pull him off.

The doctor released Claire to shove Darcey away. She stumbled, landed on her backside, and looked up at the doctor who stared down at her with adrenaline-fueled rage. When their eyes locked, Darcey was hit with yet another stunning realization. It was Ben Daniels. She didn't recognize him as the irascible cook from the Rx Diner, but from his younger self in the picture of him and his brother taken on the steps of the institute.

She also registered that he was holding something. It was a foot-long orange device that smacked of danger, and violence.

Before Darcey could react, Ben spun back to the struggling Claire and violently jammed the end of the tool into her back.

Claire instantly stiffened and screamed in pain as a powerful electrical charge stunned her.

"Stop it!" Darcey yelled and scrambled to her feet.

Before she could stop him, Ben once again stabbed the cattle prod into Claire's back. This second jolt was unnecessary. Claire was no longer resisting but Ben was out of control. The second shot was purely out of anger. She slumped over, her chin to her chest and now had to be held up by the two orderlies.

Darcey wasn't done. She grabbed Ben's arm and yanked him around to face her.

"Why?" she screamed.

Ben shoved her away, violently. Darcey stumbled back a few steps but stayed on her feet, ready to charge him again. Before she could move, Ben pointed the cattle prod at her threateningly.

Darcey stopped short.

"This is your first lesson," Ben said, seething. "Lunatics do not run the asylum."

"I'm not a patient," Darcey shot back, breathless. "I don't belong here."

Ben took a breath. He had quickly gotten his wits back, but he kept the cattle prod up and pointed at her.

"Like I've never heard that before," he said. He looked over his shoulder at the orderlies who were holding Claire and said, "Leave her."

The two orderlies abruptly let go of Claire, who dropped to the floor, unconscious. They skirted Ben and grabbed Darcey by the arms.

Darcey was more surprised than frightened.

"Don't touch me!" she shouted as she tried to pull away. "I'm not a patient!"

"Relax," Ben said, now sounding like a kindly doctor trying too sooth an agitated patient. "You'll be fine, as long as you learn from what you saw here."

Another doctor wearing a white lab coat hurried up to the group and said, "What have we here?"

He stood next to Ben and focused on Darcey.

It was George Daniels.

"Just another day in paradise," Ben said.

The two doctors strode for the exit, followed by the orderlies who roughly handled Darcey into following them.

The other patients and orderlies didn't react and went back to whatever they weren't doing before all the excitement happened.

The only person who didn't pretend as though he hadn't seen anything was Karl Iverson. He stood at the opposite side of the large room, watching Darcey as she fought to get away.

Something had finally gotten his attention.

CHAPTER 20

Darcey's prediction about how her mother would be spending the night was spot on. Terri was still in the office, her head resting in her arms that were folded on her desk. Dead asleep. She'd been up for over eighteen hours and desperately needed to re-charge her batteries before Glenville was thrust into the national news. She needed to be sharp, knowing that she'd be faced with a barrage of questions from the state and county investigators. She had to be careful of what she said, especially to the media. No doubt regional TV stations would send teams, but the discovery of a mass grave could draw national attention. She might end up on CNN being interviewed by Anderson Cooper. She wanted to look her best for that. Though she understood that in the scheme of things her vanity was inconsequential, she took some comfort in focusing on something as trivial as her appearance. She understood under-eye bags and knew how to deal with them. Everything else? Not so much.

She had placed her cell phone on the desk a few inches from her ear, knowing that when the call came in that the forensic team was near, it would serve as her alarm. She considered changing into the clean and pressed uniform she kept in the office before nodding out, but decided to wait until just before the first wave of investigators arrived. She didn't want to appear rumpled on any level, hoping that projecting a professional, capable image might help salvage her job and career.

"Sheriff? Sheriff Hirsch?"

Terri heard a man's voice through the veil of sleep. As she slowly regained consciousness, she assumed it was coming from her cell phone. It took a few seconds for her to drag herself up from the depths of sleep and once her head cleared, she wondered how a call could be connected if she hadn't answered the phone.

"Wake up, Sheriff."

Terri opened her eyes and focused on the cell phone. It wasn't connected.

"'Bout time you came to."

The voice wasn't coming from the phone. Terri turned to the office window that looked out onto the reception area, to see someone standing there, looking in at her.

It was Karl Iverson.

Terri didn't know if it was the shock of seeing the dead man standing outside her office that woke her up, or the harsh ringing of her cell phone. Whichever it was, Terri sat up quickly, having been jolted into consciousness.

What she saw was a dream, yet it felt so real. Karl felt real. It took her a few seconds to catch her breath and realize that her cell phone was still ringing. She saw who was calling, cleared her throat and answered.

"This is Sheriff Hirsch," she said, a total professional. "Yes. Hi Darren. No, I was awake. Tough to power down when something like this is going on. Is there an ETA? Zero-six-hundred. Understood. No, that's fine. It's not like they're going anywhere, sorry, that was tasteless. I'll be here at the station when the team gets here. I know, it's a hell of a thing. I'll see you at six. Good night."

Terri punched out of the call and stared at the phone. The show was about to begin. Though in truth the show had begun long before she was born. This was the final act. She dropped the phone on the desk and took a second to consider the best use of her time over the next few hours. She decided to go home, set the alarm for five, and hopefully get a few hours of solid sleep. She wanted to come back out relatively refreshed and ready to go.

She pushed back from the desk, and hesitated. The man in the window. Had it been a dream? She slowly swiveled the chair so she could look out to the lobby. She gathered her courage, raised her eyes and saw nothing. No Karl. No ghosts.

She let out a relieved breath and said, "That fucking Paper character's got us all seeing ghosts."

She hoisted herself out of the chair and headed out, looking forward to home and a warm bed.

The orderlies muscled Darcey out of the community room back into the corridor she had first come through, only now it was lit by buzzing fluorescent lights that somehow had power. The floor was polished and dust-free. She was forced into the same room where she had met Millie not long before, and saw it for what it was when High Point had patients: a cell. There was a mattress on the floor, a sink and a toilet. It fell short of being a full-on padded "rubber room," but there was nothing there that a psychotic patient could use to hurt themselves, or anyone else.

The orderlies maneuvered her toward the mattress, forced her to sit down, then released her and quickly backed away. Darcey instantly moved to jump to her feet but was backed down by Ben Daniels who loomed over her threateningly.

"That's better," he said. "Everyone is a little agitated at first. It'll pass."

"I know you," Darcey said. "And your brother. I know what's going on here."

"Do you?" George Daniels said as he stepped up next to his brother. "What is it you think you know?"

"I know about the people buried out in the woods," Darcey said. "Let's start there."

Both brothers stood up straighter. Until that moment they had been acting with smug confidence. Hearing that someone knew of the burial ground clearly shook them.

Their reaction gave Darcey a moment of satisfaction. It didn't last. It might not have been the smartest move to reveal exactly what she knew about them. What would they do to someone who knew the truth? What could they do? They were spirits. She hadn't actually gone back in time. The veil between this world and the next had been pulled aside. But was any of it real? It certainly felt real. These weren't ethereal shadows who walked through walls and rattled chains. They had a physical presence. What were the rules of this spiritual phenomenon? Whatever they were, she was at the mercy of two notorious individuals.

Millie was right. She did not belong there.

Ben collected himself, took a knee next to her, and looked her square in the eyes.

"I don't know who you are or why you're here," he said. "Or what you think you know, but we'll relieve you of your burden."

"What's that supposed to mean?" Darcey asked.

Ben stood and backed away from her.

"It won't take long to prepare," he said. "Be patient."

He nodded to George and the two headed out of the cell-room, followed by the orderlies.

Darcey immediately jumped to her feet and ran for the door, but it was closed in her face.

"I don't belong here!" she shouted as she yanked on the door handle in frustration.

There was a small, square window in the door. She peered out to see the male orderly looking back at her. He laughed and gave a taunting wave.

Until that moment, Darcey had acted with bravura. Though the reality of spirits walking among the living had been difficult to accept, it was now impossible to doubt. Once she had established that many of the spirits were seeking closure, and some level of justice, she felt compelled to help them. Coming to the High Point Institute may have been frightening, but she wasn't concerned about her own safety.

Until then.

The warning from Mr. Paper rang in her ears. He said that once a conduit to the spirit world was opened, innocents wouldn't be the only ones able to come through. What he didn't say was that the spirits would have physical abilities. She should have realized that for herself. Spirits had taken control of Scott Wilson's truck, and moved his digger to the gravesite. It had to have been spirits who killed Vera Holiday's cat, and sent the electrical surge that killed Ben Daniels. Now she was locked into a hospital cell with the possibility of falling victim to the same kind of treatment the Daniels brothers inflicted on their patients, like the poor woman who loved crows. Holly Meade's grandmother.

Not only had she miscalculated the danger she was stepping into, no one knew she was there. She wished she hadn't been so clever as to turn off her cell phone and leave it in the car.

She turned away from the door, leaned back against it and considered the grim situation. How many others had been locked into this room to wait for whatever horrible fate the sadistic doctors had planned for them? In that moment she understood the victim's need to make things right. They felt it so strongly that it persevered beyond death. She couldn't shake the grim thought that she might end up being the next victim whose spirit would be seeking closure.

There was a gentle tapping on the door. Darcey spun around to see Millie's angelic face in the window.

"I tried to warn you," the little girl said. "Now they're going to take you to the zap."

"The what?"

"Where they zap your head. It makes people forget things."

Darcey knew what that meant. Electro-shock treatments. She'd heard of those. They can be helpful, or if used incorrectly, scramble your thoughts. Permanently. Seeing the catatonic people in the recreation room made Darcey wonder how often it was used and if it was done for therapy, or for more insidious reasons.

"You're right," Darcey said. "They're going to zap me. Can you unlock the door?"

"Why are you here?" Millie asked.

"Patients are getting hurt," Darcey said. "You know that. There are some very bad people here and I want to stop them."

"You can't stop them," Millie said. "It happened a long time ago."

That gave Darcey pause.

"So you know you're a ghost?" Darcey asked.

Millie's eyes teared up and she nodded.

"We're all ghosts. But I don't know why we're still here. I don't want to be here anymore."

"Maybe that's how I can help," Darcey said. "But I can't if they hurt me."

Millie wiped away a tear.

Darcey heard the lock on the door releasing. She held her breath, pulled the handle, and the door opened. She could breathe again. She quickly opened the door and took a peek outside to where Millie was waiting.

"What are you looking for?" she asked.

Darcey was torn between running for her life and carrying through with her mission.

"Do you know where Doctor Kane's office is?" she asked.

Millie nodded.

"I need to go there," Darcey said.

Decision made. She hadn't come this far just to get this far.

Millie ran toward the atrium. Before she could change her mind, Darcey followed. When she stepped through the double doors that led back into the atrium, Darcey was so stunned by what she was confronted with that she stopped dead in her tracks.

The atrium was back to its original glory. Water cascaded from the multi-levels of the fountain. The tile floor was polished and gleaming, as was the marble stairway that led up to the stained-glass window that was now spotless, its breathtaking colors brought to dazzling life by sunlight. The reception desk was staffed by two efficient looking women who alternately answered phones and greeted people who stepped up to ask questions. It was impressive and all so incredibly normal except for the fact that Darcey was seeing it from a time that existed decades before.

"Please don't make a scene," came a quiet voice.

Darcey arms were grasped roughly by the two orderlies. She looked over her shoulder to see Ben Daniels standing in the doorway they had just come from.

Millie ran to hide beneath the fountain.

"So impatient," Ben said, smug. "I told you it wouldn't take long to prepare."

Darcey was not about to be taken back to that cell. Or allow herself to be lobotomized.

"Help!" she called out. "They're going to hurt me!"

The receptionists at the front desk looked her way but didn't know how to react. Nor did the few visitors.

Ben Daniels stepped in front of Darcey to address them..

"It's all right," he said calmly. "She'll be fine."

"No I won't!" Darcey shouted in desperation. "Somebody call the Sheriff. Please!"

Ben Daniels calmly gestured for the orderlies to "escort" Darcey from the atrium. Darcey fought, but again, she was no match.

Millie watched from beneath the fountain, helpless.

Before they dragged Darcey through the door, a screeching noise caught everyone's attention. It was so loud and piercing that they all glanced around to see what could have made such a sound.

Darcey knew what it was. She had heard it not long before.

The harsh sound happened again. It filled the large atrium, coming from nowhere and everywhere. It was the sound of a crow's caw.

Darcey looked up.

"Oh God no," she muttered.

She pulled away from the orderlies who were now focused on the woman in the pink bathrobe who was on the fifth floor of the atrium, sitting on the hand rail with her legs dangling in space.

"Claire!" Darcey shouted. "Be careful!"

Ben shot an accusatory look to the orderlies.

"You told us to let her go," the woman orderly said, defensively.

"Claire please," Ben called out. "Come down from there."

"I will," Claire shouted back, sounding almost joyous. "Watch!"

She spread her arms as if intending to fly, and leapt off the balcony.

One of the receptionists screamed in horror.

Darcey couldn't watch. She dropped her eyes but that didn't prevent her from hearing. Claire hit the top tier of the fountain, spun back, bounced off the next cistern and landed on the floor with a sickening thud. In her last moments, Claire had experienced the euphoria of flying like one of her winged friends, though it ended with her lying in a pool of her own blood that spread slowly across the tiles, staining them crimson.

She had landed near Millie, but the little girl barely reacted, as if she'd witnessed the horrifying scene before. Many times before.

"Get her," Ben commanded.

The two orderlies went straight for Claire.

No one was paying attention to Darcey. She took the chance and ran straight for Millie. She grabbed the girl's hand and without hesitation ran to the opposite side of the atrium and out of the first door they came to.

"Where is Kane's office?" Darcey asked, breathless.

Millie pulled away and ran down a long corridor, at the end of which was a door that led to stairs. She climbed, with Claire right on her heels. On the third floor they arrived at a well-appointed corridor with wood-paneled walls. There was nothing institutional about what was clearly an executive wing. Millie ran to the far end and a well-polished wooden door that was wider than the rest. It was the kind of door that would lead to the office of a hospital Director.

"Here?" Darcey asked.

Millie nodded.

Darcey opened the door and said, "C'mon."

"No," Millie replied. "He scares me."

"I don't think he's here," Darcey replied.

Millie shook her head more forcefully.

"All right then. Thank you, Millie."

"Good luck," Millie said.

Darcey took a quick breath to calm herself, and opened the door.

Everett Kane's spacious office looked exactly as Terri had described it. It felt like a comfortable living room. A sitting area to the right had a couch, two chairs and an ornate fireplace. A large window behind the couch offered a spectacular view of the forest that surrounded the institute. The heavy, wood-framed furniture and end tables looked to be antiques, as did the colorful Oriental rug. To her left was a huge, intimidating desk. It was beyond neat with a pen-set, a protective writing pad and a tray that held crystal decanters filled with amber liquor. To Darcey it looked more like a museum display of an old-timey office than a place where actual work got done. The only modern touch was the black telephone that had multiple lines. Though "modern" is a relative term. The corded phone was straight out of 1980.

She absorbed the vibe of the office quickly but didn't dwell on the fact that this was her grandfather's office. Under other circumstances she may have wanted to explore in order to get to know more about the man. These weren't other circumstances. She had to stay focused, get what she needed, and get out.

What she needed was in a secret room that was hidden behind the floor to ceiling bookcase behind the desk. She moved quickly, skirting the desk. It wasn't obvious as to where exactly the secret door was, or how it could be opened. She ran her fingers along the vertical edges of the bookcase, hoping to come across a hidden switch. She'd seen movies where pulling out a particular book would trigger a door mechanism, but that seemed unrealistic. There had to be a switch that would release a latch. Perhaps it was on his desk.

She turned around to examine the desk when she saw that she wasn't alone. A man had entered quietly and now stood across the desk from her.

"I don't believe I had an appointment scheduled," the man said. "I'm Doctor Everett Kane. Who might you be?"

CHAPTER 21

Terri drove home with one goal in mind. Sleep. She pulled her Jeep into the driveway and entered through her front door. If she had gone through the garage she would have seen that the Subaru wasn't there. The house was dark, but she didn't bother to turn on a light. She headed straight upstairs and dragged herself to her bedroom without checking on Darcey, something she had done every night since her daughter was born. She feared that Darcey might be awake, and she was not about to continue their argument. Not then anyway. She needed every minute of sleep she could squeeze in.

Terri placed her phone and gun-belt on the bedside table then dropped her clothes on the floor. It was too much of an effort to put her uniform into the hamper. After a quick trip to the bathroom she pulled on a faded Chicago Bears t-shirt, crawled into bed, turned out the light, and collapsed. The entire procedure from the time she'd left the station until her head hit the pillow was done on auto-pilot.

Before giving in to sleep, she remembered that she hadn't set her alarm. She reached out for her cell phone, and felt a tickle on her hand. A fly had landed on it. She waved it off, grabbed the phone, and focused on setting the alarm. Another fly landed on the phone, drawn to the light. It was quickly joined by another. Annoyed, Terri waved them off. But they soon returned. She shook the phone as a third appeared. The three circled the light of the phone, buzzing around her hand.

"What the hell?" she muttered. "Shoo!"

She waved her arms, mostly annoyed that they were keeping her from sleep. In frustration she reached up to turn on the bedside lamp and was shocked to see a swarm of flies circling the light. She got out of bed and clapped at them in a futile attempt to kill a few.

"Afraid that's my fault."

It was a man's voice.

Terri spun to see a man's silhouette standing in the doorway of her bedroom. She didn't scream. She didn't panic. Without hesitation she grabbed the Glock from her holster on the bedside table and raised it with both hands, putting the intruder's heart square in her site.

"Don't move," she said with trained authority.

The man held his hands out to show he was unarmed.

"Sorry," he said. "Didn't mean to scare ya."

Terri knew that voice. But it couldn't be. The last time she'd seen him he was lying in his own bed, dead.

"Karl?" Terri said.

"You were good to me, Sheriff," Karl said. "Not sure I deserved it, but I sure do appreciate it."

"I...I don't understand--"

"Not sure I do either. But here we are. You didn't know this, but I was planning on asking you for another kindness. Thought I might be of some use as a deputy, or an assistant, or anything more than a sidewalk sweeper. I'll bet you would have found something for me, too. You're a good egg. But I never got the chance."

Terri didn't waver. She kept her pistol up and trained on Karl's chest.

"How is this possible?" she asked.

"Beats me, but I think you and me talking here is the least of it."

"What do you want?" Terri asked.

"My whole life I kept to myself. Didn't pay attention to nobody, even if they needed my help. A lot of people needed it too, but I never listened. Wish I could go back and change a few things but that would take some kind of magic, right?"

"You should leave, Karl," Terri said.

"I will. You got nothing to worry about from me. But I want to do something for you. It's about your girl. Darcey."

Terri's anxiety instantly skyrocketed. It no longer mattered that she was talking to a ghost.

"What about her?"

"Don't mean to be dramatic, but this town is haunted. It ain't no dream. I've seen things I didn't think were possible. So have you. You're talking to a dead man, right?"

"What about Darcey?" Terri pressed with growing dread.

"She went to the institute. Don't know why, but she's there, and she's in trouble."

"Not true. She's right here in bed."

"She ain't. I wish I could help her but there's just so much I can do. It's like I got to re-walk the steps I took years ago, and that don't include helping out your daughter. I'm not even sure how I got here to you. It's like I'm swimming in an ocean full of riptides and eddies of time sending me every which way."

"She's at High Point? Right now?"

"Yeah," Karl replied. "I'm the last person to be telling anybody what to do, but from what I seen, she needs your help. Now. We don't want her being part of the history of that damned place."

Terri lowered her gun and took a step toward Karl.

"Help me to understand," she said, pleading.

Karl backed away and said, "It's about making things right. That's all. That's everything."

Karl walked away from the doorway as Terri picked up the pace and ran out into the hallway.

"Don't leave! Karl!"

Too late. Karl was gone, swept away by whatever tide of time put him there.

Terri stood in the dark hallway, feeling about as alone as when her father hid from her in his office. She ran to Darcey's bedroom to find her bed empty and unmade, exactly as she'd left it that morning. A lifetime ago. She quickly ran back to her room to grab her cell phone and check for Darcey's location.

"Shit," she said with frustration when she saw that Darcey's phone was turned off.

Terri's mind raced in a desperate attempt to make sense of what she'd seen, not just in the last few minutes but over the course of the day. There were multiple accounts of strange phenomena that she had discounted because she hadn't seen anything herself. Until then. Could it be true? Was Glenville haunted? Were the dire predictions of Mr. Paper coming true?

In that moment, as wild as that possibility might be, it didn't matter. Nor did the people who had lost their lives that day or the twenty-five people lying in unmarked graves. Her one and only concern was for her daughter. Had she actually been warned by the spirit of a man who died earlier that day? Or was she losing her mind?

She knew how to find out.

Darcey stood paralyzed, staring across the desk at the spirit of her dead grandfather.

"You must have recently arrived," Kane said, cordially cool. "I make it a point to meet all of our incoming patients, yet somehow you slipped by me." He gestured around his office and added, "In more ways than one."

Darcey recognized him from the few pictures she'd seen. His voice was deeper than she expected, with a distinct gravelly texture. Perhaps he was a smoker. He was a large man, well over six feet tall. He wore a sharp, three-piece suit with a perfectly snugged tie. His neatly groomed hair was near pure white, with no signs of balding. His moustache was neatly trimmed. If there was anything familiar about him, it was his eyes. They were Terri's eyes. A dazzling gray. Darcey always felt that her mother's eyes had a near-magical ability to see everything. And see through everyone. Everett Kane's eyes were no different.

"I...I'm not a patient," she said with a stammer.

Her mind raced, calculating how much, or how little, she should reveal to the man. She'd made a mistake with the Daniels brothers that almost led to her brain being fried.

"I see," Kane said. He casually lifted a decanter from his desk and poured a healthy portion of scotch into a crystal glass. "Then tell me, what brings you to High Point? And to my office?"

Darcey swallowed hard. Kane had cut right to it, and she had no answer. At least not one she wanted to give so she steered the conversation in another direction. She knew how to cut right to it as well.

"You know you're a ghost, right?"

Kane was about to take a drink but stopped and stared straight at Darcey as if seeing her for the first time.

Darcey did her best to stare back without blinking.

Kane placed the untouched glass of scotch down on his desk and strolled toward the large window to gaze out onto the forest with his hands clasped behind his back.

"And apparently you are not," he finally said. "That makes your presence here all the more puzzling."

"I'm just trying to learn," Darcey said.

"The same could be said for all of us," Kane said wistfully. "Strange how I don't feel like a spirit, not that I know what one should feel like. Perhaps we're not ghosts at all."

"Trust me, you are," Darcey said. "And you're haunting this place."

"I suppose you could characterize the situation that way," Kane said.

"How would you characterize it?"

"That's hard to say. We seem to be caught in a Mobius Loop of sorts, stuck in an endless moment where the only change is when someone passes on from life and re-joins us in this eternal limbo. Is it purgatory? Or hell? It certainly isn't heaven. Whatever it is, we have no control over it."

"So you don't know why you're stuck?" Darcey said.

Kane walked back to her.

"I must admit, there is quite a bit I don't know," he said, deadly serious. "For example, why are we now able to interact with the living? Something changed and I'd like to know what that is. Perhaps you can enlighten me."

Darcey knew, and knew that she needed to be cautious about what she shared.

"A doorway was open," she said. "A path. A rift. Whatever. It connected two worlds. The living, and the spirit world."

"How? Why?" Kane asked, genuinely intrigued.

Darcey was gaining confidence. She knew more than Kane, and it gave her a leg up.

"How? I don't know. It's all so hard to understand. But I do know why."

"Please. Share," Kane said.

"It's about what happened here," Darcey said. "The mistreatment of patients and the unreported deaths."

"It's a hospital," he said with a dismissive shrug. "People die in hospitals."

"And get buried in unmarked graves?" Darcey shot back. "This place was shut down because of the horrible things that happened, and nobody was held responsible. Not even you. You never had to answer for anything because you killed yourself."

Darcey was getting worked up. Once she started, she couldn't stop.

"There are accusations about people being tortured. Families lost loved ones. Some were children. Why? For medical research? Sounds to me like that's another way of saying it was for profit. That's worse than a crime. That's immoral. If it's true, this might actually be hell."

Kane stared straight at Darcey. This time she had no trouble holding his gaze. He downed his drink and after dabbing the corners of his mouth he asked, "How do you know all this?"

"It's out there, if you look hard enough," Darcey said. "I guess you don't know about the internet."

"How old are you?" Kane asked, as if it was an accusation. "Twenty?"

"Sixteen," Darcey said flatly.

"Sixteen," Kane repeated with a sigh. "Being righteous is a luxury of youth."

"I still haven't told you why," Darcey said. "The spirits of the dead, the victims, they're looking for closure. Maybe even justice."

"Perhaps they seek a dollop of revenge for good measure?" Kane asked with a snide smile.

Kane's dismissiveness rankled Darcey. He showed no signs of remorse.

"Yeah, maybe some revenge," Darcey said. "Don't you wonder why so many people from the past are suddenly showing up? Ben Daniels. George Daniels. Vera Holiday. Karl Iverson. They all died today. You think that's a coincidence?"

Kane poured another drink, giving himself time to let that sink in.

"I'll ask again," he said. "Who are you and why are you here? Did you know any of these so-called victims? These vengeful spirits? No you're too young. Perhaps you're an amateur sleuth looking to solve a long-forgotten mystery. Or a student journalist seeking tawdry headlines for your high school newspaper. What is it exactly that brought you here, my dear?"

Darcey saw an opening and took it.

"I want to break the loop," she said. "For all of you. Don't you want that? To be able to move on from this eternal prison?"

"And how do you propose to do that?" Kane asked, intrigued.

"The truth has to come out. The families of the victims need to know what happened to them. The world needs to know. Those people buried out in the woods should be given a proper burial. It's already begun. The state police are on the way. There's going to be an investigation and they're going to find--."

"Nothing, " Kane said curtly. "They'll find nothing."

"Those bodies aren't nothing."

"Yet there's no one left who can testify as to what happened."

"Maybe not," Darcey said. "But there has to be evidence. Hospitals keep records, but yours were never found. I'm guessing you know where they are."

Kane downed his second drink.

"You know, don't you?" Darcey said. "You have a secret room here. In this office. I'm thinking that's where the files are."

Kane focused on her with a searing look that made Darcey catch her breath. Had she gone too far?

"How could you possibly know that?" he asked.

"I'm tenacious," she said. "I take after my mother."

Darcey was trying to maintain her advantage, but Kane had regained his footing.

"And there is the answer I was looking for. You came here looking for evidence to prove our guilt. My guilt."

"Or maybe your innocence," Darcey said, though she was more certain than ever that he wasn't innocent at all.

Kane gave a wistful sigh. "All right then, let's have a look."

He slammed his glass down on the desk and headed for the bookcase.

Darcey rounded the desk, keeping it between them. She fought to contain her excitement because she was about to see exactly what she came for.

Kane stood in front of his wall of books, scanning the volumes.

"Hopefully this will satisfy your curiosity."

He reached over the top of one row of books and triggered a switch that let out the distinct clicking sound of a latch releasing.

Darcey's heart leapt. Having the spirit of her grandfather lead her directly to the missing records was not how she expected her mission to play out, but it didn't matter, as long as she found what she was looking for.

Kane grasped one edge of a bookcase and pulled. The case swung out easily to reveal a small room beyond. He reached inside, flicked on a light, then stepped back and gestured for Darcey to have a look.

She walked forward with caution, keeping her distance from Kane, and peered through the opening to see...

...an empty room.

Darcey deflated.

"It was intended to be a wine closet," Kane said. "I never got the chance to complete it."

"Then what happened to the records?" Darcey asked, undaunted.

"We're finished here," he said with finality. He was done humoring this intruder. "I admire your tenacity, but alas, you have reached a dead end."

Darcey gazed into the empty room with a growing sense of unease and ultimately, understanding.

"So it's all true," Darcey said soberly. "If you were innocent you would have turned over those records when you were alive."

"I played the hand I was dealt to the best of my ability," Kane said coldly.

"Did you?" Darcey said, scoffing. "Sounds to me like you let those people suffer and die. That's why you're stuck in this loop. That's why you all are. One way or another the truth is going to come out. Those victims buried in the woods will finally rest in peace. I doubt you will."

"Is that how you see it?" Kane said. "I'm afraid with no one left who can attest to any of this, their fate will forever remain a mystery."

"Not if I have anything to say about it," Darcey said with confidence.

"But I'm afraid you don't."

Kane gestured toward the office door. Before Darcey could look to see what was happening, she was grabbed by Ben and George Daniels.

"Would you please end this?" Kane said to them with impatience.

"It's done," George said.

Darcey looked straight at Kane and said, "You really are the monster people said you were."

"That's a matter of perspective," Kane said as he poured himself another drink.

The Daniels brothers pulled her toward the door. Darcey struggled fruitlessly.

"Do you think Granny Trish knew the whole truth about you?" she shouted.

Kane shot her a questioning look. Out of everything she had said, this was the one thing that got a surprised reaction.

Before she could say another word, George wrapped a cloth soaked with chloroform over her mouth and Darcey's world went dark.

Terri made the trip to High Point with far more urgency than on her previous visit. She sped out of town with the Jeep's lights flashing, determined to get to the old hospital as quickly as possible. The challenge was to keep her emotions in check and her hands steady on the wheel. While reality seemed to be crumbling, she forced herself not to dwell on trying to make sense of it. Her sole concern was for Darcey. Multiple people had died that day. That much was real. Whether or not spirits had anything to do with the deaths was irrelevant. She couldn't begin to sort that out until Darcey was safe.

Within minutes she made it to the turnoff and sped along the winding road that led to the institute. She had to force herself to slow down for fear she'd skid from the narrow road into the woods. She crested the rise, broke out of the pine forest, and sped up to the massive gates that were closed and pad-locked, just as she'd left them earlier that day. She skid to a stop, jumped from the Jeep, and went straight for the lock. Getting through wouldn't prove to be as difficult as it had been earlier. She knew which was the right key and found it instantly. She threw off the padlock, pushed the heavy gates open and got right back into the Jeep to make the rest of the trip.

The first thing she saw was the Subaru parked near the front entrance. It was both reassuring and frightening. Darcey was here, but why? How did she open a padlocked gate? And was it actually Karl Iverson's ghost that paid her a late-night visit to warn her? She barely came to a stop behind the car when she was out and bounding up the stairs to the front door. It was locked as well, but she had that key too. With her heart racing, she unlocked the door and stepped into the High Point Institute.

"Open your eyes."

Darcey's head was spinning. Her stomach wasn't far behind. For a long moment she thought she was in her bed at home. The nausea was so extreme that she feared she'd vomit. When she was roused enough to function, she moved to sit up, but couldn't. It didn't register as to why. Was she paralyzed? Or having a nightmare? She tried to rub the sleep from her eyes but couldn't move either hand.

Her focus sharpened quickly once she realized she wasn't in her bed. She lay flat on her back, her wrists and ankles bound by leather straps. Most disturbing was that she couldn't move her head due to a strap that ran across her forehead. In that position, vomiting could prove fatal.

Her heart raced, which cleared the lingering effects of the chloroform. Above her was a light so bright it hurt her eyes.

"Good."

Darcey squinted, filtering out some light so she could focus on the silhouette of someone standing over her. Her heart fell when she realized it was George Daniels.

"Some physicians prefer to sedate their patients during the procedure," he said matter-of-factly. "I find it helpful to monitor my patients response in real time. Let's get started."

"What are you doing to me?" Darcey said, though the words were slurred. Her tongue felt too big for her mouth.

"It's called ECT. Electro Convulsive Therapy."

George moved to a counter where he pulled on rubber gloves.

"It involves sending a mild electric current through the brain that triggers a surge of electrical activity and induces a seizure. It's an effective treatment to deal with severe depression, acute mania, and a variety of schizophrenic syndromes. None of which you are afflicted by, I should add."

"Then why?"

George loomed over her.

"Doctor's orders. The treatment will only take a few seconds but when we're through, you'll have no memory of anything you've discovered about our hospital. You may not have any memory at all, for that matter. The charge I'll be using will not be a mild one, nor will the seizure it causes."

Darcey's heart raced and her adrenaline spiked. She fought against the restraints, futilely.

"You can't," Darcey cried. "Get Kane. He won't let you do this."

"Who do you think ordered it? Now open wide."

George reached something toward her mouth, but Darcey refused to open.

"It's for your protection," he said. "Let's not make this anymore unpleasant than it has to be. We wouldn't want you biting through your tongue, would we?"

Darcey clenched her jaw and refused to open.

"Suit yourself," George said with a shrug and tossed the rubber mouth guard onto the counter.

"Please don't," Darcey cried. "I'm not a spirit. I could die."

"Nonsense," George said. "You won't die, though you might wish you had."

He rolled a cart next to Darcey that held an antiquated electric device in a wooden box. It had two dials along with a single meter and a few switches. It was a simple machine capable of horrific damage. Running from the left side were two electrical cords, at the end of each was a metal paddle with a rubber handle. George flipped one switch. The machine hummed to life. He adjusted both dials causing the machine to hum louder.

"Stop, George," Darcey cried. "You don't want another victim on your conscience."

"I stopped worrying about my conscience long ago," he said, sounding almost wistful.

He leaned in toward her, holding the paddles to either side of her head.

"It's best you relax," he said. "It'll be easier on you. Not by much, but every little bit helps."

He brought the paddles down, pressing one against each of her temples.

"Please don't," Darcey said, in tears. "Please."

"Shhh," George said calmly. "It'll be over before you know it. Or maybe I should say, you won't know when it's over."

Ben Daniels stepped up to the machine, ready to throw the switch that would send current to the paddles.

"Nighty night," he said.

"Wait," came a stern command from across the room.

"Wait?" George asked, surprised.

Everett Kane entered the treatment room.

"You said to get it done," Ben said.

"And now I'm telling you to wait," Kane replied, tersely.

George nodded to Ben, who shut off the machine. He took the paddles away from Darcey's head and stepped back as Kane approached the table. He looked down at Darcey, as if examining an enigmatic specimen.

Darcey stared back at him defiantly.

"Granny Trish," Kane said. "How do you know that name?"

"I've known it since I was old enough to understand," Darcey replied.

"Understand what?"

"Patricia Hantin? Your wife? She was my grandmother. Your daughter Terri is my mother. Surprise, Doc. You're about to turn your granddaughter into a vegetable."

Nothing seemed to have changed from the time Terri had left the institute several hours before, other than the sight of the massive stained-glass window that was now lit by moonlight. But she was at a loss. Darcey was there, but where?

With her hand on her holstered Glock, she began the search.

"Darcey?" she called out.

The only response was the echo of her own voice.

Terri moved to her left, slowly, headed for the first exit off of the atrium.

"Good you came," Karl said.

Terri spun around, ready to pull her pistol.

Karl stood beside the dry fountain.

"Where is she?" Terri asked.

Karl's answer was to walk toward the doors on the opposite side of the atrium. Terri followed right behind. She no longer questioned the fact that a spirit was guiding her.

"First room on the right," he said. "It's a treatment room."

"What kind of treatment?"

Karl shrugged. "I don't know all they did in there. Didn't want to know. I guess maybe I should have cared. Might have done things differently."

Terri pushed the door open.

"Sheriff?" Karl said. "I know this don't make up for all I didn't do when I was here. All I ask is when you think of me, try to think kindly."

Terri gave Karl a quick nod and headed through the door into the short corridor.

"Darcey?" she called again.

Still no reply.

Terri hurried to the first door on the right. It was closed. She drew her pistol and held it ready. With her foot she pushed the door open and peered inside.

Dark. Whatever this room had been used for, the only clues left were dusty counters that ran along either side of the space, and a long surgical table to the center.

Lying on the table was Darcey.

Terri rushed straight for her daughter while holstering her pistol.

"My God, sweetheart!" Terri cried as she caressed Darcey's cheek.

At her mother's touch, Darcey opened her eyes.

"Mom?" she whispered.

"Are you hurt?"

"Where are they?" she asked as she looked around the room with confusion.

"Who?"

Darcey struggled but was able to sit up because she was no longer bound by leather straps. Terri helped her up, keeping an arm wrapped around her shoulders for support.

"It feels like I was in a dream," Darcey said. "Or maybe this is the dream."

"It's no dream," Terri said. "Why are you here? Did someone try to hurt you?"

"No," Darcey said. "I mean, yes. Let's just go."

Terri helped her to her feet. Darcey was unsteady but otherwise fine. They left the treatment room, headed back into the atrium...

...and stopped short the moment they entered.

"Oh shit," Darcey mumbled under her breath.

Standing alone beneath the dry fountain, was Everett Kane.

"Hello Theresa," he said softly.

Terri's brain locked. Seeing her father, her dead father, pushed her close to the edge of sanity.

"You've grown up," Kane said kindly. "But I know my little girl. And you have a daughter of your own. She looks so much like your beautiful mother."

Darcey looked between the two, unsure of whether she should inject herself into this odd reunion.

"Please," Kane said. "Say something."

Coming face to face with the man who had lived in her memory as equal parts enigma, villain and beloved father pulled Terri's emotions in multiple directions. The fact that it was a spirit was the least troubling for her to deal with. She grasped for whatever tenuous threads she still had on reality to pull herself out of her stupor.

"You say you know me," Terri said, hesitantly. "But I don't know you."

"You must remember something of me," Kane said with an uneasy chuckle.

"What I remember is a loving father," Terri said. "But that's not who you turned out to be."

Kane flinched. "I was never anything but devoted to you, and your mother."

"Yet you committed the ultimate selfish act and left us alone."

"For that I am deeply sorry. You deserved better, but I saw no other recourse."

"No?" Terri said, gaining confidence. "You could have taken responsibility for the atrocities that were committed here. But you chose the cowardly way out."

"What I did wasn't out of cowardice. I wanted to spare your mother, and you, the years of public scorn."

"Or was it to spare yourself?" Terri asked with disdain. "Don't you feel any guilt?"

"More than you can imagine. What happened here was unforgivable, but it was inevitable."

"Inevitable?" Terri snapped back. "You think you had no control over what happened here? That your minions had no choice?"

Terri took an aggressive step toward Kane, but Darcey held her back.

"Don't," Darcey said.

"For years I pretended it was all a misunderstanding," Terri said. "I didn't want to believe that my father could have committed such horrible crimes. It was too much for me to accept or understand. So I didn't try. I buried it, just like Mom did. We pretended like it never happened, which is exactly what you wanted, right? You wanted everyone to forget. But they didn't. I don't know how this is possible but the past, your past, was dug up today. Those people buried out there were murdered. You say it was inevitable? Why? To keep the lights on? How does that justify flat out sadism? It's beyond evil."

Terri was out of breath as years of bottled-up emotion came pouring out.

Kane could only stare at the floor.

Darcey held her mother's hand for whatever small bit of support it would afford.

"Everything you've said is true," Kane finally said. "What happened here was pure evil and I can't deny my role in it. But the whole truth is far worse than you can imagine."

A man appeared at the top of the marble stairs. He approached slowly and stopped directly in front of the stained-glass window to face those watching him from below. He wore a military uniform that looked straight out of World War One, with high leather boots and a Doughboy hat. He was joined by a woman in a high-neck Victorian blouse and skirt.

Terri and Darcey watched in wonder as several more people arrived. There was a teenage girl wearing a pink cardigan sweater and a poodle skirt; a young boy with a crew-cut in a white t-shirt and jeans that had cuffs rolled up five inches; and a dapper man with his hair parted in the middle wearing a tuxedo.

"The atrocities didn't begin when I arrived here," Kane said. "They date back to the moment this cursed building opened its doors."

More people arrived. They gathered to fill the stairs leading to the ground floor and peered down from every level of the atrium.

"My time here was relatively short," Kane continued. "But it was long enough to understand that this is an un-holy place. When people came to work here, they changed. I saw it repeatedly. Basic human decency no longer mattered. There was a general ambivalence toward the needs of those who came here seeking help. I saw it in myself. To me, the patients became nothing more than numbers on a ledger sheet, and I treated them as such."

"And you blame the building?" Darcey asked, incredulously. "Seriously?"

"Something is here," Kane said. "Something dark. It turned decent people into sadistic jailers with no empathy for those who needed it most."

Terri and Darcey gazed in awe as dozens more people arrived, crowded the stairs, and loomed from every level. It was a gathering of souls whose lives spanned a century.

None wore medical uniforms.

"It didn't begin when I arrived," Kane said. "Many of these victims have haunted these halls for eons. You discovered a graveyard in the forest. It isn't the only one."

"More people are buried out there?" Darcey asked, incredulous.

Kane's answer was to gesture to the throng of spirits behind him.

"My God," Terri muttered.

"I'm afraid God has nothing to do with it," Kane said.

A few more people joined the group: the African American man in the red-plaid bathrobe, the bald woman wearing a nightgown, and the young guy wearing the Rolling Stones t-shirt.

"I told you how we're all caught in this limbo, but I believe it may actually be hell on earth."

"It's true," Claire Meade said as she stepped forward from the group at the bottom of the stairs.

Terri caught her breath, and threw a questioning look to Darcey. Darcey nodded to confirm that she was indeed the spirit of Holly Meade's grandmother.

"We're all bound by the evil that's here," Claire said. "We were victims in life, and in death."

"I don't expect forgiveness for what I allowed to happen under my watch," Kane said. "If it's any consolation, I put an end to it. I closed the institute."

"Yeah," Darcey said belligerently. "But not until people figured out what was going on."

"But closing the doors didn't end it," Claire said. "I don't know which was worse. The time we spent here when we were alive, or the evil that's forcing us to constantly re-live it."

"If you were being so righteous, why didn't you admit to the truth?" Terri asked Kane.

"To protect you, and your mother," Kane replied. "I didn't want you vilified for my failures. My weakness."

"But hiding the truth is what's keeping these poor souls here," Darcey said.

Kane looked to the throng of spirits that had gathered. His gaze wandered across the faces, as if seeing them as individuals for the first time. When he settled on Darcey, his expression softened.

"You truly remind me of your grandmother."

"Mom says I'm just like her," Darcey said. "I think I'm like my mother too. We call bullshit when we see it."

Terri said, "Haven't these people suffered enough?"

"They have," Kane said with resignation. "One of my last acts was to give your mother a difficult responsibility. Are you aware of that?"

"I am," Terri said.

"I was torn over what to do, and left it up to her. It was horribly unfair of me to give her that burden, but I wanted her to have the choice to do what she felt was right. For her, and for you."

"What's that's supposed to mean?" Darcey asked.

"She chose to do nothing," Terri said. "Because she wanted to protect you."

"I'm not surprised. So now the responsibility, and the choice, is yours. You must do what is right for you, and for your daughter."

"Her name is Darcey," Terri said.

"Darcey?" Kane said with surprise. "You named her after my mother."

"You never told me that," Darcey said to Terri.

"I hope you can do what I didn't have the strength to do in life," Kane said.

"What's he talking about?" Darcey asked.

"Why the change of heart?" Terri asked Kane.

"I believe it happened when I realized I had nearly killed my granddaughter," Kane said soberly. He looked to Darcey and added, "I'm so sorry, Darcey."

Darcey didn't respond.

Terri looked around at the hundreds of spirits that were gathered, all looking to her with anticipation. She settled on her father and said, "Good-bye, Dad."

She took Darcey by the arm and hurried toward the exit.

"Theresa?" Kane called.

Terri looked back at her father, and the crowd of cursed spirits.

"I did intend to make amends," he said. "But I was weak. I hope you can finish what I started."

"What did he start?" Darcey asked.

Terri gently pulled Darcey out of the building and down the front stairs toward their cars.

"Can you drive?" Terri asked.

"Uh, yeah, I guess. What was he talking about?"

"Go home," Terri ordered. "I'll be right behind you."

"What did he give you permission to do?"

"Later. Go!"

Darcey got in the car and though her hands were shaking, managed to put the car into gear and drive toward the front gate. Before passing through, she glanced at the rearview mirror to see her mother wasn't following. She was hurrying back up the stairs to re-enter the institute, carrying something. Darcey slammed on the brakes, threw the car into reverse, spun around, and sped back to the hospital. She skid to a stop behind the Jeep and leapt out without bothering to kill the engine. She ran up the stairs and straight into the building to discover the spirits were gone. Terri was at the foot of the stairs busily pouring gasoline over the wooden bannisters from a large yellow Jerry Can that had been attached to the back of the Jeep.

"Mom!" she called out.

Terri ignored her. She was on a mission.

"This is crazy," Darcey shouted.

"Maybe," Terri replied while splashing gas over the wooden surfaces. "Tell me one thing that happened today that wasn't."

Terri moved across the steps to the opposite banister and continued to spread fuel.

"You're the sheriff," Darcey said. "How many laws are you breaking?"

"Several. You going to turn me in?"

Gone was the pragmatic, even-keeled public servant the entire town looked to for guidance. Terri was acting on raw emotion. When the Jerry Can was emptied, she took a step back and surveyed the work, breathing hard.

"Is this what he meant?" Darcey asked. "He wanted Grandma Trish to burn the place down?"

"In a manner of speaking," Terri replied.

"Please Mom," Darcey said. "Take a breath and think for a second. Is it worth it?"

Terri looked at Darcey and smiled.

"The spirits aren't the only ones who've been held prisoner by what happened here. My entire life I tried to reconcile what the director of this place did versus the man I wanted to think was a good person."

"You think burning it down will do that?" Darcey asked.

"I don't know, but he said this place is evil and I choose to believe him."

Darcey looked around, taking in the once-opulent atrium. She lifted her gaze to the crystal dome and imagined seeing Claire sitting on the edge of the top balcony, ready to fly like her friends. With a sigh, she reached into her pocket, pulled out a Bic lighter and held it out to her mother.

Terri gave her a raised eyebrow look.

"What?" Darcey said innocently. "You know I smoke."

Terri took the lighter, sparked a flame and touched it to the base of the right banister. The gas ignited instantly and quickly spread upward. She hurried to the left banister and did the same. The heavy oak banisters were over a hundred years old and hadn't been cared for in decades. They were bone dry and burned like kindling.

The flame traveled up both banisters, growing in intensity as the gas burned away and the carved wood became fuel. Terri and Darcey took a step back as the heat grew. The bannisters were like two fuses that continued to burn upward, floor by floor, creating halos of flame that ringed each balcony. Soon the wood around the stained-glass window ignited to create a fiery frame that was both spectacular and horrifying.

"Is that enough?" Darcey asked. "Marble and stone don't burn."

"No, but the wooden skeleton will. In a couple of hours this place will be a pile of bricks. Time to go,"

Terri carried the Jerry Can, which was the only evidence of what had caused the fire. They went for the front door and stopped to look back at the inferno that now engulfed the atrium in an incongruously spectacular display of light.

"It's done," Darcey said.

"Almost," Terri said, and headed out.

Terri went for the Jeep and Darcey to the Subaru. They didn't want to be anywhere near the institute when firefighters arrived.

"You okay to drive?" Terri asked.

"Yeah."

Terri looked back at the building to see the windows were already glowing from the fire raging within. Black smoke began to seep out from every seam, as though the building was being purged of darkness.

"Go right home," Terri said. "Don't speed. Be safe."

"You're coming this time, right?" Darcey asked.

"I'm tired," Terri said. "I want to be in bed."

"Okay, you go first."

Before Terri got into her Jeep she looked to Darcey and said, "I love you."

"I love you too Mom."

Terri got in and drove toward the front gates. Before getting in the Subaru, Darcey looked up at the building, knowing it was for the last time. She saw movement in a second-floor window. It was only a silhouette, but Darcey knew who it was.

Millie stood in the window looking down at her. The little girl raised her hand, offering a slight wave. Darcey waved back.

The little ghost girl took a step away from the window and was gone.

At home, Terri stood behind her Jeep waiting for her daughter, who pulled in shortly after. Darcey got out of the car and approached her mother with trepidation.

"Well?" she said. "What do we do now?"

"Sleep," Terri said. "It's going to be another long day tomorrow."

"Shouldn't we call the fire department?"

"No," Terri said quickly. "Too soon."

"What if it spreads to the woods?"

"Not much chance of that," Terri said. "There's no wind and the grounds surrounding the building are huge so there's no fuel close by. Someone will spot the smoke soon enough and call it in. Give me your clothes, I'll wash them. Take a shower and shampoo your hair before you get in bed. We don't want there to be anything that could trace us back there."

Darcey nodded in agreement. She was too numbed to do anything else.

"No school tomorrow," Terri added. "I'll write you a note."

This was strange territory for Darcey. Her by-the-book mother was suddenly anything but.

"Are you okay?" Darcey asked. "I mean, that was some serious shit."

Terri couldn't help but chuckle. "Arson is the least of it, right?"

Darcey chuckled too, but she was troubled. "If we get caught nobody's going to believe our defense."

"I'm not worried. You shouldn't either," Terri said.

Together, they headed toward the house.

"Was that it?" Darcey asked. "Will that end it? Whatever *it* is?"

"It's a start," Terri replied.

"Is that what your father wanted you to do? Burn the place down?"

"No, I did that on my own."

"So then what was it?" Darcey asked.

Terri put her arms around her daughter and hugged her close. Darcey didn't hesitate to hug back.

"It's late," Terri said. "We'll get into it tomorrow."

"You're not going to set fire to anything else, are you?" Darcey asked.

"Not literally," Terri said.

The two went inside, finally putting an end to the long and impossible day.

CHAPTER 22

Darcey was awoken by bright sunlight that streamed through the bedroom window she had forgotten to pull the drapes across. She was momentarily disoriented, not knowing what time it was, what day it was, and wondering if she and her mother had really burned down a massive brick building in the forest that was haunted by countless ghosts.

Once she cleared the cobwebs she grabbed her phone to see that Terri had texted a few hours before.

School was notified that you're not coming in. I've been with the investigators at the gravesite since seven. Meet me at Glenville Savings and Loan at eleven. I hope you wake up in time to get this.

A quick look to her phone told her it was ten-thirty, so she bolted up and out of bed. She had no idea why her mother wanted to meet her at the bank, but she wasn't about to question it. She took another quick shower to make sure any residual and incriminating arson smells were gone, then threw on her go-to outfit of a long, muslin skirt, crop top, jean jacket, and Doc Martin boots. None of the girls in Glenville dressed that way, which was exactly why she did. Even with taking the time to dry her hair, she managed to get to the bank a few minutes before eleven and had a moment to catch her breath outside before her mother arrived.

The sky was clear, and the sun provided unseasonable warmth for an autumn day. Darcey looked up and down Main Street, thinking it was the first time the town didn't seem so gray. As much as she loathed the place, she couldn't help but feel sympathy for everyone who had been associated with the High Point Institute. She couldn't imagine how people would feel when they learned that their loved ones had been mistreated, killed, and buried in the woods. While closure was good, the news would be devastating. They'd have questions and there was no one to give answers. At least no one still living.

"Hey," Terri said as she hurried toward Darcey. "This won't take long. There's a press conference at noon."

She was back in professional-mode, complete with a perfectly pressed uniform. She'd even put on a touch of make-up.

"What about the institute?" Darcey asked.

"Firefighters got there before dawn. It's a pile of smoldering bricks."

It was a relief for Darcey to hear that they hadn't burned down the surrounding forest.

"What about the graves?" Darcey asked.

"Exactly what you'd imagine. The place is swarming with multiple forensic teams. More are coming. They'll be working for days. The town's going to be hopping for a while. Too bad the Rx is closed. They'd make a killing."

"Ooh. Poor choice of words," Darcey said.

"Yeah. Sorry."

"Did you tell anyone how the graves were found?" Darcey asked.

"They know it was Scott Wilson, but they haven't interviewed him yet. That's one of the reasons we're here."

"At the bank?"

Terri breezed past Darcey, entered the lobby, and went straight for the desk of the bank manager, an officious woman with a gray bob wearing a conservative dark pants suit.

"Good morning, Mrs. Merkyl," Terri said.

No one ever called Mrs. Merkyl anything but Mrs. Merkyl.

"Hello Sheriff, I hope you're not here on official business," the bank manager said with a slight hint of annoyance.

"I'm not. I'd like to access my safety deposit box."

"I see," Mrs. Merkyl said as she stood and walked with purpose to the back of the lobby.

Darcey and Terri followed.

"I guess news hasn't spread," Darcey said, whispering to her mother.

"It will. Might take a little longer since the Rx is closed, but it's hard to miss the conga line of emergency vehicles rolling in. And the news vans."

Mrs. Merkyl led them to a back room where a heavy vault door was swung open. Beyond were two aisles of safety deposit boxes. The brass boxes were installed in the 1930's, when Glenville was booming. Now, most only held air.

"I trust you have your key," Mrs. Merkyl said.

"Of course," Terri replied. "Can we have some privacy?"

Mrs. Merkyl stiffened, as if offended by the idea that her presence wasn't welcome.

"Of course," she said. "Please check with me before you leave."

"Will do," Terri said. "Thank you."

The two stared at one another for a long moment until Mrs. Merkyl took the hint and left.

"She's a treasure," Darcey said.

Terri went straight for one of the larger boxes.

"I didn't know you had this," Darcey said. "It's not like we have family jewels. Or do we?"

"Hardly."

Terri unlocked the door and pulled out a large brass tray and placed it on a table in the middle of the room.

"I told you that after we moved away from Glenville my father spent most of his time working in his home office. It's all such a hazy memory but I do remember how he always seemed upset and didn't want to be disturbed. He spent entire days in there and most nights. It was the first time I saw him drinking, which I'm sure didn't help his mood."

The only item inside the brass tray was a metal strong box, the size of a large shoe box. Terri lifted it out and placed it on the table. Using another key, she opened the strongbox to reveal three tightly-packed rows of what looked to Darcey like light gray, plastic cards that were roughly three inches square. Terri took one out and held it up for Darcey to see.

"And those are...?" Darcey asked.

"You're making me feel old. It wasn't all that long ago that these were common. They're floppy disks."

Darcey took the disk and examined it closely.

"Still, no clue," she said.

"It's what people used in the nineties to store computer files."

"Not very floppy," Darcey said, tapping the plastic disk on the table.

"My father spent the last months of his life scanning documents and storing the data on these. That's what he was doing in his office."

"I still don't get why—"

Darcey's eyes grew wide as the realization hit.

"You're shitting me," she exclaimed.

"I have no idea what happened to the original hard copies," Terri said. "He probably shredded them, but it doesn't matter because as far as I can tell, they've all been scanned and they're all here."

"So he did have them," Darcey said in awe.

Darcey examined another disk that had a hand-written label marked: *HPI – 1946/1947*.

"From what I can tell they date back to when the institute first opened," Terri said. "Everything is here. Patient names. Commitment papers. Waivers. Dates that patients arrived and left. Diagnoses. Session notes. It has the dates when patients were admitted, but many don't have release dates. That's ominous right there. There were extensive records of treatments, deaths, and drug purchases, many of which were hardcore psychotropics. I saw multiple contracts with pharmaceutical companies for research projects using both human and animal subjects. There are receipts for thousands of animals that were purchased. The overall dollar figures are staggering. It's all very clinical but it doesn't take much to read between the lines to see the pattern of abuse and mistreatment."

"Are relatives listed?" Darcey asked.

"Some. Not all had family. Many were homeless people who were brought here from across the country."

"And became nameless victims," Darcey added.

"That's right. There were lots of John and Jane Does. I don't know how thorough the older records are but from what I saw, these confirm the rumors."

"I'm sorry, Mom," Darcey said.

Darcey made a quick flip through the disks to see they were marked and organized in chronological order with the earliest being from 1921.

"Where did you find them?" Darcey asked.

"Granny Trish had them. My father gave them to her shortly before his death and said if anything happened to him, it would be up to her to decide if she wanted to make them public."

"Sounds like he knew he was going to, you know, end it."

"We'll never know."

"So Granny Trish knew the truth?"

"Not entirely. She swore she never read them. She said what was done was done and making them public would only open old wounds that would shame her husband and make life miserable for me. So she kept them locked away and didn't tell anyone about them. Not even me. Especially not me. For a while, anyway."

"What changed her mind?" Darcey asked.

"A man came to her looking for information about High Point. He said he was acting on behalf of some relatives of patients who were trying to learn about the fate of their children. Mom told him she knew nothing about what happened back then and sent him on his way, but it weighed on her that people were still searching for answers after all those years. The guilt got to be too much, so she gave the disks to me."

"How long ago was that?" Darcy asked

"Shortly before she passed. About a year before we moved here. I didn't go through them all, but I read enough to confirm my worst fears. It's what prompted me to move us here, Darcey. I've been torn over what to do about them ever since. I've held on to the belief that the reason my father scanned them was because he intended to turn them over to the state."

"But he didn't. Neither did Granny Trish."

"And neither did I. I've been asking myself why I didn't for a long time. I have no excuse other than to say I didn't want to publicly drag his name through the mud. And Granny Trish's. I'm ashamed to admit that I was also afraid of what it might do to my career and to your father. And frankly, to you."

Terri ran her hand over the tops of the disks, picturing the multitude of spirits who had gathered in the atrium of the hospital the night before.

"I was wrong," she said. "If nothing else, what we saw last night proves it. I'll always have to live with that."

"Do you think that's what he wanted you to do?" Darcey asked. "Make them public?"

"I think so. It gives me hope that in the end he really did want to do the right thing. Not to exonerate himself, but to give closure to the victims."

"What about the dark presence he said caused it all?" Darcey asked. "Is there anything in the files about that?"

"No. Not the kind of thing they make official records about. I have no idea how credible that is."

"None of this is credible, yet somehow it is."

"I hear you. I'm trying to expand my thinking. He said the abuse started long before he became Director. The records bear that out. There's a litany of mistreatment that stretches back to nineteen twenty-one. That's beyond coincidental. If there really was some malevolent force that compelled people to do ghastly things, I'd like to believe my father was a victim as well. It's a disturbing idea on so many levels. Maybe I'm kidding myself, but it might explain why he did what he did. Getting away from its influence might have allowed him to clear his head and led to his decision to prepare the files to become public."

"It might also have allowed guilty feelings to haunt him," Darcey said. "It could explain why he—"

She didn't finish the thought.

"It all seems like fantasy," Terri said. "But after what we've seen, I'm willing to believe most anything."

"So maybe there really is an evil presence there," Darcey said.

"Except there's no more there there. The High Point Institute is no more."

"Does that mean the evil is gone too?" Darcey asked.

Neither had the answer.

"So, now what?"

Terri put the disk back in the strong box and locked it.

"I'm going to do what I should have done when I first got them. If that doesn't give the spirits closure, I don't know what will."

"That means you're going to out yourself as Everett Kane's daughter. Are you okay with that?"

"I am," Terri said. "The spirits aren't the only ones who need closure. What about you? Are you okay with it?"

"Absolutely," Darcey said without hesitation.

"That's my girl," Terri said with a laugh. "You're like my mother and me in so many ways, except for one."

"What's that?"

"You're brave enough to cut right through the bullshit."

"I try," Darcey said with a shrug.

Terri picked up the empty tray and slid it back into the wall receptacle.

"You said this had something to do with Scott Wilson," Darcey said.

"This is complicated enough without trying to convince people that Glenville is haunted. All Scott wants is justice for the victims. These files will do that. He agreed that as long as I make them public, he won't explain how he was led to the graves. He'll say he stumbled on them while doing his surveying. He'd rather do that than be labeled a crazy Ghostbuster for the rest of his life."

Terri closed the door of the safety deposit box and turned to Darcey.

"Ready?"

"Seriously? Now?"

"I told you, there's a press conference at noon."

Terri locked the safety deposit box for the last time, picked up the strong box, and they headed out.

"What about that guy who visited Granny Trish?" Darcey asked. "Did she say anything else about him?"

"Only that he was a handsome man who dressed nicely and had a British accent."

"Really?" Darcey asked with surprise. "Was he Black?"

"Didn't ask," Terri replied. "But I sure as hell will now."

The town courthouse was hastily prepared to host the press conference. All official business was cancelled for the day. By noon, the one and only courtroom was packed to capacity with local news crews from TV stations in Madison and Milwaukee. Multiple newspapers and on-line news sites were represented and, as Terri predicted, there was a crew from CNN. The rest of the space was taken by curious locals who were rocked by the gruesome discovery, as well as the news of the destruction of a long-abandoned building that most had forgotten existed. Or tried to forget.

Facing the crowd were Glenville's Fire Chief, the President of the three-person Town Council, and Glenville's Sheriff, Terri Hirsch. The state officers and forensic investigators were too busy at the gravesite to attend.

Darcey stood to the side, trying to be invisible. She had no idea what her mother would say and didn't want to draw attention to herself. At straight up noon, Joe Flynn, Glenville's Town Council President for over ten years stepped up to the single microphone that was wired into an amplifier that was borrowed from the high school's AV department. Flynn was overweight with thinning gray hair and wore a dated suit that hadn't been out of the closet since he was first elected, which meant it hadn't been cleaned or pressed since then either. He looked decidedly nervous as he continually wiped sweat from his forehead. This wasn't the kind of task he had signed up for.

After a shrill whine of feedback, Flynn repositioned the mic and addressed the crowd.

"Good morning. To say we're all shocked at this discovery is a pretty big understatement. I'm going to run down what we know so far, but you gotta understand, the investigation is only beginning. We'll have more info as the days go on. After my statement I won't take any questions because I'm going to tell you all I know."

The crowd was dead silent. Most already had an idea of what was coming.

"Yesterday, a horrible discovery was made in the forest about six miles north of town. There are twenty-five unmarked graves. Twenty-five bodies. Twenty-five unknown victims."

Shocked gasps rolled through the room.

"I call them victims because this is not an ancient graveyard. The condition of the bodies tells us they died roughly thirty years ago. Some probably more than that. It's pretty clear they aren't native Americans or early settlers. These were modern folks, which leads us to conclude that foul play was involved."

Excited chatter broke out. Flynn raised his hands to quiet the room.

"Please, you've got plenty of time to jaw about this once we're finished here. Let's get through this."

The people settled down, but the atmosphere remained electric.

"Right now we've got state and county investigators exhuming the bodies. They'll be taken back to Madison where forensic teams will figure out who these folks are and determine their cause of death. These people are pros. They know what they're doing with DNA and such. We'll get to the bottom of this, hopefully pretty quick."

Darcey couldn't help but think how Everett Kane said there were many more bodies buried out there. The investigators would be busy for a very long time before they got to the bottom of anything.

"A few more things," Flynn said. "First, the site is secured. It's a crime scene so don't go out there snooping around. We don't want no contamination going on. Second, good news is, if you can call it that, whatever happened out there happened a long time ago. Decades. There's no reason to be afraid. We don't see any threat to anybody."

This raised more worried murmurs, as if most had only just realized that whoever was responsible might still be at large.

"That's it. I got no more for you right now," Flynn said. "Sheriff Hirsch would like to say a few words."

Flynn stepped back and nodded to Terri.

Terri tentatively walked forward and surveyed the crowd that had gone dead-silent. Scott Wilson was there. So were Holly Meade and Mikey Harper. The people of Glenville loved Terri. They trusted her. Joe Flynn may have been elected to head the town council, but he was first and foremost a florist. It was Terri they wanted to hear from. She was their sheriff. Their protector. They knew they could count on her to get them through troubling times. Since she'd been in Glenville, she'd grown to care about these people.

Though she knew she could never balance the scales with what had happened at the institute, her goal of giving back to this community in whatever way she could had worked out better than she hoped.

Now she stood before them, savoring the last few seconds before that relationship would be destroyed. She scanned the crowd and saw Darcey off to the side. Darcey smiled and gave her a thumbs up. Terri needed that. She looked to the opposite side of the courtroom and saw Scott Wilson standing alone. He gave her a slight nod of encouragement.

She cleared her throat and stepped up to the mic.

"Many of you may remember the disturbing circumstances that led to the closing of the High Point Institute outside of town. There were accusations of atrocities, malpractice, and untimely deaths, but nothing was ever proven. No one had the will to uncover what had actually happened. Not the people who worked there; not the people of Glenville who didn't want to believe that something so horrible could happen in our quiet town; and certainly not the companies large and small that benefitted from the unchecked human and animal research that went on there. It was all swept under the rug and forgotten. Last night the abandoned institute building burned to the ground. The cause is under investigation."

There were no gasps from the crowd. No murmurs. No whispers. They were hanging on Terri's every word.

"Shortly after the institute closed, there was an investigation into the accusations. A big part of that was an effort to find the official records. The hope was that they'd provide documented proof of what had actually happened. At the very least they'd show a list of the patients who were treated there. Those records were never found. The director of the institute, a Doctor Everett Kane, stated that he didn't know what had happened to them, and maintained that until the day he died. He committed suicide, actually. Shortly after his death the investigation was abandoned, and so was the institute building. Now it's a pile of rubble."

There was sporadic response to that news. Most already knew and sensed there was more to come.

"I'm here to announce that I've located those records. A few minutes ago I turned them over to representatives of the Wisconsin Department of Justice. There's reason to believe that there's a connection between the institute and the bodies that were discovered in the forest. The hope is that after all these years, the entire truth will be brought to light and with it, there will be closure for the victims, and their families. Thank you."

Terri stepped back from the mic as people in the crowd started chattering, each with their own spin on what they'd just heard.

Scott Wilson, satisfied, exited through a side door.

A reporter from Madison's newspaper, *The Capital Times* posed the inevitable question.

"Sheriff?" the young woman shouted above the growing din. "How exactly did you come across those records?"

The crowd instantly quieted back down. Everyone looked to Terri with anticipation.

Darcey held her breath.

This was the moment Terri was dreading. She stepped back to the microphone and took a last look around at her friends while they were still her friends.

"They were given to me by my mother. She had been storing them for many years."

"And how was it that your mother had these records?" the reporter asked.

Terri took a deep breath and stepped off the cliff.

"She was Doctor Everett Kane's wife," she answered. "When Doctor Kane left the institute, he took the records, scanned them, and most likely destroyed the originals. It's my belief that he was preparing to turn them over to the authorities but died before that happened."

"And this woman was his wife?" the reporter asked, incredulous.

Darcey closed her eyes, ready for chaos.

"Yes," Terri replied. "Doctor Everett Kane, the Director of the High Point Institute, was my father."

Terri braced herself, ready for the inevitable eruption.

There was dead silence. It was as though every last person was too stunned to react. Darcey opened her eyes to see that everyone was focused on Terri, all with the same look of total shock.

Terri said, "I hope these records will finally allow the truth to be made public and give some closure to those who were affected."

She stepped away from the microphone and walked quickly toward the side door with her eyes on the floor. She couldn't bear to see the looks she knew meant that she had instantly lost the trust of everyone in that room. She reached for the door handle, but someone else grabbed it first.

Terri looked up.

It was Mr. Paper.

"Bravo," he said.

He opened the door for her, and Terri hurried out.

EPILOGUE

The High Point Institute had been reduced to a sprawling pile of smoldering rubble. Once the wooden framework caught fire and its skeleton crumbled, it was only a matter of time before the entire structure imploded. Only a few charred brick walls were still standing. None of the turrets survived. Fire crews continued to hose it down to extinguish lingering embers. Smoke continued to rise, creating a dark umbrella that loomed over the wreckage, blocking the sun and casting an ominous shadow over the remains.

Terri stood on the edge of the driveway that ran past what was once the main entrance, surveying the scene. The only recognizable feature that remained were the twelve cement stairs that now led up to nothing. She'd driven straight to the institute from the press conference, partly to see the carcass for herself, but also to dodge a confrontation with disillusioned neighbors. It was a moment of calm where she could take some level of satisfaction in seeing that the notorious institute was no more.

"Quite the surprising climax," Mr. Paper said.

Terri turned to see the man standing behind her, leaning jauntily on his walking stick.

"I don't think you find it surprising at all," Terri said. "You knew where this was headed."

"Not true. I don't see the future. I make no predictions and have no expectations. All I know is what came before."

Mr. Paper stepped forward and stood by Terri. Both gazed out at the wreckage.

"Tell me something," Terri said. "With all your travels and experiences and observations, have you ever come across a building that housed an evil so powerful it could rot people's souls?"

"More times than I care to admit," Mr. Paper replied.

The answer surprised Terri, but also gave her a small bit of hope that her father may well have been a victim after all.

"And if the building is destroyed?" Terri asked. "Is the evil destroyed along with it?"

"I'm afraid a building is but a vessel. You released many innocent souls from its confines. I hope that gives you some comfort."

"It does," Terri said. "But did I also release the evil?"

Mr. Paper's non-answer was his answer.

"What happened here goes beyond my ability to comprehend," Terri said. "Just as well. I'm not so sure I want to."

"I've heard that sentiment before. Many times."

Terri looked up at the odd man and said, "I can't say you don't intrigue me, Mr. Paper. But I'm going to lock you away in a remote corner of my memory that I don't ever want to revisit. I'd much prefer to live my life in a way that makes sense."

"In my experience, that's for the best," Mr. Paper said.

"Yeah, well, we'll see," Terri said wistfully.

"Tell me, Sheriff," Mr. Paper said. "What do you imagine lies in your future?"

Terri sighed. "I'm not sure. I'd like to stay here, but I doubt the town will want me. Let alone the Sheriff's office."

"One should not be held responsible for the actions of others," Mr. Paper said.

"No, but I wasn't honest with them. It's tough to regain lost trust. And it's not like I can explain to anyone what actually happened. That would wash me out for sure."

"Perhaps. But if you're able to weather that storm, you'll be rewarded."

"How so?"

"In my experience—"

"Ahh, in your experience," Terri said with a chuckle. "I love hearing about your experiences."

"In my experience, when situations like this are resolved, it's akin to a weight being lifted from a great many people. The future of Glenville may take a decidedly positive turn."

He gestured up to the cloud of smoke that hung above the wreckage and added, "Imagine how bright this day will become once that bilious cloud blows away. You deserve to experience that. At the very least I trust you'll take some satisfaction in knowing how much good you did here."

"We'll see," Terri said with some uncertainty.

Mr. Paper reached into his inner jacket pocket and pulled out a sealed envelope.

"A signed statement. It describes the events I witnessed when Ben Daniels passed away. I trust it will be sufficient to prove Miss Holly was in no way responsible."

Terri took the envelope and said, "Thank you. I doubt it will be necessary but it's good to have."

"With that, I will take my leave." He tipped his bowler and added, "I am very happy to have met you, Sheriff Hirsch."

"Likewise, Mister Author Paper," Terri said.

Mr. Paper turned to walk away when Terri added, "For what it's worth, my mother regretted lying to you."

If this surprised Mr. Paper, he didn't show it. He offered Terri a sly smile and said, "She was such a lovely woman, much like her daughter and granddaughter."

"Good luck in your travels, Mr. Paper."

"And to you, Sheriff Hirsch. Be seeing you."

As he walked away, Terri saw that he had a ride waiting for him. Darcey stood next to their Subaru. She gave her mother a quick wave, then got in the car along with Mr. Paper.

Terri turned back to the rubble that was once the High Point Institute and looked up at the dark cloud of smoke that was ever so slowly floating away, allowing a small shaft of warm sunlight to reach the ground.

Though her future was very much in doubt, Terri was at peace.

In the car, Darcey asked, "Where to, Mister Paper?"

"If you don't mind, would you deposit me in town?"

"No problem," Darcey said and drove away from what was left of the High Point Institute.

"Have you made a decision about your near future?" Mr. Paper asked.

"I have," Darcey replied. "Mom's in for a rough time. Who knows where she'll end up?"

"She'd prefer to remain here."

"Yeah, but she might not have a choice. It's not fair."

She glanced in the rearview mirror for a final glimpse at the wreckage through the open, iron gates.

"Do you think they've moved on?" Darcey asked. "The spirits, I mean."

"I have no doubt."

"What about the evil force that supposedly caused it all?"

"It's no longer here, of that you can be sure."

"Where did it go?" Darcey asked.

"That's difficult to say."

"Can it be stopped? For good?"

Mr. Paper turned uncharacteristically solemn and said, "That is also difficult to say. But rest assured, if and when that moment comes, I'll be there."

"I'll bet you will," Darcey said. "Maybe you'll write a book about it?"

"Perhaps," Mr. Paper said.

"Where should I drop you?" Darcey asked.

"I'd like to return to that lovely establishment that serves those remarkable nuggets of fried cheese for one last sample."

"Who says the British don't appreciate fine cuisine?" Darcey said with a laugh.

After a short and mostly silent ride, she pulled the car to the curb in front of Kozak's Delicatessen and held her hand out to Mr. Paper.

"Nice knowing you," she said. "I don't know who the hell you are or how you were able to shake things up, but I'm glad you did. So are a whole lot of other people. Most of them are dead, but you know, still counts."

Mr. Paper took her hand, and they shared a firm shake.

"You are a remarkable young woman, Miss Darcey. Your future is very bright."

"Thanks. I hope yours is too. Wherever your travels take you."

Mr. Paper gave her a quick nod and got out of the car.

"Mr. Paper?" Darcey called.

Mr. Paper leaned down to look into the window.

"Be careful," she said.

"Always," he said with a smile, then placed his hat on his head. "Be seeing you."

Terri drove home. She needed a few more moments of calm to collect herself before diving back into the investigation, and the throng of demanding journalists. The first order of business was to arrange for Scott Wilson to make a public statement about how he came across the graveyard. She hoped he was up to it.

Darcey was waiting for her in the living room. As soon as Terri entered, she jumped up and threw her arms around her mother. Both were in tears.

"You were awesome," Darcey said.

Terri's reply was to squeeze tighter. After a long moment she pulled away and held Darcey at arm's length.

"You need to leave Glenville," she said. "I don't want you in the middle of this."

"That's what you want. What about what I want?"

"That is what you want."

"I know. I've been bitching about how there's nothing interesting about this place. Now all I want is for the town to go back to being the dull place I've come to know and hate."

"Hopefully it will, but I may not be here to see it," Terri said wistfully.

"You realize I'm as guilty as you are about what happened to the institute."

"Uh, not even close."

"Give me a break. When I say guilty, I mean responsible. In a good way. I deserve some credit."

Terri laughed. "Okay, agreed. But don't expect any kudos."

"Yeah, it's gonna be rough. You shouldn't have to deal with it alone and I'm the only one you can talk to about it."

"We can still talk. Chicago gets cell service."

"Chicago will always be there," Darcey said with finality. "I want to ride this out together."

Terri took a moment to let that sink in, then pulled her daughter close and hugged her again.

"You realize as soon as your father sees the news he'll be here."

"Good," Darcey said. "Maybe he can ride it out with us."

"Don't push it," Terri said. She held her daughter at arm's length and said, "I love you. I won't let anything happen to you."

"Right back at you," Darcey replied.

They stayed together for a long moment, until they heard a small voice.

"Hello?"

Both looked to see Millie standing in the center of the living room.

"I don't know where to go," the little spirit said.

Downtown Glenville was buzzing with activity. Dozens of people crowded the sidewalks while a steady parade of emergency vehicles rolled past, headed for either the gravesite or the hospital ruins. It was a procession of ambulances, fire trucks, and hearses. News vans were set up on most every corner, with correspondents recording reports for the evening news. Many reporters buttonholed locals for interviews. Most everyone gave variations of the same three comments: They never expected anything so horrible to happen in their quiet town; they had no idea of the history of the High Point Institute; and to a person they said that they would stand behind Sheriff Terri and fight to insure that she remains on the job.

Those interviews and general public opinion would go a long way toward saving Terri's career.

Mr. Paper strolled from Kozak's Delicatessen, finishing the final bite of fried cheese with his dipping sauce of preference: Ranch. He sauntered along the sidewalk, enjoying the carnival-like hum of activity. Glenville had never seen such excitement.

Once the shock of the discovery wore off, the town would settle down. But it had forever been changed. There was a general feeling of renewal, though born from tragedy. Neighbors who had been spending most of their time living in private bubbles were interacting. Store windows were cleaned. Restaurants (other than the Rx) were crowded. There was a sense of community that had long been missing. If nothing else, the world would know that Glenville existed. Would it bring an influx of people and business? That remained to be seen. What couldn't be denied was a feeling of energy that once again made the town feel alive.

For Mr. Paper, the scene was far more dramatic. That's because the local residents weren't the only ones present. Scattered among them were dozens of unseen souls. Claire Meade was there. So was the veteran on crutches and the elderly gentleman with the plaid bathrobe. The bald woman in the tattered nightgown, several children, and the kid in the Rolling Stones t-shirt were there, along with all the spirits from several generations. They stood silently, invisibly, among the living. They gazed down from second floor windows and sat on rooftops. Some climbed lampposts.

No one saw them, except for Mr. Paper. Their eyes were on him as he walked past, giving each a brief nod of acknowledgment. They didn't speak to him or reach out. They simply stared with a look of anticipation, as if Mr. Paper could provide the guidance they desperately needed.

Mr. Paper arrived at the intersection in the dead center of Main Street and scanned the busy sidewalks. Most people ignored him. He may as well have been invisible. But the eyes of the spirits were locked on him, waiting for his next move. The traffic light that had been blinking sporadically for the past ten years was inexplicably shining lock-solid bright. Mr. Paper looked up and down the street to see that there was a break in the steady line of vehicles. The street was as empty as the dawn of the morning before when he first arrived. He stepped off the curb, strolled to the center of the intersection, and stopped there. He did a slow three-sixty, lifted his walking stick, and brought it down hard on the pavement.

A sharp crack was heard that reverberated off the buildings. Passers-by looked around in wonder at what might have caused it. Seeing nothing, they went about their business.

Terri and Darcey stood looking at Millie as the forlorn little girl gazed off to what seemed like nothing and broke out in a warm smile.

"Oh," she said with a sweet giggle. "Now I see."

Millie lit up like the happy child she once was.

"That's better," Darcey said.

"You two are swell," Millie said.

"Yes we are," Darcey said.

Terri watched in open-mouthed awe.

Millie gave them a quick wave, took a step, and evaporated as though she had been blown away on a soft breeze.

"What the hell was that?" Terri asked, stunned.

"I think Mr. Paper finished the job."

Mr. Paper stood in the center of the intersection, scanning the sidewalks as one by one the spirits took a step and blew away. Some gave him a slight wave before departing.

Standing on a curb near Mr. Paper was Karl Iverson, the only spirit who was on the staff of the High Point Institute. He gave Mr. Paper a salute. Mr. Paper responded by tipping his bowler to the man. Karl stepped off the curb and was gone.

Within seconds every last spirit had disappeared, having moved on to whatever their next life held.

A black limousine rounded a corner on to Main Street and rolled to a stop next to Mr. Paper. This finally got people's attention. Mr. Paper opened the back door, took one last look around, and boarded. The traffic light turned green, and the limousine rolled on.

Many people stopped to stare at the incongruous sight of the luxury vehicle driving through their simple world. When the limo turned off of Main Street and drove out of sight, they all went back to whatever they had been doing as if it had never been there.

The limousine was soon gliding along the same country road it had traveled the previous morning. Trees adorned with dazzling fall-colored leaves contrasted brilliantly against a blazing-blue sky. There wasn't a single cloud overhead...

...except for a lone, dark cloud that hovered on the horizon.

The road headed straight toward it.

As did the limousine.

THE END

Also by D.J. MacHale

Pendragon — Journal of an Adventure Through Time and Space (Series)
Morpheus Road (Trilogy)
The SYLO Chronicles (Trilogy)
The Monster Princess
The Library (Trilogy)
Trinity
Voyagers (Book #1)
The Equinox Curiosity Shop (Audible exclusive)
The Green Grabber (Guys Read - Other Worlds)
The Scout (Redux) (Don't Turn Out The Lights Collection)
Beyond Midnight (Short Story Collection)

ABOUT THE AUTHOR

D.J. MacHale has created, written, directed, and produced many award-winning television series and movies for young people including *Are You Afraid of the Dark?*; *Flight 29 Down* and Disney's *Tower of Terror* along with many others.

As an author he has written the bestselling series *Pendragon – Journal of an Adventure Through Time and Space*; the spooky *Morpheus Road* trilogy; and the sci-fi thriller trilogy *The SYLO Chronicles* along with several other titles. D.J. lives with his family in Southern California. Visit him at djmachalebooks.com as well as on Facebook, Twitter, and Instagram.

Made in the USA
Las Vegas, NV
02 April 2025